A WORLD UNSEEN

On the other side of our trees is a place of magic and energy. And love. Everyone there has a defining power, but the Soulmate bond is universal—and unassailable. Or so say the Ones in Power.

They speak a lie. Like here on Earth, in the Commonworld there are those reviled and unwanted, like Thalia Salic, whose only crime is being Invisible. There are those persecuted for their parentage, like Sfodro Vatic. There are those coveted for their knowledge, like nine-year-old Sandy. There are the Worthless and the Loveless, and there are those who oppose evil, like Emma Mathews. In no world can we help what we're born. We can't always understand who we love. We can only decide how we're going to live.

PRAISE FOR MARY BETH BASS AND THE TRIPLE AWARD-WINNING FIRST BOOK IN THE COMMONWORLD SERIES!

"Mystical and intriguing...*everything you know* has everything you'll love—romance, magic, and characters that draw you into the story. A great new voice in the young adult genre. A truly enjoyable read."

—*New York Times* Bestselling Author C.C. Hunter

"Through astounding imagery and richly lyrical prose, Bass's memorable romantic fantasy is, at its heart, a tribute to the unconquerable spirit of first love."

—Laura Toffler-Corrie, Author of *My Totally Awkward Supernatural Crush*

"*everything you know* transcends worlds and challenges the imagination with a desperate tale of love and survival."

—Kassy Tayler, Award-Winning Author of *Ashes of Twilight*

"Bass's engagement with literature, myth and philosophy shines through the pages of her novel: *everything you know* is filled with thought-provoking and challenging ideas, and underlaid with a fair amount of philosophy. I was pleased, too, to find no trite or easy answers offered for difficult questions. It's a complicated read, a big read, bursting the confines of the paranormal romance much as Emma and Joe burst out of mundane reality into a world where anything is possible."

—Heroines of Fantasy, Harriet Goodchild

"A great twist on classic fantasy novels.... If you enjoy fantasy, mythology, adventure, portal stories, and/or romance, *everything you know* is the read for you!"

—To Taste Life Twice, Jamie Adams

all that we see

Mary Beth Bass

www.BOROUGHSPUBLISHINGGROUP.com

ALL THAT WE SEE
Copyright © 2015 Mary Beth Bass

ISBN 978-1-942886-56-3

For the lovely and amazing people who make Desert Moon on Mill Plain Road in Danbury, Connecticut, the best place in the known universe to eat guacamole, drink margaritas, and write dark stories, and most especially for April, Saquan, Alexa, Chris, Ryan, Alfonso, Kyle, Anderson, Fred, and awesome Jym. I couldn't have written this book without you guys. ♥

6

ACKNOWLEDGMENTS

Maybe you read a lot of acknowledgments. And maybe you think, that's nice, Writer Human thanked his/her/their editor. And you just accept that seemingly breezily expressed gratitude as a standard, writerish thing because really what does an editor do? I'm trying to resist answering this question with references to sorcery or alchemy or the genius loci of a manuscript, but the truth is working with an editor feels like actual magic for writers lucky enough to work with a great one. Sure, an editor helps with clarity, and cleaning up continuity errors, repetition of phrasing, inexplicable comma usage. A *great* editor sees the story you're trying to tell, the way it exists in your head powerful and exciting, the story you're trying so hard to tell in draft after draft but still isn't quite there. A great editor asks the questions and opens the doors that help you say what you want to say the way you want to say it, and the way readers will be able to hear it. Chris Keeslar has been my editor for more than ten years. If you know anything about Romancenovellandia you know that Chris has a reputation for being an insightful, innovative, elegant editor, and a fierce advocate for the romance genre and for stories in general. He is all of those things. The point in the writing process when my story is strong and pliable enough to send to Chris is my favorite part of writing. It's like finally getting a play on its feet because the actors are off book. Like running after the endorphins have kicked in. Like finding the key to the castle. Like actual magic. So, thank you a thousand times, forever and always, Chris Keeslar.

* * *

Nothing I've written over the past year, including this book you're holding in your hands or on your screen, could have been written without music. Indie-label punk rock (Altercation Records!!!). Nina Simone. Rufus Wainwright. Morrissey. Beethoven. Iggy Pop. But most of all, the two indie punk powerhouses who changed the way I see the world, propelled me through difficult periods, and made me feel happy, alive and grateful when I thought I might not feel that way again. Thank you forever to Two Fisted Law: Kyle, Jym, Tom, Andrew, Rob (and Dave and Ricky) and The Jukebox Romantics: (Mike) Terry, Bobby, Norm, (and Seth). Wherever you live, Reader Person, support the hell out of local independent music, art, dance, theatre, film and food.

* * *

I hike every morning through a forest-park and up to a ruined Victorian castle shaded by pine trees. Everything I've ever written is influenced by these woods and by poetry I recite while I'm trudging along with my big stick and my bigger hair. An apple orchard, a grape arbor, and oceans of daffodils, irises, peonies and roses wait for me on the grounds of Tarrywile Park when I come out of the woods alive to the world and ready to write. I never take this magical place for granted, and I'm amazed and grateful every time I walk up from the parking lot and see the wide hill and the mountain beyond covered with snow or mist or singing the wordless green melody of spring. The Eden-like grounds at Tarrywile Park are the wonder they are today because of the stewardship of Samuel Crews. I talked to Sam almost every day about the apples, or the grape arbor, or the beauty of the day. He was killed in an accident this spring, before the apple blossoms were really out, or the lilacs, or the peonies. I'm so grateful to have known such a lovely person who created and watched over a wild and wondrous Garden of Eden in the heart of a hardworking Northeastern city. All of my stories come from this place. Thank you, Sam.

CONTENTS

all that we see

PROLOGUE

Late May, the Catskills
West Park, New York

"That hill was considerably more difficult than the map indicated," Nancy Thornton said, emphasizing 'considerably' and nearly tripping over a fallen branch. "And don't tell me I should have worn a knee brace, Gene. I know I should have. But it's too late now."

She was lagging behind her husband, who was already out of the woods and on the path to the field. Leaning on her hiking stick, she caught her breath before continuing to the meadow. She shaded her eyes. "The air feels odd. Doesn't it? Does it feel odd to you?"

Gene didn't answer. A few feet ahead, he'd removed his sizable backpack and was digging around inside it.

"What are you doing?" Nancy asked. She'd have both hands on her hips if she didn't have to lean so hard on this damn stick. "I don't need to rest." She moved closer. "You leave that collapsible chair right where it is. I'm fine."

Gene grinned and dug deeper in the pack.

Nancy huffed at him, but that slow grin undid her even at seventy three. It always had. Since they met on the Gilbert Lake beach fifty-seven years ago, Gene Thornton had made Nancy Drake Thornton feel like the sweetest secret in the universe.

As if he'd heard what she was thinking, her imperturbable husband turned and winked. Grinning back, Nancy thought of Gene's face at twenty. His star-bright gaze and thick dark brows. His strong nose. His sweet mouth always on the verge of bending into a devastating smile. His glossy black hair, never falling in quite the right direction. All that intense color and contrast was diminished now. Loose skin gathered in folds beneath his jaw and on his neck. Most of his hair was gone; what remained had faded to granite-colored wisps. Under the hard sun and the strange air those cherished faces alternated in Nancy's imagination like changing partners in a country dance.

"Well?" she said, shaking off her reverie before she got too silly in a field with her adorable husband. "What are you rummaging around for? We have to keep moving if you want to be the first there."

Gene and Nancy had been letterboxing for ten years under the trail name Three Wishes, following clues to find small weatherproof containers hidden by other letterboxers in parks and open spaces. Once the box was located they'd write "Three Wishes" in the logbook and then stamp the letterbox's symbol in their sketchbooks.

"That red-bearded young man and those three firecracker sons of his at the beginning of the trail looked serious," Nancy continued. "All three boys had compasses, and their father was reading the clues out loud, making sure the boys memorized each one."

Still searching the backpack, Gene said nothing. Nancy resisted the urge to rub her aching knee.

"It's a near perfect day," she warned. "All the letterboxers in the area will be out. You know you get cranky when someone finds a new letterbox before you do." He wasn't the only one who got cranky, but she wasn't about to admit that right now.

"There you are," Gene sang softly into his open pack. Grinning broadly he produced a black knee brace and handed it to her. He didn't say anything about being right, or how he planned ahead while she rushed in. Or mention her stubborn refusal to accept that she needed a knee brace until she *really* needed it.

Nancy slipped the brace over her sore knee. Gene nodded then started walking through the meadow again.

"I love you, you old grizzly bear," she said.

His ears pinked, and Nancy smiled to herself. *That* hadn't changed in fifty-seven years either.

Gene called out the next clue over his shoulder. "'One hundred small steps after exiting the meadow and entering the woods on the other side, take the northeast trail. Look for the ruins of a stone chimney at the edge of a ravine ten feet after the trail bends completely to the east.'"

His rich, rough voice was all letterbox-y business, but Nancy knew better. A few yards ahead, shamelessly disregarding the PICKING WILDFLOWERS PROHIBITED notice, her husband plucked a lupine from the flower-filled meadow. He didn't turn around or stop walking. He'd wait until he thought she'd forgotten. She wouldn't forget, but she'd pretend so that it would feel like a surprise to both of them when he presented her with a single stem of her favorite flower.

The path narrowed up a rocky hill. Gene turned and held out his hand. "I know you don't need help," he said, winking. "I just like to hold your hand."

A flush of heat ran through Nancy as she took his hand. "Look," she said as they came to the top of the small rise. "That tree is growing right out of that boulder. If we stand on the roots we'll be able to see the whole meadow. And no one will be able to see us," she added, smiling at him. "We'll be like spies."

Gene pulled her close and kissed her.

Breathless, she leaned away and stroked his cheek. "What was that for?"

He whispered in her ear, "I've never kissed a spy before. Who knows when I'll get another chance?"

Voices rose from the meadow below. A man and a woman in their late thirties or early forties were standing in the high grass at the bottom of the hill. The man, who looked like a college professor, was tall and thin with light-brown graying hair, a blue plaid shirt and jeans. The woman, medium height and build with straight brown hair that fell to her shoulders, looked like a hundred other youngish, suburban-ish women, except for the ferocious expression in her eyes.

"Uh-oh," Nancy teased. "I told you we had to hurry. Now you'll have to settle for being second in the logbook. I think Mr. College Professor and Ms. Angry-at-the-World beat us to the punch."

Gene leaned over the top of the boulder to get a better look. "Maybe not," he said. "It looks like they're arguing." He turned, grinning. "Likely over which one is right about the clue. Pay attention, love. If one of them brandishes a compass, we're safe. That kind of dispute can go on a while."

Nancy hooted softly. "If you're right, we still have a chance to get there first."

She started walking then motioned for Gene to follow. "Let's just quietly move past them, all old people–like."

"We *are* old people," Gene said.

"Hush. We want them to underestimate us. Not think we're clever."

"You're clever," Gene said. "I'm dependable."

"Hush again, Grizzly Bear."

The angry-eyed woman dropped to her knees in the tall grass. Gene shook his head. "She lost the compass," he clucked. "No wonder that guy's mad."

"March," Nancy commanded in a whisper. "Now. While they're not paying attention."

The woman below stood up and pushed her hair off her face, no compass or anything else in her hands. "Let's go," Nancy heard her say.

"Hurry," Nancy urged Gene again. "They're already ahead of us."

"Would you have risked *my* life?" the man below shouted.

Nancy pulled Gene back behind the boulder.

"What?" Gene asked. "I thought we were hurrying, 'all old people–like.'"

Nancy laid her finger against her mouth. "Quiet. I want to hear what they're talking about. Maybe there's a problem on the trail."

"If there is, we can just ask them, love," Gene said, trying to move past her.

"Wait," Nancy said. "Trust me. That woman looks a little crazy. You know how some people are. Just wait a second."

Gene shook his head. "All right."

"Would you have risked my life?" the man asked again.

"No one would have asked me to," the woman replied. "You know that." She searched the sky as if expecting something to drop out of it. "We have to go." Beckoning for the man to follow, she ran a few steps toward the woods.

"There's nothing wrong with the trail," Gene realized, angry. "They probably saw us and now they're trying to beat us to the box."

The man below didn't move. "Answer my question!" he shouted.

Relieved, Gene shrugged. "Or maybe they *are* fighting about the clue," he said. "We still have time."

The woman was shouting back. "When we're home!"

The man caught up and turned her around. "Now," he commanded.

She broke away. "Fight with me all you want over hard choices and acceptable consequences when this is over. Right now, we have to get out of here before the Gatherers figure out what *that* really is." She gestured to something in the grass then headed again for the woods.

Nervous, Nancy grabbed Gene's arm. "Wait," she said. "I don't know what they're talking about, but I don't think it's clues or letterboxes."

"What else could it be?" Gene asked, sounding impatient. "They obviously think we're 'The Gatherers.' Not a very original trail name if you ask me. Might as well dub yourselves 'The Letterboxers' and call it a day."

"I don't think they know we're here," Nancy pointed out. "I don't think they can see us behind the tree and the boulder from where they're standing. We're too high above them."

"Answer me," the man shouted again from below. "Would you have risked my life to save anyone else's? Would you have risked my life for anything? Anything at all?"

The woman stopped. Her shoulders slumped and she dropped her head. "No," she said. "No. No, I couldn't have. Not for any reason at all." She turned and gazed at the man, her expression so sad and vulnerable that it was painful.

Nancy took Gene's hand. "Maybe we should forget this one," she said. "If they are letterboxers, they're too hardcore for me."

"Hardcore?" Gene echoed. "You're spending too much time with those kids at the Rec Center."

"I'm the only one they listen to."

Gene smiled and kissed her hand. "I suppose I shouldn't be surprised if you come home with a tattoo and a nose ring some day?"

"I still have a few tricks up my sleeve, Mr. Dependable," Nancy agreed. "Don't get too comfortable."

"Never," Gene said. He squeezed her waist.

Below, the woman was talking again. "I can't even think about the possibility of risking your life," she said to the man. "But this is different. I'm still not convinced he didn't manipulate her."

"*Misos,* Gwen!"

"What did he say?" Nancy asked.

"I *promised* her," the man continued. "I swore I'd protect him. I didn't think it would have to be from you. You should have been helping me take care of him, not do what you did!" He strode away and then back. "No wonder you didn't tell me. You knew I would have stopped you. A life-link—even a modified one—is unforgivable!"

"Life-link?" Nancy said. "What the hell does that mean?" She backed away from the boulder again. "I don't like this. Let's get out of here."

Gene shook his head. "No. Maybe someone is hurt in the forest. Maybe someone needs help. Wait for me."

Nancy stepped forward and stood beside her husband.

"The risk was manageable!" the woman below was saying. "I was going to reverse it. If he hadn't run…" She raised her head again and searched the sky. "We're running out of time. Please. I'll talk about anything you want once we're safe."

"You've destroyed her," the man said sadly. "Your own daughter." Then he headed for the woods without looking back.

The woman ran forward and grabbed his arm. "I had no choice!"

"That doesn't change anything."

"Of course it does. It changes everything."

"Not for me," the man said. "And not for Maude."

"If they'd found Eury…," the woman said, trembling.

"Are they Russian?" Gene muttered. "They don't sound Russian, but maybe they lost their accents. Could they be talking about something that happened in the Ukraine? It's terrible over there. Maybe someone they love named Yuri almost got left behind."

Nancy didn't care. She just wanted to leave, and she was about to respond when the couple suddenly stopped arguing and stood back to back in the bright sunlight, their hands clasped tightly together, as if they were protecting each other and themselves from some invisible or imminent threat.

"Do you hear anything?" Nancy asked Gene. "Is someone coming? Should we call for help?"

A cloud blocked the sun, shading the couple below, and then huge waves of distortion shimmering like heat from a July sidewalk surrounded the frightened pair like a circular glass wall. As the cloud moved past the sun, the distortion in the air turned red.

"Gene!" Nancy said. Frightened, she turned to him. "We should… Are you all right? What's the matter?" She touched his cheek. "You're sweating."

"I'm all right." He rubbed his jaw and exhaled then sat against the boulder. "I should have known better than to try to impress you by climbing that steep hill so fast."

"You don't have to impress me," Nancy said. "You won me over a long time ago." She touched his forehead. "You're chilled."

Gene rubbed at his chest. "I'm fine, love. Don't worry."

"Is it your pacemaker?"

"I had it checked last week," he replied. "I don't see how..." Then he turned around and saw the wall of throbbing red light. "What in the hell is that?"

Nancy shook her head. "I don't know. It just appeared."

"What is this?" the woman below and inside the wall asked, her voice shaking and her hands still clasping her companion's. "I've never seen anything like it."

"I don't know," the man answered. His earlier anger had drained away. He searched the clear red light as if he could read something inside it.

Gene moved to stand. "They're afraid," he realized. "Whoever is casting that foolish light trick is having a hell of a nasty laugh. I'm going to put an end to it."

"You will do no such thing," Nancy commanded, pushing down on his broad shoulders. "You're going to sit until you feel better."

"It's nothing, Nancy," Gene said, rising against the pressure of her hands. "I got winded from the hill. You were right. It was steeper than the map indicated." He groaned then sat down again.

"Who produced it?" the woman below asked, her voice still shaking. "Do you sense anyone nearby? Is it dangerous? Can we walk through?"

Her companion raised his hand, almost but not quite touching the throbbing red wall of light. "I don't know," he answered. "I don't where it came from, or what it is. It has all the properties of an identity shield." He turned his head, and the woman turned hers, too, so that their faces were almost touching. For an instant the man smiled sadly. He kissed her forehead then continued, "But how can anyone create an identity shield without a body to protect? Is that even possible? And why would you need to?"

"I don't know," the woman answered. She sounded scared.

"Identity shield?" Gene echoed. "What are they *talking* about? Are they on drugs? Is this a rave or whatever that drug-fueled, noise-music, hug-fest is called? The folks in Dashton had a real problem last year with drug parties in the woods. Remember?" He tried to stand up. "We're leaving."

His legs trembled. He groaned and sat down again.

"We're not going anywhere," Nancy said. "Not until you feel better. I deal with problem kids at the Rec Center all the time. Whoever is fooling around with that Halloween light will listen to me. It's the middle of the goddamn day and there are families with children in the woods. I'll go down there and straighten this out. You stay put."

Nancy walked around the boulder and the tree and saw a very tall man come out of the woods on the other side of the meadow. He was dressed all in amber, with long sleeves, long pants and boots, despite the afternoon heat. His short, dark blond hair and neatly trimmed beard glittered at the ends, spitting out light like hundreds of tiny downed power lines. The man's exposed skin—his hands, his wrists, his face, his throat—was luminous, even in the sunlight, and it cast a yellow glow over the lupines as he cut through the field of flowers.

Nancy couldn't move. This wasn't a confused, drug-addled kid. This wasn't a kid at all. He looked like a demon.

The plaid-shirted man inside the wall of red light swore loudly and tugged the woman closer. She was saying, "What is he?"

"A Chamura," the man answered.

"What? An Energy Harnesser? Not just a Gatherer?" the woman asked, her voice tinged with desperation. "Why? Neither of us is so powerful. The Ones in Power would never... Something else is going on."

Frightened now, Nancy backed up behind the boulder but watched the tall, glowing figure with the foreign-sounding name walk to the place in the grass where the couple had been arguing, where Gene had joked about the lost compass. The strange figure knelt there like the woman had done. He seemed be searching for or examining something.

From inside the circle of red light the man let go of the woman's hand then dropped to his knees for a moment before standing up again. "The energy that's trapping us is weakest near the ground," he said, his voice urgent. "You could..."

Behind Nancy, Gene groaned. She turned to see him slide from the rock to the moss below, breathing rapidly, his face and neck covered in sweat. She stared at him in terror as she heard the woman's stiff reply.

"No. Absolutely not. No way."

No longer concerned with the arguing couple or the strange red light, Nancy ran to her gray-faced husband, the onetime star-eyed boy who'd stolen her beach towel and her J.D. Salinger book of stories until she told him her name. She knelt in front of him and stroked his cheek. "It's that red light, isn't it? The woman said something about an energy harnesser. That red light must give off a kind of electromagnetic radiation or something. It has to. It did something to your pacemaker, didn't it?" She pulled her phone out of her pocket and began dialing.

Gene took it. He shook his head. "We're too far away from everything," he said. "Sit next to me."

"No!" Nancy said. She grabbed the phone. "I'm calling 911. We're not too far." She finished dialing. As she talked to the emergency operator, she vaguely heard the man below pleading with the woman. He sounded as terrified for the woman's safety as Nancy was for Gene's. She felt a surge of empathy as the man bargained desperately with the woman.

"What will happen to the kids—to *Sandy*—if both of us are taken?"

"No!" said the woman with him.

"You can come back for me," the man begged. "The Chamura isn't paying attention to us right now. Make something to dig yourself out. Burrow to the portal and get back to the kids. You can protect them better than I can. I'll stay here. He'll have to bring at least one of us back. He won't waste time chasing you."

Nancy only half heard the EMS responders as she hung up. "They'll be here soon."

Gene nodded.

Nancy couldn't help herself. Once again she peered around the boulder. The tall, glowing figure—the Chamura?—saw her. He stood up and gazed sorrowfully at her, which scared her more than anything before. He continued to stare at her in horrified pity, and she couldn't look away.

Gene groaned suddenly, his breathing labored. The Chamura broke eye contact with Nancy and walked toward the young couple, who were still frantically negotiating inside the red light.

"Okay," Nancy heard the woman say. "Okay. I'll dig myself underground." The woman dropped to her knees and gathered a handful of stones and loose soil. The man knelt beside her, his fingers in her hair as he kissed her head.

Just outside the circle, the Chamura opened his arms like a hopeful singer on a reality show. The red light poured into his hands, and Nancy felt a wave of relief that trumped any confusion about what had happened. The red light was gone; the couple was freed. The ambulance was on its way. Gene would be okay. The couple and their children, Sandy and Maude, would be okay. Whoever or whatever the glowing amber figure was, he had come to free the couple below from the red light and not to hurt them.

She turned back to her husband. Gene was sitting against the gray boulder, his eyes closed and that sweet half-smile on his face. Nancy shook her head. He'd fallen asleep. Of course he had. Gene could sleep through anything. He'd slept through a devastating hurricane the first year they were married.

Thank God for him, she thought. Although she'd give him hell later for scaring her the way he did.

His right hand lay half-open, motionless on the ground. The wilted lupine cut a green path across his gray palm.

Nancy stood still.

No, she told herself. *No.* She wouldn't move. She wouldn't think. She wouldn't breathe. She'd stand here until he woke up. She wouldn't move or think or breathe.

"Sweetheart," she whispered, kneeling in front of him.

Eugene Arthur Thornton, the black-eyed star of his high school debate team, the laughing young man who'd taken her skinny-dipping under the stars the night she'd agreed to marry him, the dependable quiet old bear who made her coffee every morning and sang her songs when she was sick had tried to give her one last flower.

And she'd missed it.

"*Nomos Apodektos,*" she whispered. "Acceptable consequences.
No one will risk the Unspeakable."
—Isia Sorgyre, *The Uske*

"All that we see or seem
Is but a dream within a dream."
—Edgar Allan Poe, *A Dream Within a Dream*

CHAPTER ONE

Protepol, the First City, the Commonworld

Her heart would burst into a hundred shivering threads of fiery longing.

Maybe it *really* would, thought young Thalia Salic, staring at her novel-reader. People died of less painful things all the time. Didn't they? If not, she could be the first. Someone could erect a statue of her and her exploded bloody heart in Syndesi Park, right next to the statue of Uncle Solymi and Hyad kissing. Maybe the broken, bleeding heart of an Invisible girl, captured in stone, standing in the middle of the most beautiful park in the city would show the world what Acceptable Consequences looked like.

Probably not.

Glancing at her unfinished homework on the kitchen table, Thalia read her favorite scene in *The Uske* one more time: *He was the man she waited for in the forest. This was the face she knew. The dark blonde hair that fell just above his shoulders, the chocolate brown eyes, the soft red mouth. Elyson knew Alder's face. His* real *face.*

His real face.

Like almost everyone at school, Thalia had read the story of Alder the Uske a thousand times. *The Uske* was so popular that the Chronicler, Isia Sorgyre, never appeared in public anymore; too many kids wanted to talk to her and ask her questions. Thalia herself loved *The Uske* so much she could read it a thousand more and not get tired. A story of love beyond all probability, beyond all sanction, beyond all hope. One that fixed the world.

This was nothing like the kiss he'd given her when she came to him because he was a Uske. This kissing—his mouth, his breath, his tongue against hers—felt dangerous, like swallowing fire....

Like swallowing fire.

Mom was upstairs playing with Thalia's little sister, Madakine, and Dad wouldn't be home from work for a while. So, changing the heroine's name to her own, Thalia activated her novel-reader's immersion feature for the first time ever and…there he was. Alder the Uske. Tall, silent, and dangerously beautiful. Standing in her kitchen.

Most of the kids Thalia knew were not allowed to use a novel reader's immersion feature. Her parents had never exactly said she couldn't, but it probably never occurred to them that she'd want to. Because they still treated her like she was five. And five-year-olds did not think about the things the immersion feature let you more than think about.

Alder held out his hand and Thalia panicked. She closed the immersion feature so hard the novel-reader almost fell off the table. Alder disappeared, and Thalia's skin prickled with shame. The image wasn't real. A Chronicler had made Alder up. He hadn't really been standing in her kitchen; the immersion just made her think he was. He couldn't reject her or make fun of her. Or sneer at her in disgust and call her an Aponomi bitch. All he could do was live out the events of his story in her kitchen while she stood in the heroine's place. Holding his hands. Kissing him. Letting him kiss her like he had Elyson.

In real life, Thalia had never kissed anyone. She hadn't met her Soulmate, and finding him could take *years.* If it did take forever, Thalia hoped she'd get to kiss someone else at least once beforehand.

Her stomach leapt. What if she'd met her Soulmate already and not known? She wasn't quite fifteen, so even if she had met him she wouldn't recognize him. Misos, she hoped she hadn't. She couldn't think of any boy at school or anywhere else she'd want to spend more than a few hours with. Or who'd want to spend any time with her at all.

Upstairs, Thalia's little sister Madakine shrieked with laughter at something Mom did.

Thalia played with her novel-reader again but didn't open it. What if she couldn't feel the kiss at all? What if she couldn't feel Alder's hands in hers, even if she could see them? *He* wouldn't notice. He would do what the story told him to do: Kiss Elyson again and again until they had to run away and Elyson almost died. Alder wouldn't know that Thalia was an Aponomi, a disgusting Invisible. He wouldn't know she couldn't easily feel, or see, or move, or speak.

He wouldn't know anything humiliating about her either. Like how she never went to the bathroom in school no matter how much she had to go because fourth year she'd missed the toilet, fell, and couldn't get up. She'd laid there all day shivering while kids came in and out, until a hygiene-and-prevention worker found her and contacted her parents. And Alder the Uske would never know the worst thing: He would never know that no part of Thalia's physical body functioned the way it was supposed to, the way ordinary bodies functioned.

Except her mind. That worked just fine. Better than fine.

Dammit, and Misos, and everything in between! She was stronger and better and braver than this. Fear did no one any good, and she was not a quitter. Ever. Thalia opened the novel-reader to the kissing scene and turned on the immersion feature again. Alder appeared just where he had a moment before and opened his arms.

Thalia stepped up to where Elyson would be if her character was activated. Alder smiled his beautiful smile, pulled her close and…kissed her. But it was an incomplete experience. She felt the subtle heat of his mouth and smelled the cold forest in his hair, but nothing else. Not his strong hands as he cradled Elyson's head and whispered in her ear. Not his hard stomach and hips crushed against hers and all that was supposed to go along with that. Nothing there. Nothing at all.

Thalia pulled away, and strong, gray-eyed Elyson flashed into the scene.

Because of the way the immersion feature was set up, a reader could hear the characters' thoughts when they weren't speaking. When unreal Alder kissed unreal Elyson, *they* felt something. More than something. They felt the something that felt like everything. Completely real Thalia had felt almost nothing. Kissing Alder was like reading about what music sounded like. Not enough. Not nearly enough.

Tiredly, Thalia watched Alder and Elyson kiss. Someday someone would kiss her like that, kiss her like he needed her to breathe. And she *would* feel it. She—

The front door slammed. Thalia jumped and closed the immersion. Alder and Elyson disappeared, and Thalia peeked into the hall. *Zino.* He was home early from work, and he rubbed his hands over his face and slumped against the door.

Thalia put the novel-reader away, started her history homework, and waited for her father to come and say hello. She hoped she wasn't blushing. She locked her thoughts, just in case he was listening. But Zino didn't acknowledge her. Or move from the door.

That wasn't like him. Usually her dad ran into the house shouting hello, picking her and Maddie up and calling them silly names.

She waited, but Zino still didn't move. Thalia knew she shouldn't listen to his thoughts if he didn't want her to, especially since she'd freaked out at her mom this afternoon when her mom did the same thing, but if Thalia didn't do it occasionally she'd never find out anything important. If Zino and Genna *could* make her five again instead of almost fifteen they would do it.

Shooting a glance at the ceiling where Mom and Maddie were playing upstairs, Thalia snuck into her father's head. Or tried to. None of his thoughts were accessible.

Weird. She should have been able to hear *something.*

Zino grunted and pushed away from the door. Ignoring Thalia's gaze, he went to the cabinet above the kitchen sink and took out the wine kana. The round-bottomed bottle glowed in the nest of his fingers. Thalia listened to the suck and pop of the stopper, and to the silvery fall of liquid into a wooden cup. Hearing was Thalia's strongest sense, and she loved the sounds of inanimate things.

Zino drank the entire cup of wine but still didn't look at her.

His silence couldn't be her fault, could it? She wasn't in any trouble in school. She'd been trying really hard to do everything she was supposed to do the way she was supposed to do it, no matter how stupid or humiliating any of it was. She'd never get an important position with the Resisters like Uncle Solymi had unless she, like him, was better than every other student in her year. Right now Thalia's assessments were perfect, even for conduct. So...it couldn't be her. It *couldn't* be.

Zino poured another cup of wine and drank it.

Had something happened at work? Had Zino made a mistake and gotten in trouble? *Oh no.* Had he lost his job so someone whose Soulmate was not an Aponomi could take his place? That was common enough, but Zino really liked working in Hygiene and Prevention, and they couldn't afford to live only on what Mom made.

Thalia stood up so that her father would know she was in the room in case he hadn't actually seen her. Like all Aponomi, her body was translucent like colored glass or dirty water and difficult to see in low light, and anything she wore became translucent as soon as she put it on. In direct sunlight her organs, muscles, bones, and blood were visible.

Zino came over and quickly pressed his cheek to the top of her head. The weight of his bearded jaw took forever to register in Thalia's brain, and by then Zino had already walked away. No wonder she couldn't feel immersion-Alder's kiss. What had she been thinking? She should have known better.

She did know better.

"Why are you locking your thoughts?" Thalia asked out loud, humiliated by the crispy whisper of her speaking voice. Mom and Maddie were Invisibles, too. Maddie couldn't speak aloud at all yet, but Mom's out-loud voice was clear and strong. Would Thalia's speaking voice always be weak? Would she always sound like she didn't mean what she said? Would everything always suck?

She was also still humiliated by the heartbreaking failure of the stolen immersion kiss.

Dad walked over, kissed her head and unlocked a portion of his thoughts. He hadn't made a mistake or lost his job; a superior's daughter had had a baby yesterday. Everyone at work would be expected to send an extravagant gift. He didn't know how they'd afford it.

Thalia waited, but Zino didn't say anything else. He brushed her cheek with his rough hand, put the kana back into the cabinet, and started making dinner.

Try not to fight any more with Mom today, Zino said as he arranged piles of chopped vegetables on a wooden board. He was not an Invisible. He was Synithi, a typical gemynd. All his senses and body parts worked the way they were supposed to. Speaking aloud was effortless for him but, until Thalia and Maddie were grown and all of their senses were as strong as they were ever going to be, Mom and Dad insisted on communicating telepathically at home.

She started it, Thalia said. *She broke her promise.*

Please, Dad said, *for me. Go easy on Genna. She has more than enough to deal with right now.*

Thalia was about to ask for the hundred millionth time how she could possibly stop Mom from worrying about every little insignificant thing when Zino's despair burrowed into her chest. His thoughts locked again, and he scraped the chopped vegetables into a pot. He didn't look at her. Which meant that whatever happened today had nothing to do with unaffordable baby gifts.

Staring at the wall behind the stove, Zino stirred the pot. It was like Thalia wasn't even in the room.

Maybe if she could make him laugh he'd feel better. Her powers instructor at school would die before he admitted it, but Thalia was the best *Teknasma*—the best Mask—in her year. At almost fifteen, Thalia could transform herself into looking like just about anything. The Ones in Power were always seeking skilled Masks, which is why she had a shot at getting a job like her uncle.

Instantly, Thalia transformed herself into a perfect Mask of her father's superior. "Goooooood work today, Salic!" she bellowed. She strutted across the kitchen, making sure Zino could see her Masked butt slosh around like a bag filled with soup.

What are you doing? Zino asked, not smiling.

Thalia let the Mask go and slowly returned to her translucent blue self. She wasn't sure how to respond.

I like you better as my beautiful daughter, Zino said, smiling slightly. He didn't say anything else and kept making dinner.

Thalia heard her mom coming downstairs. *You're lucky it's almost time for Zino to come home, little peach,* she was saying, kissing Maddie as they appeared in the front hall. *Or I'd have to eat you up.*

You can't eat me! Maddie squealed. *I'm not a real peach!*

You smell like a real peach, Mom said.

I smell like a girl! Maddie giggled, squirming in her arms.

Mom wasn't upset about anything, Thalia saw. Dad was locking his thoughts from her, too. That never happened.

Mom and Maddie came into the kitchen silently singing a song about flying potatoes Mom loved when she was a little girl. Dad looked at Mom. His locked thoughts burst open and Maddie started panting. Thalia couldn't separate what her father was saying from her mother's frantic response and Maddie's wailing.

There's been an accident, Zino said again, but this time Thalia heard him clearly. *A train's been destroyed. Everyone on board is presumed dead.*

Mom put Thalia's sister down then leaned against the wall. Maddie's translucent pink arms reached for Dad. He picked her up.

What happened? Mom asked quietly.

The Revealer reports are conflicting, Zino said, rocking Maddie back and forth in his enormous arms. *The Resisters are insisting that the Ones in Power destroyed the train. The Ones in Power are calling it a tragic accident but saying nothing more.*

Images of her mom's younger brother suddenly flooded Thalia's head—at his manifestation ceremony, that wonderful night Invisibles gained full use of all their senses until they found their Soulmates, and for a year after that. Green and gorgeous, as he and Hyad Cerus announced their Soulmate Revelation. Beaming and proud, the day the Resisters hired him as an infiltration analyst.

Was Uncle Solymi on that train? Thalia asked.

Yes, Dad answered.

She couldn't stop herself. Without thinking about it or deciding to do so, Thalia transformed into fifteen-year-old Uncle Solymi on the night of his manifestation. She hadn't been there—her uncle was more than thirty years old now—but she'd seen the memories so many times in her mother's thoughts. Especially recently, since Thalia's manifestation was only ten days away.

Holding on to the edge of the table with both hands, Thalia struggled to silence Uncle Solymi's musical voice as it came laughing out of her mouth, teasing his too-serious big sister for worrying about everything, *All the damn time! Lighten up, Charis. It's not the end of the world!*

Mom's soundless grief dragged Thalia to the floor. It felt like disappearing. Like breaking apart from the inside. Like watching all of yourself turn into nothing.

Genna, Thalia whispered, standing up and fighting to return to her deep blue shadow self. *Mommy,* she repeated. *I'm sorry. I didn't do it on purpose. I'm sorry. I'm sorry.*

Zino's strong yet feather-light-seeming hand ushered Thalia out of the room. *Take Maddie outside,* he said, gently putting Thalia's sister down. *Tell her a story.*

I'm sorry, Thalia said again. *I didn't mean to. It just happened.*

I know, Dad said. *I know. And Genna knows, too. She needs you to take care of Maddie right now. Okay, chichi? Genna needs quiet. Will you help me?*

Thalia nodded. Dad closed the kitchen door.

Thalia took Maddie's hand. She waited until her little sister sensed the physical connection, then led her out into the sunlight that their father had once visually equated to the soft, bright taste of lemon ice cream.

CHAPTER TWO

Warwick, New Hampshire, three days later

The three Mathews siblings sitting in Mr. Spencer's living room were silent. Two of them, anyway. Seven-year-old Sandy stood at Mr. Spencer's old oak desk, playing with a plastic knight, softly singing a pop song he—thank goodness—didn't understand.

Seventeen-year-old Emma glared at Elizabeth, who sat scowling on the couch, her skinny little arms crossed. Mr. Spencer watched Sandy. He and Emma had been talking in the study about how to help her missing parents when they heard something about a train accident coming from the living room. Twelve-year-old Elizabeth was a Revealer. She could make any event or story visible in the air, like a three-dimensional floating movie. Emma and Mr. Spencer had run in but it was too late; the news story or whatever it was Elizabeth had revealed about the train vanished before they could see more than a few seconds, and no matter what they did Elizabeth refused to admit she'd revealed anything at all.

Sandy finished his song about lady parts and fancy dresses and started talking to the toy knight. Mr. Spencer turned his attention to Elizabeth.

"What do you think the most important thing in the world is?" he asked her.

"I don't know." She resumed her disdainful silence.

"That's all you're going to get out of her," Emma remarked. "She might talk to Turner when he and Joe get back from town. Otherwise, forget it."

"Shut up, Emma," Elizabeth said. "You don't know everything. You just think you do."

Sandy gasped. "You can't say 'shut up.' Mommy doesn't like it."

"Mommy isn't here." Elizabeth crossed her arms tighter.

Mr. Spencer opened a desk drawer and took out paper and a pen.

"Ugh," Elizabeth groaned, scooting over as he sat next to her on the couch.

He wrote something on one of the pieces of paper then folded it in half and put it on the coffee table. "I wrote what I think the most important thing in the world is." He held out a blank piece of paper and the pen. "Do you think it's the same as your answer, or do you think it might be different? After all, *we're* different, you and I," he continued. "For one thing, I'm much older than you are."

Emma snorted.

"Shut *up*, Emma," Elizabeth repeated. "Stop making fun of me."

"I'm not making fun of you," Emma said.

"Yes, you are," Elizabeth said. "I'm not stupid," she added.

"I know."

Elizabeth grabbed the pen and paper from Mr. Spencer. She scrawled something then folded the paper and thrust it at him. "Here."

Mr. Spencer took but didn't read it. "You don't have to tell anyone what you wrote. Or what I wrote." He handed her his answer.

Elizabeth frowned then dropped her head and opened Mr. Spencer's paper. She chewed on her lip, and her huge brown eyes filled with tears.

"Did I write the same thing you did?" he asked.

She nodded.

"Not knowing where your parents are must be scary for you."

"I'm not scared," Elizabeth said, standing up. "I'm mad."

"Okay," Mr. Spencer said. "What are you mad about?"

Elizabeth snorted. "I'm not going to fall for that."

Mr. Spencer smiled, but for some reason it didn't infuriate her the way Emma knew it would have if Mom or Dad smiled that way when she was angry.

"I'm not allowed to use my phone," she said after a few seconds. "So I can't text anyone. My friends probably think I hate them. What would I say to them, anyway? 'Hey, guys, guess what I just found out? You never saw it, we have crazy illusions or something going on, but my dad has blue skin and no hair and my sister Emma looks like a strawberry milkshake. But no worries, Turner and Sandy still look the same.' I don't think so."

"Maybe you're selling your friends short," Mr. Spencer said. "Maybe they'd understand that finding out your family comes from a different world than this one, a place you didn't know existed until a few months ago, is quite painful and hard for you to accept. Maybe they'd be supportive."

"Did you even GO to middle school?" Elizabeth said. "Most popular girls don't-know-don't-care about what it's like to be the school freak, but I know what middle school was like for Emma, and—sorry, Emma—this was before she knew she had pink skin and super white hair."

"That's okay," Emma said.

"And even though Maude's ridiculously pretty, middle school was worse for her because she's so strange and quiet," Elizabeth continued. "I like being popular. I like having friends. I don't want to be the weird kid." She sat back on the couch and hugged her narrow chest again. "I hate. Everything."

"You don't hate me, do you?" Sandy asked, coming over to her. "I'm nice to you. You can have all the green Play-Doh next time if you want. I don't need it. I'll use pink. I like pink better anyway."

Elizabeth made a noise and stared out the window.

"She doesn't hate you, Sandy," Emma said, picking him up. "Nobody hates you. You're adorable. Ugh, and heavier than I thought." She put him down and kissed him on the head.

"Don't answer for me, Emma," Elizabeth said.

"Don't let him think you hate him," Emma whispered furiously. "Maybe this isn't scary for you, but it's scary as hell for everyone else. Especially Sandy. Grow up a little."

Her sister sneered, but she got up off the couch and went over to Sandy, who was tearing up a piece of paper and rolling it into little balls. "Remember," she asked him, "when Mom made that awesome roller coaster out of paper and melted crayons when we lost power last Halloween?"

Sandy nodded. "I made the monster who lived in the cotton candy truck."

Elizabeth smiled. "That's right. You did." She chewed her bottom lip and turned away, and Emma knew she didn't want Sandy to see how worried she was about Mom and Dad.

Mr. Spencer handed Sandy a box.

"I already have colored pencils," Sandy pointed out.

"I know," Mr. Spencer said. "But those are your special ones. For your comic book. These are for drawing whatever you want."

Sandy didn't say anything. He silently left the room and went upstairs. Elizabeth just watched.

"Something bad happened to Mom and Dad, didn't it?" she said. "That's why they're not here. Isn't it? That's why Turner and Joe had all those secret errands in town."

Mr. Spencer ran his hands over his face and through his hair. "Yes."

"What happened?" Elizabeth asked.

"Your mom and dad were arrested," he said.

"What?" Elizabeth looked shocked. "Why? They never do anything bad."

"They didn't do anything bad."

"So why were they arrested?"

Mr. Spencer took a deep breath. "Your mom and dad and me and Emma and Joe and Turner, and many, many other gemynd and humans—"

"I *hate* that word," Elizabeth said, interrupting him. "I'm not a gemynd, or however you say it. I'm a girl. I come from New Hampshire. From Warwick. From *this* world. The *real* world. I'm not a gemynd. I'm a girl."

"Really?" Emma said, out of patience. "Then how did you create that thing that looked like a movie, the scene of those people talking about a train accident, right in the air a few minutes ago? How come I can hear what someone is thinking all the way on Main Street if I want to, or even farther? How come Turner can make things move without touching them? How come Joe can fly? Mr. Spencer isn't just older than you are, Elizabeth, he's 900 years old. If we're not gemynd—if *you're* not—how are any of those things possible?"

Elizabeth sat down and crossed her arms again. "I won't do it then. I won't ever make a story come to life in the air. I don't have to and I don't want to."

"You can do or not do whatever you want," Emma said. "But it won't change who you are. It won't change the fact that we don't come from New Hampshire, or even this world. We come from the Commonworld, Elizabeth, as ironic as that name sounds. That's where Mom and Dad are right now. And they're in danger. And we all have to do everything we can to rescue them."

"I don't understand what they did," Elizabeth repeated in a hushed, low voice. "Why did they get arrested?"

"Well, you can't have it both ways," Emma said. "You can't pretend none of this is real and understand what's going on at the same time. You have to choose."

CHAPTER THREE

"I hate you, Emma," Elizabeth said.

"I don't care," Emma replied.

"Are you really 900 years old?" Elizabeth asked, turning to Mr. Spencer.

"Actually," he said, "I'm 914."

"You look old," she said, "but you don't look *that* old."

He laughed. "Thanks."

"Why are you so old?" she asked.

"I'm a Crossworlder," he said. "We live much longer than other gemynd."

"And humans," Elizabeth added.

"Yes," he agreed. "And humans. It takes us 300 years to develop ten normal years. If I weren't a Crossworlder, I'd be thirty."

Elizabeth thought for a second. "So, if it took 300 years for you to be ten, how did your mom and dad take care of you? Were they Crossworlders, too?"

"No," Mr. Spencer said. "They weren't. My mom and dad took care of me for their whole lives but I was still a baby. I don't remember them at all." He sat still for a second. "They wrote me letters, though. So I could read them when I grew up."

"So," Elizabeth said, still thinking. "Everyone you know dies before you do. All your friends. Everyone in your family."

"Yes," he said. "We're alive for so long we spend time in both worlds. That's why we're called Crossworlders. It's often too sad for us to stay in one place our whole lives."

"Do my mom and dad really have powers?" she asked.

"Were you paying attention at all when we were trapped in that safehouse in the Commonworld last week?" Emma asked, exasperated.

Elizabeth blushed and kept looking at Mr. Spencer.

"Your mom is a Transformist," he replied. "She can make anything she wants if she has something to make it out of."

"Like a 3-D printer?"

He laughed again. "Kind of. Except more sophisticated and much faster."

"What can my dad do?"

"He's a Seer. He can see the energy, especially life energy, in anything. He can see what it is and how it works. What its limitations are."

"Mom's power is cooler," Elizabeth said.

"Understanding how things work is pretty important," Mr. Spencer said. "It's one of the ways people in both worlds can avoid making bad choices or hurting someone else."

"How come he couldn't figure out how not to get arrested?" Elizabeth asked, angry again.

"Mom and Dad knew helping Joe's dad was dangerous," Emma said.

"Why did they do it then?" Elizabeth snapped. "Why couldn't your stupid boyfriend's dad help himself if he's so great?"

"Joe isn't my boyfriend," Emma said quietly. "He's my Soulmate. It's different. When you meet your Soulmate you'll understand."

"Ugh," Elizabeth said. "I don't want a Soulmate. I want to think for myself. I want to choose someone because I like him. Not because I can't help it."

"It's not like that," Emma said. "It's more like a seeing a part of yourself inside another person and knowing they see the same thing. It's not like a trick or a drug or—"

"That doesn't sound any better," Elizabeth huffed. "I wouldn't want anyone to know everything about me."

"That's not what I said," Emma replied. "You just want to misunderstand me. Fine. Whatever."

"Eury did help himself," Mr. Spencer interjected, answering Elizabeth's earlier question. "He's been hiding from the Ones in Power by himself since Joe was about three years old."

"Why did have to hide?" Elizabeth asked. "What did he do?"

"It's not what he did," Emma said. "It's what he *can* do. What he could do," she corrected.

Mr. Spencer squeezed Emma's hand then turned it over in his. "Does the connector scar from your cousin Isohel still hurt?"

Emma glanced at the black line cutting across her pink palm. "Not anymore," she said, remembering when the Ones in Power cut it out in an attempt to find Isohel.

Mr. Spencer sighed. "Joe's dad, Eury, was a Whole Listener. It's a very rare power. There have only been three. Whole Listeners know everything that happens in both worlds during the course of their entire adult lives. They don't ever forget anything."

"So what?" Elizabeth said. "So he was like a weird-world version of the cloud. So what? If he knew everything, why couldn't he figure out how to protect himself without depending on other people's parents to do it for him?"

"Joe's dad could be in everyone's head in both worlds," Emma said. "What do you think would happen if a bad guy learned how to do that? What do you think would happen if a bad guy had access to everyone's thoughts?"

"I'm not an infant, Emma," Elizabeth said. "If someone had control over everyone's thoughts they could make everyone do terrible things if they wanted to."

"Yeah," Emma said. "They could. That's why the Commonworld government, *both* sides—the Aythentia, they're like…conservatives, and the Eleytheria, they're like liberals, kind of—wanted to capture Joe's dad and keep him a prisoner."

"Because they both think they're the good guys," Elizabeth said, frowning. "Well, that's the same as it is in this world. Too many grownups think they're right and everyone else is wrong. Everyone is always talking, and not enough people are ever listening."

"You sound like Mom," Emma said, surprised.

"I sound like myself," Elizabeth snapped. "If you talked to me as much as you talk to Maude you'd know that."

"Okay," Emma said, taken aback.

"I thought the Ones in Power were the conservatives," Elizabeth continued, "and the Resisters were the liberals. Are there four political parties? That doesn't make sense. Especially since it seems like they're just copying each other."

"'The Ones in Power' just means the winner of the last power shift—the election," Mr. Spencer said. "'The Resisters' means the loser of that election. Both the Aythentia and the Eleytheria have been winners and losers."

"Oh," Elizabeth said. "I guess Resisters sounds better than losers."

Mr. Spencer smiled slightly. "Yes. I guess it does.

"Were Mom and Dad able to help Joe's dad," Elizabeth asked, "before they got arrested?"

Emma shook her head. "Joe's dad died. But no one, no good guys, bad guys or anyone else, took his power away before that happened."

"Well, that's good, I guess."

"Yeah," Emma said.

"Are you and Joe and Turner going to the..." Elizabeth chewed her lip for a second. "Are you going back to the Commonworld to rescue Mom and Dad?"

Emma nodded. "Yes. And Maude is coming, too. Mr. Spencer is staying here to watch you and Sandy."

Elizabeth walked over to Mr. Spencer. "Okay," she said. "I'll show you what I saw before, if you think it will help Emma and Turner find Mom and Dad. But I don't know who those people were. Or why I saw them."

"Thank you," Mr. Spencer said.

Elizabeth sat on the couch and took a deep breath. A tall red-headed man appeared, Revealed to be standing in a small dark kitchen, telling his translucent wife and their two translucent daughters about a Commonworld train accident that killed everyone onboard, including someone they all loved.

Anxious, Emma glanced at Mr. Spencer, who shook his head and turned away. Elizabeth's vision was no help at all. Three days had now passed since Mom and Dad were arrested, and they weren't any closer to figuring out where they were. Or how to rescue them.

CHAPTER FOUR

Protepol, the Commonworld

Thalia woke up to her mother sobbing. Three days had passed, but she still hadn't wrapped her brain around things. How could Uncle Solymi be dead? The smartest, nicest, funniest gemynd in the world, how could he be dead? She'd never be able to talk to him again. Or ask him the kinds of questions Mom and Dad would never answer. Angry questions about injustice in a society that acted like it was perfect. Why Invisibles were treated differently than everyone else. Why no one did anything about it, or if they did why she didn't know about it.

And Uncle Solymi would never get to meet her Soulmate, whoever he was.

Thalia loved Uncle Solymi's Soulmate, Hyad. Hyad was wealthy and handsome and haughty-seeming if you didn't know him. Uncle Solymi teased him all the time about gliding into a room instead of walking in like a regular gemynd, but Hyad took Thalia seriously and loved Uncle Solymi more than anything. Even if there were no such thing as Soulmates, Hyad Cerus would have loved Uncle Solymi forever. Misos, what would happen to Hyad now?

Maddie slept in the room next to Thalia's. She had a little song running through her head, though it probably wouldn't seem like a song to anyone else. Maddie's sense of hearing had only recently developed, and she had taken to stringing different sounds together in her head and repeating them. To Thalia, the pattern of noises sounded like music.

She got out of bed and oriented herself, counting the eight steps to the hall and the five steps to her parents' bedroom. Sight had been the last of her senses to develop, and it was still the weakest, especially when she first woke up. When she was very young she'd tried not to use her vision at all, insisting to Zino that she *was* seeing when she wasn't. He'd told her that ignoring her weakest sense was not an option.

Her parents' bedroom door opened. Thalia saw the light just in time to step back before Zino crashed into her.

Thalia! he said. *What are you doing out of bed?*

I heard Genna crying, she said. *Did something else happen?*

Zino exhaled. *The Memorium was emptied when the Masevo were trying to capture Eury Vatic.*

Every Sacerian city had a single Memorium to house the names of all its dead.

Thalia shuddered. *What do you mean, emptied?*

Gatherer lights destroyed the names and the sensor, he said. *Every name is lost.*

Thalia leaned against the wall. Like her mother, she often lost physical strength when she had to deal with big emotions. *I'm fine,* she said, refusing her father's outstretched hand. *Stop trying to help me all the time. I can stand up by myself.*

She pushed away from the wall and waited for Zino to chastise her for being rude. Well, she wasn't rude. She just wasn't a baby. It was time he accepted that.

Zino said nothing. He stared blankly down the hall toward Maddie's closed door. Mom quieted and then started crying again. Zino's hands balled into fists and then opened and closed in response, as if he could catch Genna's sorrow and crush it into oblivion.

So, Uncle Solymi's name won't be memorialized yet? Thalia asked.

Zino shook his head. The swaying motion made Thalia dizzy, which was weird.

When then? she asked. *Is that why Genna's so sad? Because his memorialization has to be postponed?*

It's worse than that, Zino said, still staring down the hall. *The current building will be destroyed and the ground consecrated so that nothing can ever be built there again. A temporary structure has been erected at the new site, but there's only enough room for the names of the new Synithi dead. The names of new Aponomi dead won't be admitted into the temporary building.*

What? Thalia said. *Is that lawful?*

Yes, Zino said.

What will happen to their identity markers? Thalia asked.

As soon as someone dies their identity marker activates, Zino said. *That activation creates the illuminated name for the Memorium.*

Thalia waited for Zino to continue or say more than that. He didn't.

Okay, she said. *I kind of knew how that worked already, I think. But you didn't answer my question.*

I don't want to answer your question, Thalia, Zino snapped. *Just let it alone. You're better off not knowing. Go back to bed.*

Her heart pounding, Thalia said, *No. If you don't tell me, I'll find out another way.*

Zino didn't say anything.

Thalia waited for a moment then said, *I'd rather find out from you.*

Zino looked at her like she was hurting him by asking. Maybe she was, but he was hurting her by not trusting her. By treating her like she was a baby or incapable of dealing with difficulty.

Please, she said.

He stared down the hall again.

As soon as a nameplate is illuminated, he said, still not looking at her, *the energy inside it—the unique energy contained in an identity marker and released by the death of gemynd—becomes volatile. It remains in that state until it bonds with the receptive energy in a Memorium. If too much time passes and it can't find that receptor...well, it tries to bond to any energy that surrounds it, like a virus seeking a host. This can damage dormant nameplates and the identity markers inside those, and if the numbers of the dead are too great...* He rubbed his hands over his face then looked at her. *My first assignment in Hygiene and Prevention was making sure all illuminated nameplates were transferred to the Memorium on the same day. It's very important.*

Thalia thought for a minute.

I don't understand, she said. *How will the identity markers of the new Aponomi dead be preserved if there's no place to store them?*

Zino made an awful noise. For a terrifying second Thalia thought he might cry.

Until the new Memorium is completed, he said, *the illuminated nameplates of new Aponomi dead will be destroyed. That process has already begun.*

Thalia's head emptied and everything stilled. The reality of what Zino said waited outside, entering slowly, as if it knew she'd need time to take it in. She wrapped her fingers around the railing that hung on every wall in the small house.

So...it will be as if they never existed? As if Uncle Solymi never existed?

He will have existed for us, Iremos, Zino said, using Thalia's baby name.

But he will be erased from the world, Thalia said, shaking her head. *That's not right. You can't be right about this, Zino. In death, we're all equal. No one life matters more than another. That's the point of the single Memorium. We just learned about this in history. You can't be right.*

A dead calm replaced the thought-noise of her mother crying. Genna's memories of Uncle Solymi as a baby, tiny, green and smiley, floated into the hall. In times of severe distress, some gemynd temporarily acquired other powers, and Zino and Thalia watched the sweet Revealer images hang in the air until, like the last note in a song, they were gone.

We'll build our own Memorium then, Thalia said. Uncle Solymi wouldn't have accepted this without a fight, and she would not accept it for him.

Zino shook his head. *No. It won't be permitted. Nomos Apodektas. Acceptable consequences,* he added ruefully.

Rage clawed through Thalia's skin. *They are not acceptable.*

They are not, Zino agreed. *Now,* he said, squeezing her hands firmly so she was sure to feel it. Not that she cared what she could feel anymore or why. *Go to sleep. You have school in the morning and you never want to give your instructors a reason to doubt your abilities.*

School? Thalia protested. *What about Uncle Solymi's memory day?*

Sorrow rose in her father's throat. *No,* he said.

So, there's to be nothing? Thalia said, incredulous. *Nothing?*

Nothing, Zino repeated. *The Ones in Power want a clean cut.*

Thalia squeezed the railing and swore to herself.

I'm not going to school tomorrow, she said. *I'm not going ever again. Why should I? Why should any Aponomi? What's the purpose? What's the purpose of serving a society that marginalizes us even as they take our contributions? After they freaking* created *us,* she wanted to add but didn't. Like most conditioned-to-be-obedient Aponomi and their Soulmates, Genna and Zino were afraid to talk about the failed weapons experiment that caused the first gemynd to be born Aponomi more than a century ago. Only Uncle Solymi would ever say it out loud. Now he was dead. Without anything to commemorate who he was or what he'd meant to any of them.

I know how you feel, chichi, Zino said, interrupting Thalia's thoughts and hearing none of them, *but we have to—*

No, you don't, Thalia said. *You're Synithi. You're typical, Dad. Until you met Mom you were never marginalized. Acceptable Consequences doesn't apply to you.*

That's not true, he said. *And not all typical gemynd believe Aponomi are inferior.*

Every instructor I've ever had believes we are, Thalia growled. *You and Mom have complained about it to the head of school every year since my first.*

That doesn't mean you should quit, Zino said. *If anything it means you should do everything you can to prove them wrong. You know that, chichi. You're just upset. We all are. It's reprehensible to rob Aponomi of all mourning rites, especially after a disaster like the train accident. But we have to pick our battles. As devastating as this is, it's not worth fighting the Ones in Power over.*

Maddie's singing-dream stopped.

Enough, Zino said, apparently ready to get back to Mom, to hide his head in sorrow and do nothing. *We've woken Maddie.*

Thalia clung to the railing while her father thought-sung Maddie back to sleep. Her father had a beautiful, carrying voice, and those *psallo thoryba* had been a favorite part of her childhood. The songs had calmed her as a child, but they couldn't calm her now.

I'm not going to school tomorrow, she said after Maddie was sleeping again and Zino was quiet. *I don't want Maddie to ever feel hate, or worse, from Synithi who think she's inferior.* She ground her teeth to keep from swearing in front of her father. *As if someone as bright and sweet as Maddie could be inferior to anyone.*

She let go of the railing. *There will be a protest tomorrow over the emptying of the Memorium,* she predicted. *And if there isn't, I'll start one.*

Zino's worried admonition rushed into her head.

Too late, Thalia decided.

CHAPTER FIVE

Warwick, New Hampshire

"What are you doing?" Emma asked her eldest brother Turner, eighteen-year-old genius and occasional pain-in-the-ass that he was.

It was after midnight, and she, her Soulmate Joe Castlellaw, her sister Elizabeth, and Turner and his Soulmate Rachel were playing Cards Against Humanity in Mr. Spencer's living room. Seven-year-old Sandy had been asleep for hours. Mr. Spencer was in his room thinking about how to rescue Mom and Dad and protect Emma, her four siblings, Joe and Rachel at the same time. A long time ago he had promised Mom and Dad and Joe's parents he would take care of their children if something happened to them. Emma supposed they were all lucky for that.

"Turner," she complained. "Let's just play. I already shuffled the cards. Come on."

"I'm not shuffling," Turner said, keeping his attention on the black and white cards in two decks on the coffee table. "I'm removing the inappropriate ones."

As he said this, individual cards took themselves off the decks and floated across the room to Mr. Spencer's desk where they made new piles of questions and answers.

"Inappropriate? That's the whole point of the game!" Emma said. "Are you 150 years old?"

Turner looked up. "Letting Elizabeth play with us was your idea, Emma," he said. "She's twelve."

"Hey!" Elizabeth said. "I want to play the real game."

"No," Turner said. Three more cards flew across the room.

"Yes," Elizabeth insisted. "I'm old enough. And I've already played this with my friends anyway. I live in the world, you know. The regular world. The one with the Internet and seventh-grade-boy idiots. And stop showing off your telekinetic superpower, Turner," she added as another card landed neatly on Mr. Spencer's big, old wooden desk. "We get it, all right? You're amazing."

Turner and Rachel both glared at her, but Elizabeth just put on her killer, I-don't-care-what-you-think face.

"Elizabeth's right," Emma said. As angry as she'd been earlier today at her youngest sister's refusal to accept that their whole family was from another world, that none of them were human, Emma realized she really had been treating Elizabeth like a baby. Worse, she'd dismissed her sister as a real person because she'd been envious of her popularity and ease with everything.

Her sister smiled at her. "*Thank* you."

Emma smiled back. "You're welcome."

"Have it your way, Emma," Turner said. "When *this* card comes up, I'll make sure Joe reads it. And then you can explain any unfamiliar vocabulary to Elizabeth if she has questions."

Joe had been sullen and silent since he and Turner came back from town, and Emma's Soulmate didn't break that silence now other than to raise an eyebrow at Turner, who ignored him.

The offending card flew from Turner's fingers directly to Emma. Rachel tucked her hand under Turner's thigh, and he smiled and kissed her. Emma glared at her brother then picked up the oh-so-shocking card, thinking Elizabeth was right; she did live in the world, and everyone had access to the Internet after all—

Shit. Emma read the card. She glanced guiltily at Turner, who stopped kissing Rachel long enough to grin smugly at her.

"Sorry, Elizabeth," Emma said. "I don't think you'll want to hear Joe or Turner or anyone else read this card. And if you're the Card Czar when it comes up, you won't want to read it out loud either."

Making sure no one else could hear her thoughts, Emma silently read the card to Elizabeth, who choked and blushed.

"You're right," her sister said when she recovered. "It's funny, but you're right. Thank you."

Emma held the card out to Turner, who floated it over to the deck on Mr. Spencer's desk.

"What about me?" Turner asked. "If Emma had her way, *someone* would have read that card."

"Emma was nice about it," Elizabeth said, pouring herself another glass of soda from the pitcher Rachel had brought out earlier. "And she let me decide for myself. You were typically, counterproductively bossy."

Emma laughed and grinned mock-smugly at Turner in return.

"Let's just play," Turner said. "You're the Card Czar, Emma."

She read the first question. "'What's that smell?'"

Everyone passed over their answers.

Emma read from the top card in her hand. "'Seventh-grade Turner.'"

"What?" her brother said, breaking away from whisper-kissing Rachel for what felt like the seventy-millionth time today. "That is *not* an official answer."

"Oh, sorry," Emma said, pretending she'd misread the card. "You're right. The *official* answer is, 'Axe Body Spray.'"

Elizabeth burst out laughing, and Rachel smiled.

"Ha-ha, very funny," Turner said. "You're hilarious, Emma."

Still giggling Elizabeth said, "I was six when you were twelve. Your bathroom is right across from my room. I still have nightmares about amorphous cloud-monsters trying to asphyxiate me."

Turner grinned a bit sheepishly. "You're lucky it was just a nightmare. I could have made that can spray-chase you all over the house."

Elizabeth squealed.

Fifteen-year-old Maude walked into the room, and Joe stood up. Maude's Soulmate Gryphon had been brutally beaten by Commonworld law enforcement agents for interfering with the hunt for Eury Vatic. He'd died of his injuries a few days ago. Maude had hardly spoken since.

"Are you all right?" Joe asked.

Maude looked at him like there was no appropriate answer to that question. There probably wasn't.

"I went into Sandy's room to get my pen," she said haltingly, as if she had to remind herself how to speak. "I let him borrow it for a few special drawings he wanted to make before he went to bed."

"Maude…," Emma began.

"I'm not finished," Maude said. "Let me finish."

"Okay," Emma said.

"It was the pen I used to ink in the temporary Masked letters in the book Gryphon made me. I wanted it back."

Rachel got off the couch. She was tall and thin, with olive skin and dark almond-shaped eyes. She wasn't very smiley or chatty, and she was so much like Turner that Emma sometimes forgot how pretty she actually was. If Rachel wore makeup she'd look like a movie star.

"Sit down, Maude," Rachel said kindly. "Do you want a glass of water or something?"

"No," Maude said. "Thanks. I'd rather stand."

Without asking any of the Mathews kids, Rachel picked up the card game and put it away.

Maude turned to Elizabeth, who suddenly seemed very small and very twelve on the big couch. Maude herself was only fifteen, but she'd always seemed older than her age. Or no age at all.

Let her stay, Emma begged, realizing her sister's intention. *We keep cutting her out. It isn't fair. And she's the closest to Sandy, anyway.*

Maude paused then nodded.

A car—driving way too fast, bass thundering and filled with noisy kids—roared from the top of the block past Mr. Spencer's house. Long lights reached through the window and onto the ceiling before disappearing, and for a moment they were all silenced by the sharp intrusion of the ordinary.

"It's weird to miss something you never had," Elizabeth said suddenly.

"You don't know that you'll never have a normal life, Elizabeth," Rachel pointed out.

Elizabeth regarded her with a mix of pity and disdain. "It doesn't seem likely."

"Your parents hid their Commonworld identities and lived here unnoticed for a long time," Rachel said.

"Things are different now, though, aren't they?"

Joe pulled Mr. Spencer's desk chair over for Maude. She sat down, took Sandy's comic book out of her robe pocket, and opened it on the coffee table, saying, "These are the drawings he made with my pen."

Until now, all the pages in his hand-drawn comic book had been made up of four or six panels. Sandy's new drawings each filled a single square on an entire page. In the first, Sandy lay in bed next to Mr. Spencer, who was reading to him. Sandy was sucking his thumb and laughing. There was a Captain Underpants book in Mr. Spencer's hand, but a copy of the same Captain Underpants story book covered Sandy's head like a helmet.

In the next square, Sandy sat on the bed with his blue blanket and the pink plastic horse Mr. Spencer had given him. His eyes were closed. His head was enormous. It filled the room, swelling to all four corners of the ceiling and draping over the sides of the bed and onto the floor.

Maude turned the page.

In this drawing Sandy sat alone on the bed. His head had exploded. His eyes, his mouth, his cheeks, his chin, his ears, and his hair, all oversized, were scattered and floating throughout the room, surrounded by meticulous blue-ink depictions of a burning Commonworld train filled with screaming people. There was also Gryphon being brutally beaten by wild-eyed men and women in uniforms; a bomb going off in a public square in this world, limbs and smoke and wailing people everywhere; and a little girl with snow white hair, pretty red shoes, and beautiful dark brown skin, bleeding and torn in half inside a tree. These images gave way to smaller and smaller scenes of death and destruction until every space in the square was filled except for Sandy sitting headless on the bed.

No one spoke. Elizabeth crawled onto Turner's lap. Joe got up and walked over to the window.

"He's so little," Emma whispered. "How is he going to handle this? Mr. Spencer said the information from Eury would come slowly, in dreams and stuff like that."

"He's sleeping fine," Maude said. "He hasn't cried or talked or woken up. Maybe he needed to get this out."

Elizabeth got off Turner's lap. She picked up Sandy's comic book and looked at the last page again.

"So, Sandy is like Eury Vatic's witness or something?" she asked. "That's what you said this afternoon, Turner, right? That after a Whole Listener dies they have someone who records everything they knew and heard and saw."

"Yes," Turner said. "Sandy is Eury Vatic's Whole Chronicler. That's what his comic book is. That Shark-Man comic of his you showed us last month? That was the last Sandy drew from himself for himself."

Elizabeth looked once more at the terrible third square then closed the book and handed it to Maude. "He needs Mom," she said. "Even if Mr. Spencer is right and he won't get all the information at once, he's only seven. And he's kind of a baby. He still sucks his thumb. He needs Mom. And Dad."

Joe came back from the window. Turner and Rachel stood up.

"Even if you guys wanted me to go to the Commonworld with you to find Mom and Dad," Elizabeth continued fiercely, "I'd stay here with Sandy. He needs me. He can't stay here with just Mr. Spencer, as nice as he is."

Turner hugged Elizabeth, and Emma thought her little sister looked tiny and enormous at the same time.

"You can't go to the Commonworld to rescue your parents," Joe spoke up. "None of you."

"What?" Emma said. "We have to." *We went to rescue your dad,* she almost said but stopped herself.

Joe heard her smothered thought. He looked stricken then said, "Your parents would want you all to stay here. To protect Sandy."

"How do you know what Mr. and Mrs. Mathews would want, Joe?" Rachel asked.

"Besides the fact that he's their kid and he's seven?"

"Yes," Rachel said. "In addition to the obvious, what makes you think Mr. and Mrs. Mathews would want everyone to stay here and protect Sandy rather than splitting up and returning to the Commonworld to rescue them so *they* could protect him? Elizabeth's right. Sandy needs his parents. You are all still young, and you've only just begun to understand how to use your powers. Everyone in the Commonworld has used them their entire lives."

"Joe," Emma said when he didn't answer Rachel's question. "We already decided to go. Even Mr. Spencer thinks it's the right thing to do. Nothing has changed since we made the decision. Why are you saying this now?"

"Because I've been thinking about it all day and it seems insane. What's to stop the Gatherers from arresting us as soon as we get there? The Masevo are everywhere."

"Mr. Spencer took care of that," Turner said. "I told you. There's a safe house."

"And then what?" Joe said. "We hide inside some old apartment the whole time? How are we going to find your parents without leaving the house?"

"Joe," Emma said again. "No one is saying it's going to be easy, but we can't just leave my parents to face the terrifying mercy of the Ones in Power. You saw what they did to your dad. You saw how he died on that beach, every thought, every feeling, every experience of his life torturously pulled out of him by that extrication weapon."

"What will happen to Sandy if we fail to rescue your parents and we're all arrested?" Joe asked in a terrible voice. "He'll be alone. He'll be all alone. Elizabeth won't be enough."

Rachel ushered everyone but Emma and Joe out of the room. Joe was shaking. Emma went to him, but he waved her off and walked away.

"Fine," he said, coming back after a few minutes. "We'll go. I know we have to. I know there's no other choice. Tell everyone I'm sorry for freaking out. We'll go. We'll go tomorrow."

He ran a hand through his beautiful blue hair and all Emma wanted to do was go over to him, but she didn't. He needed a little space. She gave it to him and bit her tongue. But she wished having a Soulmate was easier.

"Mr. Spencer has a bike in the garage," he said. "I'm going to ride around for a little while. I can't sleep."

"Sandy won't be left alone," Emma whispered. "We'll protect him. I promise."

"My dad and your parents and Mr. Spencer," Joe said, "and Fen Elos, the freaking leader of the Eleytheria for a hundred years…five full-grown Commonworlders, all with extraordinary powers, all tried to protect me and my little sister. They all failed."

Emma closed her eyes against the vision of Joe's baby sister, Edoro, violently dying inside a portal tree as Eury Vatic desperately tried to get his two children to safety. A young, brown-skinned girl with white hair and red shoes. Gone forever.

Joe kissed Emma's head and held her for a moment. "I'll be back soon," he said.

The front door slammed, and Emma was left with the image of three-year-old Joe with his spiky blue hair and beautiful wings crying alone in the woods, his sister and his guardian dead.

CHAPTER SIX

Joe did not argue any more, though he was still not sure what good they could do, and they all traveled to Protepol the next day; him, Emma, Turner and Maude.

After they'd settled into the apartment and waited a brief period, Turner went out to see if he could find any information. He told them it would be safer if he went alone at first; all four of them searching for Mom and Dad at the same time might alert the filters. Mr. Spencer had said the same thing. It was better if they took a day to ease into the search. The Commonworld was not their home.

While Turner was out, Joe and Emma took Maude to the temporary Memorium, which she had been determined to see. Turner had said the filters would likely pass over the mourners unless someone was making trouble, so it should be safe enough for Maude to wait for Gryphon's name. She couldn't bear to not be there.

A crowd had gathered outside the temporary structure. Emma's attention was on Maude, and Maude's attention was... Well, Joe couldn't think about that right now.

A little girl's crying voice broke the silence.

"Shhh," a woman hushed.

"But—," the little girl protested.

No! Her mother's thought was loud enough for everyone in the crowd to hear. "No," she repeated, out loud this time. "We're here for your grandfather." Grinding a sob between her teeth she added, "Remember that."

But it's my favorite, the girl said. She looked up to where a green and purple toy dragonfly buzzed wildly above them, stuck in a flowering tree. *Grandpa gave it to me.*

"I'll be back in a minute," Joe said to Emma, and he walked over to the huge tree as the little girl watched.

He smiled at her. She grabbed her mother's hand and hid behind her arm, but her black and silver eyes stayed on him. Joe flew up into the tree, where sharp twigs scratched his arms and face. Bracing himself on the strongest branch near the toy, he untangled its wings. The dragonfly was covered in bright blue petals and spots of pink sap, so he brushed the petals from the head and body and did his best to wipe off the sap with the bottom of his shirt. The little girl let go of her mother's hand and took a step toward the tree.

Joe held the vibrating toy against his chest and flew down to the girl. She held out her hands.

"Here you go," he said.

She kissed the toy on the head and then spit. "Misos!"

Joe laughed. "That's the sap," he said. "I think your dragonfly got in a little fight with the tree."

"She always gets in fights when she's sad," the little girl said, licking her fingers and scrubbing at the toy's purple body.

Joe glanced around at the grief-stricken gemynd who had all lost a loved one since the destruction of the Memorium. "Yes. I bet some of these…" He caught himself before he said "people" and confused the little girl. "I bet some of these gemynd wish they could get in a fight right now."

The girl looked up from her spit-bath task. "Why?"

Joe blushed and rubbed his hand over the back of his neck. "Like you said. Sometimes sad and mad get mixed up."

She nodded. "I think they get mixed up all the time."

"Dasa!" her mother called in a panicked voice. "Where are you? Don't walk away from me like that."

"Sorry," Dasa said, tucking the sticky toy under her arm.

"Stand next to me," her mother said. "And don't leave again."

Dasa stood next to her mother and clutched her skirt.

Emma came to stand behind Joe. *Did you just get that toy out of the tree for that little girl?* she asked. She slipped her hands into the front pockets of his jeans, and he shivered.

"You saw me do it," he said, leaning into her.

Last night she had snuck out of the room she was sharing with Maude and come to get him. They'd kissed for a long time in the window seat of the safe house. He'd wanted to do more than just kiss, and Emma had too, but Maude's unbalancing sorrow over Gryphon's death permeated everything.

The problem was, once they stopped kissing and Emma went back to her room, Joe was left with his own too-loud thoughts again. Of his dad dying in front of him. Of the sister he couldn't remember, also dead. And now, loving Emma more than he loved anyone or anything, even though he'd only known her for a few months. But everything disappeared. Everything died. And for what? Nothing stayed the same. Nothing lasted.

Joe had to pull away. If they weren't hiding from the Masevo, he would have flown all over the city until he was too exhausted to think. Flying was almost as good as fighting. He wished he could fly away right now.

* * *

"This is taking a long time," Emma said, glancing back toward the Memorium. "I'm going to stand with Maude."

"She wants to be alone," Joe replied, louder than Emma expected.

"No, she doesn't."

"Try to imagine what this is like for her," Joe said in a high voice. "Her Soulmate is dead, and she just met him. She must feel like she can't breathe."

"I'm sure she does," Emma agreed. "Which is why I can't believe she wants to be alone."

"I can," Joe said. "Part of her body, part of her soul, is gone forever." He picked up a rock from the construction debris and threw it into the flowering tree that had almost eaten the dragonfly toy, releasing a blue and green shower of petals and leaves. "Sometimes I think having a Soulmate is worse than being alone. It's certainly worse than having a regular boyfriend or girlfriend."

Emma was about to ask what the hell that meant, when Joe turned to her, his soft blue hair falling over his brown forehead. He took her hand and looked at it, small and rose-colored in his dark palm.

"Neither of us will ever be alone," he said.

"Isn't that a good thing?" Emma asked.

"Yeah." He dropped her hand and paced to the tree and back, kicking at the flowers and leaves on the ground. "Of course it is. I mean, it's great to be with you and not be lonely, and to know you love me just the way I am, and to love you just the way you are."

"So…what's the problem?" Emma asked. She could just slip into Joe's head and hear what he was thinking, but that wouldn't be right. If you could bite your brain the way you can bite your tongue, that's what Emma would be doing right now. If Joe was going to say something terrible she wanted to know what it was before he said it so she could be prepared. But she did nothing, just bit her brain and waited for him to speak.

Joe lowered his head and gave a tiny grin, gazing at her from under his hair. "Are you finished biting your brain, Zombie Girl?"

That grin and those eyes unraveled Emma every time. She ran her hands up his stomach and over his shoulders. "That isn't fair, you know, listening to me thinking while I'm trying so hard to stay out of your head."

He grabbed her waist and pulled her closer. "Your thoughts are so loud everyone in the city can hear them. I keep mine hidden."

"I could find them no matter where you hid them," she reminded him. "But I don't."

"I know." He kissed her forehead, and then very gently, so he was almost not touching her at all, Joe kissed her mouth. "Thank you."

"I don't remember what we were talking about," Emma said, coming out of that gossamer kiss like rising from the bottom of a deep pool in the middle of a cool forest.

Joe laughed. Several grief-stricken gemynd glared. "Sorry," he said sheepishly.

Maude turned around then, her face shimmering with silver light. Maude was a *Syche Katharos*, a Soulskin, who had the power to reveal her soul. Although they'd each seen Maude with her soul exposed before, Joe and Emma gasped at the sight of it now. The beauty was impossible.

"I'm ready to go," Maude said, shivering. "The sensor still isn't working. They're not letting anyone in." She gazed at the temporary structure with loathing, and her soul sank slowly back into her skin.

CHAPTER SEVEN

The three of them were halfway down a shady street not far from the Memorium when Maude pulled Joe and Emma behind a curving staircase that led to a flower-decked balcony above.

"Wait," she said.

At the end of the block a group of teenagers was circling a girl or a boy about Maude's age. The kid must have been a Teknasma, because he or she kept transforming into something different, provoking shouts and laughter from the others.

"Mask yourself into anything you want, Aponomi bitch," a beautiful girl with dark red hair said. "You'll still be revolting when you're finished showing off."

We can't, Emma said to Joe, who had already started to walk toward the group.

The Teknasma dropped the last Mask, and a deep blue, translucent girl stood trembling before her tormentors. She tried to run away, but the red-haired girl grabbed her wrist. "Do you want to see what the Aponomi had for lunch?" she asked the others.

We have to, Joe said to Emma. *Look at her. She's terrified.*

"No way," one of the kids said, laughing and shaking her head.

There are too many of them, Emma said to Joe. *And Maude's still fragile.*

"Misos, no," a tall boy said. "I just ate."

Don't coddle me, Emma, Maude said. *It makes it worse.*

"Well, I want to see," the red-haired girl said. She dragged the protesting Aponomi into the sunny center of the street.

I'm sorry, Emma said to Maude. *But we're here to help Mom and Dad. We can't risk getting caught. We don't know who those kids are or what they—*

"Oh my God," she said aloud. "You can see that blue girl's heart beating." She took a step nearer, speaking without thought. "You can see her entire skeleton. She was translucent in the shade, but in the sun you can see right through her. And her clothes!"

The red-haired girl turned to Emma and grinned. "Here," she said to a winged boy who looked to be around eleven. "Hold her for a second. I don't want to touch her any more than I have to. I don't want to turn Aponomi."

When she waggled her eyebrows at the winged boy, he jumped back. "Me neither!"

"I'm kidding, Lyka," she said, messing up his curly hot pink hair. "It's not catching. Misos, do you think I would let you get this close to her if it was?" She took off a bracelet and rolled it around in her hands until it looked like a pearly cane, then poked the exhausted Aponomi girl in the stomach. "Is this what you had for lunch today? Did Genna make you soup because you still can't eat like a big girl?"

Trembling all over now, the Aponomi fell to ground. The red-haired girl leaned down to whisper something, and the others closed in like menacing, laughing wings.

Something happened, some flash of movement, and the circle, still taunting, backed away. The translucent girl reappeared, and focusing hard on Lyka, the pink-haired boy, she transformed into a shrieking man in his fifties, spitting and screaming obscenities.

"Stop," the boy suddenly begged. "Be quiet. Stop it."

The towering man kept screaming.

The boy pulled a knife out of his pocket. Some kind of liquid dripped from the blade, and the red-haired girl grabbed the boy's arm.

"Zino told you never to take that knife out of the house!" she said as the man lunged closer before turning to threaten the others. "He needs it for work. He'll get in trouble if anyone finds out you took it. We have to get home right now and put it away before that happens."

Lyka ignored her and covered his ear with his free hand. "Stop," he begged again.

"It's not real, chichi," the red-haired girl said soothingly. "She's just a Mask, remember? It's not real."

The man shouted something vile and raised his fist.

Furious, the red-haired girl turned and snarled, "That's enough." She took the wet-looking knife and sliced the blade across the towering man's forearm before he had time to react; then she retracted the blade into the handle. "Stay out of this neighborhood and away from my brother, Aponomi *skyta*. It'll be worse next time."

The man roared in anger, and hurt or not, Mask or not, his action was effective. He reached for the boy, who fled, the red-haired girl and the other kids close behind him.

Maude ran forward. Emma and Joe followed.

The translucent girl reappeared, dropping the Mask of the terrifying man and looking at Maude. Then, before Maude could say or do anything, she transformed into Gryphon, bloodied and beaten by Gatherers, pleading with them to stop.

Maude shrieked. Joe caught her before she fell onto the sidewalk. She wanted to die; Emma heard her sister say it over and over again in her head.

"What the hell did you do that for?" Emma snarled at the false Gryphon, who instantly became the image of Emma herself failing to save everyone she loved from some unseen attacker. "She was trying to help you!" Emma added, trying to ignore the illusory, violent deaths of everyone in her family.

The Mask turned back into the shadowy blue girl. "Leave me alone," she said. Then she walked away, clutching her arm and holding on to the side of a building for support.

In the middle of the next block, her legs gave way and she sank to the ground. Emma went to help. Joe and Maude were right behind.

"Don't touch me," the girl commanded in a dry whisper as Emma bent to pick her up.

"We're not going to hurt you." She gently took the girl by the arms to help her up...then screamed and let go.

"What happened?" Maude asked, reaching for Emma's hand, which was shaking and covered with white lines that rapidly crossed over one another, sinking deeply into her skin.

Joe snarled. "What did you do to her?"

"Don't touch her hand," the girl said in a voice like sand rubbed across a window.

"Why?" Joe asked angrily.

"She didn't do anything," Emma explained through her teeth. "She warned me. This stuff is all over her arm."

"What is it?" Joe asked, only a little more gently.

"Venom from the *dilitirio* knife," the shivering blue girl said, almost too quietly to hear this time. She clutched her arm and made no other sound.

"We can't stay here," Maude said. "We've been out too long already."

"I'm sorry I made you see that boy again," the girl whispered.

Maude shrank.

"He was your Soulmate, wasn't he?"

"Yes," Maude said.

"I'm sorry."

"Maude's right," Joe said. "Can you walk?" he asked the blue girl.

She shook her head and whispered, "Not yet."

"Can I carry you?" Joe asked. A group of silver-suited Gatherers crossed the street less than two blocks away, so he didn't wait for an answer; he picked the girl up. "I thought you'd be lighter."

"I'm Invisible," she said, "not insubstantial." Then she wrapped her dress, which was also translucent, over her arm so the venom didn't touch Joe's skin as they all headed back to the Mr. Spencer's apartment.

CHAPTER EIGHT

Mr. Spencer's safe house was near the Kena, the Refuge of the Worthless, in a place that had belonged to a friend of his who'd fought in the Fourth Revolution a century before. The apartment had been used as a hiding place for Eleytheria ever since.

Safe inside now, the Invisible girl, who said her name was Thalia Salic, told Emma, Maude and Joe that her father would be able to help get rid of the poison. Almost everyone who worked in Enforcement or the Detainee System had a dilitirio knife, she'd said, but sometimes they got into the wrong hands. Her dad worked in Hygiene and Prevention so he had to help when that happened.

"Can you call and ask him to come over?" Emma asked.

"Not from here," Thalia rasped in her unnervingly thin voice. "It's too far for me. One of you could contact him. If you say I'm hurt he'll definitely respond."

Wow, Emma said to Joe, locking her thoughts so Thalia wouldn't hear. *That was close. I forgot no one has a phone here. I guess they still say "call" when they mean contacting someone from a distance. Do you think she can't call her dad herself because she's Invisible?*

Yes, probably, Joe answered Emma. "Where do you live?" he asked Thalia. "Or, rather, where does your dad work?"

She sat on the dusty couch, caught her breath, and told him.

"I'll get him," Joe said.

"Wait," Emma said. "I'll go with you."

No, Joe growled. *You stay here. If Thalia needs something I don't want Maude to have to take care of it by herself.*

What if someone follows you? Emma asked. *Or tries to access you? You still can't consistently hear thoughts, can you? How would you know?*

Joe glanced at Thalia, whose eyes were closed. In the dimly lit room her insides weren't visible at all. *I get can get around by myself just fine,* he said. *Without being followed, by Gatherers or anyone else. You forget that, except for my mom, I've been alone for most of my life.*

I didn't forget, Emma replied. *I just think it would be safer it I went with you.*

I'll fly. I like being alone, he replied, and Emma felt a little piece of her break.

Thalia opened her eyes. "It's not a long way from here," she said softly. "He'll be fine. Your identity shields are really good, by the way. We just finished a semester on identity shields at school, so I'm kind of an expert." She grinned at them then wrapped the skirt of her dress more tightly around her injured arm and shut her eyes again. "If you're trying to hide from someone, you're safe enough for now."

"Thanks," Emma said, not sure whether to be grateful for the insight or pissed that Thalia had been listening to a private conversation.

Joe left. "I'll be back as soon as I can," he shouted from outside.

What the hell? Emma stared stupidly at the closed door like he was going to come back and apologize for having been an asshole. He didn't, so she peeked at Thalia. The girl's eyes were closed, and she was clutching her injured arm. Emma looked at her own throbbing palm as if it belonged to someone else's body. If felt like tiny, burning teeth were slowly chewing through her skin.

Maude and Thalia were both lost in their own thoughts, so Emma took a deep breath and slid into Joe's head. Seriously? All he was thinking about was getting Thalia's dad then coming back as quickly as possible? Did he really not know what a jerk he'd been before he left?

Emma looked at Maude to complain, but curled up on the window seat her sister was replaying in her head the memory of the last time she saw Gryphon alive, when they were all with Mom and Dad at Joe's parents' house in the middle of the Commonworld forest.

"Maude never would have been able to give him her Nevma if it wasn't true," Dad said. "It would have rejected him."

Mom closed her eyes. Her hair curled into itself like a burning leaf.

Maude laid her hand on Gryphon's thigh. He made a sound of sad pleasure.

"She only just turned fifteen," Mom said.

"That's old enough," Dad remarked. "You know that."

Gryphon squeezed Maude's hand. She leaned over and kissed him on the mouth.

"Chi Psalla," Mom said quietly. "Dear child."

Maude couldn't have kept her soul inside her skin at that moment even if she'd wanted to.

So easy. The love part had come so easy to Maude. *Why?* It didn't matter that Maude and Gryphon had only known each other for a few months; they would have felt the same if they'd known each other for a hundred years. It wasn't fair.

Emma immediately gasped at her selfish, unfeeling thought, praying Maude hadn't heard. Maude hadn't. She was still thinking of Gryphon lying on that bed under the thistledown blanket Mom made, of Gryphon squeezing her hand and kissing her gently when she lowered her mouth to his.

I am a terrible sister, Emma thought, A terrible human being—or gemynd, or whatever I am. True, Maude had known and never doubted her Soulmate, but she, the person Emma loved most in the world after Joe, had then lost him. She would only ever be differently sad than she was at this moment. She would never be the same as before Gryphon died. Whose life *really* wasn't fair?

Not that anyone was listening, but Emma locked her thoughts. She left the room and sat in the kitchen. If she had to be alone with her bad thoughts, without Joe or Maude to talk to, she wanted to be physically alone, too. She looked around the small dark room, in case someone or something was lurking, but there was nothing. So she shut the kitchen door and sat at the table.

She loved Joe. She knew that. She could *feel* it. It came without thinking, like pleasure at the scent of the woods in winter or a hot July meadow filled with flowers, or Oreos and ice-cold milk. But...

For a second, Emma really wanted an Oreo. Would that fight off her confusion? She put her head down on the table like she had in elementary school when the teacher was reading to them. She missed her dad. He always knew what to say when she lost perspective or was overreacting to something. But maybe she wasn't overreacting now. She loved Joe, but she didn't know him. Not really. Elizabeth had been right that there were problems with the Soulmate system, as ideal as it seemed at first glance. After their connection, Emma didn't immediately know what it was like to grow up with no brothers and sisters and no real friends, always worrying about where you were going to live or if you had enough money. She didn't know how Joe acted when he was bored or angry for a long time. She didn't know what he wanted to do after he graduated from high school. *If* they got to graduate from high school.

Emma took a shaking breath and faced her scariest thought. They'd connected and had sex; one time, but still... They'd done everything she'd ever hoped to do with a boyfriend. She'd told Joe things she'd never told anyone. He trusted her and she trusted him. She loved him, more than she even knew how to explain. But...but was she really ready at seventeen to know that Joe Castlellaw was the person she wanted to spend the rest of her life with, when she didn't know anything else about what she wanted to do or be?

Maybe, she considered, the Soulmate bond was weaker if you'd grown up completely separated from the Commonworld and your gemynd nature. Maybe it only half-bloomed, like a flower that doesn't get quite enough sun. And didn't flowers like that eventually die?

* * *

An hour later, Joe returned with Thalia's dad. Mr. Salic was tall and muscular, with huge arms. He looked like a football player who fought dragons on the side. His red hair and rough new beard were flecked with sparking gold and copper, as if he were partly made of metal. He ran to his diaphanous daughter, who was almost impossible to see on the dirty couch in the dark alcove. Joe closed the door and gazed for a moment at Emma, who was holding her hand to her chest.

I'm okay, Emma said.

No, you're not, Joe said.

She looked away from his concerned face.

"Help Emma's hand first," Thalia whispered from the couch. "It hurts her more."

"It hurts her differently," her father corrected, taking three vials out of his pocket and glancing over.

Maude went into the kitchen and brought back a bowl and a spoon. "Do you need something to mix those in?" she asked.

Mr. Salic smiled. "Yes. Thank you." He poured measured drops into the bowl and stirred the mixture vigorously until it seemed to emulsify.

"What is it?" Maude asked, peering into the bowl.

"The antidonai," he said, "for the dilitirio venom. Dilitirio produces both pain and exhaustion. It's meant to weaken and demoralize an enemy or opponent."

Maude looked furious and heartbroken at the same time. "Because getting stabbed isn't enough," she said to no one in particular, "the knife needs to be poisoned, too. It's the same everywhere, isn't it? Nothing is ever enough. It's not enough to have a gun to protect yourself, you need an assault weapon. You need a basement full of assault weapons that your son can use when he's angry. Isn't anything ever going to change? Are we never going to learn anything?"

Mr. Salic put the bowl down. "I don't know why an Otherworld girl is here in this neighborhood, and I'm not going to ask," he said, talking to Maude but glancing at Thalia. Turning back to Maude he said, "I know both worlds seem terrible, and they are terrible in some ways all the time." He took her narrow shoulders in his huge hands. "I also know that people in both worlds are working to change that all the time, too. That's what's important, chichi," he said, chucking her on the chin. "That's what we all have to remember." He picked up the bowl again and turned to his daughter.

Thalia held her arm away. "Help Emma first," she insisted in her rough, small voice, and Emma felt Joe's swell of relief as Mr. Salic obeyed and gently took her hand.

"It will hurt at first," Mr. Salic said, holding a spoonful of the smooth black liquid over Emma's fingers and upturned palm, which he'd positioned above the bowl. "But not nearly as much as the poison does. Are you ready?"

Emma nodded. Her heart pounded as Mr. Salic dripped the antidonai into the white crevices covering her pink skin. It felt like blades of ice. She sucked in a mouthful of air and gazed at Thalia, who smiled reassuringly.

Thanks for helping me, the girl said in a clear, musical voice.

Thanks for letting me go first, Emma replied as the pain in her hand subsided.

Who are they? Mr. Salic asked his daughter as he gently poured the rest of the antidonai into the crevices covering Thalia's arm.

She shivered but didn't make a sound. *I don't know.* She glanced at Emma. *They're wearing identity shields.*

Neither Thalia nor her father knew she could hear them, Emma realized. They were locking their thoughts to everyone but one another. All gemynd could hear unlocked thoughts, but *Thoryba Exocho*, Super Telepaths like Emma, could hear past such simple barriers.

Are you all right, Thalia? Mr. Salic asked.

His daughter nodded, but Emma felt the pain deep in the girl's arm. It did feel different than the pain in her hand had, but it didn't hurt less. If Emma's pain had been hard and bright, Thalia's was dark and pervasive. She felt it everywhere.

Their identity shields are very well made, Mr. Salic said. *I can't see through them. Maybe Mom could.*

No, Thalia said. *They helped me. Leave them alone.*

Mr. Salic stood up. "Is there someplace I can wash my hands?" He put the tops back on his vials and slipped them into his pocket.

Maude led him toward the kitchen. "We only have bottled water here," she said. In some of the oldest, poorest sections of the city, they had learned from Mr. Spencer, like the area where this apartment was, it was still drawn from ancient community-shared pumps connected to underground water valleys. "I mean, it's all in containers. There's no running water."

Mr. Salic smiled curiously at her then followed her into the kitchen.

Can Joe hear me? Thalia thought purposefully to Emma.

Yes, Emma said. She sat next to Joe on the couch and slipped her hand under his warm thigh. *But it's easier if you let him know you're talking first, so he can concentrate.*

He's your Soulmate? Thalia asked.

"Yes," Joe said, putting his arm around Emma.

There's no need to be possessive, Thalia said, laughing. *I have no plans to steal her.*

Neither Emma nor Joe laughed back.

What happened *to you two?* Thalia asked.

CHAPTER NINE

Emma glanced at Joe. "We don't know you," she said in response.

Fair enough, Thalia admitted. *I'll ask my dad to erase our memories of this place after we leave. That way it will continue to stay out of the filter system. That's what you want, isn't it?*

Emma and Joe both nodded.

You've done a good job so far, Thalia remarked. She gazed curiously around the room. *I've never seen or heard of a place better protected. My Uncle Solymi was an infiltration analyst. He would have loved it here.*

As Thalia spoke, something throbbed beneath her skin, like a flush of emotion, except instead of intensifying her skin color, such as it was, it intensified the sense of absentness. It was as if feeling something unexpectedly or too deeply made her less visible. Emma was fascinated.

"What happened to him?" Joe asked, leaning forward. "Your uncle."

Thalia sat up straighter, her translucent body still almost invisible. *He was in that train wreck.*

Emma watched Joe stare as Thalia's chest disappeared.

The Ones in Power are calling it a 'deeply regrettable malfunction,' Thalia continued. *But you know them. I think they destroyed it.* She turned toward the closed kitchen door, behind which her father and Maude were talking quietly. *They're still mad to capture Eury Vatic.*

Emma felt a rush of heat flood Joe's throat. She looked at him but he didn't look back, just looked vaguely ill. His dad, she thought with a jolt of guilt. How could she have forgotten how recently that happened? In the past few months Joe had found and then lost his father. Again she fought the impulse to read his thoughts without him knowing.

I'm sorry, Thalia said, apparently sensing the mood shift, her translucent body somewhat visible again. *Did you know someone on that train?*

"My cousin," Emma said, lacing her fingers through Joe's. He leaned into her and she felt him calm down.

Thalia glanced at their joined hands. *As you can see,* she said, raising her arms and turning her hands like a magician indicating empty sleeves, *I'm not old enough to have met my Soulmate yet.*

"You will," Joe said, sitting up straighter, seemingly anxious to be reassuring. "Unless you're a Loveless and you don't have a Soulmate of course," he said. "If you are Loveless, I'm sorry. I didn't mean to be rude."

Thalia laughed then covered her mouth, even though she hadn't opened it. *I shouldn't laugh. No, I'm not a Loveless.* She sighed. *There is nothing sadder than an Invisible Loveless. Even Anaxio pity Invisible Loveless.*

"Why is an Invisible Loveless sadder than any other Loveless?" Joe said. "And aren't there Anaxio Loveless, too? Anaxio have no powers, but they're just like every other Commonworlder in other ways, right?"

Thalia looked at him strangely, but before she could answer the kitchen door opened and Mr. Salic came back in, followed by Maude, who looked upset. Joe and Emma both stood up.

"Thank you for helping Thalia," Mr. Salic said to Emma, not looking at Joe.

"We all helped," Emma said.

What? Thalia thought to her father, still unaware Emma could hear all of her thoughts.

I'll tell you when we get home, he said.

Behind him, Maude stared at the window facing the courtyard. She twisted a stalk from a weed she'd picked earlier between her fingers.

I was going to ask you to erase our memories of this place, Thalia said to her father.

We'll talk at home, Mr. Salic repeated. "Thank you again," he said to everyone else, glancing at Joe.

The apartment door burst open, and Turner appeared. "I found—," he began, coming into the room. "Who the hell are you?" he said to Mr. Salic, and then he stared at Thalia. "She's the Invisible girl from Elizabeth's Revealer image."

Emma looked more carefully at Thalia. She'd been trying so hard to help Mr. Spencer hear anything in Elizabeth's image about the train accident that might lead to information about her parents she'd hardly noticed what the family looked like. "You're right," she said after a moment. "But why would Elizabeth see a family she didn't know?"

"Because the mother and the two daughters are Aponomi," Turner explained. "The glitch in the filter system, remember? The nameplates of Invisibles aren't allowed in the temporary Memorium. That created a huge reclassification of names that overwhelmed the filter system, and it shut down for a few hours that day."

"How the hell do you know that, Turner?" Emma asked. "And how do you know that's the reason Elizabeth saw them?"

Turner was about to say something like, "Because I pay attention," or some other super Turnerish thing, when Mr. Salic said, "Close the door." He repeated himself when Turner looked mutinous.

"Not until you tell me who you are and what you're doing here."

"They helped me get away from some *klasisa* assholes on the street," Thalia said. Her voice was like something underground.

Turner stared, seemingly surprised Thalia could speak at all.

Mr. Salic pushed past him to close the door. Turner whipped his head around and slammed the door without touching it.

Showoff, Thalia thought.

Emma bit back a smile. Thalia grinned at her, but Turner frowned.

"Everyone sit down," Mr. Salic commanded.

"This isn't your house," Joe said quietly.

"You're right," Mr. Salic said. "I'm sorry."

"He knows who we are," Maude said suddenly. "I couldn't help it. He said something about Gryphon. I guess Gryphon was a year or two ahead of Thalia at school." She clenched her teeth and breathed through her nose, obviously trying not to cry in front of anyone. "I didn't mean to. He didn't realize. He was just proud of Thalia and what a skilled Teknasma she is." Maude took a halting breath and sat down.

"What happened?" Turner said quietly.

"I told him everything," Maude said.

"What does that mean?" Emma asked.

"I told him about Joe and Eury Vatic," Maude said. "And about Mom and Dad."

What does Joe have to do with Eury Vatic? Thalia asked her father.

Emma glanced around the room. Thalia had forgotten to block access, so everyone heard her question.

"Eury Vatic was my dad," Joe said.

You're Sfodro Vatic? Thalia asked. *I thought you were dead.* She turned to her father, having just understood what Joe hadn't said. *Is Eury Vatic dead?*

Mr. Salic nodded.

Was he on the train? Thalia asked. *But that doesn't make any sense. Why would the Ones in Power destroy the train if Eury Vatic was on it?*

"The destruction of the train was an accident," Turner said. "Eury Vatic was already dead. The Resisters extracted everything from his consciousness. The extrication lights they used were on that train. The Ones in Power were trying to capture the train, not destroy it."

Right now, Eleytheria are the Resisters, Thalia said to Turner. *You know that, right? Eleytheria have been out of power since the last power shift. The Aythentia are the Ones in Power now.*

"Yes," Turner said. "I know Eleytheria are the Resisters right now."

Eleytheria *killed Eury Vatic?* Thalia asked. She shuddered, and Mr. Salic helped her to the couch. *I could have stayed standing,* she said, making sure everyone heard.

"Don't be stubborn," her father said out loud.

I'm not stubborn, Thalia thought. *I'm just so much stronger than you think I am.*

You're not nearly as strong as you want to be.

Brilliant insight, Zino, Thalia grumbled, her visibility diminishing almost completely. *Did you learn that in Elimination Studies?*

Mr. Salic's face darkened. *That's not fair, Thalia.*

She smiled at him. *Fairness isn't a useful concept. 'Acceptable Consequences,' remember?* She paused. *I went to the Memorium today.*

Yes! he snapped. *You did. And look what happened. Some klasisa miscreant sliced you with dilitirio knife.*

We didn't even know Eury Vatic was killed! Thalia shouted.

Emma was surprised how loud Thalia's thought-voice was. The noise didn't hurt her ears, but it seemed to pound in her brain.

"What difference does it make?" Mr. Salic shouted back, this time aloud. He sucked in a short breath. "I'm sorry," he said to Joe.

"Stop," Turner said. "Who are you? And what are you going to do now that you know who we are? You know they're looking for us. They think we know something about Eury, but we don't."

"We're not going to inform anyone," Mr. Salic said quietly.

"It doesn't matter if you *tell* anyone," Emma said. "If you think about us in the wrong place or at the wrong time the filters might catch it and find this place and us. You have to erase your memories. Thalia told us you would."

"I can't," Mr. Salic said.

"Why not?" Joe asked.

"Thalia is too close to her *protanosi,*" Mr. Salic said. "It would be dangerous to erase her memory now. Her energy could fragment as a result, making it difficult for her Soulmate to recognize her."

I forgot about that, Thalia said.

"What's a protanosi?" Joe asked.

Mr. Salic eyed him quizzically. "You really don't know anything about this world, do you?"

"I know more than you think," Joe growled.

"I'm sorry," Mr. Salic said. "It's just so hard to imagine you grew up with no knowledge at all. Sfodro Vatic." He stopped and stared at Joe for a moment. "You're Volucris, aren't you? The Revealer images of you and your sister after Eury Vatic disappeared showed a winged boy."

"My wings were cut off in the Otherworld," Joe said.

Mr. Salic glanced at Thalia, who glared stonily back at her father. There was a brief silence.

"Let's sit down," Turner said. Then he led everyone to the alcove where Thalia sat like a memory on the couch.

CHAPTER TEN

Protanosi is the Sacerian world for manifestation, Thalia said, making sure everyone heard her.

Manifestation, she continued, *is a period between an Aponomi's fifteenth birthday and one year after they meet their Soulmate. During that time we have full use of all our senses. We see and hear and speak and feel just like every other gemynd. And we look like everyone else. No one can see what we had for lunch or watch our hearts beating no matter how sunny it is where we're standing.*

Emma felt angry embarrassment crush Thalia's chest. The center of her shadowy body disappeared completely.

"A fully manifested Aponomi is nearly as beautiful as a Soulskin," Mr. Salic said, glancing at Maude, who blushed.

"Why does it last for only a year after you meet your Soulmate?" Joe asked.

Because it does, Thalia said. *Everything we are—all gemynd, not just Aponomi—everything we can do, all of our powers are different means to find and connect with our Soulmates. It's all linked to that.*

"So Aponomi Loveless never manifest?" Emma said.

Thalia shook her head. *No.*

"I can and will erase my memory," Mr. Salic spoke up. "But I can't erase Thalia's."

"Can she stay with us, then?" Turner said. "Until her manifestation? Then you can come here and erase her memory because she'll be stable enough. Right?"

"Yes," Mr. Salic said. "But…"

A protanosi is a really big deal, Thalia said. *Imagine that for your whole life you only got one holiday, one celebration. That's kind of what it's like. There are parties and dinners. Synithi…* She frowned then clarified, *Typical gemynd try to touch you for luck. Because it's not enough to marginalize us, they have objectify us, too.* She exhaled and shook herself. *Anyway, my mom's been preparing for my manifestation ceremony for two years.*

"But you can go home as soon as it happens," Turner said. "As soon as your dad erases your memories of us."

It's the actual transformation that is the big deal, Thalia said, her chest disappearing and reappearing. Emma realized she was trying to control her emotions and stay as visible as she could. It seemed exhausting.

At midnight on your fifteenth birthday all your friends and family come to watch you manifest, Thalia said. *If your birthday is in a warm season, it's usually done outside. But I think the most beautiful manifestation ceremonies are in the snow under the stars.*

Turner stood up and walked angrily into the kitchen.

Joe glanced after him then back at Thalia. "Their parents were arrested. That's why we're here." He looked at Emma. "They're not in a regular prison. They're secreted. That's what we've been told, anyway. We heard no one ever comes home after they're secreted."

"That's right," Mr. Salic said gently. "Officially, the Ones in Power insist that the secret Synektos prison doesn't exist, that it was destroyed almost a century ago. Most Aythentia and some Eleytheria accept that statement, but..." He exhaled and turned sympathetically to Emma and Maude. "It does exist. No one has ever escaped. And no one has ever been released."

"That doesn't mean it's impossible," Emma said. "It just means it hasn't been done yet."

Mr. Salic didn't say anything. No one did.

"I'm sorry," he finally said, breaking the silence. "Truly I am, but I can't ask Thalia's mother to miss Thalia's manifestation because you believe you'll find your parents. You won't. I'm sorry." He stood up, and a conflicted expression crossed his face. "I don't know what would have happened to Thalia injured and alone on the street if you hadn't brought her here. I will be forever grateful that you helped her."

Thalia said nothing.

"I don't know what Thalia told you about being an Invisible," Mr. Salic continued. "Probably nothing. She's proud as... Well," he said, taking a deep breath. "Aponomi have fewer rights than Synithi, than ordinary gemynd. It's permissible to treat them differently. Acceptable consequences," he added, taking another halting breath.

"What I am trying to say is, most gemynd wouldn't have bothered. So, thank you." He shook all their hands. Then he said, *Thalia, we have to go.*

"But our mom and dad," Maude said.

Mr. Salic looked saddest when he regarded her. "It is unbearable, I know," he said, "but you simply won't find them. I'm sorry. And I'm profoundly sorry for the loss of your Soulmate."

Maude sucked in a mouthful of air and was silent.

"The smartest thing to do," Mr. Salic said, "is to bring the rest of your family here. Register with the Ones in Power. Promise to behave yourselves and then make good on that promise." *Come, Thalia.*

Emma watched Thalia follow her father from the dingy apartment. She didn't look at any of them on her way out.

As soon as the door closed, Turner said, "I found an Anaxio who says he can help us find Mom and Dad."

Emma looked incredulously at him. "Didn't you hear what Thalia's dad said? Forgetting about the terrifying fact that no one has ever been rescued from wherever the hell the secret Synektos prison is, he won't erase Thalia's memory. How is she going to stop thinking about meeting Eury Vatic's son, or that Eury Vatic is dead when apparently no one else in the Commonworld knows? Aren't these the kinds of things the filters are set up to catch?" She looked at Joe and Maude. "We have to go home. Now. While the identity shields are still working. We have to think of a new plan in a safer place than this."

"I'm not leaving," Turner said. "This kid promised he could help, and I believe him."

"Kid?" Emma repeated.

Turner reddened and set his jaw. "Aubrey is almost thirteen years old."

"Turner," Emma said, a little more quietly than before. "You're not thinking straight. I know this is horrible. I know you think this is somehow your fault, that you could have saved Mom and Dad, but…even if she tries not to, Thalia might accidentally reveal our location and our identities to the Ones in Power. We can't stay here because you found someone Elizabeth's age who thinks he can help us. And Anaxio aren't trustworthy anyway. They hate everyone because they have no powers. You know that."

Her brother paled, and Emma felt instantly guilty.

"How can you make such a sweeping statement about any group of people?" Turner asked. "'Because they have no powers all Anaxio hate everyone'? What the hell, Emma?"

"I didn't mean it like that," she stammered. "I meant—"

"Aubrey isn't helping us for nothing," Turner said. "I promised to find him a place to live in the Otherworld. He won't be segregated or despised there."

"What about his family?" Emma asked. She tried to swallow her thick sense of shame.

"He doesn't have one," Turner said. "Well, he did, but they left him in the Kena, the Refuge, as soon as they realized he was Worthless."

Emma sat down.

"How do you know he can help?" Joe asked.

"Because he told me what he can do. He told me in secret," Turner added. "There's a bar where he goes to steal food."

"I thought gemynd gave food to the Anaxio," Maude interrupted.

"Aubrey doesn't want donated food. He wants to get it himself. So he steals it."

"What does this have to do with anything?" Emma almost shouted. "We still have to find a new place to stay before Thalia or her dad accidentally give us away."

"The bar has an 'inaccessible spot,' something totally protected from the filter system," Turner continued, ignoring her. "Aubrey breaks in after the bar is closed. It's where he plans how to steal food or anything else he needs."

"Can Anaxio hear thoughts?" Maude asked.

"No," Turner said, "and they can't block anyone from reading theirs, either."

"How did he meet you there during the day?" Joe asked. "Doesn't he have school or something?"

"The inaccessible spot is in the bathroom," Turner said. "I walked in, locked the door and waited. Aubrey came up through an opening in the floor that's used for garbage. And no, Anaxio aren't educated. The Ones in Power believe it's a waste of resources."

"So, you think because he went through all that to tell you in secret, he told you the truth?" Joe said.

"Yes," Turner said. "And because of what he said. Aubrey ran away from the Refuge as soon as he could get food for himself. He knows almost everything about the city and the surrounding woods. He foraged from spring until fall, and then he got caught and was brought back."

"How did he forage without getting sick or poisoned?" Maude asked. "Some plants only look innocuous."

Emma and Turner exchanged glances. For the first time since Gryphon's death, Maude sounded something like herself.

"He's smart," Turner said. "And lucky."

"Where does he think the secreted gemynd are kept?" Joe asked. "Did he actually say he knows where the prison is? How could a kid know if adults don't?"

"He doesn't know where it is," Turner said.

Emma leapt out of her chair. "We are seriously wasting time."

"Calm down," Turner said to her before answering Joe. "He doesn't know where the prison is, but he thinks he knows how to find it."

"How?" Emma said. "Tell us something now, something that makes sense, or I'm making us all leave this minute."

Turner crossed the room to stand in front of her, his arms folded and his expression immovable. "How are you going to do that?"

Joe moved to stand beside Emma, and Turner glared at him.

Emma sighed. "Listen," she said. "If the Masevo come after us, we'll have no chance at all of finding Mom and Dad. I'm not asking you to ignore what the kid said. I'm just saying we can't wait here until Thalia accidentally gives us away. The identity shields only work up to a point. If the Gatherers suspect something—which they will if they discover a hundred-year-old safe house—they'll look harder, and the shields aren't impervious. *Thalia* saw through them."

"Thalia didn't see through them," Maude said. "She saw that we were wearing them. That's bad, but it's not as bad."

"And *I'm* saying," Turner interjected, glaring at Joe, his arms still crossed, "stop interrupting me, give me a chance to explain, and *then* we'll leave."

"We'll have to tell Mr. Spencer there's a possibility this apartment will be discovered," Maude murmured.

"Explain," Emma said, ignoring her sister and unintimidated by Turner's posturing.

CHAPTER ELEVEN

Don't leave the house without permission again, Zino said as he and Thalia walked back to their neighborhood.

I won't, Thalia said. *I'm sorry.*

Zino didn't say anything.

I'm not sorry for myself, Thalia said, struggling to keep up. If her legs started to feel any weaker he'd have to carry her, which she hated, hated, hated.

He stopped and let her catch her breath. They'd both decided that there might be Gatherers on the train or at the stations, and that it was safer for Joe, Emma and Emma's family if they walked home. The filter system was constantly recording but not constantly viewing information, but the Masevo might stop and harass them anyway just because Thalia was Invisible.

I don't care about the dilitirio knife, Thalia said.

Zino made an angry noise between his teeth.

I'm sorry for the others, Thalia continued, careful not to be specific. *I'm sorry that someone could get hurt for helping me.*

I know. Zino hesitated.

I'm fine, Thalia insisted, walking ahead of him.

He caught up to her in two strides. *You could make yourself disappear completely, and I could carry you on my shoulders. No one would see.*

I would know, Thalia said. *What do you think it feels like to know that your weakness might put someone else in danger—someone only trying to help you? To know that you can't walk because you can't really do two things at once, like feel and walk?* Despite her best efforts, Thalia started to cry, which made her legs give way completely, which made her cry harder.

A thin woman with a beautiful, lemon-yellow face appeared on the footpath ahead. She walked around Thalia, who had collapsed in the sunniest part of the path—of course. The woman stared, clucking her tongue in disgust.

"Fuck you, periskata," Thalia hissed.

Thalia! her father admonished.

What? Thalia said, choking over her attempts to stop crying. *Should I have thanked her for not stepping on me?*

Iremos, Zino said, using her baby name, which meant "quiet one." *Don't fall prey to self-pity.*

Thalia took a deep breath and stood up shakily, daring her father to try to help her. He didn't. *You're right,* she said when she was upright. *I won't. I'm sorry.*

Don't be sorry, chichi, he said.

But I am, she said. *I hate gemynd who complain. I don't feel sorry for myself.* She took another breath. *Let's go.*

Let's eat, Zino said, glancing at a restaurant across the street.

I don't want to go in, Thalia said.

I'll get something and bring it out. We can eat in Syndesi Park. He pointed up the street to a carved iron gate covered with moonflowers. *It's after four and you haven't eaten since early this morning, have you?*

No, she said. *Okay. I'll have bread and cheese and fruit. Raspberries,* she added, smiling slightly.

Raspberries, he said, smiling back. He tapped her on the nose. She didn't feel it, but she felt what he felt, which was sweet.

Thanks, she said, squeezing his hand.

There was no one in the park, which was lovely both for its emptiness and for the flowers and greenery that covered the stone and iron walls. Zino set up the food on a bench far away from the statue of the kissing Soulmates the park was named for. Syndesi was the Sacerian word for connection. Before Thalia was born, Uncle Solymi and Hyad were the models for the black marble sculpture. They were young and had just had their *Kiryx Eynosyndeo,* their Soulmate revelation. Thalia didn't think she could bear to see the statue so soon after Uncle Solymi's death.

Zino heard her thoughts and smiled sadly at her. He poured each of them a small cup of wine from a narrow-throated blue kana.

What has Genna been doing today? Thalia asked, holding a crushed raspberry in her mouth until the taste of bright, sharp sweetness reached her brain.

What do you think? he said, sipping his wine. *After we realized you were safe, she went back to planning the ceremony. She bartered with someone at work for silks. The woman makes blue silk in the exact shade Mom imagines your skin will be when it's opaque. And all the music spheres will be purple for your hair.*

Does Mom think my hair will be purple? Thalia asked, picking up a strand. Right now it was translucent blue.

Her mother's hair was purple, Zino explained. *And you favor her.*

Thalia smiled. Her grandmother had had a famously beautiful manifestation. *What did Mom barter for the silk?*

A song sphere, Zino said. *The woman's sixteen-year-old son is Loveless. She wants a song for his Xere Kiryx, which she thinks will happen soon. Genna went to their house this afternoon to meet the son and write a Soul Song.*

Thalia's mother was an *Exocho,* a Telepath, but she was also a *doro,* an Aponomi with one exaggerated sense—her hearing—and her connection to sound and beauty was finer and more subtle than that of most gemynd. Commonworlders had begun to value art and beauty for its own sake only within the past fifty years. Thalia's mother made song spheres primarily for rituals and celebrations, but sometimes gemynd wanted them just because her spheres were so beautiful. If Genna been Synithi instead of Aponomi their family would have been *chrim,* wealthy, because of her extraordinary talent.

What if the boy has an ugly soul? Thalia asked, grinning.

Thalia, Zino scolded. *Everyone has some goodness.*

Thalia groaned and looked away.

Everyone, Zino repeated. *No exceptions. Let's go,* he said, standing up and gathering the garbage into a bag when they were finished. *I told Genna we'd be back before dark.*

Thalia glanced down to see if she had any crumbs on her clothes. She did.

Clean? she asked after she brushed them off. Anything that was touching an Aponomi or his or her clothes became difficult to see. Thalia was always worried about looking dirty and not realizing it.

Zino examined her dress and brushed something off the skirt. *Clean,* he said.

Do you think I'll meet my Soulmate soon after my manifestation? Thalia asked, walking with him, stronger now after having eaten and calmed down.

It's hard to say, Zino replied, putting out his arm to stop her from walking in front of a vehicle she would have seen too late. *Some gemynd don't meet their Soulmates until they're in their twenties or thirties. Some meet them later than that. Genna and I met when she was nineteen.*

Was it hard for her? Thalia asked. *When she went back to being completely Aponomi?*

No, Zino said. *Genna worries about the gemynd she loves, but she's very happy with who she is. She doesn't ever want to be anything else. And she never did. She doesn't envy anyone.* He took Thalia's hand and led her across the busy street. *Her happiness with herself was one of things that drew me to her even before I knew she was my Soulmate.*

How did you know? Thalia asked. *How do you know someone is your Soulmate?*

They'd crossed the street, and Zino gazed at her. *You know,* he said. *You know like you know your own self. Like you know your own thoughts. You* know. *And it is the most wonderful, single miraculous element in the world, save existence itself. Come on,* he said. *Mom is waiting.*

Thalia smiled to herself. She couldn't wait to feel things like Synithi. Sounds, tastes, smells; seeing and feeling everything completely… And she couldn't wait to know what it felt like to meet her other half and recognize him as her Soulmate.

CHAPTER TWELVE

Emma, Joe, and Maude waited in a park for Turner to come with Aubrey, the Anaxio who'd offered to help them. Gemynd came in and out to talk, or argue, or in the case of a bright pink couple to kiss until it was embarrassing for anyone else to sit there anymore. Maude, Emma and Joe walked over to the restaurant across the street. Joe had seen it on his walk to Thalia's dad's office. Her dad had said the family lived nearby. Maybe he and Thalia even passed it on their way home.

The kissing pink couple came out of the iron gate looking glowier than Turner after spending time alone with Rachel. Emma was trying not to stare at them when Joe whispered, "Here comes your brother."

Turner was alone.

"Where's Aubrey?" Emma asked.

"He's already in the park," Turner said. "He didn't want to walk with me. If he's caught out of the Refuge he'll get punished."

"What will happen?" Maude asked.

"He won't tell me," Turner said. "Come on."

They walked back into the park, which seemed empty until a purple-haired boy, slightly taller than Elizabeth, with a dirty face and a fierce expression, climbed out from under a tree dripping with red-flowered branches that hung to the ground like a circus tent.

"Why are there so many of you?" Aubrey asked, and Emma was shocked by how resonant his voice was. "Never mind," he said. "Forget it."

He glanced at the gate and dropped to his knees near the crimson tree, but Turner grabbed him by the arm. "Wait. You have to help us."

For a minute Emma thought Aubrey was going to bite her brother's hand.

"I don't *have* to do anything," Aubrey said. "I'm Worthless, remember?" He tried to pull his arm away but Turner was stronger. "Let go of my arm," the boy said in a voice both scary and mesmerizing.

"Let go of him, Turner," Maude said.

"I don't need your assistance or your pity," Aubrey snapped, seeming angrier with Maude than he was with Turner.

"You promised you'd help," Turner said, still not letting go.

"You promised you wouldn't tell anyone about me," Aubrey said, sounding a little more like a twelve-year-old boy.

"I told you I was here with my sisters," Turner said. "I told you we were looking for our parents."

"Who the hell is that, then?" Aubrey said, standing up and glaring at Joe.

Turner let go of Aubrey's arm. "My sister Emma's Soulmate."

"No," Aubrey said, backing away and shaking his head. "You lied to me. You never told me about anyone else. Find your parents yourself." He crawled under the tree then turned around. "And if you tell anyone about me or my place at the bar, I'll tell the Masevo where you live." He gave Turner a look of triumph and loathing. "I'm not an idiot. Everything I do, I do myself. I don't need powers to help me."

"Wait," Joe said, and he dropped to the ground near Aubrey.

"What?" the boy said icily. "Turner already offered me the only thing I want, and I'd rather not have it than be lied to or patronized. You can't give me anything I can't get for myself."

Joe picked up a stick and wrote something in the dirt. He covered the words with his hand. "Think quietly when you read this," he said.

"I'm not an idiot," Aubrey repeated slowly.

Joe moved his hand. *I AM EURY VATIC'S SON* was written on the ground.

Aubrey looked at him as he wiped away the statement. "Are you telling the truth?" he asked.

Joe nodded.

"That's why I didn't tell you about him," Turner said.

Aubrey sat on the ground. "Are the Masevo looking for you? You do know who the Gatherers are and what they do, don't you?"

"The Gatherers don't know we're here yet," Turner said. "They think we're still in New Hampshire—the Otherworld," he added, matching Aubrey's condescending tone. "But we don't know how long that will last."

"Why?" Aubrey said, alert and suspicious.

Turner glanced at Emma. "We met someone who came to the place where we're staying. She and her father discovered who we are. She said she'd try not to give us away. Her father agreed to erase his memory but he refused to erase hers because it's too close to her manifestation."

"You risked being caught by the Gatherers because of an Invisible?" Aubrey spat. "Are you crazy? What a waste."

"Well, now we have to worry about you," Maude said. "You're just as likely to accidentally think about us in the wrong place as she is."

"Yeah," Aubrey said, snarling. "But I had something to exchange, so the risk is balanced. An Invisible is less than nothing. You might as well walk up to a Gatherer and say, 'Here I am! Take me to the Detainee Tower!'"

"This is stupid," Emma said. "We have to stop arguing all the time." She knelt next to Aubrey so they were at eye level. "Are you going to help us or not?"

"Are you really who you said you were?" Aubrey asked Joe.

"Yes," Joe said.

Aubrey made a noise and turned away for a minute.

"All right," he said, leaning back on his heels. "I'll help you. I think the place where gemynd are held is accessible through a portal that leads to a chain of entrances, kind of like a series of mazes with a door at every change in direction. If I'm right, and if I can determine where that portal is, I'll meet you tomorrow to tell you. Got it so far?" he asked, not waiting for an answer. "But we'll have to be careful." He glanced at Joe with a mix of awe and annoyance. "*He'll* attract the Masevo more readily than the rest of you."

"He's wearing an identity shield," Emma pointed out. "Did *you* know who he was?"

"An identity shield doesn't mean anything to me," Aubrey said. "I have no powers. Remember? I can't read thoughts or anything like that, so how could I see an identity shield? It's not literally visible. You know that, right? It's only detectable telepathically." He made a noise that sounded like a mixed sigh and a growl, stood up and brushed the newest layer of dirt from his knees. "Why were your parents secreted?"

Turner reddened slightly. "I think the less you know the better."

"Why?" Aubrey said. "My thoughts are too easy for the Gatherers to access? Is that it?"

"No," Emma said. "It's arithmetic. The fewer people who know, the less likely it is—"

"'People'? I'm a gemynd," Aubrey said. "I'm not human any more than you are."

"This isn't going to work," Joe said to Turner. "He's too young. Let's get out of here."

Aubrey rubbed a small stone into the ground with his foot, made that growling sigh again, scowled and said, "All right. Fine. I'll tell you everything I know. The filters won't sweep this area again for a little while anyway."

"Thank you," Turner said.

Aubrey nodded then said, "After the Fourth Revolution almost destroyed Saceres, the Aythentia and then Eleytheria decided to work together to create a weapon so terrible that no one would risk upsetting the balance of power again. They called it Synektos or The Unspeakable System. Sounds like a foolproof plan, right?"

No one said anything, but they didn't leave, either.

"I'll answer," Aubrey said. "It wasn't. There were problems from the beginning—rumors of experiments on gemynd that broke Sacerian law, way past the boundaries of Acceptable Consequences…which is a morally ambiguous law to begin with. Yeah, sacrifices have to be made," he continued, pacing in the grass, "when the safety of an entire society is at stake, but who the hell ever thinks of themselves as an acceptable consequence? No one. Not me, not any one of you either, unless you're all idiots. Sacrifice should be freely chosen, not forced on anyone."

"Didn't anyone do anything?" Joe asked when Aubrey stopped ranting. "Did people—*gemynd*," he corrected when Aubrey frowned, "just accept it?" *Is everything the same everywhere?*

Only Emma heard Joe's unspoken thought. She tried to catch his eye but he wouldn't look at her.

"Of course they didn't just accept it," Aubrey said, insulted. "There were all kinds of protests, but the Ones in Power ignored them. Or it seemed like they did. Then one of the experiments caused a mutation in the children of the gemynd who were working on the weapon. That mutation created Invisibles. When the information got out, the Ones in Power announced that they'd stopped working on the Synektos weapon. All records and chronicles were destroyed."

"If they stopped working on it, why did they destroy the records?" Emma asked.

Aubrey glanced at Joe, who was standing very still. He said, "Some gemynd suspected the work wasn't abandoned and the records were secreted not destroyed. That's why everyone started calling it the 'secreting system.' Like calling it a stupid name would be enough to piss off the Ones in Power and make them stop working on it. Anyway, gemynd who wanted to prove that the work was continuing began a coded chronicle to track information about the experiments and the secret prison where they took place. Just before Eury Vatic disappeared those gemynd thought they may have found the location of the Synektos prison, but they and their chronicle disappeared before they could make the discovery public."

He bent down and picked up a rock, turning it in his hand to catch the dying sunlight. "This is dangerous for you to talk about," he announced, tossing the stone into the branches. "I'm Anaxio. The filters are set to pick up on Worthless chatter about bribery and leaving the Kena, but otherwise they kind of ignore us. You're not Worthless," he added. "You should be careful where and how you mention it."

"Well, where is it?" Turner asked. "The thing you're talking about."

"I already told you, the filters won't sweep this area for a little while," Aubrey said. "You're safe to talk about it here. I was just saying—"

"So where is *the secret prison?*" Turner asked, exasperated.

"I can't be sure," Aubrey said. "I only have a chronicle that references the original lost chronicle, but it seems a veiled portal leads to a series of entrances in the Otherworld—the maze thing I mentioned earlier—and eventually back here. I have an idea where that veiled portal is, but I want to make sure."

"What's a veiled portal?" Emma asked.

"A portal that doesn't officially exist," Turner said before Aubrey could respond.

"How do you have access to this kind of information?" Emma asked Aubrey, unable to keep incredulity out of her voice. "I thought Anaxio weren't allowed to go to school. And as young as you are—"

"Fen Elos," Aubrey interrupted. "If you don't know who he is, who he *was,* you should. Fen Elos was a Crossworlder and the most recent Eleytheria leader. He was murdered by the Masevo in the hunt for Eury Vatic a few days ago." The boy stood up straighter and crossed his thin arms over his narrow chest. "Fen hated the Refuge and the way Anaxio are treated. He gave me a small library of reading stones and books. And I read them. They can't stop us from thinking. Not yet anyway."

"Why did he bring you books?" Maude asked.

Aubrey turned on her, ready to be insulted again, but Maude's face was utterly without malice or mockery. "I asked him to," he said quietly.

Maude said nothing, but Emma saw her wrap her fingers around Gryphon's book, which she kept in her pocket.

"Maude loves to read, too," she told the boy.

"Is that a book?" Aubrey asked, his eyes going to Maude's pocket.

"Yes," Emma said.

"What's it about?" Aubrey asked.

Emma almost blurted, "Why are you so suspicious?" but changed her mind. She glanced at Maude, who nodded and then walked away toward a nearby statue of a gorgeous young man kissing another. "The book is kind of a love letter from Maude's Soulmate."

"Is she already fifteen?" Aubrey asked, looking embarrassed and irritated at the same time.

Emma nodded.

Aubrey gazed at Maude, who sat on a low-hanging branch near the blissful statues. "Is her Soulmate dead?" he asked, genuine empathy in his face, which Emma realized was beautiful in its own stark way.

"Yes," Emma said. He was…" She hesitated. "He thought he might die, so he made her the book."

Aubrey looked stricken. He didn't say anything for a long time. "Have you met your Soulmate?" he asked, turning to Turner. "I'm sorry to ask. You don't have to tell me if you don't want to."

"Yeah," Turner said. "I have."

Aubrey looked at Emma and Joe. "And you two?" He paused and shook his head as he realized. "Right, Turner already said you were her Soulmate."

"What difference does this make?" Joe asked.

Aubrey sighed as if he were very old and Joe was an exasperating toddler. "If something happens," he said, "you two will be together. But Turner… What happens to his Soulmate if…?"

The Anaxio boy trailed off then looked at Maude as if he hadn't really seen her before. "When I agreed to help you, I wasn't thinking about you," he said to Turner, "I was just thinking about how to get the hell out of here. I wasn't thinking about what might happen to any of you. Or your Soulmates."

"What about you?" Joe said. "You have a Soulmate somewhere. You're not a Loveless, right?"

Aubrey shook his head. "No."

"Well, your Soulmate is out there, too," Joe said. "What will happen to her—him?—if something happens to you?"

"Her," Aubrey answered quietly. "And nothing will happen to me."

"How do you know?" Emma said.

"I'm smarter than all of you."

Emma nearly smiled, but something in Aubrey's expression stopped her.

"I have to be," he added.

A group of laughing women passed in front of the gate. Aubrey waited until they passed out of earshot and ordinary thought-access distance.

"You can't sleep in the Kena with me," he said. "If anyone discovers who you are they'll give you away for a sandwich. Or just for the fun of it. Do you think your house is still safe?"

"I don't know," Turner said.

"Well, you have to sleep. And it's too dangerous to sleep during the day."

"We can sleep here," Joe suggested. "The park is big. We'll wake up early and meet you here."

"I can't meet you here again," Aubrey said. "Meet me in the Library of Useless Information tomorrow morning."

Emma laughed. "I forgot about that name. Some kids in Warwick probably think that's the name of every library."

Aubrey glared at her. "Are you incapable of maintaining a stream of serious thought? How can you be a Super Telepath in a constant state of distraction?"

"Well, I am," Emma said. "And it's not constant."

Aubrey shook his head. "The final consecration ceremony is being held at the site of the destroyed Memorium tomorrow. Almost every gemynd in the city will be there, and it's nowhere near the library. Go to the Otherworld art section. Only half-dead scholars ever go there."

"Will the library let us in?" Turner asked. "Do we need identification or something?"

"Tell the guards you're on school punishment," Aubrey said, pacing as he thought it through. "That you were barred from attending the Revealer images of the consecration at school and instead have to come to the library to record information about symbols in Otherworld art. Are any of you Transformists?"

"No," Turner said.

Aubrey sucked in air through his teeth and swore.

"Why?" Emma asked.

"Because Turner is right," Aubrey said, frowning. "You'll need something that proves you got in trouble at school and had to come to the library as punishment." He swore again. "And I don't know how to make anything like that. Not before tomorrow morning anyway."

"Can we sneak in?" asked Maude, who had been listening, coming over to join them.

"No," Aubrey answered, blushing with renewed empathy at Maude's sorrow. He exhaled and brushed his plum-colored bangs off his dirty forehead. "Are any of you talented Teknasma?"

"No," Turner said. "Why?"

"A Mask could become an instructor and maybe get into the library that way," Aubrey said. "And if he was skilled enough, he could become an instructor that the guard—if she was young enough—might recognize. Because you're pretending to skip school."

"Thalia's a Mask," Maude pointed out.

"Who's Thalia?" Aubrey asked, his face flushed with sudden anger. "I thought you only had two sisters."

"Actually, we have another sister and a brother," Turner said. "But they're younger."

"Thalia is the Invisible girl we met," Joe said.

Aubrey made a sound of revulsion.

"Do you think she'll help us?" Emma asked Joe.

"I don't think her father will let her out of the house again," Joe said.

"The nameplates of Invisible dead are barred from the temporary Memorium," Maude called out in a thin voice. "When I was waiting, I heard a man say that no Invisible—including the ones who were on that train—would be memorialized until the permanent Memorium was complete."

"So their names are just lost?" Aubrey said. "Their identity markers? Everything? As if they never existed?"

Maude nodded.

Aubrey made a face like he was trying to reconcile two very different beliefs.

"Thalia's uncle was on that train," Emma said. "Do you think that's why she ran away?"

"There was supposed to be a protest," Maude said. "The man I heard said Invisibles were coming to protest, but I never saw any."

Aubrey smiled. "Of course you didn't." He sighed uncomfortably. "I hate Aponomi, but I can't believe even the Aythentia would let their names be lost forever. That's really filthy."

"Isn't that what happened to the names the Gatherers destroyed in the old Memorium?" Joe said. "All *those* names are lost. Those Revealer images and nameplates are gone forever, too, aren't they? Those families will never see or experience anything connected to those names again."

"Yes," Aubrey said. "But the Ones in Power weighed the tragedy of that loss against the potential benefit of finding Eury Vatic. That's what Acceptable Consequences means. What it should mean anyway. Barring the names of Invisible dead from the temporary Memorium is about convenience."

Emma moved toward Joe.

Don't. He held up his hand so she couldn't come any closer and walked away. *I don't want to talk about it.*

Emma turned. Aubrey exhaled again and dug his heel into the soft ground, and she realized what he needed.

Say you're hungry and go get enough food for all of us, she thought quietly to Maude. *When you come back, distribute it evenly and thank Aubrey for helping us.*

"I'm hungry," Maude announced to Turner. "I'm going to get something to eat. Do you think that restaurant is still open?"

"The women who walked by a little while ago were meeting someone there, so it should be," her brother said.

"I'll be back, then."

"Someone should go with you," Turner said.

"No," Maude argued. "We're less conspicuous apart. I'll be back soon," she added and disappeared through the gate.

CHAPTER THIRTEEN

Thalia felt her mother's anger before she realized her mom was back in the house. Genna didn't get mad very often, but when she did, everyone in the house felt the heat.

Charis, Zino said. *The kids will hear you. Hush your thoughts.*

Genna ignored him.

She didn't have any silks at all! Not blue, not gray, not anything. I stayed with her sullen, patronizing son and patiently asked him questions. I tried hard to come up with a song that reflected whatever small beauty there was in such a spoiled and dull boy— and I did exactly that, she continued, moving excitedly around the kitchen until Thalia felt her father hold Genna still so she wouldn't accidentally hurt herself. *I wrote a sublime song about that acrid, sour-souled boy. It took me nearly half the day. I knew I would miss Thalia when she came home, and I wanted to see for myself that she was all right. And then this woman, this...*

Thalia's mother hesitated. As angry as she ever got, Genna never swore.

She told me she had no silks. That she'd given the ones she promised me to a neighbor who wanted curtains. Given, Thalia's mother repeated. *Not sold, not bartered, but given. She said she'd make more in a few weeks, but what difference does that make? The ceremony will be over. She let me give her the song for nothing.*

At this point Thalia felt her mother let her father put his arms around her.

I know I should have asked her to pay me upfront, Genna said. *But sometimes that doesn't work.*

I know, Zino said.

Some gemynd like to feel like they're being charitable, Genna continued. *As if the work done by Aponomi isn't real.* Then she locked her thoughts and Thalia couldn't hear anything else.

Maddie's sugary pink outline appeared in Thalia's bedroom doorway. Thalia focused on it and walked over to pick up her little sister. She did so carefully, waiting until both of them had adapted to the contact.

What are you doing out of bed? she asked.

I escaped, Maddie said in her baby thought-voice. She couldn't speak aloud at all yet. Some Invisibles never mastered it. Some didn't want to.

You escaped? Thalia repeated, sitting on her wide bed with Maddie. *Why?*

I heard Genna, Maddie said.

Oh, Thalia said. *Were you scared?*

Maddie pressed her head to Thalia's chest. Her sister was too young to hear thoughts clearly unless she was physically very near someone, but she sensed emotions at a greater distance, especially intense ones.

Were you scared Genna was angry with you? Thalia asked.

Maddie nodded and whispered, *Yes.*

Well, she wasn't, Thalia said, letting her sister's warmth seep into her skin. *She was mad at someone who didn't play fair.*

Oh, Maddie said. *Is Genna still mad?*

I don't think so. Zino made her feel better, Thalia said. She felt Maddie smile in response.

Mom's translucent apricot form and rock-solid, red-haired Dad appeared in the doorway. Genna moved carefully to the bed and picked up Maddie. *Did I scare you?* she asked.

Yes, Maddie said.

Should Zino take you back to bed and sing you a story?

Okay, Maddie agreed.

Thalia watched her clear orange mother pass her tiny, snow-pink sister into Zino's visibly solid arms. Before she'd realized that Synithi hated Invisibles, Thalia had felt sorry for them. Typical gemynd looked harsh and heavy, with all their flaws so vivid and apparent. Thalia loved her mother's gentle, pellucid beauty, and she had loved her own deep blue reflection in the mirror. She used to pretend she was a piece of twilight sky that had fallen on the ground.

Are you all right? Genna asked her when Zino and Maddie had left the room. *Let me see your arm.*

Thalia held it out. *I'm fine. Dad fixed it.*

Genna laid her hand on the place where the venom had eaten into Thalia's skin. *He got to it quickly enough. I don't think there will be a noticeable scar for your manifestation.*

Thalia pulled her arm away. *I'm fine,* she repeated. *Really.*

I understand why you wanted to fight back for Uncle Solymi, Genna said. *He would have done the same thing, and I would have felt the same way. But you have to pick your battles, Thalia—*

I don't want to talk about it, Thalia said, cutting her off. She left her bed and crossed the room to sit on her desk. Genna was always afraid of Thalia falling but didn't say anything.

Zino's sweet voice drifted into both of their thoughts, and Maddie sang back in her funny little thought-voice. Thalia smiled at her mom, and Genna closed her eyes. Neither of them said anything for a while.

Thalia opened and closed her lesson reader and felt awkward. Her hot-tempered speech about never going back to school rang in her head. What had she been thinking? Of course she had to go back to school. What other option was there?

We told the school you were sick today, Mom said when the silence got to be too much for both of them. *They pretended not to have realized you weren't there.*

Thalia groaned. She got off the desk too quickly and fell painfully to the floor. Genna knew better than to run to her.

I'm fine, Thalia said, standing up again. She exhaled but didn't feel any better. *You should take the song sphere back.*

I can't, Genna said. *As soon as I gave it to her, she put it in a glass cabinet filled with all sorts of useless chrimy garbage. Everything in it was shiny and fragile and silly. She locked the cabinet and then turned around and told me about the silks.*

Genna shook her head. Thalia watched the graceful movement and the shift of the light in the room as it made way for her mother's fruit-colored shadow. *So pretty,* she thought, blocking her mom's access for a moment. Genna was so pretty.

Was he really that bad? she asked afterward, sitting back on her bed and taking her toy sun into her lap. When she and Maddie were born, Zino made each of them soft replicas of the sun and all the planets and moons in the solar system. Maddie loved Venus and called it her "snowflake," because the feeling of snow was the first thing she'd thought of when Zino handed her the toy.

He was that bad, Genna said, sitting beside her and stroking Thalia's long hair. *Or he was too sullen and obstinate to let me see anything else. The mother is appalling. I don't know why I trusted her.*

You trust everyone, Thalia said.

Zino trusts everyone, Mom corrected. *I think I just loved her silks so much I convinced myself she was better than she is.*

Don't worry about the silks, Thalia said. *I'd rather have Grandma's anyway.*

They're in pieces, Mom said.

Thalia sighed and leaned against the wall. After a few seconds she felt the cool of the stone sink into her skin. *Can we patch up the holes with your silks?*

I gave mine to my cousin, Genna said.

Thalia crossed her legs and tucked her sun to her chest.

You could have Uncle Solymi's, Genna said, almost too quietly to hear.

Okay, Thalia said, not wanting to talk about Uncle Solymi or how her mom felt. Or how she herself felt. She pushed the sun to the foot of her bed.

Go to sleep, Genna said, kissing her on the head. *You have school in the morning.*

Can I cut tomorrow? Thalia asked. *I'm not really going to quit— obviously—but I don't want to go to the destroyed Memorium site consecration ceremony. That's all we're doing tomorrow, sitting in the atrium and watching Revealer images of the consecration. I don't want to go.* A lump rose in her throat and she was afraid she was going to cry.

Okay, Genna said. *You can skip the morning. The ceremony won't last all day. But you have to go back in the afternoon.*

I will, Thalia said. *I promise.*

CHAPTER FOURTEEN

"What are all your powers?" Aubrey asked, his eyes on the gate as it closed after Maude.

"Super Telepath, Volucris, and Telekinetic," Turner said, pointing to Emma, Joe and himself. "And Maude is a Soulskin."

Aubrey's gaze shot to Joe, who said, "I can still fly."

"They were cut off," Turner explained when Aubrey kept staring at Joe's wingless back.

Aubrey looked horrified. He broke away and paced the garden, finally asking, "Do you think she'll be back with the food soon?"

"She just left," Turner said. He kicked a rock into the hanging branches of the red-flowered tree. "Be patient."

"Turner," Emma admonished quietly. "Don't be a jerk."

"How am I being a jerk?"

Emma sighed.

"Did it hurt?" Aubrey asked Joe.

"I don't remember." Joe stared almost blankly past Aubrey at the flowering tree. "I don't remember anything from that time."

"After you show us the way in—," Emma began, trying to change the subject.

"I only *think* it's the way in," Aubrey said. "I told you I don't know for sure yet."

"What makes you think it's the way in?" Joe asked. "You said you only had a chronicle that referenced the original one. How do you know it's correct?"

Emma wanted to take Joe's hand but didn't. He glanced at her with an expression of irritation and gratitude, then irritation again.

"Fen Elos gave me history reading stones so I could memorize how the city was constructed," Aubrey explained. "The more I could learn about how the city was built, the more I'd know about where to hide and how to get out of the Refuge."

"You memorized the architectural history of the whole city?" Emma said, astonished. "How old are you again?"

Aubrey sighed. "Almost thirteen. And I told you," he said, "I'm smarter than all of you."

This time Emma did smile when he said it. She glanced at Turner, who was still being mysteriously surly and glaring at the red-flowered tree. What the hell was up with her brother and Joe and staring at trees? But at least now she knew why Turner trusted Aubrey; they were practically the same person.

"Anyway," Aubrey said, miffed—very Turnerishly—at being interrupted, "there was an inconsistency in the construction records of a certain building that matches some of the dates in the chronicle about the nature of the experiments and where those experiments took place. There are never unexplained inconsistencies in Sacerian histories. They're always written by both Aythentia and Eleytherian Chroniclers so the perspective is as balanced as possible."

"What was the inconsistency?" Joe asked.

"One record mentioned a portal," Aubrey said. "None of the others mentioned it at all." He blushed and looked at his feet. "I almost didn't read that record at first. It was written by an Aponomi."

"No other record mentioned the portal?" Turner asked.

Aubrey shook his head. "And by tomorrow I will have cross-checked that record with every history chronicle Fen Elos gave me. I've read them all more than once so it won't take me very long."

Emma gaped at him, and Aubrey smiled.

"I didn't have anything else to do," he said, grinning proudly now. The lopsided expression made him look his age. "I had nothing but time to read. And I don't need a lot of sleep. I didn't even go out for food. I just ate the shit they brought us. Sorry," he said, glancing away from Emma.

"I don't care if you swear," she said.

Maude ran through the gate, a mesh bag of food in her hand. "There are Gatherers in the restaurant," she said breathlessly. She handed the bag to Aubrey. He took it and stuffed it into a deep jacket pocket. "They're not looking for us. Or you," she added, glancing toward Aubrey who was already under the tree.

"What should we do?" she asked Turner. "Should we hide here? If we go back on the street, I'm afraid they'll see us. They have clarifiers."

"Clarifiers?" Aubrey said. "What the hell are they looking for?"

"I don't know," Maude said. "They didn't say anything. They just shined the clarifiers on everyone in the restaurant. As soon as I started walking away they shined one right where I'd been standing."

"We have to get out of here," Turner said. "Where does the tunnel under the tree lead? Where did you come from?"

Aubrey hesitated for a second. "It leads to a basement across the street. No one lives in the building anymore," he added. "It's where Gelon Lira encausted all those Soulskins before the last power shift."

"We'll follow you," Turner said.

* * *

The tunnel was dark and not very wide. Aubrey and Maude slipped through easily, but Joe and Turner almost got stuck when it narrowed as it inclined toward the basement.

"Are you okay?" Emma whispered to Joe once they were all in the pitch-black room.

"Yes," Joe said. "Why wouldn't I be?"

"I don't know," Emma said. "You've been acting kind of weird. I thought maybe you were upset about—"

"I'm fine," he interrupted.

"Okay," Emma said.

"Later, okay? I don't want to talk about it now."

Okay, Emma said. But it wasn't. Not really.

"It's so dark," Turner said. "How do we find our way out?"

"You're not getting out until morning," Aubrey said. "I'm going back to the Kena before they cut off the lights. Now that you know where it is, you'll sleep here. It's the safest place if the Masevo are on the street."

"I can't see anything," Emma said to the Anaxio. "How will you find your way out?"

"I can do it in the dark," Aubrey sniffed. "For you...there are cracks in the foundation near the ceiling. In the morning, some light will come through. You'll see a broken floor-stone in a corner of the room. Lift it and jump in. Don't forget to replace the stone. The passageway below is an abandoned train track. It leads to a station bathroom. Listen to make sure the bathroom is empty before you come out. And clean yourselves up before you come to the library."

"We can't get into the library without identification," Turner reminded him.

"Your friend," Aubrey said, sounding surprised and annoyed at having to explain. "The Invisible. The Mask. You'll have to get her to help you."

"But we don't know where she lives," Turner said.

"Emma can access her," Aubrey grunted. "She's a Thoryba Exocho, right?"

"Yeah," Turner said, "but—"

"Calm down," Aubrey said, his voice fading as he walked toward the broken floor stone. "You can't do anything but sleep right now anyway. Oh," he added, and it sounded like he'd turned around. He inhaled deeply and then choked on the dank air. "If you want a little light…"

"What?" Turner asked when the Anaxio didn't finish his suggestion.

Aubrey spoke again, but his voice was almost too quiet to hear. "If Maude reveals her soul, there will be a little light in the room. At least enough to see where everything is and find a kind-of clean place to sleep." He sighed then faced them. "You probably don't realize this, because you all grew up in the Otherworld, so your thinking isn't nuanced. You value the obvious and overt and distrust the subtle and hard to explain. You want to *see* things. Actions. Answers. Results.Things you can identify. Things you can name."

"What are you getting at?" Turner asked.

"Cut it out," Emma scolded him. "Knowing everything isn't a competition."

Aubrey regarded them. "That's what I'm talking about." He looked to Maude and, though he couldn't communicate telepathically, Emma felt his empathy for her sister's grief touch everyone.

"A Soulskin might seem like a nearly useless power," the Anaxio continued, "because it doesn't *do* anything. But it's actually the most powerful gift a Commonworlder can be born with, especially for someone like you. It reveals what love is in a way we can all actually see, if only for a moment. That's why an exposed soul is so hard to look at, like gazing directly at the lighting god of one of your old stories. An exposed soul reveals what we call *fos katharos*, what Otherworlders think of as holiness or the sublime. It's...an overwhelmingly beautiful thing."

He left quickly, then, and Emma realized he didn't want to see Maude with her soul revealed. She reached for Joe's hand and nearly lost her balance in the silent darkness—which was punctuated only by Maude's halting exhalation.

CHAPTER FIFTEEN

"I don't know if I can," Maude said. She made a frantic sound. "It's too painful. I feel him more when my soul is exposed. I don't know if I can."

"Stay where you are," Emma said. "I'll find you."

"I don't even feel alive," Maude continued, half to herself.

Emma made her way through the dark. She didn't know what to say to her sister; all she knew was that Maude needed her.

"I'm still here because of you and Turner and Elizabeth and Sandy," Maude whispered.

Emma reached her, took Maude's hand, squeezed it briefly then let it go.

"And don't," her sister continued, "tell me Gryphon would have wanted me to stay alive. Don't tell me he sacrificed himself for my sake. He didn't."

The barely controlled fury in Maude's voice unnerved Emma.

"You have no idea what this feels like," Maude continued. "It's like waking up and finding half your body missing, and every place where you were torn apart is still bleeding and exposed to the air. It's unbearable."

Something throbbed under and through Maude's wild grief. Emma couldn't quite hear what it was. Maude seemed to be both trying to kill and release it at the same time.

"I'll sit here as long as you want me to," Emma said. "You don't have to say anything."

Maude spun on her so quickly that Emma almost fell off the rickety bench they shared. She said nothing, though.

What? Emma asked. *What is it? What aren't you saying?*

Maude shook her head. She stood up.

It's okay, Emma said. *Don't worry. I won't pretend to understand what this is like for you. You can say or do whatever you want. I won't leave. You can tell me I'm an academic fuckup or a terrible dresser. Or I eat too many Oreos. Or pink skin is not my fucking color. Whatever. You can say whatever you want. I'll stay right here. I'll just be quiet if that's what you want.*

"Oh," Maude said brokenly, crying for real now.

Emma hugged her, and Maude sobbed into her shoulder. Red light blazed from her hair and skin. Aubrey was right. Maude was the most painfully beautiful thing Emma had ever seen.

While Maude cried, Turner and Joe looked around the room and found chairs and boxes. They dusted these off and put together makeshift beds, all near the broken floor stone. Finally, when they were done, Maude pulled away and looked down at herself, at her chest and arms and legs, all glowing red and far too exquisite for Emma to describe. Then the light from her sister's soul shivered and went out.

Turner and Joe came over and led them to their chair and box beds.

I'll stay awake if you want to talk later, Emma thought to Maude alone, but her sister's response was a cracking sob that resonated in Emma's chest. The feeling was…indescribable. She and Joe were Soulmates, but she and Maude were something else, connected in a different way than Emma was connected to anyone.

She heard Turner kiss Maude then roll over and go to sleep. Joe laid his head in her lap, and Emma ran her fingers through his hair and resisted the impulse to read his thoughts, feeling guilty and lucky he couldn't read hers when she didn't want him to. Would Maude have ever been annoyed at Gryphon? Would she ever have questioned anything about their Soulmate connection?

Joe. Emma worried again that she didn't know much about him. Gryphon and Maude were so different that Mom had initially refused to believe they were Soulmates. Maybe Mom still had a hard time believing it, even though Gryphon was dead. Once she believed something, it was almost impossible to convince her otherwise. Only Dad could do that consistently.

Joe's standoffish attitude and his refusal to confide in her shot up in Emma's thoughts again. How would Maude have felt if Gryphon did something she thought was wrong? He'd been Aythentia. What if he'd sacrificed the life of some innocent gemynd in order to save more? How would Maude have lived with that? What if Emma now found out something about Joe that she couldn't accept? What if there was something about her that Joe would hate so much that it changed the way he felt about her, Soulmate connection or not? She supposed the only answers would come with living.

Emma was almost asleep when Maude finally spoke. It was so dark and so late, Emma couldn't quite tell if her sister was speaking or thinking.

"The book Gryphon gave me is a story. It starts with the first time he heard my voice in the woods at home. I was always looking for him, you know. I always knew he was somewhere. Even when I was little—like Sandy's age—I'd stare into the bathroom mirror and try to see him, what he looked like and wherever he was at that moment. Sometimes I thought he was looking in a mirror at the same time, trying to see me. *Anyway.* He heard me in the woods and realized I didn't know anything about the existence of the Commonworld, but he also knew I was looking for him. He wrote, in his beautiful, *beautiful* handwriting, everything he thought or felt about me, from that first moment in the woods, to when he saw me with you on the bench under Ozymandias, to the first time we actually spoke at school when he gave me the dress that..."

Maude stopped and breathed slowly. Emma waited.

"The dress that revealed my soul on my skin before I knew how to do that myself."

God, why wasn't there anything she could do? Emma hugged her chest and wished she had a different power, one that could help her sister in some way. Was there no power that could take away the pain in the worlds, or somehow make it easier to bear? Wasn't love supposed to cure all ills or some garbage like that? It sure wasn't helping anyone she knew.

"The hardest part to read," Maude continued, "is the section where he says how he felt when I gave him my Spirit Sphere and he realized I wasn't going to take back any of my life force that I put inside. But he would have died sooner if I hadn't!"

Emma said nothing. She heard Maude take the book out of her pocket and open it.

"The book is a complete record of everything Gryphon ever thought about me and everything we ever did together. He remembered everything, Em. *Everything.* Inconsequential things, like my expression when you said something funny. The way my skin smelled when I touched his face." She drew in a slow breath, and a pearl-gray light rose from her skin and hair. Emma had to look away.

"The last page is a little story of what might have been," Maude said. "What he wanted to do with the rest of his life. Asking me what I wanted to do with mine. Sex. Babies. Being old. How I would still be beautiful and he would have to constantly Mask himself to look young and hot." Maude took a shaking breath, and Emma heard her stand up. The gray light in the room faded. "It ends with him telling me how much he loves me, right now, in that moment. And how much he'll still love me after he dies."

Emma heard her sister walk away in the dark. She herself slid down beside Joe, wrapped her arms around his warm, strong, breathing chest, and cried herself to sleep.

CHAPTER SIXTEEN

Right in the middle of a dream about a boy with silver hair and green eyes, Thalia heard the voice of the girl who'd helped rescue her from the Synithi attack.

At first she thought Emma was in the dream and trying to take the boy away from her, but when he disappeared the girl's urgent voice remained. *Thalia!* she heard again. *Are you awake? We need your help.*

She sat up, oriented herself to her sitting position and searched her room. Even after her eyes adjusted, she couldn't see Emma anywhere.

Where are you? she asked.

I can't tell you, Emma said.

You're not here in my room?

No, Emma said. *I'm somewhere else. But we need your help. Can you cut school today and meet us at the Library of Useless Information?*

Why? Thalia asked. She'd only just met Emma, and despite the intensity of that situation she'd promised Zino she wouldn't leave without permission again.

Emma sighed. *I can't tell you that either.*

I'm sorry, Thalia said. *I promised my parents. I can't.*

That's okay, Emma said quietly. *I understand.*

It's just that it's dangerous for me to be outside by myself, Thalia said. *Because of the train accident and the destruction of the Memorium. Tons of gemynd are upset, and Invisibles are an easy target. You can't attack a Gatherer but you can torment an Aponomi and get away with it. Otherwise I would help you.*

Thalia stood up and felt the change from darkness to dim illumination in her room as morning sunlight spilled through the window. Uncle Solymi's green silks lay over the back of her desk chair. Genna must have put them there after she'd fallen asleep.

I get it, Emma said. *I don't want you to get hurt. We'll think of something else. I'm sorry about your uncle. I don't think I said that yesterday. Have fun at your manifestation ceremony.*

Thanks, Thalia said. *Tell Joe I'm sorry about his dad. I don't think I said that yesterday, either.*

Emma didn't say anything, but for some reason Thalia didn't want to say goodbye.

The silks caught the first streaks of sunlight as if they'd been waiting for it, tossing the rays back across the room and painting the foot of Thalia's bed a mossy green. Thalia felt a wave of anger rise up from the bottom of her stomach, that Uncle Solymi was dead and Joe lost his dad and so many other gemynd lost someone they cared about. And for what?

I'll help you, she blurted, turning away from the silks and letting the incoming sun blind her for a second. *But I have to be back at school in the afternoon—after I join the protest at the consecration ceremony,* Thalia thought but didn't say. She was tired of hiding and capitulating. Someone had to be a model for Maddie.

You'll be back before then, Emma said, relief in her voice. *We only need you for a few minutes.*

Where is the Library of Useless Information? Thalia said. *I've never been there.*

Emma gave her the address, thanked her, and said goodbye.

Thalia dressed and ate breakfast. Her parents left for work. Maddie's guardian Nysa came into the kitchen, breathless and apologetic for being late. She'd had to come the long way to avoid Gatherers looking for protesting Invisibles.

Don't worry about it, Thalia said to Nysa as she found Maddie's stuffed toy Venus and handed it over. *Genna is letting me cut the morning so I was here. I'll be in my room now. I have a lot of work to catch up on before the interim break next week.*

Okay, chichi, Nysa said. She picked up Maddie and kissed her. *What do you want for breakfast?*

Peaches! Maddie said.

Sometimes being Aponomi had its advantages. Just before lunch, Thalia snuck out without Nysa noticing.

Except for a few old women murmuring evilly about her cutting school, she made it to the library without incident. The four from the previous day—Emma, Joe, Maude and Turner—were waiting outside the Library of Useless Information when she got there, and Thalia stepped out of the sunlight and into the shade of the building, but not before Emma and Maude stared at her for a second.

Thanks for coming, Emma said, smiling.

You're welcome, Thalia said.

Yeah, thanks. Maude had glanced away, obviously embarrassed.

I don't mind if you look, Thalia told them. *I guess you've never seen an Aponomi in the sunlight before me.*

I didn't mean to—, Emma began.

Really, Thalia said, cutting her off before she started over-apologizing. *You can look for a minute. Just don't feel sorry for me. Okay? I don't feel sorry for myself.*

Emma glanced at Maude—for approval probably, although she didn't seem the type to admit it—and then looked at her. Thalia listened as Emma silently marveled at her strong heart pumping blood through her whole body, watching her lungs swell and contract and her muscles shift as she tossed her blue-raspberry lollipop-colored hair over her shoulder.

What the hell was a lollipop? Was it a good thing or a weird thing?

"That's amazing," Emma said, beaming at her. "Your life, *alive.* Right there for all to see."

I guess. Thalia shrugged. *Your life is alive right here, too.* She tapped Emma's chest.

I know, Emma said. *But somehow it seems more real when you can actually see it. It's awesome.*

Thank Misos you're a Super Telepath, Thalia said. *Otherwise gemynd could take advantage of you. You say everything you think, don't you?*

Emma blushed. *Not everything.*

"Come on," Turner said. "Let's get inside."

"Is Aubrey here?" Joe asked.

Emma paused for a second. "Yes. And he's pissed that we're late."

Who's Aubrey? Thalia asked, making sure the group could access her thoughts.

"He's helping us," Turner said. "Did Emma tell you what we need you to do?"

No, Thalia said.

Emma explained that that she would access the guard at the library so Thalia could then Mask herself into whoever the guard would let in without too many questions. A former teacher would be the best, since they were all pretending to be kids out of school today.

Luckily for them, the guard was pretty young and a huge crush on her former history teacher. Using the information Emma accessed, Thalia Masked herself into a hot young gemynd with dark brown skin and long black hair.

"Awesome," Emma said, smiling. "She can't stop thinking about him. His face is practically in the front of all her thoughts."

"Doesn't she have a Soulmate?" Joe asked.

"Not yet," Emma said.

"Sometimes you don't meet your Soulmate until you're in your twenties or thirties, or even later," Thalia explained in the teacher's deep, silky voice.

Emma laughed.

"Don't," Turner said. "We're in trouble, remember? Come on."

CHAPTER SEVENTEEN

Getting past the guard was easy. Emma couldn't believe someone with skin that red could turn even redder, and she had to stop herself from feeling too openly sorry for the young woman. Other than by using a clarifier, was there any way to see through a Mask? And, Thalia was amazing. No wonder the guard had a crush on that teacher. He was wicked hot.

Joe gave her a look. Emma blushed and took his hand.

Aubrey was standing near a table stacked with brightly colored reading stones.

"Why are there reading stones in the Otherworld section?" Maude asked, lightly stroking the bindings of books she passed.

"For a while Commonworlders chronicled Otherworld art," Aubrey said, crossing his arms. He had cleaned himself up a little since the previous day. "Until they realized it was without quantifiable value. Is this the—?" He stopped and sucked an irritated breath through his teeth. "Is this Thalia?"

"He's Worthless," Thalia said.

"And you're a periskata Invisible," Aubrey said, genuine loathing in his voice.

The center of Thalia's teacher-chest disappeared.

"She's the reason we got in," Maude said.

Aubrey snorted, but he didn't say anything else unkind.

"Take a book and start reading," he said. "The filters are especially alert at transitions, right? Beginnings, endings, changes of situations. So, before we can talk, we have to do what we told the guard we came to do. That way, if the filters are sent to sweep this area, which I doubt, they'll stay uninterested in us."

Maude's face lit up as she reached for a book about poetry and Pre-Raphaelite paintings.

"Don't get too excited," Emma said, smiling.

"Is she…?" Aubrey began. "Is Thalia coming with us to—?"

"No," Emma said. "She has to get back to school."

"She'll have to stay with us until we've done what we came here to do," Aubrey said, gazing intently at a book on ancient cave paintings in France. "It shouldn't take too long. Maybe three quarters of an hour."

"Okay," Thalia said.

¬"You're a really good Teknasma," Aubrey added after a moment.

Thalia's teacher chest flashed in and out of visibility. "Thanks."

"You're welcome," Aubrey said, glancing down the empty aisle. "Is there anyone else in the library?"

Emma concentrated for a moment. "No," she said. "Except for the guard and two other gemynd working in an office, we're the only ones."

"Is the guard thinking about us?" Aubrey asked.

"No," Emma said, listening to guard's thoughts again. "She's still trying to make herself believe the teacher is her Soulmate. Why, though? If you know you're going to meet your real Soulmate someday, why would anyone try to make themselves believe something that is so clearly not true?"

"Most gemynd are idiots," Aubrey said, staring at an image of a horse. "Okay, go read or whatever. And keep your thoughts mundane."

They headed off to spend some time looking through the books and making use of the materials at hand before they would all meet up again in a little while.

Aubrey was hiding at the end of an aisle of dusty books and ancient reading stones when they found him again. "Okay," he said when they'd gathered around him. "If everything I read last night is correct...and there is no reason why it shouldn't be." He glared at everyone except Maude.

"No one is questioning you," Turner said. "We've followed you this far, haven't we?"

Aubrey frowned then continued. "If everything I read last night is correct, the first portal is somewhere in the Aftokinito."

"What's the Aftokinito?" Turner asked, and Emma looked at him, a little surprised there was something he hadn't heard of.

Aubrey rolled his eyes. "The Erevno," he explained, emphasizing the word as if Turner were a fool. "Aftokinito is what it's called by gemynd who know what really goes on there."

"What is it?" Maude asked.

"The Erevno is a research and development facility," Turner explained, flushed. "It's mainly used to develop weapons and better information-extricating systems."

"And," Aubrey added, seeming to try to master his tone, "the work is done just at the edge of Commonworld law. Aftokinito basically means 'to experiment without scruple.'"

"Let's go," Joe said. "Let's get out of here."

"We can't all go together," Aubrey pointed out. "We're too big a draw for the filters if we're together."

"Are you coming with us?" Maude asked.

Aubrey blushed. "Turner promised that one of you would take me to the Otherworld as soon as I helped you—" He only sounded like a twelve-year-old he was when he was talking to Maude, and he blushed again and frowned, clearly annoyed. "I thought that would be today," he continued. "I don't want to ever have to go to the Refuge again."

"Someone will take you to the Otherworld today, Aubrey," Turner said. "I promise."

"So we'll split up," the Anaxio said, wiping the blush from his face. "Emma, you go with Joe. I'll go with Turner and Maude."

"Someone's coming," Emma whispered.

The pretty, red-skinned guard from the door approached, beaming and breathless. "Here you are," she said at the end of the aisle, seeming to simultaneously stare at Thalia and avoid looking at her. "I'm sorry to bother you when you just got here, but the Gatherers need the library. Everybody has to leave."

Don't worry, Emma thought to Thalia alone. *You're really good at this.*

Thanks, Thalia said. *We practice in school all the time, but I don't do it in real life too often—Mask myself for strangers who aren't trying to hurt me, I mean.*

Emma nodded. *I understood.*

* * *

Thalia took a deep breath, feeling better than she had in weeks. Emma grounded her and helped her remember that she *was* good at this, was the best Mask in her year. She smiled at the guard and said smoothly, "No need to apologize. You're just doing your job." She smiled again. "I knew you'd turn out well."

For a minute, she worried the guard might fall over.

"Well," the red-skinned woman finally stammered, "You were a really good teacher."

"Thank you," Thalia said, smiling kindly. "That's always nice to hear."

She turned severely to Emma and the others, continuing the ruse. "It looks like you got off easy, but you'll still have to write the reports when we get back to school. And you're still barred from attending the ceremony. Come," she said, striding confidently out of the library. Behind her she heard Emma ask Maude to take Aubrey's hand, pointing out that the Masevo would notice if they were all treating him nicely.

"I can't believe Mom and Dad made me take you with me today," Maude whispered fiercely as they passed several Gatherers who were talking in the lobby. Tugging Aubrey behind her she added, "Come on! I can't wait until you have to move to the Kena."

Once they were outside Aubrey said, "Split up. When we're far enough from the library I'll tell Maude how to get where we're going and she'll think it to Emma who'll tell everyone."

"Why can't you just tell us here?" Joe asked, that dark, strange irritation again in his voice. Thalia wondered why he seemed angrier today than he had yesterday.

"Are you an idiot?" Aubrey snapped. "Gatherers are in the library. The filters are always on alert wherever Gatherers are. And we can't be sure that they didn't catch anything when we were in the library. It's safer to split up and let some time pass." He stood still. "You either trust me or you don't."

"We trust you," Turner said. "We trust you. How many times do I have to say it?"

Everyone quieted as a woman and two young children approached walking quickly. The woman was complaining into a crystal *ergal* about the appointments she'd had to cancel because of the consecration ceremony today. Her kids squabbled below her in hushed voices over whether a *Kino* or a Volucris had better powers, and Aubrey smirked as if he expected Turner to jump in and take the Kino kid's side.

Turner messed up his hair without touching it.

"Hey, quit it!" said the Anaxio, smoothing it back.

Turner grinned. "Telekinesis for the win," he said to Joe.

"Yeah, you wish you could fly," Joe said, grinning back. "If you could, it would be like the greatest thing ever. You'd fly everywhere. You'd probably never use stairs or a ladder ever again."

"What am I doing on a ladder in your little fantasy, Joe?" Turner asked, but Thalia stopped listening and waited for the kids and the woman to be out of ordinary thought-hearing distance.

When they were far enough away, she let go of the Mask of the teacher. She was exhausted. It was always harder for her to let go of a Mask after holding it for a long time than it was to create it.

"Are you going to be okay going home?" Emma asked.

What? Thalia said, slightly dizzy as her awareness of everything turned slowly to mush. But she would get home, even if she had to hide in a park somewhere and rest along the way. *Yeah. Sure.*

Aubrey turned and saw her, and he groaned in disgust at what she looked like as she stepped into the late-afternoon sunlight. She swallowed a wave of sadness. Stupid. It was always the freaking same. Even the few gemynd who liked to think they were cool with Aponomi recoiled when they had to see them in the bright sun, all of their organs and bones and bodily functions moving and visible.

It's not catching, Thalia wanted to hiss. She ground her teeth and frowned at Aubrey instead.

Good luck finding your parents, she said to Emma, Turner and Maude. Not that they'd find them. Any more than an Invisible would ever blend into Synithi society on an equal status. And now she was too tired to go the protest. It wasn't fair. None of it. Like fairness was a thing. Or a useful idea.

Thanks, Emma said.

Thalia smiled at her and started to leave, but a feathery resonance thrummed suddenly from the base of her spine. She gasped and stood still, and everything quieted.

Everything retreated.

Everything stopped.

Deep inside her body, Thalia heard music. Felt harmony. A surge of light roared from her feet to her head, and she felt herself smile. She would have laughed. But she didn't want to move.

Everything quieted. Everything retreated. Everything stopped. There was nothing in the world but her and the silver-haired boy she'd felt before she would actually see him come up the street behind her. Surrounding her now. Part of her. Inside her skin. Swimming in her hair. Singing through the air in her lungs.

He swept past then, taller than she was, with an intense gaze, beautifully-made clothes, and markings on his forearms like streaks of green light embedded in his skin. And he spun around.

Thalia smiled and stepped forward.

"Quit staring at me, Aponomi *skyta*," he snarled.

CHAPTER EIGHTEEN

So…that couldn't have just happened.

There was nothing in Thalia's head now but loose gray silence. Maybe she was having a reality slip. Before your manifestation, your energy and emotions supposedly became unstable. Maybe your ability to separate fantasy from reality got muddled, too. She didn't know. They certainly didn't study elements of the protanosi in school. And she was so, so tired. Too tired to be standing, really.

Thalia took a shallow breath and waited for her head to clear, but nothing moved. Nothing changed. Until a strange fire ignited and burned uncontrollably from the center of her stomach. She watched as her body darkened and became more solid-looking. Her legs were shaking, but she didn't sink to the ground.

The fire inside her died as suddenly as it had begun. Something like ice pulled her violently inward as if she were a black hole.

No, she said. *No, no, no, no, no.*

She hadn't had a reality slip. She was unmistaken about the reality of who the silver-haired boy was, and of what she'd felt before he saw her and called her an Aponomi bitch. She knew, just like Zino said she would.

Her legs still shaking, Thalia looked down, certain she must be bleeding. Because some unseen dagger had just torn a jagged hole in her chest.

"Disappear, Aponomi," said a soft-featured, orange-skinned boy Thalia hadn't noticed before. He waved his hands as if she were a bad smell. "You can do that, can't you?"

She couldn't move.

"Don't get your hopes up, you ugly piece of shit," a different boy chimed in.

Where were they coming from? Were they popping out, fully-formed and hideous, from the footpath?

"My chrim boy wouldn't touch you if he was Loveless," the second boy continued in a voice like scissors and silk. He and the orange boy laughed then strutted around the corner onto the next block.

The silver-haired boy, who'd been silent, glaring at nothing across the street, turned his attention back to Thalia. A vicious insult died on his lips. He gaped at her, not moving, until one of his friends came back, smacked him on the head, and pulled him away.

What? Emma said, coming to stand beside Thalia.

Nothing, she said. *Nothing.*

"Let's get out of here, then," said Turner.

"Wait," Aubrey called. He turned to Thalia. "Where do you live?"

"Why?" Thalia asked, out loud because Anaxio couldn't hear thoughts.

"Where do you live?" Aubrey repeated.

She told him.

He swore. "That's too far."

"I managed to get here all by myself this morning," she hissed.

"Well, it's different now. Isn't it," he replied.

Thalia glanced at Emma before turning back to Aubrey. "What do you mean?"

"I have to be smarter," he said, emphasizing every word, his expression fierce. "I can't depend on telepathy or anything else to *tell* me what's going on. I have to be observant and analytical."

"About what?" Emma asked, sounding exasperated. "What are you talking about? Turner's right. We should leave."

Aubrey exhaled and clenched his fists. "The Soulmate connection takes precedence—"

"That periskata Synithi is not my Soulmate," Thalia interrupted. "He can't be. I'm not fifteen yet."

Aubrey raised an eyebrow at the increased volume in Thalia's voice. "It's possible to recognize your Soulmate just before you turn fifteen. Especially if one of the pair is Aponomi."

He was right.

"You're wrong," Thalia said.

"Explain the fear on his face, then."

"Why would Thalia's Soulmate be afraid of her?" Emma asked.

"Shut up," Aubrey said. "Misos, don't you know anything?"

"I know Soulmates are a good thing," Emma said. "Maybe the only good thing." She glanced nervously at Joe.

Misos, Thalia said bitterly to herself and locking her thoughts. Kids like Emma had no idea how easy they had it. *'Oh, poor me, maybe someday my freaking Soulmate won't like me for five minutes.' That is not a real problem!*

"Not always," Maude said.

"What do you mean?" Emma asked.

"Gryphon said some Soulmates have an *Atiryx Syndesi*, a Hate Match."

"Wait. Everyone has said that Soulmates are always true," Joe spoke up. "Everyone. Isohel told us it was an unbreakable biological connection, the literal other half."

"Yes," Maude said, "the connection is always true, and it's always painful if something happens to…to one of the pair. But in rare circumstances, if a trauma occurs at the moment of Eynosyndeo recognition, and if the pair is on opposing sides of the trauma, a Hate Match can form. An Atiryx Syndesi is a physiological response, and it's usually irreparable."

"I still don't understand why—," Emma said.

"Shut up!" Aubrey commanded. "Are you going to keep arguing about this?" he asked Thalia, in a slightly less aggressive tone.

"That asshole was not my Soulmate," she repeated. "Hate Matches are so rare that some gemynd don't even believe they happen at all. He wasn't my Soulmate."

"And you look less translucent, why?" Aubrey asked. "Just because? Because that just happens? Because sometimes the shitty hand life deals you just goes away? And a tall, chrim Synithi was afraid of you because…what? He thought you could take him in a fight?" The Anaxio swore and shook his head. He walked a few steps away then came back to say, "You look less Aponomi but not enough like everyone else. Now gemynd will notice you more, but they won't wonder why. And the real klasis out there will follow you and torment you. You can't go home alone. You'll have to come with us."

"She can't," Turner said. "We can't risk her getting caught if the Masevo find us. Her dad said it's legal to treat Aponomi differently."

Aubrey shook his head like Turner was focusing on something irrelevant. "Keeping the Masevo away from her is not the problem. Ordinary gemynd are the problem."

"Couldn't you Mask yourself?" Emma asked Thalia.

"Not all the way home," she admitted. "Remember, it's an illusion, not an actual transformation. I'd have to keep accessing whoever was around the corner or up the street and maintain a single Mask or change without anyone noticing. Either way it's difficult, especially if the walk is far."

"Is Aubrey right?" Emma asked. "Could that silver-haired asshole be your—?"

"You can't ask that," Aubrey interrupted sharply. "I'm only talking about it so much because she's too proud to do what she needs to protect herself. Don't ask."

Emma looked surprised, but Maude took Thalia's hand. "You can come with me and Turner and Aubrey."

"No," Aubrey said in an awkward voice. "She has to go with Joe and Emma. We're trying to keep our numbers small, remember?

"Okay," he said after a pause, exhaling and swallowing the vulnerable edge to his voice. "You three go five blocks north. We'll go five blocks east. The building is between those two neighborhoods. Emma, listen hard for Maude. She will tell you how to get there."

CHAPTER NINETEEN

Emma was shocked how much the walk seemed to exhaust Thalia. How had the girl gotten to the library so easily?

Thalia answered Emma's thought question in a tone that said she did not want to talk. *I took the train.*

Joe, Emma said, not letting Thalia hear. *Thalia is about to pass out.*

Joe and Emma stopped walking. Thalia stopped and turned, swaying like she was drunk. Her skin had a weird sheen that had nothing to do with the silver-haired asshole, and Emma realized she was sweating.

Thalia grabbed the side of the building but said fiercely, *I'm fine.* Then she pushed away from the wall. *Let's go.*

"I'm pretty strong," Joe said.

Don't even think about offering to carry me.

Thalia walked away, but Joe ran up to her. "You could Mask yourself as a baby," he said. "And I—"

I wouldn't be as light as a baby, Thalia said. *And I hate… Never mind. I'm fine. You're not going to carry me.*

Emma didn't know what to do. Thalia was so upset and exhausted she seemed ready to throw up.

Thalia realized Joe had stopped walking, swore viciously and turned around.

"I'm not going any farther until you let me carry you," he said.

Thalia laughed and then made a noise like she was going to cry. *Fine*, she said, her voice both breaking and squeaking. *I'll go without you.* She took a long shaking breath and made her way up the street again.

"You don't know where we're going," Joe shouted after her.

Thalia whirled, swearing, and fell to her knees. Joe started to run to her.

"No," Emma said. "Let her get up by herself." She and Joe walked over to Thalia, who struggled to pull herself back to a standing position. "You can turn yourself back before we get there. No one else will know."

Thalia stared hard at Joe, who was gazing at her with an expression of concern. Emma felt jealous before she remembered she didn't have to be. God, what if Aubrey was right and that jerk was Thalia's Soulmate? What if Joe had said something horrible to her when they first met and made her hate him?

Joe gave her a weird look. Oh. Yeah. *She'd* said something that made him almost hate her when they first met. But the silver-haired jerk sounded like he'd meant what he said to Thalia. Emma didn't know what "skyta" meant exactly, but it didn't sound good.

Okay, Thalia suddenly said. She took a shaky breath and turned into a baby boy with black eyes, inky blue skin, and no hair at all. Joe picked her up, and she laid her adorable baby head on his shoulder.

"You are so cute," Emma said, stroking Thalia's soft cheek. *Misos, how did anyone ever get used to the beautiful magic in the Commonworld?*

It's not magic, Thalia said, closing her eyes. *There's no such thing as magic.* She took a slow breath. *And don't even think about kissing me.*

"But you are so seriously cute," Emma whispered.

Thalia scowled, which made her even cuter.

Seriously, don't kiss me.

"I won't," Emma said. "But I can't promise Joe won't."

Joe blushed. "I can promise that I won't kiss you, Thalia," he said, glaring a little.

I think I hate you, Emma, Thalia said, her eyes still closed and her outrageously cute baby face still frowning.

They reached the address Maude had given Emma just as Aubrey, Turner and Maude appeared at the other end of the street. Aubrey asked, "This is only a block from your house, right?"

Thalia, back to her Aponomi body, nodded.

"Mask yourself into something innocuous and walk home quickly," the Anaxio said.

She nodded again.

"Thanks for helping us," Aubrey added.

"You're welcome," Thalia said, her voice louder than it had been earlier but still exhausted.

"Mask yourself and go home," Aubrey repeated, now in that bossy, angry tone.

Thalia's eyes flashed in indignation, but she turned into a big yellow dog. Tongue flying and tail wagging, she jumped on Aubrey and licked his face.

"Ugh," the boy shouted, wiping his face as she bounded off down the street, fluffy tail aloft.

"So, how do we get in?" Joe asked. "To the portal."

"Follow me," Aubrey said, still wiping his face.

* * *

A few feet from her house Thalia let go of the dog Mask and looked down at herself. Her body was as translucent as usual; the nearly opaque solidity was gone.

Maybe the change in her skin had been temporary, like the seeming disappearance of body parts that occurred when Aponomi felt embarrassed. She hadn't known that temporary opaqueness could happen at all. Very few gemynd recognized their Soulmates before they turned fifteen. She didn't know anyone who had.

How had Aubrey known the reason her skin changed? Anaxio weren't allowed to go to school. So, maybe he was wrong. About everything. If Thalia were less tired, she might have been able to fool herself that he was.

She held the railings outside the front door with both hands until the chill of the metal penetrated her blood. Only when she was strong enough to reveal nothing of what had happened or how she felt about it, Thalia put on an energetic happy face and walked into the kitchen.

Where were *you?* Nysa demanded.

School, Thalia said dismissively. *I told you I was cutting my morning—"*

You didn't go back to school, Nysa said. *I contacted the administrator's office at lunchtime to ask you something about Maddie and they said you weren't there.*

I snuck out to see some friends, Thalia said, pretending to look for something to eat. *I'm sorry. It wasn't a big deal. It's not like school cares if I show up or not.*

I didn't know where you were, Nysa said. *I could have lost my position. Do you have any idea how difficult it would be for me to find a new one? Your mom and dad would be right to fire me.*

Nysa was both Aponomi and Loveless. Her parents were dead. She had only herself to depend on, and Invisibles were always the first to be fired and the last to be hired, no matter what the economy was like.

I'm sorry, Thalia said.

Nysa sighed. *Start prepping for dinner. I've been too upset to hide my emotions from Maddie. She's hysterical.*

Thalia opened herself up to her sister's feelings and cringed. *I'll help Maddie. She'll be better for me.*

Fine, Nysa said. *But don't ever leave without telling me again.*

I won't, Thalia said. *I promise.*

She left and walked into Maddie's room. Her sister was in the crib, crying, but Maddie sensed Thalia before seeing her and stood up, holding out her arms.

It's okay, Thalia said, picking her up. *Don't be scared.*

I'm not scared, Maddie said, still crying. *I'm sad.*

Okay, Thalia said. *Don't be sad. I'm here.*

I'm not scared, Maddie repeated.

Okay, Thalia said. *I believe you, you're not scared.*

Maddie pressed her head to Thalia's shoulder. After a minute she asked, *Did you go to school? Nysa was scared.* She picked up her head gazed seriously at Thalia. *I wasn't scared.*

I know, Thalia said, walking carefully to the center of the room. *I know you weren't scared. And I didn't go to school. But I should have told Nysa. When you're a big girl you always have to tell Nysa where you're going if you leave.*

I am a big girl, Maddie said, squirming in Thalia's arms. *Genna says I'll be a big girl on my birthday. Is it almost my birthday?*

No, silly, Thalia said, setting her sister on the floor and rolling the soft, pale green Venus toy toward her. *It's almost my birthday.*

Then you'll meet your Soulmate, Maddie said.

No, Thalia replied, shivering as she thought of the silver-haired jerk on the street. She pushed him out of her mind so she wouldn't upset Maddie, who was hypersensitive to every negative emotion. Maybe Maddie would be a Teknasma, too.

Maddie rolled the Venus back to her, and Thalia caught it. She said, *Then I'll have my protanosi. Genna is planning a party. There will be lemon ice cream and colored lights and song spheres and games. And then,* Thalia thought-whispered with another roll of the Venus, *you'll see me.*

I already see you, Maddie said, catching the toy and sending it back.

You'll really see me, Thalia said. *I'll be just like Zino.*

Maddie's lip started to quiver. *I don't want you to be a boy. I don't want a brother. I only want a sister.*

I won't be a boy, Thalia said, laughing.

Don't laugh at me, Maddie said. *I hate it when you laugh at me. I'm not a baby.*

I know. I'm sorry, Thalia said. *I won't laugh. But I won't be a boy. I'll be me. I'll be a girl, but you'll see me. Everyone will be able to see me. That's what a protanosi is.*

Will I have one? Maddie asked.

Yes, Thalia said. *When you're fifteen.*

Did Genna have one? Maddie asked.

Yes.

I can't see Genna like I see Zino, Maddie said.

It goes away, Thalia said. *One year after you meet your Soulmate.* She couldn't help it; she shuddered again.

Why?

I don't know.

When are you going to meet your Soulmate? Maddie asked in a cautious little voice.

CHAPTER TWENTY

There was a noise in the kitchen. Genna and Zino had just come home. They were upset about something.

Selfishly, Thalia breathed a sigh of relief. She didn't know how much longer she could hide her despair from Maddie, and Genna and Zino would be easier to fool. They would think she was sad about the Memorium and Uncle Solymi.

Thalia gasped. She'd forgotten about Uncle Solymi. How could she have forgotten that her beloved, sweet, funny, brilliant uncle had died? Maybe that Anaxio boy Aubrey *was* wrong. Maybe she truly was experiencing some kind of pre-manifestation madness.

Nysa, Mom said in a guarded voice downstairs, *will you take Maddie outside?*

What did Genna say? Maddie asked.

Nysa is going to take you outside to play Volucris, Thalia answered, picking her sister up. Nysa had made a pair of pink wings and Zino suspended a harness on a cord between two trees so Maddie could pretend she was flying.

Maddie beamed and said, *I love my wings,* wiggling in Thalia's arms as they walked down the steps and into the kitchen.

Careful, Thalia said. *I don't want to drop you.*

Nysa took Maddie from her.

Where are my wings? Maddie asked.

Outside, Nysa said, kissing Maddie on the head. *In the box where we left them.*

I want my wings, Maddie said as the door closed behind them.

Before Thalia could sneak off to her room Genna said, *School is cancelled tomorrow. And I'm glad you didn't go this afternoon.*

How did you know I didn't go? Thalia asked, instantly regretting her confession. That kind of stupidity wasn't like her. Maybe everyone was lying. Maybe manifesting sucked. And they must have been watching her more carefully since the dilitirio knife. She had to get upstairs before they sensed anything about what happened today.

Genna didn't answer.

Zino said, *There was a Resister who somehow got off the train.*

Thalia's mother turned around and covered her eyes with her hands.

Why is that a bad thing? Thalia asked. *Did the Resister know something about Uncle Solymi?*

She took something, Zino said. *The Ones in Power and the Resisters are both denying it, but I was working in the Kena today and the Anaxio are saying that the Resister—a girl about your age—escaped the wreck with something the Resisters took from Eury Vatic.*

Thalia was about to tell her father to stop believing everything he heard, and to remember that Anaxio would exchange a beautiful lie for a sandwich, but Aubrey was the first Worthless Thalia had actually met and he was nothing like she'd expected.

Why do they have to close the school? she asked. *And why are you and Mom so upset?*

Because, Genna said, feeling for her chair and sitting down. *No one can find her. If it's true—and it must be, because there are Gatherers with clarifiers everywhere—the Ones in Power will stop at nothing to find her. And the Resisters won't be much better.*

Genna stopped talking, so Thalia looked at her father.

Rights are suspended, he said. *Gatherers will be legally permitted to search any house, any building, and any gemynd whenever and wherever they want.*

Genna drew in a deep breath. *There is also a renewed call to destroy inaccessible places and make them illegal.*

What? Thalia said in disbelief. *What does this girl Resister have that's so important?*

Dad exhaled. *The Anaxio I spoke to said she has 'the way of listening.'*

What does that mean? Thalia asked.

The Ones in Power and the Resisters both think she has the secret to the way the power of Whole Listening works, Zino said. *It's why Eury Vatic's daughter was killed, and why he hid his son for all those years. And it's why he died. Emma's sister Maude told me that when the Resisters captured Eury Vatic they used extrication lights to rip everything out of his consciousness. He died in the process.*

Poor Joe, Thalia said. Then fear grabbed her chest. *Will the Gatherers go after him and the others?*

Of course, Zino said. *As soon as they realize they're in the Commonworld. I'm sorry I forgot to erase my memory about your friends. I can't erase it now because it might alert the Gatherers to them and to you. I'm sorry.*

What about Emma's younger brother and sister? Thalia asked. *They're in the Otherworld.*

I don't know, Zino said.

No one spoke for a few minutes. Dad gazed at Mom, who was obviously trying not to cry. He turned back to Thalia.

We have to cancel your manifestation ceremony, he said.

Why? Thalia asked.

Because the Masevo will investigate every major energy release, Zino said. *And a manifestation releases nearly as much energy as a Soulmate revelation, but it's not legally protected the way the Soulmate connection is. Rights are suspended. We can't put you and Maddie or our friends in danger. The Gatherers will come, make a mess, and then leave. They won't have to justify or explain anything they do. To anyone. And they won't take the time to figure out what's going on. They'll hunt for the girl and leave as soon as they don't find her.*

So, what are we going to do? Thalia said. The ceremony had always been more important to her mother than it was to her, but now, with the possibility of no party at all, she felt terrible. *What about everything Genna's done already? What about all her work? What about Uncle Solymi's silks?* she asked, biting her cheek.

We have to put the whole thing off until the Resister girl is found, Zino said.

What would be the point? Tears welled in the corners of Thalia's eyes. *I'll already be visible. It would be a joke.*

Dad glanced at Mom. Thalia felt his pain at her sorrow, and sucked in a mouthful of air.

When rights are suspended, he continued, *the Gatherers are legally permitted to act without fear of consequence. It isn't worth it to bring attention to ourselves.*

Thalia sat down, and Maddie's squealing, laughing voice broke into her thoughts. Every Eleytheria knew the terrible story about how Joe's little sister Edoro had died in a portal tree when Eury Vatic was trying to hide his children in the Otherworld, and Edoro had been younger than Maddie when she died.

I'll still manifest, she pointed out. *Nothing can stop that. Should I go away or something?* Her throat swelled again, but she swallowed hard.

I don't know. Iremos, Zino said, taking her hand and squeezing it. *This fugitive girl has the only thing that's left of Eury Vatic, and the Ones in Power and the Resisters both want to get to her first. Genna and I have to figure out the safest place for you.*

What about the Whole Chronicler? Thalia asked, remembering something from her Hierarchies of Power class. *Won't Eury Vatic have a Whole Chronicler?*

He will, Zino said. *And I'm sure the Gatherers are hunting for him or her right now, too. But they don't know who the Whole Chronicler is. They know who the girl is.*

CHAPTER TWENTY-ONE

"Surround me," Aubrey said to Turner, Joe, Emma, and Maude, who were standing with him near the Erevno, a wide, low, windowless structure with most of the rooms below ground level. "Surround me and think threatening thoughts.

"Everyone can tell I'm Worthless," he continued, "and if you hang on my every word it might draw the attention of the Gatherers. So think vicious things about me."

He smiled at their obvious reluctance. "It's not hard. Everyone needs to hate something. But," he added, glancing up the street, which was strangely empty for the late afternoon; gemynd should already be heading home after work, "listen to me while you're thinking. I'll only be able to say this once."

Turner nodded and moved threateningly toward Aubrey, and Emma felt an appalling wave of accompanying elation as all four of them concentrated negative thoughts in the same direction. The elation was Maude's. The thing Maude had been hiding from herself and Emma when they were sleeping in the basement now clawed to the surface; Maude wasn't just grief-stricken over Gryphon's death, she was furious. And for a second that rage was directed not at Aubrey but Joe, who stepped back.

Maude refocused herself, and the circle of energy that linked the four of them was both horrifying and exhilarating. Emma nearly felt sorry for Aubrey. He shot her a furious warning glance, as if he could read her thoughts, but he couldn't. He was just a periskata Anaxio. He couldn't do anything.

"One more thing," Aubrey said, standing ringed by them, small and uncharacteristically pale. "Don't argue with anything I say. You decided to trust me, so you have to listen to—"

"We don't have to—," Joe began.

"Shut up," Aubrey hissed, and Emma felt afraid.

Joe's thoughts weren't about Aubrey at all. They didn't seem to be about anything specific, or they never rested long enough on anything for Emma to catch. She felt incoherent rage uncoil inside her Soulmate, nothing like Maude's, and again she had to resist the impulse to read his thoughts without permission.

"You'll never be as pretty as Maude or as smart as Turner," Aubrey purred to her, and Emma crushed an impulse to smack him in his ugly little face.

"Shut up," she said as Joe leaned forward to perhaps do the same.

"I said *think* negative thoughts," Aubrey snarled. "Now, listen," he said. "Because Maude is a Soulskin, she has the power to recognize unregistered portal trees. We'll go find one right after this and she'll take me to the Otherworld, where we'll wait for the rest of you. Turner, you're going to break open the wall of this building to create a diversion so that Emma and Joe can climb inside and find the veiled portal. They're the best team."

Aubrey took a shaking breath and looked at Emma. "He's strong, and you're a Thoryba Exocho. You'll be able to hear things none of the rest can. After you two pass through the veiled portal, look for traces or any evidence of the way back to Saceres and the prison. There should be a pattern. Look for it. That's the best I can do. The rest is up to you two."

"That's your plan?" Turner said. "Are you crazy?" He shook his head and whispered harshly, "You want me to destroy part of the Erevno? Every Gatherer in the city will come to investigate. You call that a good diversion?"

"No," Aubrey said, "I call it the only way you will ever see your parents again. How else will Emma and Joe be able to get inside? Constructive chaos. Don't you believe in it?"

Turner glared at him.

"Good," Aubrey said. "You're going to break open the wall, and then you're going to hide."

"Hide!" Turner repeated.

"Stop arguing," Aubrey hissed. "Making a hole in that wall will be the hardest thing you've ever done. I hope your powers are as strong as you said. You won't be able to follow Emma and Joe, at least not right away. There's a refuse containment center across the street. Stand in front of the entrance and break this wall open"—he nodded at the building's plain front—"and then go into the refuse center. Hide in the back. As soon as you feel ready, leave through the garbage door and keep moving. Hide every time you feel tired."

Aubrey took another deep breath then turned to Emma and Joe. "Stay right here. As soon as Turner creates an opening, get inside the building and find the portal."

"How will we know what to look for?" Joe asked.

"The chronicle said it was near a vessel for storing *theama peritta*," Aubrey said. "Revealer detritus. Theama peritta is the sound element of Revealer images. After the image dissipates, the noise sinks into the ground." He glanced at Maude. "Okay," he said. "Let's go. This all must happen quickly."

Turner crossed the street. Maude grabbed Aubrey's hand and walked up the block toward a pretty house. Emma and Joe stood still.

Joe took Emma's hand. They both watched Turner. Emma felt a wave of dizziness and fear, but it was overcome by a sense of the tremendous energy it took Turner to even try to break open the wall. She unconsciously moved to go to him, but Joe pulled her back. Then suddenly the sidewalk shook and there was a huge noise.

Joe lost his balance and Emma caught him. They both choked on the dust. An alarm shrieked. Across the street, Turner was gone.

"He'll be okay," Joe said. "Come on."

He pulled her through the hole in the side of the building. Emma felt dizzy again as she climbed over the broken chunks of stone and some other material she didn't recognize.

"What?" Joe said when she stopped moving just inside. "We have to hurry. Can you figure out where the vessel is that Aubrey mentioned?"

Emma shook her head, realizing a flaw in the plan. "Not unless someone thinks of it." She concentrated, opening herself to as many gemynd as she could, listening for any mention of the vessel or a portal, or perhaps even the very thing they were looking for: the entrance to the prison where gemynd were secreted.

The alarm wailed over shouting in the building and on the street.

"Em," Joe whispered. "We have to move."

Emma grabbed her head. "I'm trying." She was trying as hard as she could but something was scrambling her attempt to hear anything beyond where she stood. "I hope Turner's okay," she murmured. "For a second I felt what he did when he finally made the hole. He almost passed out." She looked up into Joe's eyes. "He felt like Isohel—"

The first siren still shrieked, but a second, louder alarm sounded as soon as she said Isohel's name. Emma felt cold and hot at the same time.

"What?" Joe said.

"My cousin," Emma said. "Everyone is looking for her. She took something important when she escaped the train wreck. That's why I could hardly hear anything. The filter system is almost entirely focused on Isohel. It must be blocking almost everything else."

The alarm crescendoed, and footsteps sounded.

"Run," Joe said.

Emma followed him into the building, but she had no idea where they were headed. "You should go without me," she said. "They only heard me. They're looking for me because I said her name. Your identity shield will hold. Find the portal."

Joe whipped around. He wore a ferocious expression. "I am *not* going without you. And I'm not leaving you here."

Emma ran with him. More footsteps sounded behind them, and it wasn't just the gemynd who worked in this building anymore. There were too many.

"Gatherers are here," Emma realized.

At the end of the hall swung a black door, broken, in an open doorway.

"The explosion must have opened it," Emma guessed.

"Come on," Joe said.

They ran through the doorway. It led to a staircase that went down to what seemed like a basement level of the building.

"Yes," Emma said. "I have a good feeling about this. Theama peritta would be collected underground."

She and Joe ran down the stairs, Gatherers somewhere behind. The stairs ended at another door. This one was closed.

Joe swore and smacked it. Voices sounded on the other side. He jumped back.

"Here," Emma whispered, "under the staircase."

She pulled him into the dark space. Joe crouched next to her, his fingers laced with hers. Emma felt his heart pounding. The door hissed open, and three gemynd came out talking rapidly, hurrying toward the stairs. Joe took off his shoe and slid it into the doorway before the door shut.

"What the…?" one of the gemynd said, turning around on the stairs when the door didn't close. A soft alarm beeped repeatedly.

"Forget it," another gemynd said. "What's going to happen? This place is crawling with Gatherers. Rights have been suspended. Anyone could be detained, even if the workday is ending early and the building is being shut down on account of the security breach. I have to get home. Maybe you don't have anything to hide, but I do. My neighborhood will be the first to lose our inaccessible places. That wretched girl lives on my street. Her father's been a maniac since the train accident. You'd think the kid was his Soulmate the way he's acting. "

The three headed up the steps, and there was a noise followed by cursing voices as they crashed into Gatherers or someone else just as determined to get downstairs. Joe and Emma ran for it. Joe grabbed his shoe and the door closed behind them.

"Is that it?" Joe said, pointing to something that looked like an expensive, iron-colored umbrella stand.

Emma squeezed Joe's hand, thinking again of how crazy everything in this world looked compared to home. But yes, this was the detritus vessel they sought, and she thought her heart was going to jump out of her body.

"God, I hope Turner, Maude and Aubrey are okay," she whispered.

"This must be the portal," Joe said, pointing to a slightly worn spot on the polished wood floor. "It really is veiled."

Emma hoped so. She stood with Joe and they thought themselves through.

CHAPTER TWENTY-TWO

The portal led to an empty chamber with smooth colorless walls and no doors or windows, which surprised Emma. "Do you think Aubrey lied to us?" she asked.

"No," Joe said. "You would have heard it if he was lying. I think he was wrong."

He grabbed Emma's hand as an opening appeared in one of the walls, and three harried-looking gemynd, a man and two women, entered through the opening, which disappeared seamlessly behind them.

The woman in the center frowned. "Who are you?" she asked.

Emma stepped forward, not letting go of Joe's hand. "We're part of the protest against the injustice of the temporary Memorium," she said fiercely. But she also listened to what the gemynd were thinking.

"What are you doing *here*?" the woman asked.

"Constructive chaos," Emma hissed. "Barring Aponomi dead from the temporary Memorium is unconscionable, and it demands a response that the Ones in Power will hear."

"Neither of you is Invisible," the woman remarked.

Emma growled and swore, transferring all her terror and frustration into the lie. "What the *Moklu Dynami* are doing is vile!" she spat, using the official name for the Ones in Power. "The names of the dead, all of them, are sacred to their surviving Soulmates and families. Acceptable consequences," she sneered, as if the phrase were a terrible curse, "are not—"

"Enough!" the frowning woman said. She glanced around the empty room and exhaled. "They can stay here," she said to the gemynd at her sides. "It's as secure a place as any. We'll deal with them later. Idiotic Aponomi sympathizers are not a priority right now." She glared at the male gemynd for a moment before they all turned around and left through another sudden opening in the wall.

The opening disappeared. Emma fell to her knees. She breathed slowly. She thought she might throw up.

"What's wrong?" Joe asked, immediately beside her.

Emma took a deep breath and sat on the cold floor. "I need a second," she said. For some reason talking to the gemynd and listening to what they were thinking at the same time had exhausted her.

When her head cleared she said, *There is no Synektos prison. No actual place at all.*

Joe stared at her. *What?*

The silent man believed the frowning woman was wrong to think we weren't important, Emma explained, *because the portal we came through wasn't a real portal. He knows what happens to secreted gemynd, but his thoughts about it are blocked really well. I saw a flash when he tried to convince the frowning woman that we were more important than we seemed.*

But Thalia's dad knew about the secret prison, Joe said. *He also said some gemynd don't believe it exists. Maybe—*

I didn't say gemynd weren't secreted, Emma said. *I said there was no one specific place.*

So, where are your parents? Joe asked. Then he turned away, and for the first time since they'd met, Joe locked his thoughts. It corresponded with another spike of his fury.

"What are you doing?" Emma said.

Don't ask me.

What?

I mean it, Joe said. *Don't ask me. We're here to find your parents.*

But something flickered again and then shut down in Joe's head.

Do you know something about my parents you're not telling me? Emma asked. *I could just take it out of your head. Tell me what it is.*

Don't, Joe said.

How could you keep a secret from me? Emma asked. *We're Soulmates.*

Do you tell me everything?

Emma blushed.

Okay, Joe said. *And that's fine. We don't have to tell each other everything.*

We have to tell each other the important things, Emma growled. *And something you know about my parents that I don't know is important.*

You don't want to know this, Emma, Joe said. He stood up.

How do you know?

Because I wouldn't want to know if it was me, okay? Just drop it. He paced to the colorless wall and back. *You have no idea how lucky you are to have grown up the way you did.* He turned away and wouldn't look at her. *How lucky you still are.*

Just because I didn't have the same problems you did doesn't mean I didn't have problems, she pointed out. *My life wasn't perfect, you know.*

No one's life is perfect, Emma. But yours was pretty close.

How can you say that?

How can you not see it?

"You don't know anything about me!" she said. "You don't know how I feel! Or what I think!"

Joe stood still. "I guess I don't."

For a few terrible minutes, neither of them spoke.

How do we get out of here? Joe asked at last.

I don't think we can, at least not the way we came in, Emma said. *The veiled portal, or whatever it really is, must be one-way.*

We'll have to leave through the opening the others did, Joe decided. *I didn't notice any of those three touch anything, so it must be done by thought. Were any of them telekinetic?*

I don't think so, Emma said. *But I don't know how else you could open the wall.*

Unless the opening works just like a portal... You simply think yourself through one of those. Maybe the wall opening works on the same principle.

But you can't think yourself through a portal unless you're touching it or standing in a specific spot, Emma said. *That didn't happen with them.*

Maybe there's a code.

An icy deadness in Joe's voice washed over Emma's skin. She couldn't unsay what she'd said, but how could he keep a secret from her if it was about her parents? Would he forgive her if she listened to his thoughts without permission? Would she forgive him if something happened to her parents and his information could have prevented it?

There was no question about it, then. She had to listen if he continued to refuse to tell her.

Are you listening to me? he asked.

What? she said. *No, of course not.*

I mean about getting out of here, he said. *Maybe it's a code.*

What do you mean? she asked.

A code, he repeated. *Maybe there's a sequence of words that instruct the door to open.*

Oh, she said. *To open the wall. Like 'Open Sesame?'* she added, grinning slightly.

Maybe, he said. *But I'd imagine something more personal, like a user name and password. Do you remember anything that sounded like a series of unconnected words they were thinking?*

Something like that would probably have been blocked by them, she pointed out, pushing the hollowness of his tone and her decision out of her head. *But I'll try to remember if I heard anything I didn't initially pay attention to.*

Go ahead. He nodded then turned away.

She wanted to think about how to open the wall but instead Emma thought of the day they'd met two and a half months ago. He'd been so angry. She didn't know what she'd said to him until much later, as it had spilled from her lips without her being aware. Even now that story came to her in unexpected fragments, bursting into her head like an exhausted messenger: *The terrified old woman is running. The winged little boy keeps falling down. The baby girl in the white dress and the tiny red shoes is screaming. The dragon is diving toward them. The old woman pushes the boy through the tree and then the girl, but the baby girl doesn't want to go. She fights back. The dragon grabs the little red shoe. The tree—*

"Stop," Joe said. *What are you doing? Stop!* Wild-eyed, he ran his hands over his head. *What the hell is wrong with you, Emma?*

Nothing, she said. *Nothing is wrong with me.*

She closed her eyes and focused, going back over the conversation of the recent gemynd. The frowning woman had cut off the protestations of the male, and then…she had silently recited five unrelated words.

Okay, she said. *You were right. Get ready.*

She recited the five words in her head. The door slid open and she and Joe ran out.

CHAPTER TWENTY-THREE

Zino made dinner while Genna and Nysa gave Maddie a bath. Thalia set the table and listened to Maddie splash Mom and complain that the bath belt was *too tight!*

Bathing an Aponomi child was dangerous. The water temperature had to be constantly monitored, as hot water would burn an Invisible child long before he or she would actually feel the heat of it. A tight belt held the slippery child in place so he or she couldn't wriggle out of anyone's hands.

Is Genna okay? Thalia asked her dad, hoping Mom wasn't listening.

She's really upset, Zino said, scraping a bowlful of chopped vegetables into a simmering pot. *But she's even more committed than I am to postponing or canceling the ceremony.*

He stirred the pot. Thalia tried hard to ignore how sad he was, and the thoughts he was trying and failing to block.

Zino stopped the movement of the long wooden spoon. *If anything happened to you or to Maddie...* He stopped talking and stirred the vegetables too vigorously, splattering his shirt with hot broth. Swearing out loud, he grabbed a cloth from a hook and wiped at it. *If something happened...especially now...after Solymi and the...*

He didn't continue, but Thalia heard his smothered thought. If something bad happened to her or Maddie now, their names would be lost forever.

I'll be more careful, Thalia said. *I promise.*

Zino nodded and plunged his hands into a bowl of protein mix, which they ate because Maddie still needed very soft foods. There was a noise at the door and Zino groaned. He glanced down at his hands and forearms, which were covered in a sticky brown mess.

I'll get it, Thalia said, moving toward the rude and insistent noise at the door. *It's probably just some jerk trying to sell fake nameplates again.*

She chewed on the fury in her mouth. Since the announcement that the names of new Aponomi dead wouldn't be admitted into the temporary Memorium, some gemynd had begun selling nameplates to bereft Invisibles, promising nameplates that would fool the sensor and be accepted. It was a fat lie, of course, but that didn't stop some Aponomi from falling for it.

Thalia set her jaw and opened the door.

"Tell your skyta mother she can have her shitty song back."

Thalia's heart fell to her feet as the silver-haired boy from that morning thrust a song sphere at her. She clung to the door. He looked like he wanted to say more but didn't.

For a snatched instant, Thalia longed to move closer to him, to feel his moonlight hair under her hand. To hear him say her name. Then *Tell your skyta mother* echoed again in her head as she remembered exactly what he'd said.

She let go of the door and stood taller. He opened his mouth to speak.

My mother was wrong about you, she interrupted, not making the effort to reply out loud for him. *You're much worse than just spoiled. I can't believe she found enough of anything genuinely beautiful in you. You don't deserve this.*

She grabbed the blue and silver song sphere and tried to close the door, but he stuck his foot in the doorway.

"Wait!"

"Too late." She kicked his foot off the threshold, slammed the door and locked it.

* * *

For a second Rede stood motionless, his hands pushing against the rough metal door. The girl inside hadn't moved. She was locking her thoughts, but he could feel her emotions. He pounded the door once with his fists and felt her spin around in anger.

"I didn't know!" he shouted, banging on the door again.

"Thalia!" came a deep strong voice from inside the house. "Who is at the door? Are you all right?"

I'm fine, Zino, the girl shouted back. *It's just a fake-nameplate-selling jerk. I locked the door.*

"I'm coming anyway," her father said.

"Let me handle it, Dad," Rede heard just barely. "Maybe if he realizes an Aponomi sees what he's up to he'll stop doing it."

Rede listened to her father consider her point then say, "Call me if you need me."

Leave, the girl thought to Rede through the door.

Please, he said. *I didn't know.*

That makes it worse! she said. *If you didn't have an Aponomi Soulmate you would have kept despising us without ever considering the consequences. You would have continued to insult my beautiful and brilliant mother, and someday my little sister would have been nothing but an Aponomi skyta if she made the mistake of looking at you. You would have thought it was acceptable that my uncle's name is lost forever because Aponomi are not the same as Synithi. We feel different, look different, move and sound different, so it's okay to treat us like shit? To fire us when a dumbass Synithi needs a job? To make sure we live in shitty neighborhoods? To punish us more severely when we commit a transgression, and to punish anyone who hurts us less severely because we feel less, matter less? Leave, or I will call for my father. He is not Aponomi. And he's stronger and smarter and better than you will ever be. Leave. Now.*

Rede stepped back from the door.

I didn't know I had a Soulmate, he said. *At all.*

* * *

Emma and Joe were out of the windowless room.

"How are we going to get out of the building?" Joe asked. "The opening Turner made will be guarded now. That can't be good," he added when the lights suddenly dimmed.

Emma ignored the change in the light level. She was so angry. Did Joe think it was easy to have terrible things burst into her head without warning? Did he think she wanted to see his baby sister die again? And what the hell could he know about her parents that was worse than that?

"We're not getting out of here until we find that gemynd who knows what secreting really is," she snapped. She led Joe down the dimly lit hall. *Think about nothing,* she ordered.

Are we underground? Joe asked after they'd been walking for what seemed like a long time.

I think so.

This place is huge.

Shhh, Emma hushed.

She and Joe reached the end of the hall and came to a strange dead end. Emma thought of the woman's five words in different sequences. On the third arrangement, the wall slid open to reveal another down staircase.

This silence is not good, Joe remarked. *There should be some noise everywhere, especially after what Turner did. I don't like it. If we saw or heard something, we'd know which direction to run.*

This is the only way, Emma said. *The other way is just back where we came from.*

Joe walked down the stairs. Emma followed him and then stopped. The hallway ahead ended in a door.

What? he asked.

"If we separate…," she began.

"Even if I wanted to separate," he said, "which I don't, you just said this is the only way."

"I meant, when there is a choice of two directions to follow." Emma took a deep breath. "One of us has to get out. No one knows Aubrey was wrong about the prison."

"No," Joe said.

"Turner might come after us."

"I don't care," Joe said. "I'm not leaving you here, and I'm not letting you leave without me."

There was a noise at the top of the stairs, and also one from the door in front of them. Then silence.

Emma listened carefully and heard thoughts from behind the door. She pushed Joe against the wall of the stairwell landing, whispering about the filthy Ones in Power and the plight of the Invisibles. *It's not Gatherers or the gemynd from before, I don't think,* she passed to Joe alone, trying to slow her increasing heart rate. *I don't know. I can't hear who it is. Everything is scrambled.*

Joe took her hands and played his part in her ruse. "I don't think we should go to the protest. Your parents don't like me as it is—especially your dad. If I take you to the protest it will only make it harder to convince him that I'm your Soulmate."

Pretending to be fake Soulmates when Joe was angry and she was so uncertain made Emma want to cry. Worse, he stared at the underside of the staircase and refused to look at her. Fuck him, then.

"But we don't have to convince my dad," Emma said, continuing the charade. "Once we have our revelation everyone will know. He won't be able to say anything."

At the same time, she motioned to the door in front of them. *Whoever is behind the door is still there. Should we run back up?*

Joe shook his head. *Not yet. Until you can figure out who they are, I think we're safer hiding than running. We don't want them to think we're important. We said we were here to protest. Let's keep that story consistent.*

"You're right," he said aloud. "Don't worry. We *are* Soulmates, and your father can't do anything to change that."

An alarm sounded. Emma and Joe both jumped.

"It's okay," he said.

No, it isn't. They're still behind that door. What are they waiting for? Is it us?

Joe lifted his head and listened. *I don't know.*

The door above them suddenly opened.

"Here they are." The frowning woman and the silent man from before were on the landing before Emma and Joe could move. The woman grabbed Joe's arm, and the man held Emma.

"Let go of her," Joe said, struggling to pull free.

The woman gently traced a thin bright blade across Joe's throat, leaving behind a hair-thin scratch. He sucked air through his teeth and kept struggling.

The man holding Emma leaned forward, and two gemynd appeared through the door at the bottom of the stairs and ran up.

Stop struggling, Emma said to Joe, wanting to cry. *That was a poisoned knife.*

CHAPTER TWENTY-FOUR

"She's right," said the frowning woman. She pointed the poisoned instrument at Emma's throat. "Be still," she warned Joe. "If you're not, I won't be as gentle with her as I was with you."

"You're not authorized to use a dilitirio knife on underage gemynd," said the man who was holding Emma, the man who knew what Synektos really was and what it did.

"I am today," the woman replied. She turned to the two gemynd who'd come up the stairs. "The situation is under control, Lukas. We don't need your help."

"You were wrong to disregard Hyad before, Pheone," said the gemynd she addressed. Emma reached for Joe's free hand and grabbed it, but Lukas separated them. In that moment Emma listened hard to the thoughts of the gemynd named Hyad. He alone had given an inkling of the possible fates of her parents and others who'd been secreted.

"Please!" she said wildly, reaching again for Joe. "Don't separate us!" she begged, transferring her despair over what she had seen of the Synektos weapon in Hyad's thoughts earlier. "We're Soulmates. You know that. Keep us together."

Lukas watched her.

Emma quieted.

Lukas smiled.

"You'll find I'm not so easily fooled," he said.

He doesn't know who we are, Emma thought with a start.

Lukas smiled again. "No. I don't. But your identity shields are so well-made I can only assume that you and your Soulmate are too important to leave alone. That and," he added icily, glancing at Pheone, "the fact that you came through the false portal."

The man turned his attention back to Emma. "At least you won't have to think about imaginary Aponomi any longer. Although your performance was thrilling." He leaned closer, and Emma was appalled to notice that he smelled delicious, like forest and ocean and snow. "I almost believed you cared for the Invisible friends you fabricated for our benefit."

Briefly, Emma flashed on Thalia. She felt something distant and painful at the same time, like watching someone step on a long nail. An inaudible gasp—more sorrowful for being kept silent—gripped her throat. Something terrible had happened to the gemynd named Hyad, the one who knew the truth about secreting. She didn't know what it was, though, and right now she didn't care. She kept her thoughts quiet and her eyes on Joe.

"Go home," Lukas said to the frowning woman. Then, as if drawing a curtain across a window, he took Joe, who was reeling from the dilitirio venom, from Pheone and handed him to the gemynd who'd followed him in through the downstairs door. "Once they're both secured," he instructed, "give the boy an antidonai, Regulus. We want him lucid."

Emma breathed a sigh of relief.

"You're welcome," Lukas said.

The frowning woman stayed where she was.

"Go home, Pheone," Lukas said again, his voice shifting slightly like a song changing key.

Emma's hair stood on end and her heart beat faster.

"You're right to be afraid," he whispered.

Pheone left, albeit angrily, and Lukas led everyone else to the door at the bottom of the stairs. He thought of the code sequence and grinned back at Emma as if she were a favorite student.

The door opened to another hallway. This one, like all the others, was dimly lit and lined with glossy, colorless walls. Emma walked slowly, trying to trail behind.

Lukas laughed. "I'll still hear your thoughts, no matter where you are."

It didn't matter anyway. Hyad's thoughts were impenetrable to Emma now. He walked beside Lukas and said nothing.

"Where are you taking us?" she asked, and felt Lukas smile.

"I'm afraid it won't be so easy as that," he said. "I know you're not as full-hearted and empty-headed as you've been pretending to be—although I'm not sure about your blue-haired darling." He inclined his head back toward Joe. "He seems to be nothing but emotion. All hate and lust, and no thinking." Lukas turned, as if he and Emma were best friends gossiping about a hot stupid boy at school. He raised an eyebrow and grinned again. "But you're a different story, aren't you? I don't have to tell you that we're headed someplace we'll be able to determine who you are and what you want. And then," he continued brightly and easily, "we'll take you somewhere else."

He stopped walking. The smooth bare wall disappeared to reveal a huge, nearly silent room broken up into smaller areas separated by light grids, each a different pattern, color and density.

"Impressive," Lukas said, almost flirtatiously. "Isn't it?" He was short, round and bald, but he moved lightly and gracefully as if gravity had a crush on him. His red, flashing eyes made swift promises of enchantment.

Don't trust him, Joe thought.

"Ah, he speaks," Lukas said, smiling slowly as Joe's face darkened.

"Don't let him get to you," Emma said.

"Right again," Lukas agreed, crisp as an apple.

We can't think in here, Emma thought to Joe.

"You won't have to," Lukas said, nodding to Hyad and Regulus to release them to a group of gemynd standing watch at the front of the enormous room.

"Oh, go ahead," he said suddenly and irritably to Hyad, "ask your questions." He turned to the watching gemynd who had surrounded Emma and Joe, and said, "Take them after Hyad has made his private inquiries."

Emma tried not to cringe as the pain Joe felt from the poison gradually increased, and Lukas glanced at Emma with something like sympathy. "Be quick about it," he said to Hyad. "The boy needs an antidonai."

Hyad nodded, and Emma thought he was silently asking Lukas a question.

"Yes," Lukas replied, genuine compassion in his voice.

Hyad turned to Emma, and she believed he spoke to her alone. *Did Thalia Salic's parents cancel her manifestation ceremony?*

What? Emma asked.

Please, he said, glancing at the others. *I don't have a lot of time.*

I don't know, Emma said. *She didn't say they had. Why?*

Hyad looked at her the way Maude had when she'd asked about Gryphon's book. Emma swayed where she stood.

"What are you doing to her?" Joe asked weakly.

"I'm okay," she said. Then, to Hyad, *I'm sorry.*

Stop, Hyad said. *I don't need sympathy.* He took a slow breath, and Emma was shocked to see that none of the anguish he felt was revealed on his amber face.

She glanced at the guards. Lukas was talking to Gatherers she hadn't seen a minute ago, so she asked, *Why do you want to know?*

Hyad glanced almost imperceptibly at the Gatherers talking with Lukas. *A manifestation releases a degree of energy greater than that of a Soulmate revelation.* Light flickered in his yellow eyes and then was gone. *Until the Resister from the train is caught, every energy release will be vigorously investigated with no regard to private property. Only the Soulmate connection is protected, and even that is…*

Emma wanted to take his hand, or something. She couldn't believe someone could be in that much pain and reveal none of it.

There are things that belonged to Solymi, he said slowly, *that I would like to have. Silks. Revealer images encased in crystal. I think Charis might still have one from when he was a baby and she had to look after him.*

How would you see him? Emma asked. She remembered that Solymi was Thalia's uncle's name, the one who died in the train accident. Hyad must be his Soulmate. *Do Aponomi appear more visible in images than in real life?*

I would see enough, Hyad said. *I would see his outline. I would see his face.* He took a shallow breath, and a new pinprick of light shone from his eyes for a split second. *His name is lost.*

"That's enough," Lukas said gently. He came over and squeezed Hyad's hand. Emma felt a wave of gratitude wash through Hyad in response, but it was nothing compared with the loss he felt.

Lukas gazed searchingly at her. Emma stiffened.

"Can I ask him one more question?" she asked Lukas.

Do not abuse my kindness, Lukas said seriously. *I will not offer it again.*

Emma nodded and steadied herself.

If you can, she said to Hyad alone, *when you go to ask for Solymi's things, can you do anything to protect Thalia and her family? I know she's really close to her sister and her parents.*

Lukas turned to the Gatherers as Hyad replied to her question. He told her he didn't know what he could do, if anything. Emma listened in a half-concentrated way, softening the edges of his thought-voice so she could access what he knew about the Synektos weapon. This time she took in the information dispassionately, as if it were part of the light in the room, or the buzz of sound, or the golden glow of Hyad's face. She took the information and shaped it around innocuous memories: the train, food, buildings, sunsets.

"Thank you," she said to Hyad. She wanted to say how sorry she was for what he had lost, but she didn't. Still, she felt her unspoken apology touch Hyad, and she was glad to have helped him even a little without speaking. Then, before she could stop herself, Emma thought of Maude and her father's favorite line of poetry that she always associated with her beautiful Soulskin sister, *'Heard melodies are sweet, but those unheard are sweeter.'*

Lukas was at her side before she could cut off vivid mental images of her father and Maude. *Shit. Shit. Shit!* Dad's face must be all over the filter system.

Lukas gazed triumphantly at Joe then back at Emma. "You have saved me the trouble of removing your identity shield, Emma Mathews."

Panic swelled in Emma's chest. She tried not to think of Joe and whether she had betrayed him as well.

"Yes," Lukas said. "I know who your blue-haired Soulmate is." He turned gratefully to Hyad. "Your foresight will be remembered. Come," he said to the circle of guards. "Take them to the detainee chamber."

CHAPTER TWENTY-FIVE

"The antidonai!" Emma shouted, pulling against the grasp of the guard. "Give Joe the antidonai or I won't cooperate at all."

"You'll only make it that much more painful for yourself and Eury Vatic's boy if you struggle," Lukas said calmly.

"I know," Emma said. "But it will be inconvenient for you. You'll have to work a little harder and a little longer than you wanted. And it will be messy."

Lukas frowned.

"We're caught anyway," Emma said, ignoring Joe's silent pleas for her to stop. "We can't get away. You're going to do whatever it is that you want to do. It will be easier for you if you give Joe the antidonai."

She glared hard at Lukas, who was silent. "I'm not making an idle threat. I'm promising you. And because I know you're not easy to fool, because I know you are the same as I am, with the same degree of power, even if I am uneducated, I know you know I'm telling the truth."

Lukas stepped closer, smelling like tranquility. "Don't be stupid. You are not in a position to make threats or promises. Make it inconvenient for me and I promise I will make it devastating for you—and for your emotionally-stunted Soulmate. You have no choice but to quietly do everything I ask of you."

Emma still had some of the weight of Eury's last few hours in her head when the Whole Listener had taken her into his consciousness and she had felt, briefly, the terrifying madness of hearing and seeing everything in both worlds. The scenes had begun to deteriorate the moment Eury disconnected from her, and the remaining incoherent, chaotic information itself wasn't valuable; it was nothing but the echoes and remnants of the words and thoughts and feelings Eury had absorbed before he died. It was nothing of Eury Vatic, or Lukas wouldn't have been talking with her right now.

But it was powerful, and if she was able to release it to every gemynd in the room…

Lukas's eyes flashed, but he didn't have time to stop her.

Using almost all the strength she had, Emma implanted the incomprehensible chaos into the consciousness of every gemynd in the room. The guards, the Gatherers, Hyad and Joe collapsed. Lukas fought to remain standing.

Emma staggered and ran to Joe, connecting to a memory of Isohel on the day they'd first rescued Joe from the detainee tower, when Isohel drew up Joe's adrenaline so he'd have the strength to fly out of the tower carrying Emma and her dad. Emma drew Joe's adrenaline up now.

"Come on," she said to him, struggling for power. She accessed Pheone, whom she sensed was not too far away. The woman was still so angry at being dismissed that her thoughts were like low-hanging fruit.

Lukas reached for Emma. Joe hit him in the face, knocking him to the floor.

"Run," Emma whispered.

They used Pheone's password to leave the room, and Emma followed the woman's thoughts down one corridor and then another. Pheone was walking to a room where gemynd were temporarily implanted with something that acted like a hallucinogen before they could leave the building, stopping in that office to record a complaint, and to take something Emma couldn't access.

"We're in the Impenetrable Defense Building," Emma related to Joe. "All the gemynd who work here are drugged or something before they enter and exit so that nothing of the building's location is remembered. That room is at the top of these stairs." She pointed, speaking aloud because she'd realized the filters prioritized thoughts before voices. "Pheone is there. She'll come down. We'll wait until she does. Hopefully she'll be too angry to notice us here in this corner."

Joe didn't answer.

"Are you okay?" Emma asked.

He nodded.

"I increased your energy level when I raised your adrenaline, but it increased the pain from the venom, too, didn't it?"

"Yes," he said in a harsh whisper.

"We'll fix it as soon as we're out," she said.

Joe nodded once.

Pheone came down the stairs with quick, angry little footsteps. The door at the bottom opened and closed, and Emma took Joe's hand and pulled him forward.

"Wait," she said suddenly.

"I told you," he said in a halting, furious voice, "I will not—"

"No," she said. "I'm not talking about separating. We have to figure out how gemynd get in and out of this building but also immediately shock everyone in that room."

Joe clenched his teeth. He was shaking uncontrollably. "Why don't you…?"

"You can't endure *that* shock again," Emma said. "And I can't draw your adrenaline up again."

"I'm not leaving you," Joe said, clutching his chest.

Emma wrapped her arms around him and whispered as emotionlessly as she could, "Calm down. No one is leaving anyone. I need you to connect with me the way you did when we had to find your dad. Then you'll feel the chaos leave me but it won't enter you."

Joe shook harder. "No," he said. "You'll feel what I'm feeling. You won't be able to handle it. I'm stronger than you are."

"I don't think that's true," Emma said. "And even if it was, what difference would it make? We only have each other right now. You have to trust me."

Joe exhaled. "Okay."

Emma took a deep breath and opened herself to him. "Hold my hand and connect with me," she said. She shook at the familiar pain of the poison knife. "Once we're inside, I'll access information about the exit and then release the chaos."

Joe nodded, shaking less with Emma inside him.

They continued up the stairs and opened the door. The room was silent and dark, but she accessed the thoughts of gemynd who were wearing special glasses to see in the dark and saw the exit. It looked like a medical diagnostic tunnel. Squeezing Joe's hand, she released the chaos of Eury Vatic's thoughts into the room. Everywhere she felt people drop.

"Let's go," she said.

Joe couldn't see, and he cried out as he tripped over someone crumpled on the floor and smashed into the corner of a table.

"It's a tube, like the beginning of an MRI or something," Emma whispered. "Right here." She guided him toward where she remembered seeing the exit, her share of Joe's pain making her dizzy. "Get in with me. It's activated by gemynd being inside. We have to get in together."

Not letting go of Joe's hand, she helped him then climbed in herself. An instant swift movement made them both feel sick. Emma saw Joe's memory of the motorcycle rocket Isohel had made, then panicked about thinking Isohel's name and tried—almost unsuccessfully—not to throw up. Then she realized something else.

"Joe," she said, keeping her teeth close together.

He made a noise.

"There are no filters in this tube," she said as they hurtled through the darkness. "Only drugged gemynd pass through. Why would they waste money putting filters here?"

Joe groaned. "I think I'm going to puke," he said, panting. Then Emma cringed as he did.

Miraculously, as much as she wanted to, she did not sympathy vomit. "You have to think clearly, Joe. Listen to me," she commanded. But before she could tell him what she'd learned about secreted gemynd from Hyad's few moments of unprotected thought, the movement in the tube slowed.

"Get ready," Emma said, unsure she had the energy to shock anyone again. Joe didn't seem much better, so she prayed there'd be no one at the other end of the line.

There were others. She sensed them, and Joe took her hand. The mouth of the tube opened. Emma took a huge breath, prayed she'd be able to use Eury Vatic's memories one last time…and the unseen gemynd in the silent, dark room collapsed to the floor.

CHAPTER TWENTY-SIX

Panting and shivering, Joe climbed out of the tube and into the completely dark room.

He reached for Emma's hand to help her. Maybe someday they'd go on a normal date. See a movie. Eat pizza. Talk about things they hated. Kiss for hours in a car. Talk about school and the future. What they wanted to do with their lives. *More than kiss* for hours in a car.

"Shit," Emma said.

"What?" Joe asked. Was she listening to his thoughts about kissing? Did she want to kiss him now, too? Did she not want to kiss him?

"I forgot to connect with…" She stopped talking, turned away from him and threw up on the floor. He laid a hand on her back.

"Sorry," she said, her teeth chattering. "God, how embarrassing."

Joe laughed and then made a sad noise when the movement hurt his chest. "Why is embarrassing for you but not me?"

"It just is," Emma said.

"No, it isn't." He took a huge breath.

"What?" she asked, still shaking slightly.

"I don't feel the venom anymore. Maybe puking in the tunnel sucked it out. Or maybe there's some sort of purifier in the tunnel."

"Awesome," Emma said. "But no talking about puke for a few minutes, okay?"

"Okay," Joe said, taking her hand. "Let's get out of here."

"I forgot to access the thoughts of one of the gemynd who could see in here before I blasted them. I don't know where the door is."

"Where was the door in relation to the tube on the other end?" Joe asked. "Maybe they're set up identically."

"Directly across from us."

"All right," Joe said, squeezing Emma's fingers in one hand while feeling for the mouth of the tube with the other. "I have a good sense of direction. I'll find the door."

"Okay," she said. "But the code probably won't be the same in two different buildings. How will we open it?"

"I don't know," Joe admitted. He helped Emma step over a groaning gemynd on the floor. "Careful."

Emma held them still for a moment. Then: "Okay. I got the code from this one. Let's hurry."

Joe found the door, and Emma opened it. The light blinded them both for a second. They stepped through, then, and the door disappeared behind them. They were in some kind of storage room or waiting room or something.

Emma looked at Joe's disgusting, vomit-covered shoes and bit her cheek. "Gross."

"Yeah," he said, half-smiling. "Well, you don't look much better."

"Oh yes I do," she said, lifting her clean shoes.

"I guess you do," he admitted, smiling and leaning toward her.

"Gross! No kissing until we brush our teeth."

"Baby," he accused. Then he saw something. "Hey. That looks like a regular door."

* * *

Emma followed him across the room. *I love you, Joe Castlellaw.*

Joe spun on his heel, his soft blue hair swinging in the dusty semi-darkness of the room. *I love you, too, chi Erama.*

Emma almost went back on her no-kissing pledge.

The door Joe had found opened without a code, and it led into what looked like an elevator. Joe didn't let her pass through, though. He closed the door again.

"What?" Emma asked. "That has to be the way out."

"It isn't that," Joe said. "We have to move fast but…you're a mess and I'm disgusting."

Emma smiled.

"Thanks," he said. "But seriously, we don't want to attract too much attention if this elevator, or whatever it is, leads someplace there are a lot of gemynd."

Emma took off her sweater. She was wearing a pink tank top a shade darker than her skin underneath, and she heard Joe sigh. It made her tingle inside.

"We can use my sweater to clean ourselves up," she said. "But we have to do your shoes last."

Joe rolled his eyes.

Moving as fast as she could, Emma scrubbed the dirt and she-didn't-want-to-think-what-else off Joe's face and hands and forearms.

"Your face is fine," Joe said. "But your hair... You look like you've been riding in a convertible during a thunderstorm."

"Shut up and fix it," Emma said, smiling back.

Gently Joe ran his fingers through her hair, and the tingling got worse. She could not possibly want to kiss him. They were still lost. They weren't out of danger. He had puke on his shoes. But his hands in her hair made her long to kiss him anyway.

Joe pressed his mouth to her forehead. "How's my hair?" he asked.

"Gorgeous," she said, beaming.

He grinned slowly, and she thought she might fall over. How could she be so furious at him, over something really serious, over hiding information from her about her parents, and then want to kiss him five minutes later? Was this a Soulmate connection thing, or was it a being-in-love-and-being-seventeen thing? For an aching moment Emma just wanted her mom to talk to. The last time she'd seen her, they were in the cabin and Gryphon had just escaped to find Eury Vatic. Emma fought back tears.

"Say goodbye to your sweater," Joe said, bending over to scrape off his shoes. "Not that I'm going to miss it," he added, glancing up at her tiny, close-fitting shirt. "Are you all right? You look sad."

God, Emma thought, watching him clean his shoes, the muscles in his forearms flexing and shifting, his night-blue hair falling over his face. The waistband of his jeans gaped at the small of his back, revealing a narrow strip of smooth brown skin. *God.* She had to get a hold of herself; she was ping-ponging back and forth between sadness and desire like she was crazy.

"Yeah, I'm all right," she said, hoping she sounded at least half convincing.

"Okay," Joe said, standing up. "Done." He gazed for a second at her expression, which must have been one of blatant longing, and she seriously considered staying a few minutes longer. She even hoped he'd want to stay almost as much as she knew they shouldn't.

"We can't," he said in a ragged voice. "We have to get out of here. We aren't any closer to finding your parents than we were the day we got here, and..." Again, that odd look iced his features.

"You're right," she agreed, waiting for him to say something in explanation. This time he would.

He didn't. Which meant she had to do what she'd planned.

They opened the door and got into the elevator-thing. Emma stared straight ahead and slipped into Joe's head. He was guarding the thought very carefully. She almost didn't find it; then she remembered Maude glaring at Joe when they were outside the Erevno. Without looking at it closely, Emma implanted whatever Maude had confided to Joe in her own head, planning to go back to it later. She didn't want to access it now. Not when it seemed like they'd made up.

God, she really wanted her mom or Maude to talk to.

It *was* an elevator, and it opened onto the first floor of Protepol's detainee tower. Emma remembered the wide lobby from the last time she was here. Now it was filled with gemynd, running and talking, trying to stem the crisis that had erupted when the train carrying Eury Vatic's information had been accidentally destroyed. Emma never thought she'd be glad for a crisis of those proportions.

CHAPTER TWENTY-SEVEN

Rage shot through Thalia, filling her legs with strength, darkening her skin. She didn't move. She couldn't think.

Are you all right? Zino asked, coming from the kitchen into the hall. *Did that charlatan upset you?*

"I'm fine." Thalia started to go up the stairs.

Thalia, Zino said.

"I have homework."

Zino took her slightly more opaque hand and turned it over in his. *What happened?*

Nothing, she said. *I'm fine.*

He studied her for a second then dropped her hand and opened the front door.

"Wait!" Thalia pushed past him and out onto the front steps, but the silver-haired boy was gone.

"Never mind," she said.

Zino took her chin and turned her face to his.

Don't, she said.

Oh, Thalia, he whispered.

Thalia ground her teeth so hard she was surprised her jaw didn't break. *I don't want to talk about it,* she said. Zino wouldn't push her. He shouldn't have noticed anything at all. No one should know until the Soulmate pair was ready to reveal themselves. But she wasn't quite fifteen. Maybe that made a difference. And maybe Zino knew something about the temporary change in her skin and the strength of her voice.

If he did, he should have freaking told her to look the hell out for it.

The silver-haired boy had apologized only *after* he'd realized what he might lose. What he'd already lost. It would have made all the difference if he'd come to apologize for what he'd said without knowing Thalia was his Soulmate, but he hadn't. It was the biological imperative of the connection that made him regret how he'd treated her.

Thalia dropped her head. Zino held her smaller hand in his huge warm one. She was so angry and sad that she wondered how she was standing at all.

Atiryx Syndesi, she thought. Hate Match.

She clenched her teeth again. She couldn't say it. She could hardly think it. She'd never heard of anyone who'd actually been cursed with one. What did it mean? Would she never love anyone else? Never have children? Would she still manifest?

Zino squeezed her hand.

Will this make it easier or harder for Mom? she asked. *Because now my manifestation will kind-of suck. Right? I mean, what's the point?*

Do you want to talk about it? Zino asked.

I guess, Thalia said. *I'm still standing here. Are Genna and Maddie upstairs? Because I don't want to talk to Mom about it. And I absolutely don't want Maddie to know. Okay? Promise you won't tell Mom.*

I can't promise that, Zino said.

"I don't want anyone to know," Thalia commanded. Her temporarily powerful voice roared in her throat. *I can't help it that you were here when he came to the door.*

Is it possible you've leapt to the wrong conclusion? Zino asked gently.

Thalia shook her head. *He walked past me on the street and thought I was staring at him,* she said. *I guess I was, but there was no reason I shouldn't have been.* "I knew." *Just like you said I would.* She ground her teeth again.

Zino wanted to speak but kept silent.

"He called me an Aponomi skyta before he actually saw me," Thalia said.

Zino closed his eyes. Thalia heard him muffle an ugly curse in his head.

The Atiryx Syndesi is because of me, she continued. *Just now he wanted to explain. He told me he didn't know I would be Aponomi. Like that makes it better.*

Perhaps he—

Thalia cut Zino off. *No. He didn't come here to see* me. *Or to apologize. He didn't know I lived here. He's the jerk Genna made the song for, the one whose mother cheated her out of silks. He came to return the song sphere. He called Genna an Aponomi skyta, too, as soon as I opened the door. So, no, I don't think I made a mistake.*

Zino didn't say anything.

Thalia lifted her nearly opaque arms and turned them over. *This isn't my manifestation, is it?* she asked. *You guys didn't mess up my actual birth date did you? I'm not fifteen yet, right?*

No, chichi, Zino said. *We didn't mess up your birth date. You turn fifteen next week. And it isn't your manifestation. An Aponomi can recognize his or her Soulmate just before they turn fifteen, and temporary protanosi-like changes can occur. But it's usually in cases when one of the pair is in danger or extreme distress.*

Like Uncle Solymi's death? Thalia said. *Or the loss of the names of Aponomi dead?* "Why didn't you and Genna tell me this could happen? I could have been prepared. Maybe I wouldn't have—"

No, Zino said. *Not like those things.*

What then? Thalia said. *What could be worse?*

The noise of the door buzzer made them both jump.

Zino pushed Thalia into the living room, but she turned around in his strong grip. *Answer me.*

If one of the pair is in some kind of mortal danger, Zino said, *and the Aponomi is not quite fifteen, he or she will become more visibly apparent when physically near the Soulmate.*

Am I in mortal danger? Thalia asked. *Because of the Gatherers? Because rights have been suspended?*

The door buzzed again.

If it's the boy at the door..., Zino said.

"It isn't him," Thalia replied.

I don't know if you realize this, Zino said, *but you're alternating between speaking telepathically and out loud.*

Am I? she asked.

Yes, he said. *I thought you'd want to know.*

He went back and opened the door. *Hyad,* he said in surprise.

Thalia came out of the living room and saw that Hyad trembled slightly.

"May I come in?"

Of course, Dad said, stepping aside to let Hyad pass.

Mom appeared, walking into the hall, bright and beautiful as an apricot firefly. She took Hyad's gold hands and kissed them.

Zino closed the door. *Nysa,* he shouted into the kitchen. *Dinner's ready. Will you please feed Maddie?*

I'm not hungry, Maddie called back.

You have to eat, Zino replied. *You want to be strong enough to open your presents on your birthday next month, don't you?*

There was a short silence.

Well, I'm not hungry, Maddie said. But Thalia soon heard her enthusiastically eating dinner.

Come, Zino said, leading the way into the living room.

I've come to ask a favor, Hyad said quietly.

Of course, Mom answered. She sat next to him on the couch and briefly laid her hand on his.

I know this time is painful for you as well, Hyad said carefully. His sorrow was so intense and explosive Thalia could hardly bear to be near him. *But I was wondering if you'd be willing to give me some things that belonged to Solymi.* He shuddered as he finished the sentence, as if every time he said the name it made Solymi's death more real, as though he believed that if he never said the name, Solymi could sneak back into life again.

Of course, Mom said, *whatever you want. With the issue of the Memorium…* She couldn't continue.

Hyad stared into the center of the room.

Which of Solymi's things do you want? Zino asked.

Hyad told them. When he mentioned the silks, Genna's attention shifted to Thalia.

It's more important that Hyad has them, Thalia said. *No matter what happens with my manifestation.*

All right, Genna said, standing up. *I'll get everything.*

She left the room, and Zino followed. Thalia and Hyad sat in silence in the living room. Hyad's grief was so raw, so private, and so loud—at least to Thalia's heightened sensitivities as a Teknasma—Thalia didn't know where to focus her attention. She had never been this close to a gemynd who'd lost his Soulmate. Hyad looked terrible, as if he'd swallowed poison. The memory of Emma's willingness to suffer the dilitirio knife in her defense popped into Thalia's head. Hyad turned suddenly to her then glanced at the empty doorway.

Emma and her Soulmate were caught in the Impenetrable Defense Building today, he said in a strained voice.

What? Thalia asked, horrified. Since she was twelve she'd practiced with Hyad and Solymi at blocking her thoughts, and she'd gotten good enough to stop even them most of the time. Had she accidentally revealed something somehow? She hoped she hadn't unwittingly endangered Emma. *Are they okay?*

I don't know, he said, not looking at her. *They staged a dramatic escape, but I don't know how far they got.*

Thalia felt a stab of fear.

Hyad stood up and anxiously stared again at the empty doorway. *Can you determine how much longer your parents will be?*

Sure, Thalia said. Hyad could access her parents' thoughts as easily as she could, but it would have been unacceptably rude.

Still staring at the doorway, Hyad sat down again. Thalia listened to her parents for a moment and cringed. *They'll be a while longer. Genna is really upset. Do you need to leave soon for something?*

I don't require everything I asked for, Hyad said frantically, not answering Thalia's question. Again, he stood up then sat down.

It isn't that, Thalia said, trying to think of a way to be helpful. *She wants you to have everything you asked for. She's just still so sad.*

Oh, Hyad said. He sucked in a mouthful of air then stared blankly into the center of the room. His mouth was moving slightly, like he was trying to talk himself into something. *Is your inaccessible place in here? Your family has one, no?*

It's the wall behind that table, Thalia said. *I thought you knew. Mom always teased Uncle Solymi about spending too much time in here with you when you came over.*

Hyad exhaled. *We didn't need an inaccessible place to spend time together.*

Thalia blushed as she thought of Uncle Solymi kissing or doing something more with Hyad, and her heart ached in protest at the memory of how amazing and happy she'd felt before the silver-haired boy turned around and saw her.

Hyad was staring hard at her now, but she didn't feel him trying to access her thoughts. Maybe she wouldn't feel it. She sat up straighter and tried to access him to figure out why he was acting so oddly, if it was because of something more than despair over

Solymi's death, but she couldn't. He'd completely locked his thoughts.

Come, he said suddenly, and he led Thalia to the inaccessible spot. He moved the table, leaned against the wall and motioned for Thalia to do the same.

The Ones in Power want to make inaccessible places illegal, Thalia pointed out.

Hyad nodded but didn't say anything for a minute. Thalia didn't try to listen to his thoughts. Instead, she thought of the silver-haired boy pounding his fists on the door, saying he hadn't known.

Before Eury Vatic resurfaced, Solymi joined a covert team of Eleytheria and Aythentia who were investigating the secreting system, Hyad said.

Wow. Thalia felt a moment of awe that Uncle Solymi had done something so brave and important. *Were you scared for him?*

Hyad was quiet. Thalia had forgotten that for the very private Hyad certain kinds of sympathy and insight were painful.

He finally spoke. *I didn't know about it until a few days before he died. And yes. I was terrified.*

Thalia looked away. A chrim, Synithi, Aythentia Chamura never admitted anything like weakness or fear. Did Hyad know something about the secreting system, she wondered. Maybe he could he help Emma find her parents.

I think Emma already knows something about the secreting system, Hyad said.

Thalia shuddered in fear for her friend, but Hyad didn't seem to realize he'd answered her private thought. He was quiet for a long time, and then he began shaking so violently Thalia held his hand for a few minutes.

Genna and Zino are coming back! she realized. She started to move away from the wall, but Hyad kept her frozen for a moment as her mom and dad's footsteps sounded in the hall.

I've implanted a thought in your head, Hyad said, not looking at her. *Don't access it until you can get back to the inaccessible place by yourself.*

He and Thalia moved away from the wall and replaced the table just as Mom and Dad walked back into the room, Genna's apricot-colored outline bruised from crying and Zino's face exhausted.

CHAPTER TWENTY-EIGHT

She snuck out of bed that night, and Maddie's dream caught her as she passed her sister's open door. In the dream Maddie was flying—free from the harness—and Genna, Zino, and Thalia were flying with her. Thalia exhaled and went into the living room.

An inaccessible place was always cold. Thalia shivered as the chill seeped into her skin. She couldn't help wondering what things would feel like after she manifested. Would she prefer it? Or would it just seem different, not better? It would be easier if she didn't like the experience because it could only last for a little more than a year.

She closed her eyes until the face of the silver-haired boy disappeared from her thoughts. She didn't even know his name. She shouldn't want to know…but she did.

Hyad's thought opened in her head, and Thalia almost lost her balance. The revelation of an implanted thought felt like falling in a dream, unexpected and uncontrollable. Hyad's voice murmured over images of unfamiliar, terrified gemynd, including one who looked like Isia Sorgyre, the Chronicler of *The Uske.* Under Hyad's urgent narration, one by one the terrified faces melted away, morphing into others and then disappearing.

After a few minutes Hyad's voice silenced and the images stopped. Thalia slid to the floor. She kept her back against the wall. When she stood up again she'd have to keep her emotions calm; she didn't want to wake up Mom or Dad or Maddie. But, right now, she sat alone in the dark living room and cried. How did the gemynd who'd come up with and worked upon such an unspeakable idea sleep at night? How did they walk around? Eat breakfast? Kiss their Soulmates? Have children? Why had Hyad told her about this? Some part of Thalia, a big part, wanted to stand outside and scream and scream until everyone in the Commonworld knew what the secreting system, the Synektos weapon, did. Maybe if everyone knew, the Ones in Power would stop using it. It wouldn't be so easy to live in a world if everyone knew you spent your days destroying the bond that held everything together.

* * *

Rede sat up in bed, out of breath and sweating. His mother and father were screaming at each other, but that wasn't what woke him; he had learned long ago to shut out his parents' hatred of each other, or to kill something inside himself so he didn't have to feel what they felt. Something else had terrified him enough to wake him tonight.

He listened for a few minutes through the vitriol downstairs but heard nothing. It must have been just a random nightmare. He lay back down.

As soon as Rede's head touched the pillow, the nightmare thrust full-force back into his head. But now he was wide awake. Thalia was upset. And it wasn't about him. She was terrified and sad, alone with a horrifying secret.

Rede crushed the pillow around his head as Thalia paced in her room, trying not to cry. She wouldn't want him to help. So, why couldn't anyone in her stupid family hear her?

He got out of bed and walked to the window. Thalia lived in a neighborhood two trains away from his, but she might as well have been in the next room. Or in this one. He stood helplessly listening to her fears, feeling her struggle not to scream or cry out. Rede would have given anything—almost anything—to take back what he'd said on the street. Distracted as always by the one terrible mistake he could never undo, he hadn't seen Thalia. Hadn't felt her. Hadn't recognized that she was his Soulmate until it was too late. He'd ruined everything. Again.

She was crying now. Rede sat on his bed. He grabbed his arms and dug into the *fos charasso* marks until his skin almost bled.

Thalia was pacing unsteadily. She was dizzy, and he knew how fragile Aponomi could be. Rede stared wildly around his room as if there were someone who might help, or something he could do from this distance away. Then she tripped over something and fell.

Rede jumped from his bed and listened, and listened, and listened.

Thalia was silent.

* * *

She woke to someone turning her onto her back and shaking her.

Thalia. Thalia!

She opened her eyes. It was dark. The panicked face above hers gradually came into focus.

Misos, Thalia, Zino said, leaning back onto his heels. *What were you doing out of bed?* He tucked his hand under her head, gasped and pulled his hand away. *You're bleeding.*

No, I'm not, she said, dizzy on the floor.

Zino turned his wet palm toward her. *You would argue with the sun,* he said, twisting as Genna came into the room and asked what he needed. Zino ran his hands over Thalia's skin, obviously trying to figure that out.

I'm fine, Thalia said, trying to wriggle away.

He ignored her.

Moragia, he said to Genna. *She cut herself when she fell.*

Where? Genna asked.

Just above her collarbone. Zino pressed his hand to where Thalia's shoulder met her throat, and Genna left the room.

I don't feel any blood, Thalia said.

Zino pushed the hair from her forehead with his free hand. *What do you feel, chichi?*

Why did you come in here? Thalia asked.

He just continued to stroke her hair and gaze worriedly at her.

"You couldn't have heard me," she said out loud. "I sealed off my room."

Zino exhaled. *You can't seal off your room, Thalia,* he said. *You know that. If something happened...something like this*, he continued, shaking his head, *we would have no way of knowing. We respect your privacy, Thalia, but we have to be able to hear that you are all right.*

Genna doesn't respect my privacy, Thalia snapped. *She listens when I ask her not to.*

I'll talk with Genna. Okay? Zino said, caressing her cheek. *But no more sealing off your room.*

Why did you come in here? Thalia asked again.

Genna came back with the moragia and a wet cloth. Zino cleaned the blood off and spread the moragia over the lacerations. Thalia waited for the sting to penetrate her skin. She gasped when it happened.

Zino picked her up and carried her to her bed. *Let me talk to Thalia alone for a minute, Charis,* he said to Genna.

Is she all right? Genna said. *Are you keeping something from me, Zeph?*

Yes, she's all right, Zino said. *And yes, I'm keeping something from you. But it's Thalia's story to tell. Not mine.*

Genna sucked in a mouthful of air and gazed at Thalia.

Please, Charis, Zino said.

I love you, chichi, Genna said to Thalia, and she left the room.

Rede told me you'd fallen and he couldn't hear you anymore, Zino said after Mom shut the door.

Who is Rede? Thalia asked, even though there was only one gemynd it could be.

He called your name, and when you didn't answer he called me, Zino said. *I was awake or I don't know if I would have heard him. Do you want to tell me what upset you?*

"No," Thalia said.

All right, Zino said. *But if you do, I'm ready to listen.*

Thanks, Thalia said, and she leaned over to let him kiss her on the head.

Please be more careful.

This doesn't change what he said or how I feel, Thalia remarked.

Zino nodded and opened her bedroom door.

"It doesn't change what he said or how I feel," she said again, out loud this time after sucking in a halting breath. "But you can let him know I'm all right."

Okay, chichi, Zino said. *I will.*

"I don't want him to contact me, though," she said. "Okay?"

Zino nodded. *Okay.*

He left the room.

CHAPTER TWENTY-NINE

The elevator door opened.

Holding hands and talking dispassionately about the consecration ceremony at school, Emma and Joe walked out of the detainee building and down the street toward what seemed to be a residential neighborhood.

We have to find a portal tree, Emma said, still talking out loud about the consecration ceremony and her imaginary parents' resistance to her Soulmate connection. But she told Joe what she'd learned and prayed the filters wouldn't pick it up. *I connected with Hyad before we escaped. Secreted gemynd are sent to the Otherworld, our world. We have to go home.*

Joe nodded.

A few blocks away from the detainee building he dropped her hand. "Were you ever going to tell me?" he asked. "Or did you think you wouldn't have to because you thought I'd never find out?"

"I…," Emma began.

"Don't lie," he said. "It's bad enough that you did the one thing I asked you not to do."

"I tried to be patient," Emma said. "I tried to give you a chance, but you wouldn't tell me what it was. I couldn't wait any longer."

Furious, Joe spun around to face her. "Why haven't you listened to it yet?"

"How do you know I haven't?" Heart pounding, Emma gasped. "Can you listen to my thoughts without my knowing?"

"Why?" Joe asked. "Are you hiding something else?"

No!

Are you? he demanded, his low voice full of apprehension.

"No," she said. "Of course not."

"What the fuck, Emma?" Joe walked ahead of her onto an expensive-looking tree-lined street.

She ran to catch up. "Can you listen to my thoughts without—?"

"No!" he said, cutting her off. "I can't. Does that make you feel better? You can keep all your secrets."

"I don't have any," she said quietly. "Not anymore."

"You don't sound very convincing," Joe said. "You might want to work on that."

"How did you know I haven't listened to the thought I—?"

Stole? he interrupted.

Took from your head, she finished.

"Because the thing I know is unforgivable," Joe said. "And once you hear what it is, you'll never be able to forget it." He gazed at her. "Do you really think that if I knew something that could help you find your parents I'd keep it from you, no matter what it was? What do you think of me, anyway? Besides the fact that I don't know anything about you," he added, throwing her words back in her face.

"That's not fair," Emma said.

"Fair!" Joe echoed. "What the fuck in either world is fair?"

"Ow!" Emma said. It felt like a bee stung her hand. The blackened remains of the connector scar she'd shared with her cousin Isohel was suddenly bright with fluid.

"What?" Joe growled. "Are we not finished with the All About Emma show yet?"

She pressed her hand against her chest. "Why didn't you tell me that what you knew wouldn't help me find my parents? I wouldn't have snuck into your head if I knew that."

"I did tell you," Joe said.

Emma stared at her palm, listening to something Joe couldn't hear. The implication was terrifying. *The Gatherers are coming,* she relayed to him. *Here. It's the scar. I think they picked up something from the scar.*

There, Joe said. He indicated an alley that likely led to gardens behind the row of houses.

They climbed over a fence and into a small garden, then over a white stone wall into another garden, and then another, all searching for a way out.

We're trapped, Emma said. *None of these gardens lead anywhere except into another garden or house. By the time we get out they will have surrounded the street.*

Look at that tree, Joe said, pointing to a something like a maple in the corner of an untidy garden two houses away. *Remember what Maude said about the bark and leaf patterns? That's a portal tree.*

They ran for it. As they did, Emma repeated, "You didn't tell me that what you knew wouldn't help me find my parents. You said you wouldn't want to know what it was."

Joe stopped running. "Isn't that the same thing?"

"No!" Emma said. "It isn't. Joe! I thought you knew something that would help me find them and, for some crazy reason known to you alone, you stubbornly refused to tell me. How the hell was I supposed to think otherwise when you wouldn't say anything other than *I wouldn't want to know if it was me!?*"

Emma felt Gatherers break into the house behind them, waking up an angry woman who'd fallen asleep listening to a music sphere that shattered into a dissonant wail when it rolled off her lap. Beside Emma, Joe's face fell.

"Maybe I don't know you," he said. Then he climbed into the portal tree. "Are you coming?" he asked before he moved through it.

How could everything unravel so quickly? Emma contracted her stomach so she wouldn't cry and grabbed the lowest branch.

Before she could do anything else, strong hands descended. They pulled her out of the tree and lifted her to her feet. Volucris Gatherers surrounded her, and one of them released a narrow, spinning cylinder of energy into the portal tree. It burst into flames and burned to the ground.

CHAPTER THIRTY

Thalia couldn't sleep. The moragia irritated her skin, and everything else hurt from her fall.

By now Zino would have told the silver-haired boy—*Rede*—that she was okay. She shouldn't care or even be curious about how he felt, but Thalia couldn't stop thinking about him. Trapped in a detainee tower of her own mind and heart, she couldn't turn her thoughts away from him. She wanted to scream.

In her weakest moments, Thalia almost forgot what Rede had said and the vicious way he'd looked at her. He'd hated her before he knew her, so she should despise everything about him. If it weren't for the stupid Soulmate connection, she would loathe him without question. She was a traitor to herself.

Nothing, nothing, nothing was what she'd expected. Uncle Solymi was dead. Her manifestation ceremony was cancelled. And her *Eynosyndeo*, her Soulmate, whom she'd been waiting her whole life to meet, was a despicable jerk.

The sound of Rede's fists banging on the front door and the words *I didn't know* rang in Thalia's head. A memory. An unwanted memory. She shook herself and got out of bed, carefully walking to the window to watch the sun come up.

Sunlight was the first thing Thalia had actually ever seen, when she was very young and her ability to see finally developed. Even as a toddler she'd loved the feel of the sun on her face. Zino would sit her outside every day, telling her that someday she would see the sun and it would look lovelier than ice cream tasted. Sunlight looked the way music sounded, he'd said.

Thalia sank into the soft window seat and let her eyes adjust to the gradually fading darkness. Nysa must have left the box that held Maddie's wings and other outside toys open, because Maddie's harness was just visible hanging between the two trees. And in the shade, the open box looked like someone was sitting on it.

Thalia pulled her knees to her chest and wrapped her arms around them. They were dark and solid-looking again. She ran her hands up and down her skin wondering if she'd like the way she looked when she was fully manifested.

Her stomach suddenly felt warm, the way it had when she was little and Zino brought home presents unexpectedly. The way it felt when Uncle Solymi told her someday she'd be the best Teknasma the Ones in Power ever had, if they were Eleytheria by the time she was grown up. And maybe even if they weren't.

Thalia leaned into the slowly expanding gray light and saw Rede sitting on Maddie's box of toys.

He stood up. *I just wanted to make sure you were okay.*

My dad said he would tell you, Thalia said as Rede turned to leave.

He did, thanks. I just wanted to see for myself.

Thalia remembered what Genna had said about how difficult it was to find anything in Rede worthy of a Soul Song, and she tried to access something of the thoughts he kept hidden, but she couldn't— which was weird. Even without her considerable skills, she should have been able to access almost anything about her Soulmate unless he locked his thoughts. Rede's thoughts didn't feel locked, but Thalia's attempts to access them bounced back. There was something Rede didn't want anyone to know.

Thalia kept trying. Every time she thought she came near it, he pulled it away. Whatever it was, it made her afraid. And not for herself.

I'm glad you're okay, Rede said. *I'll leave you alone.*

Wait, Thalia said.

No. You'll wake up your dad. I promised him I wouldn't contact you. He said you didn't want to see me. Ever.

I don't, Thalia said. *I mean, I didn't. Just wait a minute, will you? I can't move that fast. I hurt myself when I...*

There was a noise outside, and Rede was suddenly at her window. He'd climbed the flowering vine Zino planted when he and Genna first bought the house.

Thalia opened the window. For a second she just stared at Rede. His bright green eyes were so fierce they were almost hard to look at, and his silver hair was combed back like the hero of a story chronicle. Thalia flashed on Alder, the beautiful damaged hero of

The Uske, then remembered the humiliation of the failed immersion-kiss.

She stepped away from the window. In a few minutes sunlight would be streaming in, and, unlike Alder, Rede had already looked at her in disgust. And she'd been in the shade then. What would he have done if Thalia were standing in the sun and he could see her blood sloshing through her veins? Or worse.

"Do you want me to leave?" Rede asked, gazing at her like he could see inside her. Not just her body, though. Her soul. Her heart. It gave her shivers.

No, Thalia said. *I want you to come in.*

Your father, he said.

She blushed and grinned sheepishly. *I forgot to unseal my room.*

Rede looked like he was afraid to smile back at her.

"Come in," she said again, out loud this time. *My room is still sealed off, but my dad might hear you if you're talking outside. Even telepathically.*

Rede climbed into Thalia's room. She backed up, not quite sure what to do now that he was here, and the awkward uncertainty felt a lot like the immersion-kiss had. Misos, wasn't there at least *one* thing that was easy to understand? Maddie was so lucky. All she ever wanted was to eat peaches and play Volucris, and she got to do both of those things every day.

I forgot what I wanted to ask you, she said.

Rede swallowed a laugh before it was finished then turned away and rubbed a hand over his forehead. Thalia watched the marks on his forearm fade in the light from the window and then brighten again as he dropped his arm to the shade at his side. Rede saw her watching. He held his arms up for her to see.

"It's the first book of the Idrysi song," he said. "That's the ancient telling of the creation story, if you didn't know. The creation of this world and the Otherworld." He seemed to smile slightly, but the expression fell away before Thalia had time to be certain it happened.

"I carved it myself," he continued, turning his arms over so they faced him. "I'm a Chronicler, so I'm good with my hands and good with language." He exhaled, and Thalia thought he might have blushed but wasn't sure. "My mom hates fos charasso marks and piercings, anything like that. She says they make gemynd whose powers are weak look even more pathetic." He glanced at Thalia, seeming to want her to contradict that statement, then shook his head and laughed derisively.

Are they always so luminous? she asked as he turned away.

Yes, he said, turning back. *That was one of the reasons I did it.* He frowned.

So you could always read the song? she said.

He nodded. Then, clearly worried she might not have seen him, he said, *Yes.*

A reminder, Thalia said. *I understand. You wanted a reminder of something important to you. Something that no one could alter or dismiss.*

He didn't smile, but he looked at her so intently Thalia swayed where she stood. Rede caught her arm until she was steady and then let go.

You're a Teknasma, aren't you? he asked.

Thalia nodded. *Yes.* Suddenly she wanted to transform into a perfect Synithi girl. Someone he wouldn't have hated. Someone he wouldn't have called a terrible name. Anger roared through her again.

Rede colored and turned away. "I should go."

"Okay," Thalia said.

I won't come near you anymore, he said, fighting to keep his voice steady. *Unless you're hurt or something. I don't think I could stay away then.*

"I can take care of myself," Thalia said.

He laughed. *Your dad said you'd say that.*

He walked to the window and climbed out. Thalia followed him—to shut the window after he'd gone, she told herself.

Rede turned and faced her, his hands wrapped around the thick vines, the fos charasso marks beaming like tiny melodies under the shade of the leaves. He wanted to tell her something; Thalia could feel it, like rain or sunlight on her face. But she didn't ask him what. And he didn't say anything.

Goodbye, Thalia, he said, and he climbed down the vine.

* * *

Something cold dripped on Joe's face. Was there a leak coming from the upstairs apartment? He groaned and swore. His mom would rather move his bed and put a bucket on the floor than have to talk to the neighbors. Shit, his head was *killing* him. He reached for a pillow and hurt his hand on something sharp. Bolting up, Joe smashed his head on a branch of the half-burned portal tree that had fallen over him.

Emma. What the hell happened? He smelled smoke but it was raining and the tree was cold.

"Emma!" Joe shouted. He broke the branches that were trapping him and climbed out from under the nearly destroyed tree. "Emma?" He ran to other trees nearby. Maybe she'd moved through a different portal. But, didn't they all connect with different places in this world? Where could she be? Where the hell was he? A park in a city? He saw trees and flowers but heard the heavy roar of traffic.

"Emma!"

God, had she been in the tree when it was destroyed?

Emma! Joe thought loudly and insistently. *Emma!*

She didn't answer, but Emma was not dead. Emma could not be dead.

His head was still killing him. What time was it? It looked like early morning. But it was late afternoon just a few minute ago.

The air shifted behind him. Joe whirled.

"Hey, dirtbag," someone on a bike shouted. "Get your drunk ass out of the park. It's fucking Sunday. Where's your fucking sense of decency?" The bike curved past a green kiosk and disappeared.

Sunday? Joe thought. It was Friday. Friday afternoon. Where was Emma?

It stopped raining and the wind picked up. Joe smelled the ocean. He looked around. Silver buildings surrounded a hilly, fenced park. An old stone church with a clock tower stood on the other side of the street, and a few nicely dressed old people were climbing the steps and entering it. Joe looked at the clock again. Eight? In the morning? Two days had passed? What the hell happened? Where was Emma? Had she made it through the tree? Did the Gatherers take her?

Two more cyclists flew past, followed by a man running with a stroller and a sleek, fawn-colored dog. Joe looked around for, found and ran to the nearest park exit. He had to get back to the Commonworld. Emma had to be okay. She had to be.

He shoved down the guilt and sorrow over how they'd parted. Emma was okay. She really had to be. Maude had screamed the second she knew Gryphon was gravely injured, before they'd had any idea where he was or how to find him, so Joe would feel something. He would feel something if anything terrible happened to Emma; he wasn't so severed from his gemynd-self that he couldn't feel his own Soulmate if she—

A seriously fucked-up kid around his age or maybe a little younger paced outside the park, talking animatedly. "The windows are wrong," the kid said repeatedly to no one. "They open when they aren't supposed to, but they never get stuck, never get stuck." He was skinny, with terrible skin and the hollow eyes of a drug addict.

Joe watched for a second, horrified. Without his mom, without books and time to bike alone in the woods, without the secret hope that he did have a father out in the world somewhere, this lost kid could have been him, strung out, homeless and alone. Sometimes Joe forgot how lucky he really was. Somebody always had it worse. Always. If the kid asked him for money or something, he'd give it to him.

As if he heard what Joe was thinking, the kid turned and walked over, his gray eyes piercing and hyper-focused. Joe dug into his pocket and found three quarters. He pressed them into the kid's palm. It was soft like a woman's and felt smaller than it looked.

The kid stared at the silver discs as if he didn't know, or had just remembered, what they were. "The window is wrong," he said urgently to Joe. "The window is wrong." He grabbed Joe's arm. "The window is wrong."

"I'm sorry," Joe said, "that's all I have." He pulled his arm away. "I'm sorry."

"The window is wrong," the boy repeated desperately.

"Okay," Joe said. "Okay. Thanks for telling me."

He walked away, guilty and unnerved, thinking about his Otherworld mom and wishing he could remember something about his biological mom. If only he still had that picture of his parents. Or something. Anything. And he hadn't seen his Otherworld mom since running off to find his father in the Commonworld with Emma. Mr. Spencer said she was okay, that she'd eventually been convinced that Joe was away on a school thing and would be back soon. Would he ever see her again, though? What would he say? Would she be proud of him for fighting so hard to do the right thing?

Joe turned and watched the homeless kid stumble away, wondering if his Otherworld mom would have taken the boy in. Most parents warned their children to stay away from strangers, especially strangers who seemed mentally unstable, but one of Joe's most vivid memories was of a field trip to the New England Aquarium in Boston when he was in second grade. Uncharacteristically, his mom had not only allowed him to go on the trip, she'd come along as a chaperone.

An old homeless guy had approached the class as they stood outside the aquarium gift shop window. The teachers and the other chaperones quickly ushered the kids back inside, but Joe and his mom stayed. She had already told him he couldn't get a souvenir; she only had five dollars and wanted to hold on to it in case of an emergency.

Joe remembered her hand clutching his way too tightly while he turned around to look through the gift shop window at the other kids buying whale puppets and undersea snow globes. The old man had approached to only a few feet away, saying something about a sandwich, and "God bless you." Joe was torn between staring at the man's tanned face and a stuffed, bottlenose dolphin in the window—and a yellow stick with a red-handled biting shark head on top. That's what he *really* wanted. He remembered planning what he could do with it, who he could bite and what he could pick up, when he'd heard the old man say "Thank you," and without looking he knew his mom had given the five dollar emergency money away.

Even then he'd known not to say anything. He'd glared at the empty food stand across the courtyard and hated her as the other kids noisily exited the gift shop, showing off their toys and biting each other with their shark heads. His mother pulled him away and knelt in front of him so her pale blue eyes were level with his, and she said, "Once that old man was seven years old just like you."

Joe remembered watching the filthy, fuzzy-haired thief of his shark toy walk over toward a couple who crossed the street to get away. Joe's mother took his chin and turned his attention back to her.

"Once that old man was seven years old just like you, Joe," she repeated in her whispery monotone. "He went to school. And had homework. And wanted presents for his birthday."

The rest of the class, most clutching bags lumpy with souvenirs, moved toward the garage where the bus waited. His mom stood up and didn't say anything else, and Joe hated her—*hated* her—the whole bus ride back to New Hampshire. Tommy Mulvaney kept using his shark head to steal a green stone turtle out of Dakota Cassidy's hand; he got in trouble and had to sit with Mrs. Weigand in the front of the bus. Joe hated his mom, hated the bus, hated the other kids, hated Tommy Mulvaney. He considered stealing the shark toy that Tommy left on the bus seat, but he eventually decided he would only get caught and in trouble, and he didn't want anyone to talk to him ever again.

He'd tried to imagine the old man with dirty feet and skin like an overcooked hot dog being in second grade. It hadn't seemed possible. Old people were never actually young. Joe didn't want to ever look like that old man, and he never wanted to have to ask people for money, *ever*. Where was that old man's mom? he'd wondered. Why didn't she help him? Why didn't *she* give him money? Maybe, he'd thought back then, she'd left the man the way Joe had heard his real mom and dad left him near that garbage can.

From the front of the bus Joe's mom had turned around and smiled at him. She'd glanced at the other moms, who were asleep, and at Mrs. Weigand, whose angry, whispering head was bent toward Tommy Mulvaney. Then Joe's mom held up her fist and opened her fingers to reveal a tiny airplane made of blue paper and decorated with small pictures. Glancing once more at Mrs. Weigand, who continued to quietly scold poor Tommy, Joe's mom threw the plane. It curled through the air, dropping bits of colored paper onto the floor of the bus, and finally landed in Joe's lap. It made him look up at his mom and smile back.

CHAPTER THIRTY-ONE

The red-eyed gemynd named Lukas entered the room where Emma had spent the night suspended in air the way she and Joe had been before they found Joe's father. Emma dropped to the floor, breaking her fall with her hands. It felt like she'd sprained her wrist. She gritted her teeth, fiercely thinking about nothing.

The door opened again. Emma glanced up to see Isohel, gray and nearly unconscious, in the arms of a tall Gatherer. Lukas nodded at a long flat piece of furniture, a table or a bed or something, and her cousin was carried to it.

Isohel swore quietly, and Emma gasped. Deep in the palm of her hand her connector scar burned. Isohel stopping making any sound or movement.

"Proximity won't make a difference," someone said.

Emma recognized Hyad's voice. Two gemynd who had come into the room with him were thought-speaking into what looked like palm-sized reading stones, both pointed at her.

Lukas shot his attention to her, and Emma felt a sharp pain like someone had ripped off a Band-Aid inside her head. "No," he said. "I want her to see."

"I understand your anger…," Hyad began.

Lukas smiled. Emma smelled the pure, delicious, oceany scent that had surprised her the first time they met. "I am angry, yes," he said calmly. "She destroyed equipment and slowed our progress when she escaped with her Soulmate. Two days! But then…"

Emma felt his desire to turn and smile triumphantly at her. He resisted the impulse until he realized she sensed it. Then he turned to her. Emma felt seduced and terrorized at the same time.

"But then her cousin tried to destroy what was left of the connector scar," he said.

With a jolt of nausea, Emma saw that most of Isohel's palm was destroyed, her fingers hanging like dead flowers from the remains of her hand.

"I guess she was not as dedicated an Eleytheria as she thought," Lukas added.

Don't let him get to you, Emma thought to Isohel.

"She can't hear you," Lukas said.

"Well, if she can't hear me, she can't hear you," Emma said, "and you won't be able to get what you want."

Again Lukas smiled.

"Stop smiling at me," Emma said.

He laughed. "She doesn't have to hear me for me to get what I want from her," he said. "In fact, it's easier for me if she doesn't. She might have abandoned her political affiliation and not given them what they want, but she has not abandoned herself. She won't release anything willingly."

"What are you going to do?" Emma asked.

"You know what I'm going to do," he said. "But if you need me to say it, I'm going to use extrication lights on your cousin."

Emma held her injured wrist to her chest, but she didn't close her eyes or turn away. Would Isohel die? Would the trauma of the extrication kill Isohel the way it had killed Joe's father?

"I don't know," Lukas said, answering Emma's unspoken questions. "She made her own choices, though, running away with that information. As Eury Vatic made his own choice. We all live with the consequences of our actions." He eyed Emma and said, "Oh, yes. We gave him a choice."

Emma hissed. "That he surrender to the Ones in Power or his children would be executed? And after you slaughtered him with extrication lights in a room just like this one, who would have watched over those children, their father's killers? You didn't give him a choice. You gave yourselves a justification so you could sleep at night."

A strange look shivered across Lukas's face. He nodded to the Gatherers, who aimed the blue lights at Isohel.

Emma felt Hyad shudder, but his face was as serene as ever. She clenched her teeth and every muscle. She tried not to think of Joe or remember his dad, and she prayed that Isohel would be okay.

Not knowing what would happen to Isohel or what her cousin felt, the process was excruciating to watch. Her cousin trembled less than Eury had. Maybe she was stronger. Maybe she was weaker.

Hyad began to lose his composure, though his face still revealed nothing.

Don't worry, Emma said. *Everything will be okay.*

What an idiotic thing to say, Hyad replied.

A memory of his laughing Soulmate clung to Hyad's words, echoing them in Emma's mind with a different but melodic voice. *Everything will be okay,* Solymi had whispered. He kissed Hyad's neck. *You worry a great deal for someone who has had everything handed to him on a golden plate, Hyad Cerus.*

As Solymi kissed Hyad on the mouth, the memory faded. Emma turned back and watched Isohel tremble almost languidly on the table. The Gatherers replaced the swollen lights they held with fresh ones.

Lukas saw it a second before she did. "Stop!" he cried. He pushed the Gatherers aside then leaned closely over Isohel and swore.

Emma stared at her cousin, pale and small on the bed.

"What happened?" Hyad asked.

Lukas ignored him. He took a small red vial from his pocket, opened it and drank. The sugar-flower smell made Emma feel sick. For a second she thought—hoped—that it was poison.

He laughed at her again. "Nothing is ever that easy."

He turned to the Gatherers and indicated Isohel. "Clean her up and put her back in her room. I'll meet you there in a few minutes." He turned to Hyad. "Don't let her out of your sight," he said about Emma.

Hyad nodded. "I know. I won't."

Lukas glared at Emma. "She'll explain what happened," he said. Then he left the room.

"Don't try to use whatever information you have to bribe me to help you," Hyad said immediately. "If you don't tell me, Lukas will. And I don't care anyway. I see that the extrication didn't work, and won't work, so it doesn't concern me anymore."

Furious, Emma held her breath.

"Let me see your wrist," Hyad said, walking over to her.

She held it out, and he took it.

Hyad turned to the Gatherers, who were wiping clear fluid over Isohel's arms and legs. "After you get the girl back to her room," he said, "send someone back here with an arnica binding."

The Gatherers left with Isohel, who lay still but was breathing. Gently, Hyad released Emma's arm back to her.

"Hold it up like that and try not to move it."

"Isohel—the girl on that table," Emma clarified, "destroyed the part of her brain that remembered where she hid whatever she took from Eury Vatic."

Hyad stared at her.

"She didn't simply erase the memory," Emma continued. "She made a tool that located and obliterated it. The seat of that memory, and probably other memories and functions, is completely gone. It wasn't in any layer of her consciousness. The extrication lights— which I guess from hearing Lukas's thoughts are difficult to make, super expensive, and can only be used once—were wasted."

"Does anyone know where she hid what she took?" Hyad asked.

"Her memory of that information was destroyed as well."

"She must have been an extraordinarily gifted Dimiorg," Hyad murmured.

"Yeah," Emma said. "She was. And that gift is wasted now, isn't it? Whatever she might have been, whatever she could have done, is over. I guess that's what 'acceptable consequences' means."

Hyad shook so violently that Emma forgot her fury over Isohel and grabbed his hand, which he immediately pulled away.

"I don't want your sympathy," he hissed.

"What is the fucking point?" Emma asked. "Whenever anyone gets power they just fuck it up, don't they?"

"No!" Hyad cried. "No. Most gemynd, even Aythentia," he added, sneering slightly at her, "work to make circumstances better for everyone."

"Aythentia are the Ones in Power," she said. "*They* destroyed the train your Soulmate was on. You realize that, don't you?"

Finally, for the first time, everything Hyad felt showed on his face. It was painful to look at, was something like Maude with her soul exposed except this was utterly naked and without beauty. The expression in his eyes was so raw and desperate that Emma wished more than anything she could take back what she'd said.

"I'm sorry—," she began.

"It was an accident," he said, breathing in an odd rhythm as if he were being forced to inhale and exhale. "The blockage we'd set up and the shield the Resisters used were incompatible. Both were new technologies with unprecedented power. Neither had been tried in an uncontrolled environment. We realized too late that the reaction would be incendiary."

Emma held her breath. Hyad stared wildly at her, as if she could do something or say something to make everything different.

"Did you know he was on the train?" she asked quietly.

Hyad shook his head. "No."

Emma felt so much violent upheaval inside him that it was all she could do not to reach out and hold him.

He pulled himself out of it. "It wouldn't have made a difference if I had known." He exhaled unevenly. "I would have tried just as hard to avoid injuring any gemynd whether Solymi was on the train or not. Maybe this is difficult for you to understand, since until recently you thought of yourself as human, but the Soulmate connection is sacred to us, no matter which side of the power spectrum we're on."

Hyad paused, hardly breathing. The image of a skinny teenage boy with the terrible skin and hollow eyes of a drug addict flashed from his thoughts to Emma's, but lost in uncontrollable sorrow he didn't notice that she had seen.

He shook his head then continued, "Whenever anyone is injured or killed, every gemynd feels, even if it's only for a moment, empathy for the Soulmate left behind. Ugly actions are sometimes taken, yes, but only when they are necessary. And sometimes mistakes are made, but the Law of Acceptable Consequences is deeply thought out and considered."

"Nobody seemed to care about plowing through Isohel's consciousness," Emma said. "Or about possibly killing her with those extrication lights."

"Isohel is Loveless," Hyad said. His voice was gentle but firm. "No one would lose her. She would only lose herself."

"What?" Emma almost gagged, her throat closing over. These gemynd truly only believed in the value of those with Soulmates?

Someone came into the room and spread something cool and soothing around her injured wrist. The pain stopped, and her forearm felt numb. Hyad watched, his face serene and unreadable again.

"You'll be able to use it again in a few hours," he said. "In the meantime, try to keep it still. Come."

CHAPTER THIRTY-TWO

How did this *get here?* Genna asked later that morning. She took the song sphere from the shelf where it had been placed.

Oh, Thalia said, getting up from the couch where she'd been trying to concentrate on her homework. *The boy you made it for came to return it yesterday.*

Genna turned the sphere over in her hands. Pale music drifted out, and Thalia wanted to take it away.

That's odd, Genna said.

What? Thalia asked, feeling spiky and defensive.

That he would have returned it.

You said he was a jerk, Thalia said. *He obviously didn't want it.*

I'm not surprised he didn't want it, Genna said, eyeing her curiously. *I'm surprised he returned it.*

She put it back on the shelf. Thalia dug her fingers into her clothes so she wouldn't reach for it.

He could have thrown it away, Genna pointed out. *Or destroyed it.*

He wasn't nice when he returned it, Thalia said. She wanted to condemn and defend Rede at the same time.

Are you all right? Genna asked.

"Yes!" Thalia said. "Why is everyone always asking me that? You'd think manifesting was dangerous or something."

It can be, Genna said, *but that's not what I'm talking about.*

"What else is there to talk about?" Thalia said. "Some chrim jerk didn't want a song sphere made by an 'Aponomi skyta'—"

Thalia!

"That's what he said when he returned it, Mom," Thalia said. She wanted to cry. Or break something.

Genna moved closer. Thalia stiffened and prepared for a lecture, not that she had any intention of listening. She needed to get out of the house.

What? she said. *Stop staring at me!*

Oh, Genna said sadly, taking a strand of Thalia's hair between her fingers.

"Zino promised he wouldn't tell you," Thalia hissed. She gnawed on the inside of her cheek.

Zino didn't tell me anything. And you don't have to talk about it.

"I don't want to talk about it," Thalia said. Which was a lie. She didn't want to talk about anything else. She couldn't think about anything else. The problem was, the only one she wanted to talk to was Rede.

It's not fair, she said.

Genna nodded. She let go of Thalia's hair and walked back to the sphere.

What are you thinking? Thalia asked. *You're locking your thoughts.*

Genna turned around and smiled sadly. She didn't say anything about Thalia demanding privacy for herself and then asking others to unlock their thoughts. She said, *Just that now I know why I couldn't truly access him.*

You're wrong about that, Thalia snapped. She looked down at the couch and realized that not once during this painful conversation had her legs felt weak or any part of her seemed to disappear. *We hadn't met when you made the sphere. He wasn't trying to hide anything from you. He really is a just a spoiled chrim jerk.*

Genna moved to pick up the sphere then decided against it. *Rede—*

You know his name? Thalia interrupted.

Yes, Genna said. *It means 'Translator of Dreams.' Did you know that?*

Thalia didn't, but it kind of made everything worse.

Rede's parents told him he was Loveless, Genna said. *His mother asked me to make the song sphere for his Xere Kiryx.*

How could they make him believe it if it wasn't true? Thalia asked. *I thought there was a physical marker or something.*

Small openings line the skin of a newborn Loveless in the places where the physical connection to the Soulmate should have been, Genna agreed, *but the marks close and disappear after the first few weeks of life. You've never seen any marks on Nysa, have you? Rede's parents simply told him he didn't have a Soulmate, and he had no reason to doubt them. Unlike a real Loveless,* she added quietly, *after Rede turned sixteen he would have felt something of you. Because of his parents' deception, I suspect that awareness has felt more like the death of a Soulmate.*

* * *

"Where are you taking me?" Emma asked. She didn't move.

Hyad didn't answer. He waited, calmly looking at her until she decided to follow him without a fight, and then he turned without a word and left the room.

The walk to wherever they were going was labyrinthine. Emma tried to memorize the sequence of where and when they turned or went up stairs or down, but the trip went on too long and sometimes seemed to repeat itself. Everything looked the same, like running down a hallway in an old cartoon.

"Are you trying to confuse me?" Emma asked.

Hyad turned. "We're not taking any chances this time."

Despite her intention to think of nothing, Joe's face popped into Emma's head. She shut the image out and clamped down on any fear she had for him.

Hyad stopped. "It was you we wanted," he said. "Joe will be safe wherever he is." He glanced over Emma's shoulder at the door they'd just passed through. "Unless he tries to find you."

"You know he will," Emma said.

Hyad nodded. "I'm sorry."

"Why do you want whatever Isohel took, anyway?" Emma asked.

"She took the last of Eury Vatic's extrication lights," he said.

"So what?" Emma said. "What could they tell you? You won't be able to use them to discover the secret to the way Whole Listening works."

"We won't be able to discover it easily or quickly," Hyad said, "but the answer will be there."

"It could take years to uncover," Emma said.

"Decades," Hyad agreed. "Aythentia Crossworlders have been lining up to volunteer to help."

Emma stared at him. "If it could take so long, why were you in such a hurry? The capture of the train could have been planned better if you'd taken more time." Hyad gasped, but she didn't care. "Everyone on that train was someone's Soulmate!"

"The longer the Eleytheria had the lights, the less likely it became that we could acquire them," Hyad said. "The party who possesses the possibility of understanding the way Whole Listening works is in the best position to hold on to power longer."

Emma opened her mouth to interrupt him.

"And is therefore," he continued, "in the best position to rule wisely and effectively. We are not like Otherworlders. We don't want power for power's sake. Because of the Soulmate connection we—all of us, Aythentia and Eleytheria—want to help as many gemynd as we can. Our differences are solely concerned with the best methods to accomplish those goals."

"You've both done terrible things and ignored injustice in the pursuit of power," Emma said. "That sounds just like us in the Otherworld."

"Before the Fourth Revolution, yes," Hyad argued. "Not since."

"What about Gelon Lira?" Emma asked. "He murdered and burned all those Soulskins because he thought he could use their ashes to cure disease!"

"Gelon Lira was right," Hyad said. "Many diseases would have been eliminated. "But," he continued, "the consequences of that research and development were not 'acceptable.' Gelon Lira continued to encaust Soulskins after an enforceable exhortation, and he was caught and punished."

"You're so cold," Emma said. "Anything can be justified to you, can't it?"

"No," he replied. "But everything can be explained."

Hyad turned and starting walking again, while Emma stayed still. "Why won't you tell me where you're taking me?"

"I'm taking you to Isohel's room," he said. "We don't give up easily. Lukas hopes that by examining what you know of Isohel, a missing or forgotten thread might be found."

CHAPTER THIRTY-THREE

The air in the living room felt like it was clogging Thalia's throat.

"I'm going outside," she said to her mother.

All right, Genna said. *I'll keep Maddie busy or she'll sense whatever you're feeling. You'd think she was Eury Vatic's Whole Chronicler, she's so perceptive.*

She's not, though, right? Thalia said, suddenly afraid.

No, Mom said. *Don't worry. The Whole Chronicler is born with an innocuous-seeming mark that opens into a receptor when the Whole Listener dies. Maddie doesn't have any marks. Don't worry. Call me if you need to talk.*

Genna went upstairs. Thalia walked into the backyard and sat on the box where Nysa kept Maddie's outside toys, where Rede had sat. Uncle Solymi had warned her that too much empathy for the fears and desires of other gemynd could overwhelm a young Mask, but too little could make her manipulative and cruel. She'd have to learn to keep her heart open but her head clear, he'd said, especially if she wanted to work for the Ones on Power someday.

An open heart and a clear head, Thalia reminded herself.

What could it have been like for Rede to believe he was Loveless and then to cause a Hate Match with her the moment he recognized Thalia was his Soulmate? It didn't justify what he had called her, or the loathing he felt for Invisibles; "Aponomi skyta" was out of his mouth before the door was even open. He thought of all Invisibles with equal derision, when and if he thought of them at all, and yet…

He'd returned the song sphere rather than destroying or discarding it. And he'd called Zino when he realized Thalia hurt herself and no one knew. He must have sensed her despair over what Hyad told her about the secreting system. Was it hard for him to hear her and not be able to help? He'd practically flown to her window when she mentioned hurting herself when she fell.

Why would Rede's parents tell him he was Loveless? How could that even be lawful? And what would she feel if something bad happened to Rede? Would a part of her be destroyed the way a part of Hyad was destroyed? The way Rede must have felt when he realized he'd destroyed something of her.

A group of winged Gatherers flew over the street, dropping down for a moment before rising back up. Thalia retreated to the shade of the bigger tree and sat on the cold ground, a wave a pity for the fugitive girl sweeping through her. Even though the Resisters were the reason the train was destroyed, the reason Uncle Solymi was dead and the reason Hyad was heartbroken, no one deserved to be treated the way whoever caught that girl was going to treat her.

The swarm of Gatherers suddenly turned and headed toward what she knew was a residential area a few blocks away. An alarm sounded. Thalia heard shouting, and the panic of gemynd who were attempting to run away entered her skin like heat from a fire. A moment later, Thalia couldn't draw in enough air. Her skin, her recent physical changes despite the fact that she hadn't manifested: it all meant…

She wasn't the one in mortal danger.

Rede.

Somehow she jumped to her feet. She didn't know where he lived, but she knew it had taken Genna two trains to get there. She tried to access Rede's thoughts but couldn't hear anything. How had he heard her last night? She'd sealed off her room and…

She concentrated and tried again, but she couldn't access anything of what Rede was feeling or thinking. Or figure out where he was. Did Rede not want to be found? If so, it seemed there was only one way to find him. The only way to get Rede's attention was to put herself in danger.

The alarm continued to wail. Cars and gemynd filled the street, fleeing the neighborhood where Gatherers hunted the fugitive girl. Thalia left the backyard and walked as fast as she could toward the noise.

As soon as she got close, she saw Masevo breaking down doors.

"Girl!" A male gemynd with a kind face and clutching a fat black dog under his arm shouted as he came toward her. "Aponomi girl! Turn around. Gatherers are up ahead." He stopped and gazed right at Thalia. "Rights are suspended, girl! Turn around. Run. Run!"

The little dog yapped excitedly as if in agreement. Thalia kept walking toward the chaos. The gemynd shook his head then briefly soothed the dog and ran in the opposite direction.

Widespread terror poured into Thalia's brain as she entered the neighborhood where Gatherers stormed through houses. She hesitated for an instant then stepped between a gray-skinned Gatherer and a terrified old woman. The Gatherer didn't give Thalia a second glance; she swung a powerful arm and slammed her out of the way.

Knocked to the ground, Thalia couldn't see anything for a moment. Her ears rang, and the street vibrated beneath her skin. Gemynd screamed above on the footpath as they ran away.

Thalia turned her head to see a speeding car headed right for her.

Everything slowed.

* * *

Rede slipped between buildings, making his way through the shadowy darkness to the broken window that was his destination. Looking behind him to make sure he hadn't been followed, he climbed through and into the empty room.

He took a lightstick from his jacket pocket and set it upright on a table in the far corner. The room hadn't changed at all since he'd last been here. Well, it was filthier. But nothing else had changed. None of the furniture was moved. The story chronicle was right where he and Allasso had left it five years ago, rolled up and stuck in a hole in the stone wall near the broken couch. He wouldn't look at that, though. The story chronicle would stay where it was, untouched and unread.

Even in the low light, the loveliness of the table in the middle of the room was unmistakable. Someone had worked hard, long ago, to create the complex design of swirling metal and colored glass. Kneeling at it, Rede pulled his sleeve over his hand and wiped away as much as he could of the thick dust. Once he'd considered taking this table and keeping it in his room at home. After all, this apartment still belonged to his parents, though they hadn't been back since Allasso's death. He'd come here once and thought about taking the table home. He'd cleaned it and carried it to the window, but when a rebellious shaft of sunlight jumped through the broken window and threw itself on the riot of color and twisting veins of black metal, Rede had turned around and returned the table to where it was before, where it had always been. He couldn't bear to look at it every day. Not if the sun was going to shine on it like that.

Three vials of Novo should be enough to practice with. It wouldn't kill him but would make him violently sick and powerfully distracted. If he could handle that degree of sickness and frenzied perception, he'd have the strength to do finally what he'd wanted for such a long time, the thing he'd been carefully planning when he glanced up and realized that the blue Aponomi girl staring at him on the street was his Soulmate. Most gemynd could just let go of their life force if they wanted to end their lives. No matter how many times Rede tried, he couldn't. An excess of Novo was the only way out for him.

After last night, Rede had convinced himself Thalia would recover. Maybe it would be easier for her once he did this. His parents' Hate Match had destroyed his whole family.

Rede opened the first vial and recoiled from the sugar-flower scent of the drug. For some gemynd the smell alone was enough to bring on the sweet, deadening, bliss. Not Rede. He hated the smell of it. Novo smelled like artifice. Like everything ugly in both worlds.

Lowering his head to kiss the image of the blue and green bird half-hidden in the iron vines on the table, Rede threw the contents of the first vial down his throat.

* * *

The tall, gray-skinned Gatherer had knocked her into the street, but Thalia hardly felt it. Everything slowed, almost to the point of actually stopping. Thalia knew a car was speeding toward her. She knew she'd be hard to see, even if the panicked driver wanted to stop or avoid her.

Like she was watching a series of Revealer images at school, Thalia saw Rede kneel at a low table in a dark dirty room. Gray illumination from a lightstick pooled like water over a blue and green bird embedded in the top of that table. Rede leaned away from a vial, kissed the bird, then poured lavender fluid into his mouth.

The noxious liquid landed in Rede's stomach, and fury shot through Thalia. She rolled away from the car, which splattered hot, foul refuse from the street into her eyes and mouth. At the same time, she screamed, "No!"

No, she roared in her head, violently enough, she hoped, for Rede to hear.

CHAPTER THIRTY-FOUR

Rede vomited a few seconds after the drug dropped into his stomach. He stood up then fell. Someone, a Gatherer, had knocked Thalia into the street. She was terrified. A car was headed toward her. She was terrified.

He stood up again but he couldn't catch his balance. His head was swimming.

No! Thalia's voice burst into his head like an army. She was shouting at the car? He stumbled toward the window, fell again, and almost hit his head on the corner of a shelf.

No! Thalia screamed again.

Where was she? He couldn't see where she was. The drug was clouding his ability to see anything.

Rede, Thalia said. *Rede, don't. Don't take any more. Where are you? I'm coming. Don't take any more. Wait for me. Where are you?*

A rush of dizziness and nausea overwhelmed him. He clung to the window frame and sucked in mouthfuls of dirty air. That was all he could manage.

Please answer me, Thalia begged.

Where are you? he asked.

Misos, Thalia said. *I thought you'd taken more. I thought...*

Where are you? he asked again. He couldn't focus on anything. His brain felt like it was being swung around from the end of a rope, and his stomach felt worse.

I asked you first, she said.

Are you joking?

Why would I be joking? Anger illuminated Thalia's voice. *I'm not the one who just took enough Novo to incapacitate three men. Tell me where you are and then stay there. I'm coming.*

* * *

Thalia thought the twenty-minute train ride might actually kill her. Still, she'd scared off a Synithi, who'd thought he could intimidate her out of her seat, just by glaring at him. He'd hissed, "Aponomi skyta," but retreated to the next car. *Good.* She was in no mood to pacify an asshole.

Rede was on the ground floor of an abandoned building in a lost neighborhood between the Kena and the newly chrim downtown area where the stores with the costliest merchandise catered to deluded gemynd who'd convinced themselves that their ability to purchase beautifully-made, useless things validated their superior sense of themselves. Or that's what Uncle Solymi said when he teased Hyad for purchasing all his honey-colored clothing there. The train station was a few blocks away. Thalia was afraid she'd be exhausted by the walk but she wasn't. The closer she got to the building, the stronger and more powerful she felt.

Rede had come outside. Slumped against one of the building facades at the mouth of an alley, he pulled himself to a swaying, standing position when he saw her. His complexion was gray, and his flashing eyes were much too bright. She didn't know what to do now that they were face to face.

"What were you thinking?" she asked.

"Did you run straight into that neighborhood where they were hunting the fugitive girl on *purpose?"* he asked, ignoring her question. "I've been going over it, and I can't think of why you would. Of course you got smacked around by a freaking Gatherer. You're lucky it wasn't worse! Why did you go?"

How did you know about that? Thalia asked, surprised.

You're not the only one with heightened perceptive abilities, Lady Teknasma, Rede said, bowing extravagantly then groaning from the effort.

I'm the only one capable of standing for very long, Lord Handsome, she retorted, catching him before he fell. *Hey! I'm a little bit stronger than I was a few days ago. I caught you.*

Rede grinned, and Thalia sucked air through her teeth, horrified. She made a face.

I called you Lord Handsome, didn't I?

You did, he agreed, smiling and swaying.

She held him still, making him grin more broadly.

I didn't mean it, she said, trying not to notice the warmth of his waist in her hands. Was her manifestation beginning now? Or did she feel things more intensely because of Rede?

Oh, too late, Lady Teknasma, Rede said, his pretty green eyes sparkling in the filthy, dark alley. *You said it. I heard it. You can't take it back. What's said cannot be unsaid.*

Thalia felt her face fall, and Rede made a noise like he'd been stabbed in the heart.

I didn't know you were there! he cried, pulling out of her grasp. *I hadn't seen you at all. I felt something but I pushed it away.*

I thought I was Loveless, he continued. *Your mother must have told you. My parents told me I was Loveless. I've even spent time with a Fallwell so at least I could talk about connecting when my friends inevitably did. My father told me that everything I ever believed about having a Soulmate was a fantasy; that all young Loveless dreamed of Soulmates and all of them are devastated when they find out the truth. He said he was only trying to help me. I didn't know. I didn't know. I'd give almost anything to take back what I said.*

He looked down at where he'd clutched Thalia's arms again, let go and held on to a building.

It doesn't really matter whether you said it or not, does it? Thalia said. *You* meant *it. Didn't you? And if I wasn't your Soulmate, you wouldn't have thought about having said it.*

That's one of the reasons I took the Novo, Rede acknowledged. *I did mean it. And you're right. I wouldn't have thought about it again, except maybe to make fun of you with my friends.*

Thalia gasped and stepped back. It was one thing to know how some Synithi really felt about Aponomi, but she'd never heard it stated so quietly and matter-of-factly. To her face. Rede felt something for her, something good, she knew he did, but how would she ever learn to accept that fact that he would have hated her if they hadn't been Soulmates? It made it seem like their connection would always feel fake or like a trick.

For a long moment Rede stood there gazing at her as if he'd never seen anything before, not his own face, not sunlight, not darkness. He caressed her cheek once then moved away, saying, *My parents have a Hate Match. They can't stand each other, and they can't be away from each other. It's horrible. It's worse than a dead Soulmate.*

It isn't worse, Thalia snapped.

Do you know any gemynd who have an Atiryx Syndesi?

No, she admitted. *But—*

Then you don't know, do you? Everyone knows someone devastated by the death of a Soulmate. Family and friends take care of those gemynd. They're never alone in their sorrow. Everyone abandons anyone unlucky enough to have a Hate Match. No one comes near you. They're afraid it's catching. You *already didn't want me to contact you ever again.* Rede folded his arms over his stomach. *And I needed something to give me the courage to do what I've wanted to do for a long time. You'll be happier without me.*

Fury spiked Thalia's blood again. *My happiness or unhappiness shouldn't have anything to do with it.*

"Your happiness has everything to do with it."

Why? she asked. *Isn't there enough in your own life—with or without me—that makes you happy? Isn't there something you want to do, something you want to accomplish? There are so many things I want to do that don't have anything to do with you. What do you want for yourself? What do you want to do with your life? Love is the sacred thing, but it's not the only thing.*

Rede stepped back. He was so surprised by the way she'd yelled at him and what she said that he forgot to hide his thoughts, that he'd stopped thinking about his life and the future and anything he wanted for himself five years ago when something happened that he kept so hidden Thalia still couldn't see it.

CHAPTER THIRTY-FIVE

Somehow Rede had let Thalia convince him to come to her house until he felt better. He told himself that it couldn't be worse than going home, but that wasn't the real reason. The real reason was that he wanted to spend as much time as he could with her until she didn't want to see him anymore.

He thought he couldn't feel any sicker than he had on the long train ride, even when he almost got in a fight with someone making nasty comments at her. Now, as Rede looked up at Thalia's enormous father standing in the doorway of their small house, he realized he was wrong. The prospect of facing this angry gemynd who loved his daughter made him feel worse.

Lecture me later, Zino, Thalia said, taking Rede's hand. *Right now he just needs your help.*

Rede pulled his hand from Thalia and stood in front of her. If he spoke to his father like that, he'd get smacked for insolence. He wasn't sure what Mr. Salic was about, but he wasn't about to let anyone hit Thalia.

His thundering heart made him feel more and more like he was going to throw up. He held himself still as Thalia's father walked down the front steps, and he said, "It's my fault she left the house without telling anyone."

Thalia is responsible for her own actions, Mr. Salic said. He held out his hand then and introduced himself formally. *Zeph Salic.*

Rede looked at Mr. Salic's hand for a second before he shook it. *Rede Onerio.*

Mr. Salic nodded then took one of Rede's arms. Thalia took the other, and together they helped him up the stairs and into the house. His head spinning, Rede sat at the kitchen table.

Can you help him? Thalia asked.

I don't know, Mr. Salic said, lifting Rede's chin and looking into his eyes. *What happened?*

Thalia glanced at him, and Rede felt strange. He told his parents almost nothing. He would never tell them he'd taken Novo, not even if he'd taken just a tiny bit for pleasure.

Mr. Salic leaned away from him. *Were you trying to harm yourself?*

Rede sat up straighter, ready to pull on his second self. Reveal nothing. Be no one. But after Mr. Salic's question Thalia made a mournful sound, and Rede turned to her, wanting to apologize again but not ready to say anything.

Let me feel your pulse, Mr. Salic said. He pressed a finger onto Rede's wrist, but Rede just stared into Thalia's worried gaze.

Mr. Salic let go of his arm. *Did you ingest anything other than the Novo? I can smell that much on your breath. And your parents would be able to smell it, too, whether you told them about it or not.*

I only took Novo, Rede said.

Mr. Salic stood up and squeezed his shoulder. Rede flinched, and Mr. Salic exhaled. *Your pulse is almost normal,* he pointed out, squeezing Rede's shoulder again, more gently this time. *Have your sensory perceptions stabilized? Are your thoughts clear again?*

Rede nodded. "Yes."

Novo never quieted his thoughts. No matter how much he took, his thoughts were always loud and clear and constant.

You'll feel less sick as the drug moves through your system, Mr. Salic said. *I'm afraid I can't do anything to speed up that process.*

Thalia spoke. *So, he'll be all right?*

Yes, chichi, he'll be all right, Mr. Salic said. *Perhaps you could do me a favor, Rede?*

Fear rose up again, but not as powerful as before. *What?*

Mr. Salic smiled at Thalia. Her gorgeous deep blue skin darkened then almost disappeared and then darkened and disappeared again. Was she blushing, actually seeming to disappear at the exact moment she didn't want to be noticed? Misos, Rede thought, what could it be like to have your vulnerabilities constantly screaming for attention in a world that treated you like shit?

Teach my daughter a lesson and let your parents know you're here and you're all right, Mr. Salic said. The man was grinning, but he also seemed serious.

I'll tell them, Rede agreed. *I'll contact them right now if you want.*

Mr. Salic relaxed and turned to Thalia. *You see?* he said. *It's not so difficult.* Then he mussed her hair and left the room.

"Your dad is nice," Rede said after he'd telepathically contacted his parents to let them know he was fine and visiting a friend. Not that they cared. He'd known they wouldn't care, but it seemed important to Mr. Salic to let them know, so he did.

Thalia laughed and stood up. Her soft-looking, translucent blue hair fell from her shoulders and down her back. Sunlight from the window washed through it, and he thought of the bright green wings of the bird on the glass table.

"What?" he asked. "Why are you laughing?"

"You said my dad is nice like he eats rocks and likes it. Don't you know any nice gemynd?" She turned around and leaned over to look out the window above the sink.

Rede swallowed a sigh and wished he could hold his heart in his hands so it wouldn't feel like it was breaking all the time. "No," he said.

Thalia spun around, but before she could say anything, a high-pitched thought-squeal broke into Rede's head.

"What was that?" he asked.

"My little sister Maddie," Thalia answered. "She's outside with my parents. My dad hung a harness from a rope so she can pretend she can fly. Come here."

Thalia turned to the window, taking Rede's arm and pulling him over. He looked at her sun-touched fingers tucked around his arm. The bones in her hand visible through her twilight-sky skin made him think of unworldly jewelry or intricately-wrought gloves that protected from the inside.

"See?" Thalia said. "She's even got fake wings." They both jumped as an exceptionally loud squeal burst into their heads; then Thalia said, "She can't speak out loud at all yet."

"How old is she?" Rede asked.

"Almost three," Thalia said. "We develop differently than Synithi. Our skills and senses come more slowly."

She shifted her weight and brushed her hair back over her shoulder again, and all Rede wanted to do was kiss her. If someone had told him less than a week ago that he'd want to kiss an Invisible, even the realization that he had a Soulmate, that he wasn't Loveless, wouldn't have been enough to stop him from wanting to retch. But now… He was in awe of her. He'd never met anyone so aware of the world and yet so happy inside herself. This didn't feel like simply the reputed biological imperative of the Soulmate connection. Rede didn't need Thalia like he needed food, or water, or air. He needed her like music, like poetry. Like beauty that required no explanation.

* * *

Laughing, Maddie ran into the kitchen—and smashed her face against the door frame. She sat down and hysterically, silently sobbed.

Surprising Thalia, Rede picked her up. *Are you okay?*

Maddie was surprised, too. So surprised that she stopped crying.

Did you hurt this? Rede asked, tapping her tiny nose. *Is it still there?*

Maddie brought her hands to her face and gazed curiously at him. *Yes?*

Rede smiled. *Yes,* he agreed.

Misos, he is hotter than the Uske awakened, Thalia thought, remembering that awesome scene in the story chronicle when Alder wound his arm around Elyson's waist, took her expectant face in his hands, tilted her head back until her hair covered his fingers, and kissed her.

Kissed her.

Rede grinned. Thalia blushed from the soles of her feet. When had she started sucking so hard at locking her thoughts?

You look funny, Maddie said to her.

Thalia didn't say anything.

Rede put Maddie down. Mom and Dad came into the room. They each took one of Maddie's hands.

Let's go, little peach, Zino said, smiling at Thalia and then at Rede before walking out with the others.

Rede stepped forward. *Do you think your parents would let me take you somewhere as long as we were back by before dark?*

You're not that hot, Thalia said.

Really? he asked. *I thought I was hotter than the Uske awakened.* He grinned again and waggled his thick, dark silver eyebrows at her.

Thalia shoved him, but Rede took her hands in his. He wanted to kiss her. She knew he did. But he wouldn't. He was still willing to stay away from her if that's what she wanted. Forever. If she wanted.

She didn't want him to stay away forever.

Thalia held Rede's waist and pulled him close, his warm body soft as a whisper against hers. She took his face in her hands and kissed him. This kiss didn't feel like a subtle heat against her mouth, or a bright taste like raspberries slowly registering in her brain, either. Thalia kissed Rede and a vibrant wild radiance washed through her, making every part of her body feel more alive than it ever had. And maybe because she was a Teknasma, or maybe because she was an Invisible, or maybe both, Thalia also felt what Rede felt when she kissed him.

She pulled away, laughing.

What? he asked, his hands in her hair.

I didn't expect that, she said, smiling.

You didn't expect what? He slid his hands to her waist and held on.

I didn't expect it to feel so…

What? he asked.

"Amazing," she said, kissing him again.

Out of breath, Rede pulled away and gazed down at her. "*You* didn't expect it," he said. "I thought no one would ever feel anything for me."

Thalia thought of Rede taking the blame for her leaving the house without permission and saying he didn't know any nice gemynd. *Rede.* He didn't know it, but she'd heard his mother's uninterested response when he'd told her he was okay. What a different life he led than the one she'd originally imagined.

"I feel something for you," she whispered.

"Yeah," Rede replied, picking up her hand and letting it go again. "But you kinda have to. Biological imperative and all. Not that I'm not grateful. I didn't know an Atiryx Syndesi could be undone."

"I think it can only be undone if the Soulmate who wanted it chooses to undo it," Thalia said. "But I don't really know. It probably doesn't happen very often."

"Yeah," Rede said bitterly. "I've never heard of it happening."

"You're wrong about why I undid it," Thalia said, turning his face to hers. "There was no biological imperative. The Hate Match freed me from that. I *chose* to want you. I chose to undo the Atiryx Syndesi. I chose to come to you. Because I wanted to."

"You thought I was hurt," he pointed out, running his fingers through her hair but not stepping any closer. "I know what that feels like—to know your Eynosyndeo is in pain or in danger. It's horrible. It's worse than being in pain yourself."

"You're right," she agreed. "But I didn't undo the Atiryx Syndesi because I felt sorry for you. I chose you because I want to know you. Because you came to return the song sphere instead of destroying it or throwing it away. Because you picked up Maddie when she was crying and made her laugh. Because you were willing to stay away from me because that's what I wanted, no matter how hard it would have been for you. I chose you, Rede, because something inside you calls out to me, and I want to hear it every day for the rest of my life."

Rede gazed at her but said nothing.

"I feel something for you, Rede Onerio, Translator of Dreams," Thalia repeated. "And this is what I see when I look at you."

She smiled and then Masked herself into him, tall and lean, his beautiful face almost feminine with its wide green eyes and soft red mouth, except for his angular jaw, dusted with stubble a shade darker than his silver hair. She did not forget the words of the Idrysi song luminous on his strong arms.

> *Silence swallows me*
> *Every breathing thing retreats*
> *Eynosyndeo, Eynosyndeo!*
> *I hear none but you*
> *Kiryx Eynosyndeo*
> *I am you.*

CHAPTER THIRTY-SIX

What are you going to do?" Emma asked, keeping her thoughts and emotions quiet. "You're not going to use extrication lights on me, are you?"

"No," Hyad said. "Not yet, anyway. There aren't any more. We're going to use something similar to the connector scar your gifted cousin made, along with a replica of the way we think you connected with Eury Vatic."

"There's nothing valuable left of what I saw in his consciousness," Emma said. "You know that."

"Yes," Hyad admitted. "We saw that immediately, or it would have been you under the extrication lights and not Isohel. It's your extraordinary power of connection that we want to exploit."

"I know what the secreting system is really is," Emma said.

Hyad paused, and a flicker of fear traveled over his face. "I know. That you so easily accessed me was the reason Lukas wanted you."

"Why?" Emma asked. "Are you so hard to access?"

Hyad exhaled and looked away. "Nearly impossible. Only Lukas can do it without my cooperation. Even Solymi couldn't penetrate my thoughts if I didn't want him to."

"Are the Singers of the Apocalypse the only ones who can access anyone's thoughts?" Emma asked. "Other than a Whole Listener?"

"The Singers of the Apocalypse aren't real," Hyad scoffed.

Emma bit back shock. Educated gemynd still believed that? How had Fen Elos turned a real danger into an unreal story?

"They're a myth," Hyad continued, talking over her thoughts. "Only a few weak-minded gemynd cling to the belief that the Singers—the *Phylotelas*—are real."

"They *are* real," Emma said. "They wanted Eury Vatic to join with them so they could bring about the end of everything."

"The Phylotelas are a myth," Hyad repeated calmly. "They were created by weak and fearful gemynd who couldn't bear taking responsibility for their own actions any longer. Eleytheria leader Fen Elos spent the last years of his very long life fighting to educate gemynd on the dangerous lie of the Singers of the Apocalypse. It was one thing we Aythentia always admired about him. We believe in the necessity of authority and rule by reason, not because of baseless fear. Perhaps that's why you believe in the Singers of the Apocalypse. Because Otherworlders so frequently gain power by, and rule by, fear."

Emma exhaled. "Fine," she said. Let's go."

Hyad led her down the hall. She followed.

"How do you block access so well?"

Without turning Hyad answered, "I'm an Energy Harnesser, a *Chamura*."

"What's that?" Emma asked, hurrying to keep up.

"A special kind of Seer," Hyad said. "Seers detect energy. A Chamura can harness, shape, and direct energy almost any way he or she wants. Because thoughts and emotions are accessed through energy, I can send the energy attempting to access me right back before it even comes near."

"My dad is a Seer," Emma said.

"I know," Hyad replied in a strained voice. "Thalia's father is a Seer as well."

Emma walked beside him and thought about her parents, wondering where they were. She thought about Joe and prayed he was okay. She thought about Isohel and wondered what she'd be like when and if she recovered.

"Nearly there," Hyad said, but Emma had already stopped.

The Singers would have known where Isohel was and what she did with the lights, she realized suddenly. *They don't care. They don't want the lights.* Then, very carefully, looking at Hyad, Emma distilled her concentration to a single idea. "The Singers of the Apocalypse are not a myth and I can prove it."

"They are a myth," Hyad said, calm as ever.

Emma clenched her teeth and prayed her instincts about him were accurate. "The Singers wanted the key to Eury Vatic's power as much as the Eleytheria and the Aythentia."

Hyad didn't say anything.

Emma's stomach tightened. Maybe her plan to save herself and Joe by proving the existence of the Singers was too dangerous. Hyad had said acceptable consequences were thought about and considered. He didn't say they were avoided at all cost. But maybe if she helped the Ones in Power by showing them the *most* dangerous enemy, they would let her and Joe and her parents all go free. She couldn't think of another way out. For any of them.

"There *is* no way out," Hyad said, so gently she was distracted by the genuine regret in his voice. He exhaled. "My only hope for you is that Lukas can be persuaded to detain rather than secret you." He shuddered, as if he had participated in the secreting of other gemynd and it scarred him.

Emma didn't care. She said again, "The Singers of the Apocalypse are not looking for the extrication lights Isohel took. They were hovering around Eury Vatic the whole time the Resisters were slowly killing him. They probably saw Isohel take the lights. And they probably know what she did with them, too."

"I know you believe that what you're saying is true," Hyad remarked, his serene face sympathetic.

"It *is* true," Emma said. Part of her brain screamed at her to stop, but another part insisted this was the only way, that she was right about Hyad and what he would choose.

"You don't know me, Emma," he said carefully. "You accessed the surface of my consciousness, what I was thinking at that moment. You don't know me. You have no idea what I would choose in any given situation."

"Bind me somehow," Emma said. "You're part of the detainee system, so do something so that I can't possibly get away and let me prove to you that the Singers are real. You have nothing to lose if I'm wrong and everything to gain if I'm right."

CHAPTER THIRTY-SEVEN

Thalia sat on the couch in the living room in the quiet fulcrum of the night, cradling the song sphere her mother had made for Rede in lap. She could think more clearly when everyone was sleeping.

Are you awake?

Rede's melodic voice was both unexpected and familiar as it melted into her thoughts. Thalia sat up straighter, even though he was far across the city and not in the room with her. *Yes. I'm awake.*

Good, he said.

Why are you *awake?*

I couldn't sleep, he said. *What about you?*

Thalia's chest contracted. She held the sphere tighter.

What is it? Rede asked. *Did something happen? Did Gatherers come to your house after I went home?*

No, she said. *Nothing like that.*

Have you changed your mind about choosing to be with me? he asked quietly.

No, she said.

Will you tell me if you do?

Yes, she said, passing the sphere back and forth between her hands. *But I'm not going to change my mind. Unless you do something really vile again. Then no promises,* she added in a light-hearted teasing voice.

Rede was utterly silent.

I'm sorry, she said. *I was kidding.*

He was still quiet, like he'd cut himself off from everything again.

I wouldn't joke about it if I was really thinking of changing my mind, Thalia said. *I would tell you. I promise. But you have to promise that you'll tell me if you're going to hide inside yourself again. I understand if you need to be alone in your own head sometimes, believe me I do. My parents are always hovering around my thoughts. You'd think I spend half of every day falling into vats filled with dilitirio venom.*

That's not funny, Rede said.

How do you think I felt when I realized you were going to take enough Novo to—?

It wouldn't have killed me, Rede said. *I measured it out so it would only be enough to* almost *kill me. I wanted to practice.*

Practice? she said.

I'm sorry, he said. *I thought you'd be happier without me. And I—*

I wouldn't have been, she interrupted. *Even when I hated you I wouldn't have ever wanted you dead.*

Why not?

What do you mean, why not?

I felt what you felt when you realized what I'd called you, Thalia. I felt what you felt before I said it, when you recognized me as your Soulmate. I can't believe you would have cared what happened to me after that. The Soulmate connection is sacred, and I nearly destroyed ours.

My friends' parents have been secreted, she said, almost telling Rede the truth of the Synektos weapon. But she wouldn't. He didn't need to know something so awful, even if it affected everything she'd ever again think.

What? he said. *I thought secreting was an anti-Aythentia myth perpetrated by Eleytheria.*

Thalia laughed.

Why is that funny? Rede asked, sounding pissed off.

You're an Aythentia, too, she said. *An Aponomi-hater* and *an Aythentia.*

Of course, Rede said, half to himself. *You would have to be Eleytheria.*

What does that mean? Thalia asked, irritated herself now.

Aren't all Aponomi Eleytheria?

No, she said. *Just like Synithi, we think for ourselves.*

They both sighed in exasperation at the same time.

This doesn't make you feel any different about me? Thalia asked, already certain of his answer.

No, he said. *I still feel broken and incomplete without you. I still want to spend every waking minute of my life with you. I still want to kiss you more than I want to eat or breathe.*

Me, too, Thalia said, staring at her skin and watching as the blue deepened. She drew in a slow breath and thought she could taste Rede in the air.

What? he asked, so sweetly she could have cried. *Why are you upset? Is it your friend's parents? What did they do? It must have been pretty bad if your friend thinks they've been secreted. Even if secreting's not a myth—and just so you know, I think it is—her parents must simply be detained somewhere.*

It's not a myth, Thalia said. *My uncle was part of a special team of Eleytheria and Aythentia who are investigating it.*

And he told you? Rede asked, appalled. *Didn't he realize the danger that would put you in? If it is true, that's just the kind of thing the filters are set up to catch. Especially now that everyone is so crazy over this fugitive girl.*

He didn't tell me, Thalia said. *He's dead. He died when the Ones in Power destroyed that train.*

That was an accident, Rede said.

Thalia swallowed hard. *He's dead,* she repeated, *and his Soulmate told me about the secreting system.*

I'm sorry, Rede said. *But what can you do about any of it? You're fourteen and—* He cut himself off before he said *and you're Aponomi,* but Thalia heard him anyway. He exhaled and continued. *You can't bring your uncle back, and you can't help your friend's parents. Try to forget about it.*

From her room, Maddie began to cry. Her dreams must have shifted into a nightmare, and from the sound of her whimpers she was being chased by a Gatherer with an animal's face. Zino got up to check on her.

Just a minute, Thalia said. She laid Rede's song sphere down and then crawled under a table to lie against the family's inaccessible spot.

Is everything all right? Rede asked.

You worry a lot, Thalia said. *Yes. Everything's fine.*

I guess..., he began.

Thalia waited.

I guess now that I've found you I'm terrified something will happen to you, he said. *I'd accepted the idea that I was Loveless, and now…now that I know I'm not, now that I know what that means, what it feels like to be connected to someone, I don't ever want to lose it. I never want to lose* you, *Thalia. I don't care how weak that sounds. I feel like we're woven together, like I can't breathe or think without you.*

I know, she said simply. *I feel the same way.* She felt him smile, and she lost herself remembering again their kiss that afternoon. Like she was swallowing fire.

Yes, he whispered. *It's all I've thought about all day. It's why I was so willing to wake you up, just to see if you were thinking about it, too.*

Thalia smiled in the darkness. She said nothing.

I'd kiss you now if I could, he said.

Me, too, she said.

She felt him close his eyes, and without moving or leaving the room she melted into Rede's dream of kissing her. This was why love was sacred, she thought to herself when he pulled away, happy in the darkness of his bedroom; why it was protected above everything else. Because it was better than anything else.

What would it be like to be without him? How did anyone bear it? She thought of Uncle Solymi and Hyad. Then she remembered what Hyad had shown her and she decided to tell Rede. Maybe it was important that someone else know.

There is no secreting system, she said.

What do you mean? Rede sounded confused. *You just said there was. You said your friend's parents were secreted.*

There is no place, Thalia said. *No detainee building or tunnel or tower. Gemynd are secreted, but not to a single place, and not together.*

What, then? Rede asked.

Thalia took a long breath. This, Rede, everything, was going all right. Gatherers had searched this and the surrounding neighborhoods and likely wouldn't come around again. And with her manifestation ceremony cancelled everything might just stay okay. She should just let it go. The fugitive Resister girl would be caught soon and this all would be over. Hyad had said that Emma might know already about the secreting system, and the girl would have to find and help her parents on her own. Thalia didn't owe her anything. She hardly knew Emma.

Please, Rede said. *I feel how upset you are. Please, please tell me. It's more painful for me to know that you're sad and I can't reach you than to feel anything for myself.*

Well, that's it, Thalia said quietly, trying to keep her emotions under control. *That's what it is. The secreting system, Synektos, is a weapon. It strips gemynd of their perceivable identities, their ability to say what they want and to communicate anything about who they are.* She exhaled and considered not telling him the worst part.

Trust me, Thalia, Rede said. *Please. Whatever it is I don't want you to have to know about it alone. I know what that's like.*

Okay, she said, grateful. *The Synektos weapon permanently separates Soulmates from each other. They can't recognize one another ever again. Then they're dumped in Otherworld cities, permanently Masked to look like Worthless or homeless humans who've lost the capacity to function in their world, completely incapable of saying anything they mean to say unless it has to do with basic needs like food or shelter. Secreted gemynd are entirely dependent on the compassion of Otherworlders, are separated from their Soulmates with no way to find them.*

Rede was silent.

They never ever forget who they are on the inside, though, Thalia said. *Even if their faces and bodies look different, fixed in some perversion of a Mask, they always know who they are and what they want and what they need. They are trapped forever inside themselves.*

Has it ever been used on anyone? Rede asked.

Yes, Thalia said. *But I don't know why. What kind of crime is terrible enough to warrant this kind of punishment? And if the weapon is such a big secret, how is it any kind of deterrent? The faces of the secreted gemynd Hyad showed me didn't look like monstrous criminals who'd done unforgivable things. They looked ordinary—and so, so scared. One of them looked like Isia Sorgyre, the Chronicler who wrote* The Uske. *But maybe I just imagined that she looked like her. Because* The Uske *is about a virus that almost destroys the Commonworld after the Ones in Power use Synektos too many times.*

I thought it was about kissing, Rede said sweetly, trying to lighten the mood. *I've only ever heard you talk about the amazing kissing parts.*

Well, the kissing parts are amazing, Thalia agreed, reaching out to dream-kiss Rede across the city again. *Maybe that's the point. That sacred things like love and life and the connections we have with one another are worth protecting.*

And kissing, too, Rede said, reaching across the city to dream-kiss her back.

Yeah, she said. *Definitely kissing, too.*

CHAPTER THIRTY-EIGHT

"Why are you doing this?" Hyad asked Emma. "Why are you trying to make me believe in something that doesn't exist? You're already in danger, Emma. Pushing me to waste time will make asking for lenience more difficult, for you and for Joe if he tries to rescue you."

"Because the Singers of the Apocalypse do exist," she said. "And if *they* find the key to Whole Listening before the Ones in Power or the Resisters, nothing else will matter ever again."

Hyad glanced at a door Emma hadn't seen a minute before.

"Is that Isohel's room?" she asked.

Hyad nodded.

"Is she okay?"

"It's too soon to tell," he answered, distractingly sympathetic again. "She's alive."

"What about her father?" Emma said. "Does he know where she is? Have you brought him here?"

"No."

"You should," Emma said. "He'll be going crazy."

Hyad said nothing.

"Do you really think he loves her less than he loved his Soulmate?" Emma asked. "Do you really believe that the Soulmate connection is the only connection that matters?"

"It's the most important connection," Hyad said.

"It's *one* connection," Emma said. "Claudeo Arismapsi needs to see his daughter. Do you think Thalia's mom would be okay if something like this happened to Thalia?"

"Thalia is not Loveless," Hyad said.

"What if she was?" Emma almost shrieked. "Do you really think her parents or her sister would love her any less? Do you think Solymi would stand by if Thalia was in Isohel's place?"

Hyad paled. "All right," he said. "I'll make sure Claudeo Arismapsi is brought in to see his daughter before the Three Leaders decide what to do with her."

"Thank you."

Hyad turned away. Emma knew he was thinking about what she'd asked him to do about the Singers of the Apocalypse, but she couldn't hear him clearly. It sounded like his thoughts were scrambled.

"I wish I knew how to do that," she said, half to herself.

Hyad ignored that and looked searchingly at her. "Very well," he said at last.

Emma heard his thoughts clearly now. He was telling Lukas about her claim to be able to prove the existence of the Singers. She couldn't hear Lukas's response, but it was apparent from Hyad's replies that Lukas was not pleased to be asked to waste more time.

The one-sided conversation reminded Emma of hearing Fen Elos thought-speaking to Odym Chadia when she first met him. That had been the first time she heard the Singers of the Apocalypse, and an echo of what she'd felt that day resonated lightly through her. Hyad glanced strangely at her, but at the same time Lukas reluctantly gave his permission for Hyad to life-link to Emma.

"If you try to break the life-link," Hyad said, "you'll die. Are you certain that this is what you want?"

"What are you going to do?" Emma asked.

"I'm linking to your life force with a finite tie," Hyad said. "You cannot move out of my sight or too far away or the tie will break and your life force will spill out as if an artery was severed. I won't be able to help you."

"What if you choose to let me go?" Emma asked.

Hyad's face darkened. "I will not choose to let you go. Don't be stupid. You set the terms, I am agreeing to them. I will not change them, and you won't be able to."

Emma took a steadying breath, but her heart was in her throat. "What I was asking was, is it possible for you to choose to let me go once the tie is set. Not, is it likely that you would."

"Of course it's possible," Hyad said, angry and out of patience. "The tie isn't permanent. But I will not release you until we are back in this building."

"Okay, then," Emma said, stepping close. "Go ahead."

"Think of Sfodro," Hyad said, begging her to change her mind.

Emma shuddered. "I am thinking of him," she lied. "Please. Set the tie or whatever it's called."

Hyad clenched his jaw and turned away then exhaled and pressed his fingers to the base of her throat. The lightest sensation wound around her neck, as if she'd put on a scarf made of spiderweb, and she thought of the net-like thing Eury Vatic made for Gryphon before Gryphon died. The feeling sank deeply into her skin, and Emma was left cold and a little dizzy.

"The vertigo will pass," Hyad said, his expression still angry. "Your body is reacting to the danger. It's something like standing at the edge of a cliff. Tell me when your heart rate returns to normal and you don't feel dizzy anymore."

Emma nodded. "How close do I need to stay to you?"

"I have to be able to see you. And you can't be more than ten feet away. Please, stay close."

"I will," Emma said.

"Ready?" Hyad asked after a minute.

"Yes," she said.

"Where are we going, then?"

She gave him an address close to Fen Elos's store. She wanted to make sure she wouldn't endanger any Resisters who might be inside. She hoped she'd be able to tell their presence without Hyad accessing her thoughts. She planned to practice scrambling her thoughts while they were walking. She thought she understood something of how he did it.

Hyad swore quietly. "Even if you succeed in blocking my access to your thoughts, you cannot escape me, Emma. You'll die. It will be painful, and Sfodro will be destroyed."

Emma took a deep breath. "I promise I won't try to escape."

"Very well," Hyad said. "Let's go."

He took her arm, but she stopped him, saying, "Wait."

He glared at her.

"In case something happens—"

Hyad opened his mouth to protest.

"Like an accident," Emma explained. Her stomach clenched. "I want to know that Claudeo will get to see Isohel."

"I already asked Lukas to instruct the Gatherers to bring him in."

"Thanks," Emma said. "Let's go."

CHAPTER THIRTY-NINE

To her shock, Thalia's parents allowed her to go out in the city with Rede the next day. The fugitive girl had been caught, they heard, and Maddie hadn't stopped asking about the chrim gemynd with the leafy eyes since he promised her she still had her nose. Thalia and Rede had been talking every night regardless.

"Are academic classes especially easy for you?" she asked as they walked toward a store that sold raspberry ice cream sandwiches.

"No," he said. "Why? And how can you be thinking about ice cream so early in the day?"

"You're a Chronicler," she explained. "I thought academics would be like...a subset of your power. And I wasn't aware there were ice cream times and no-ice cream times. That must be an Aythentia thing. Eleytheria eat ice cream whenever the hell we want."

He grinned and pushed her. When she pushed him back, Rede pulled her close and kissed her.

"That's why we're the Ones in Power," he whispered into her neck. "Although 'Resister' seems like a curious name for gemynd who do nothing but eat ice cream."

Oh, we do other things, she promised. Full of an energy that was entirely new to her, she ran down the street, spun around to smile at Rede and almost lost her balance.

Be careful, he shouted, running as if she'd fall to her death.

Thalia stared at him. "What the hell happened to you that you're so easily scared? I don't think there are many deaths caused by tripping."

Nothing happened to me, he said in a strange voice. They passed a little white-haired girl who gaped at them until Rede flashed a dangerously dazzling smile. The girl paled and ran away.

"And I'm not scared for *me,*" he said.

"You don't have to worry," Thalia promised, but she was suddenly staring at the end of the block. "Not about me. I do okay."

"You fell and were bleeding alone in your room a few days ago," he said, then turned. "What are you looking at?"

That's Emma Mathews. She's...my friend. The one I told you about.

Oh, Rede said. *Are you all right? Who's the guy?*

Thalia sighed. *Hyad Cerus. He was my Uncle Solymi's Soulmate.*

The uncle who died in the train accident?

Thalia nodded, and Rede squeezed her hand. She was about to ask him if he'd mind if they said hello when she noticed Rede gazing hard at them. Hyad and Emma walked slowly closer.

Please don't stare, Thalia whispered. *Emma is a Thoryba Exocho, and Hyad is extremely observant. He's a Chamura. Whatever you're thinking, they'll hear it.*

He's life-linked to her, Rede said.

What? Thalia looked harder at Hyad and Emma. *That can't be right. How do you know? Hyad would never...*

I am right, Rede said. *I've seen one before. That's how I know. If you look carefully you'll see the threads glittering around her throat. It's not permissible to life-link to a kid.*

Rights are still suspended, Thalia said, still unwilling to believe. *Acceptable consequences.*

Rede shuddered.

Emma smiled and waved to Thalia.

Does she see you already? Rede asked. *How?*

Thalia groaned and rolled her eyes. *I already told you we're friends, and she's a Super Telepath. She might have heard us talking. Besides, I'm easier to see since I met you.*

He grinned slightly, and she forgot to be irritated.

They're coming to talk to us now, Rede pointed out. *Are you okay with that?*

Why wouldn't I be?

Because of what you told me last night, he said.

Thalia nodded. *We have to be careful. Don't think about it.*

No. We can't help her, Rede said.

No one can, Thalia agreed sadly. *That's what's so devastating. All of those gemynd are lost.*

If it is true, Rede said, *and the Ones in Power really did come up with such reprehensible system, there's probably* some *useful information somewhere. Aythentia keep information on everything. Nothing is too small, and nothing is insignificant. When my dad was a kid the Aythentia wanted to incorporate the Library of Useless Information into the Registry of Information. The Aythentia were the Resisters then, so that measure failed, but I think some gemynd in the Ones in Power now want to revive the idea.*

Thalia squeezed Rede's hand, appreciating that he was rambling nervously as Emma approached but needing him to stop. The girl smiled sweetly, but she was standing unnaturally close to Hyad, who looked as distraught to Thalia as he had when he'd come to the house to ask for Uncle Solymi's silks.

"Hey, Thalia," Emma said.

Hey, Thalia said, aware this was all absurdly mundane. *This is my friend Rede.*

* * *

"Nice to meet you, Rede," Emma said. She smiled again and glanced at Thalia but noticed Rede did not smile back. Was this the asshole from a few days ago?

The asshole glared at her. Shit. She forgot sometimes that gemynd could hear her thoughts.

"Sorry," she said out loud.

"Emma is helping me with something," Hyad said beside her. When she glanced over, Emma saw that he was staring hard at Rede and Thalia. "Don't," the gemynd said when he heard what the pair were thinking. Emma heard it, too. About the life-link.

"Don't think about that," Hyad commanded. "Don't tell anyone."

"How can you?" Rede asked.

"I said, *don't,*" Hyad repeated, his voice so calm that Emma thought he must be talking about something unimportant, but Rede's face paled and he pulled Thalia closer.

"I'm sorry," Hyad said to Thalia, then, "It couldn't be helped."

Of course it could have, Thalia said. *There is always a way to do things without hurting someone else.*

"It's not his fault," Emma broke in. "I asked him to."

"Please," Hyad said, urgency rising in his soft voice. "Forget about it. Go home."

"I thought the fugitive girl was caught," Rede said. "I thought everything was okay."

"It's not," Hyad said.

"What's on your arms?" Emma asked, trying to break the tension. She couldn't risk drawing the attention of the Gatherers or the filter system. "It's pretty."

Rede blushed and Thalia beamed at him. Their sweet exchange made Emma's heart clench. God, she hoped Joe was okay. Hyad squeezed her shoulder, and Emma suddenly wanted to cry.

"It's Sacerian, right?" she asked in an embarrassingly squeaky voice.

"Yes," Rede said, holding out his arms for her to see. "It's the first book of the Idrysi Song. I'm a Chronicler," he explained.

Before Emma could stop it, Sandy's face, his comic book, and the mark on his back came into her head. Hyad stepped back.

"No," Emma said, instantly realizing what she had done. "I won't let you. I won't let you. I'll pull away and die in front of you. I'll make you watch. I'll make you think of Solymi's death. Don't," she said desperately. "Please, please. *Please.*"

"What is going on?" Rede asked, moving aggressively toward Hyad. "Why is she so upset? What the hell are you doing to her?"

Ignoring Rede, Hyad completely blocked his thoughts. Emma couldn't hear anything in his head, so she started to run. He held her arm.

Rede tried to grab Emma and unlock the tie.

"No!" Hyad roared, throwing him to the ground.

Thalia screamed and knelt beside Rede on the footpath.

"Let me think," Hyad said to Emma. "Let me think."

Emma didn't know what to do. It had all been for nothing. Gryphon's death, Eury Vatic's death, her parents' arrest—everything meant nothing. "Please," she said again, crying now. "Please."

Rede shivered on the sidewalk. It seemed Hyad had done something more than push him away.

I'm okay, Rede said to Emma. *Don't worry about me. Make him undo the tie. Please.*

I'm sorry, Emma replied. *I can't. Not yet. I'm sorry.* She turned to Hyad. "Can you block my thoughts the way you can block yours?"

Hyad didn't answer.

"I want to tell you something, but I don't want anyone else to hear," she said. "And I don't want the filters to catch it."

Hyad shook his head. "This isn't about you or your brother," he said sadly. "My first responsibility is to the safety of the Commonworld. I cannot let this go, and I won't let you break the tie. I'm stronger than you, and I have weapons at my disposal that you don't have." He glanced down at Rede, who still seemed incapable of standing up.

"What about Sandy's Soulmate?" Emma asked, her voice stuck like half-swallowed vomit in her throat. "What will happen to him or her?"

Hyad shook his head. "I'm sorry, but that doesn't matter. I am sorry, so very sorry."

"He's only seven," Emma said. "He's practically a baby. Can't you keep it a secret? Can't you wait until he's older?"

"You know I can't," Hyad said, and Emma saw that he had made up his mind. "You and your family would try to hide him."

You're disgusting, Thalia cried, leaping to her feet. *How can you devote your life to a government that permits the atrocity of permanently separating gemynd from their Soulmates? Uncle Solymi could not have lived with it if he knew you supported that system.*

"Thalia," Hyad begged, "you don't understand. It's complicated. And I don't support the secreting system. I don't. But I can more easily fight it from within the power structure than from outside it."

What is Emma so upset about? Thalia asked. *What is she talking about?*

Hyad shook his head. "I can't," he said. "I'm sorry."

Emma stared blankly at the ground. She stared at Hyad's shoes and the smooth footpath intermittently sparkling with mica. She thought of Joe and how he'd swept up the jelly beans on the sidewalk at home so long ago. She thought of the first time he'd kissed her, how she'd opened her eyes and seen that they were flying through the trees and above the waterfall. "I'm telling you the truth about the Singers," she said softly. "I am."

"I know you think you are," Hyad said—so sweetly. "I'm sorry."

He took a slow breath then leaned over and brushed his fingertips over Rede's chest. Rede sucked in a mouthful of air and stood up.

"I can't forgive you," Thalia said.

"I wouldn't expect you to," Hyad replied.

"I'm telling the truth," Emma repeated. "I'm telling the truth. The Phylotelas are real."

"Even if you are telling the truth," Hyad said, "it doesn't matter. We have what we want."

"No, you don't," Emma said, sick that she hadn't realized the truth earlier. "Not for long anyway. Sandy is what the Singers have been looking for while you've been wasting your time torturing Isohel and slaughtering Resisters. We're almost there. Let me prove to you that the Singers of the Apocalypse are real. Because if you don't nothing will matter anymore. They'll find him and then everything will be over. Be true to the promise you made when we left your evil boss."

Hyad glared at her.

"I didn't make this shitty world," she said, glaring back. "You did. And the blood of both worlds will be eternally on your hands when this is over."

Hyad made a terrible, unholy noise under his breath. "Five minutes," he said hoarsely. "You have five minutes."

Emma grabbed his hand and ran toward Fen Elos's store. She didn't turn around to see if Thalia and Rede were following.

CHAPTER FORTY

"Joe." Mr. Spencer's worried voice buzzed through the static on the laundromat pay phone and into Joe's ear. "Thank Misos. It's been two days. I thought... Where's Emma? And Turner? Are they with you? What are you doing in Newport?"

"Emma and Turner are still in the Commonworld," Joe said. "I don't know where."

"Maude said—," Mr. Spencer began.

"Maude is there?" Joe gasped. "Thank God. What about Aubrey?"

"He's here, too," Mr. Spencer said, somewhat recovered. "Were you successful?"

"No," Joe said. "Turner got us into the building, but Aubrey was wrong. The portal led to an underground detention chamber."

There was silence on the other end of the phone.

"I need you to help me," Joe said. "Emma was right behind me in the portal tree. I got through, but she didn't. Gatherers were chasing us. I don't know what happened. I don't have any money. I need you to help me get back to the Commonworld. I have to get back and find her."

"I can't leave," Mr. Spencer said. "It's too dangerous for the other kids."

"I have to get back," Joe said again. "The Gatherers were right behind us."

"I can't look for an unregistered portal tree," Mr. Spencer said. "Any serious inquiries will be picked up by the filters."

"I can find a portal," came a voice from the background.

"Aubrey?" Joe said.

"No one can search for a portal without the risk of alerting the filters," Mr. Spencer said.

"I don't have any powers, remember?" Aubrey said contemptuously. "I'll look in books. There are libraries here, right? Otherworld books are not part of the filter system."

"Portal places won't be in Otherworld books," Mr. Spencer said.

Joe heard Aubrey curse.

"That's a bad word," Sandy said.

"I know," Aubrey replied. "That's why I said it. Don't *you* hate it when someone thinks *you're* stupid?"

"No one thinks I'm stupid," Sandy said. "Do they, Maude?"

Joe didn't hear Maude answer.

"Let me talk to Aubrey," he told Mr. Spencer, and Mr. Spencer passed the phone over. When he heard Aubrey take it Joe asked, "How can you find portal locations from Otherworld books? And I'm not being condescending. I'm really asking."

Thanks, Joe suddenly heard Maude say. Ever since the day at the temporary Memorium, Joe could hear her thoughts almost as easily as he could hear Emma's. *About Aubrey. He's so sensitive.*

I know, Joe said. *Are you okay?*

"Are you listening to me?" Aubrey snapped.

"Give me a second to talk to Maude," Joe said.

Aubrey growled but didn't protest.

No, Maude said, *I'm not okay. But Emma is. I can hear it in your voice. You would know. You would know if something terrible had happened to her. And I would know, too. She's okay—for now.*

Thanks, Joe said. "Okay, Aubrey."

Aubrey swore again, but even through the phone Joe could feel how much he liked Maude. "You're an Otherworlder," the boy said, "or you might as well be. I can't believe you weren't smart enough to think of this yourself, but whatever. The Otherworld has always been aware of the Commonworld, but we easily mask the truth of our existence in stories of ghosts, vampires, witches, wizards, and that kind of stuff, and you guys eat it up like sweets or candy or whatever. Of course, if an Otherworlder is a little too bright-brained or they've seen too much, a Gatherer will just erase their memory." He laughed without mirth. "Anyway, I'll research legends set in Newport. It's possible—it's *likely*—that the site of some ghost or witch story is the site of a portal tree."

"Good idea!" said Maude.

Aubrey must have blushed, because Maude felt for him.

"We can all help," Maude continued. "I'll go to the library with you, and Mr. Spencer and Elizabeth can search online. You haven't met Elizabeth yet. She's upstairs."

"Another sister?" Aubrey said. "Misos, how many are you?"

"Seven," Sandy said. "Including Mommy and Daddy."

"I'm sorry I was wrong about the secret prison," Aubrey said to Joe.

"You couldn't have known," Joe said. "The chronicle you read must have been wrong. That's not your fault. How could you have known?"

"Misos," Aubrey said again. "Maybe that's how they do it?"

"Do what?" Joe asked.

"The Ones in Power," Aubrey said. "Maybe they've been working on the Synektos weapon all this time and are leaking false information about a secret prison. Otherworlders are not the only idiots in the universe."

"Nobody said we were," Joe said.

Aubrey was silent.

"What?" Joe asked. "Don't be so damn sensitive. I'm not insulting you."

"That's not it," Aubrey said.

"What then?" Joe asked.

"If I'm right, and the Ones in Power have been leaking false information about Synektos for decades, maybe they're using it."

"I can't think about that right now," Joe said. "I'm sorry. I have to find Emma. Put Mr. Spencer back on. Please."

Aubrey handed the phone over.

"What should I do?" Joe said to Mr. Spencer. "Should I wait here until you find something?"

"I don't think you should go back to the Commonworld," Mr. Spencer said. "You'll be caught, and if Emma is safe she'll risk herself to find you. You're both safe now. Be patient."

Joe felt the same sick, hot sensation rise in Maude's chest that he felt in his own. Emma was *not* safe.

"Emma is powerful," Mr. Spencer continued. "If you haven't sensed that she is in terrible danger, you have to trust that she'll find her way back to you."

"You're not serious," Joe said. He turned and saw the homeless teenager he'd met earlier standing in the doorway, strung out, staring, and pissing people off because he wouldn't get out of their way. *"Move,"* Joe mouthed at him before someone knocked him over. Was this fucked-up kid following him?

"I'm completely serious," Mr. Spencer continued. "And…"

"What?" Joe said. "Because I'm about to hang up the phone."

"There's something else to consider," Mr. Spencer said. "Something Emma would risk anything but you to protect. Don't think about it or answer me," he warned. "But I know you know what I mean."

The kid in the doorway made a terrible noise. Someone must have finally pushed him out of the way.

"So I'm helpless then?" Joe said, pushing Mr. Spencer's implication to the back of his head. "That's what you're saying? I should just come home and sit and wait while Emma endures everything on her own? Is that it?"

"Don't be dramatic," Mr. Spencer said. "That's not what I'm saying at all."

"It might as well be," Joe said. "'Cause that's what you're asking me to do."

"Emma is safer with you here," Mr. Spencer repeated. "She's more powerful than you are, Joe. Now that the whole Commonworld is on the alert, she's safer without you."

Joe dropped the phone and leaned against the cold cement wall of the laundromat. The kid was digging through someone's purse. Maybe he was hungry in addition to whatever else was wrong with him.

Making that terrible noise again, and holding something in his hand, the kid staggered over to Joe.

"I'm sorry," Joe said. "I don't have any more money."

"The window," the teenager said wildly, passing the thing rapidly from hand to hand. It was a tube of lipstick. "The window is wrong."

"I'm sorry." Joe shrugged. "I don't know how to fix it."

The kid put the dark red lipstick all over his mouth.

Wasn't there someone who looked after kids in trouble? Joe wondered. God, this one couldn't be more than fourteen.

Mr. Spencer's worried voice came up from the hanging, black receiver: "Who are you talking to?"

The kid slowly turned his head to the phone then picked it up and kissed the mouthpiece, smearing lipstick all over it. "The window," he repeated over and over, turning around and lowering his head to keep the phone away from Joe.

"No one," Joe said to Mr. Spencer after he finally got it back and wiped most of the wet lipstick off with his shirt. "Please," he said to the kid. "I can't help you. I'm sorry."

The kid sat on an orange plastic chair near a loud dryer that was vibrating and clanking with loose change. He dropped his head into his hands and cried horribly, like his fucked-up heart had finally given up and broken into a million pieces.

"Joe," Mr. Spencer said. "Listen, I know it's hard—"

"You don't know anything!" Joe said. "You don't know what it's like to be separated from the only person in the world who means anything to you. To know that she's in danger, and that *you*—the person who's supposed to protect her—are fucking powerless."

Mr. Spencer said nothing, but a moment later Maude's soft voice came through. "Joe, stop. Of course he knows. He's a Crossworlder. He's been alive for hundreds of years, and only sixty of them were spent with his Soulmate. He had to watch her grow old and die while he stayed young."

"I don't care," Joe said. "I'm sorry, but I don't. I can't stay here while Emma is alone in the Commonworld. I can't. And all of you should have known that. Thank Aubrey for the ghost story idea. I'll find a portal tree myself. I'm sorry."

He hung up the phone and left the laundromat.

CHAPTER FORTY-ONE

Emma's voice seemed to die in her throat when a third Masked door opened on a completely empty room in the back of Fen Elos's store. Thalia stared. She had never known there was a back room, and she didn't know what had been inside it or what Emma now hoped would be there.

"What is this?" Hyad asked, turning on Emma. "Answer me!"

Emma sank to the floor. Thalia and Rede knelt beside her.

What is it? Thalia asked. *What happened?*

Emma shook her head.

Rede leapt to his feet and glared at Hyad, but Thalia stood up and took his hand. *Whatever it is, it isn't his fault,* she said. *He didn't do anything to her.*

"He let her bring him here," Rede said. "He life-linked to her. Do you know what happens if someone breaks the tie? It's horrible." Rede glanced away for a second. "It doesn't matter how it happens, whether the break is intentional or not. And once it's broken, no one can do anything to stop it."

Emma isn't going to break the tie, Thalia said. *And Hyad won't either. He's not a monster. He's not klasis.*

"It was klasisa to life-link to a kid," Rede said. "That is a monstrous act. Unfit for an Aythentia to contemplate."

"What!" Thalia said. "What about the temporary Memorium being forbidden to Invisibles? That's an Aythentia idea."

Rede turned away.

Thalia ignored him and concentrated on Emma and Hyad. Their intense silence cooled her anger. She felt ashamed, as if she'd been gossiping at a Memory Day ceremony. *I'm sorry,* she said to Rede. *This political crap doesn't matter. He won't hurt her, I promise.*

Hyad was standing, but his expression was the same as Emma's. Thalia tried to access their thoughts but couldn't.

What? Rede asked, suddenly close by.

How do you sense what I'm feeling so quickly? Thalia asked. *You're a Chronicler, not a Seer or a Teknasma.*

Rede ignored the question, but when Thalia gazed at him he laid his hand on her cheek.

I don't know what's going on, she said, a little scared. *Both of them are acting like we're not here. Not because they don't see us, but because we don't matter. And I can't access any thoughts from either of them. Can you?*

Rede shook his head.

I'm going to try to Mask into whoever Emma is feeling strongest about, Thalia said. *Maybe that will help us figure out what's going on.*

Don't, Emma whispered.

Thalia knelt beside her again. *Tell me what happened. Please.*

Emma turned to her. *It's not what happened.* She was almost panting. *It's what will happen. Everything that was in this room is gone.*

What was in here? Rede asked, kneeling on Emma's other side.

"I don't know what to do." Hyad spoke in a terrible voice. Emma looked at him for the first time since they'd entered the room. He glanced down at her then turned away again.

"What the hell is going on?" Rede said, frustrated and on his feet again.

Hyad ignored him. "I can't even unlock the tie until we're back in the detainee tower," he said to Emma.

Emma stood up. "Can you sense what was in here?"

"I can see what happened to it," Hyad said. "Traces of something…not quite alive, but not dead either, were left behind. Like a shadow of life force staining the walls and floor."

"Then you know," Emma said, exhaling and wearing a relieved smile. "You know I was right! You know the Singers of the Apocalypse are real. You know what they want, and why they should never get it." She turned excitedly to Thalia and Rede. "Everything will be okay."

"Emma," Hyad said in that terrible voice again. He rubbed his hands over his eyes. "There isn't any way to protect your brother. Any movement, any movement at all, to shield him or hide him will alert these"—he exhaled heavily—"will alert the Singers to him. And when they find him, and they *will* find him, they'll incorporate him completely into their substance until they find the key to Whole Listening. You know this is true. It's why you brought me here. Why you demanded the life-link."

Why can't you unlock the tie here? Rede asked.

"Lukas made me set it up so it could only be unlocked in the chamber where it was created."

Thalia swore.

"He didn't trust me not to be persuaded by whatever Emma had to show me," Hyad said.

"But now that you know I was telling the truth," Emma said, "won't you be able to convince him to fight the Singers?"

"You can't fight them, Emma," Hyad said. "They have nothing to lose. By making them a myth Fen Elos diminished their power. That's all you can do. Gemynd are less likely to be seduced into killing themselves by something that isn't supposed to be real. They are less likely to allow them into their heads."

"I thought you said you didn't know what was in this room," Emma said.

"I didn't," Hyad said. "Then I found what Fen Elos was thinking the last time he was here. I didn't sense it at first, it was so well hidden."

How did you find it? Thalia asked.

"He left it behind," Hyad said. "A thought implanted in the walls. He meant for someone to find it, but…" He pressed his hands to his eyes again, and Emma burst into tears.

Rede turned to Thalia. *What?* he asked. *I can't hear anything.*

Emma's little brother, she said, *will have to be killed.*

* * *

Most of the Newport ghost stories Joe could find were set in buildings. The only one that took place outside was in the park he had come through when he got here, and that portal tree was destroyed. If only he had money, he could take a bus back to New Hampshire and find a portal tree there.

The library was a few blocks from the beach, so Joe walked there and stared at the ocean. He could fly for part of the way. He could swim out and then fly just above the surface of the water. If he was far enough away from the shoreline, no one could see him. He'd have to keep the shoreline in sight so he wouldn't get lost. He thought he'd be able to recognize the Portsmouth skyline. If it was dark when he got there maybe he could fly home through the woods, keeping below the treetops so he wouldn't be seen. He'd never been so grateful for paying attention in geography class.

His shoes would make it difficult to swim, so he stole a backpack from a blanket on the sand near the steps after dumping the contents. When he was far enough away from the blanket, Joe took off his shoes and shoved them into the backpack, which he then flung over his shoulders. He dove into the water and swam as fast as he could.

At first the weight of the wet backpack made it hard to swim, but he got used to it. He listened for the lifeguard whistle and swam underwater as much as possible. Finally, when he was far enough out that he could just barely see the shoreline, Joe pulled himself just above the surface of the water and stayed there so no passing boat or low-flying airplane would notice an airborne blue-haired teenager.

He'd forgotten how exhilarating it was to fly. How fast it felt. How free of everything. He wanted to rise higher, to really fly above the ocean, but it was still daylight and he didn't want to be seen.

After a few hours, a feeling of strange panic struck him. At first Joe thought Emma was trying to talk to him, but then he realized he could simply sense what she was feeling. Not that she knew it. His stomach touched the cold waves as his concentration broke, and he choked on a mouthful of salty water.

She couldn't hear him, she wasn't listening to him, but something had changed. She was ready to give up or give in. He couldn't reach her, either. She couldn't or wouldn't hear him, and he couldn't fly any faster. He was still hours away from New Hampshire, and even when he finally got there he couldn't be sure that Gatherers wouldn't be posted at every portal tree on the other side. Worst of all, Mr. Spencer and Maude were wrong about Emma. She wasn't safe. She was in pain and…she had given up.

CHAPTER FORTY-TWO

She'd betrayed her little brother.

She couldn't stop crying. Emma didn't fight back, and she didn't help when Hyad and Rede ushered her out of the Masked room in back of Fen Elos's store. She didn't listen to whatever they were saying. She kept Sandy's little face out of her head, but she couldn't stop crying.

It started in the middle of her stomach, a sudden cooling sensation like she had just eaten ice cream. The sweet smoothness wrapped around her waist and over her shoulders and legs like a blanket that sealed in the perfect temperature, not too hot and not too cold but just right. She heard herself crying, but the sound was distant and disconnected, as if she were in a room next to her crying self. So when the soft, seductive voices of the Singers started, Emma was ready to listen. It really did seem they were everywhere, ethereal, predatory, just waiting for their chance. Or maybe it was just for those gemynd with whom they'd already interacted, a highly attuned sense of their despair.

Yes, she realized. This is better. Death is better. It's easier. Her crying self was choking and sobbing in that other room. Emma just wanted quiet. She just wanted everything to stop. She wanted to stop thinking and feeling.

Someone was shaking her other self. It didn't matter, though. Soon she wouldn't feel anything. Soon everything would just be peace and quiet.

She smelled the ocean and felt a cold mist on her face. It was so nice. Maybe death was like always swimming in the cool ocean of the universe. Being a tiny part of the connected everything had to be better than life as a sharp-edged, separate piece of disconnected noise. She didn't want to be separate and individual anymore. She just wanted to sleep in the quiet connection of all things.

The delicious scent of the ocean grew stronger, but if Lukas was here he couldn't hurt her anymore. Emma almost felt sorry for him. He would never get what he wanted.

Someone was still shaking her. Someone was saying her name, but it melted away. The cold of the ocean seeped into her skin. Maybe she was already dead. It didn't feel bad, except for the increasing cold. The air was freezing, and her skin felt wet.

Don't give up.

It was Joe's voice, desperate and urgent, in her ear. *Don't give up. Don't give up. I'm coming to get you. I'm coming to help you. Don't give up. I love you, Emma. I'm sorry about what happened. I'm sorry I didn't trust you to make your own decision about Maude's secret.*

The Ones in Power are going to kill Sandy, Emma said. *It's my fault. And I can't stop them.*

Why wasn't she dead yet? Emma wondered dreamily. Why hadn't the Singers succeeded? Maybe she wasn't gemynd enough to kill herself by letting go. Maybe she'd have to do it like an Otherworlder.

"Stop shaking me!" Emma said out loud.

"Thank Misos," Hyad said. His terrified face, flanked by Rede's and Thalia's, came into focus. Hyad hugged her. "I'm sorry," he said. "We have to go."

* * *

Joe watched the ocean, tumultuous and gray, pass swiftly beneath him. He swore as loudly as he could and turned toward the shore, diving under the waves as soon as he was close enough to be seen. He wasn't sure where he was, but he had to get in touch with the others.

He checked the doors of empty houses a few blocks from the beach until he found one that was unlocked. Dripping water and tracking sand all over wooden floors and braided rugs, Joe found a phone and called Mr. Spencer.

Maude picked up.

"Tell Mr. Spencer," Joe said, "that the thing he was afraid of is about to happen."

While he talked to Maude, he searched the house for cash. A shiny bronze, fake leather purse hung on the back of a bedroom door, and he took out eighty dollars. "As soon as I figure out where I am, I'm going to look for a bus station and come home. Mr. Spencer has to leave right now and find a different place to stay. You and Elizabeth should go with him." *And Sandy,* he tried not to think.

"I'm not leaving," Maude said.

"Mr. Spencer will need help."

"He won't need me," Maude said. "I don't have any helpful powers."

"You can take care of him," Joe said. "Make him feel better."

"Mr. Spencer doesn't need me to take care of him," Maude said. "I'm staying here."

"That's not what I meant," Joe said, and he felt Maude finally understand that Sandy needed to go, too. *Especially.* "Take Aubrey with you. He's smart. I'll wait there until I hear something from Turner."

"What about Emma?"

"Don't ask me that," Joe said, clenching his teeth. A car pulled up outside, and Joe tried to remember if he'd seen a back door. "I have to go. Leave as soon as possible."

* * *

"I won't move until I know Rede and Thalia are safely on their way home," Emma said to Hyad.

We're coming with you, Rede said.

"No, you're not," Emma snapped. "You're going home. And you're both erasing me and my family completely from your memories as soon as you can."

No, Thalia said.

Hyad nodded. "Emma's right."

"I won't leave here until I know they're safe," Emma repeated.

What are you going to do? Thalia asked.

"Nothing," Emma said. "Unless you try to follow or help me. Then I'll break the tie."

Hyad will stop you, Thalia pointed out.

"He can't," Emma said. "Not if I want to break it. No matter what Lukas did, if I want to break the tie I can. I see that now. It's a condition of any life-link." She looked directly at Rede, who shut his eyes.

How did you know? he asked.

"I saw you remember it when you were talking before," Emma said. *It wasn't your fault. You didn't know.*

What is she talking about? Thalia asked.

Nothing, Rede said. *No, not nothing. I'll tell you later. I promise. We'll do what you asked, Emma. Come on, Thalia, let's go.*

"Don't give up," he said out loud to Emma. *I'm still here,* he added just to her. *What would have happened to Thalia if I'd given up? If you know my secret, you know I've thought about giving up every day since that one.*

Maybe you're stronger than I am, Emma replied. *I think I've been pretending to be strong this whole time. Saying yes to every challenge. Pretending I can handle anything and everything. Well, I can't. I can't handle this. I understand the consequences. I can't see any other way out for me. I'm glad you found Thalia, though.*

"Hey," she said out loud to Thalia, who moved with Rede toward the doorway. She clutched Hyad's hand. "Maybe you can have your manifestation ceremony now. I bet you'll be beautiful."

CHAPTER FORTY-THREE

It was close to midnight when Joe finally got back to Mr. Spencer's house. The bus ride seemed to take forever. Turner's Soulmate Rachel was waiting, sitting on the couch in the living room. She stood up when Joe walked in.

"What are you doing here?" Joe asked.

"Are you hungry?" she said, ignoring his question. "I picked up ravioli from Mario and Luigi's." She sniffed and made a face. "Did you swim here? You smell like exhaust and dead fish."

"I'm not hungry," Joe said. "Is Turner here?"

"You have to eat something," Rachel said. "Take a shower. I'll heat up the ravioli. I ordered a salad, too."

"Where's Turner?" Joe asked.

"He's still hiding in the Commonworld," Rachel said, the confident, bossy edge to her voice softer. "He's too weak to move much, but he said he's okay and I believe him. Mr. Spencer told me to tell him that you and Emma didn't find the place where her parents are, so I did."

"Where is he?" Joe asked again.

"I told you, he's hiding. He's okay. Leave it at that." She crossed her thin arms. "Seriously. Take a shower. Borrow some of Mr. Spencer's clothes. I'll heat up the ravioli." She turned around, her dark brown ponytail swinging behind her, and disappeared into the kitchen.

The hot shower was a good idea. Joe tried to reach Emma with his thoughts, but he couldn't. Or she wouldn't let him. The thought of Emma alone and hopeless made him sick. Worse, he couldn't believe that after everything they'd been through she would cut herself off from him.

Mr. Spencer's clothes were too big and too short, but at least they were dry. Luckily his feet were the same size, so the shoes fit.

Joe walked into the dining room. Rachel pointed to a plate of ravioli and salad. He hadn't realized how hungry he was until he started eating.

"Don't go so quickly," Rachel said. "You'll get sick."

"Are you always so bossy?" Joe asked, swallowing a mouthful of lettuce and cucumber.

"Yes."

Joe just stared at her.

Rachel smiled. "That's why Turner likes me."

Joe laughed. "Does Mr. Spencer have any milk?"

Rachel disappeared into the kitchen again and came back with a glass.

"I could have gotten it myself, you know," Joe said.

Rachel said nothing.

"Did everyone get out okay?" Joe asked when the milk was gone.

She didn't answer his question. "Do you want anything else?"

"No," he said. "Thanks. I guess I was hungry."

Rachel smiled at him again, somehow irritatingly condescending and sweet at the same time. "Everyone got out okay," she said.

Joe was exhausted. He pushed away from the table.

"I think you should go back," Rachel said.

Joe stared at her.

"Everyone has a breaking point," Rachel said. "From what Mr. Spencer told me, Emma must have reached hers. Go back and help her." Silently, she picked up Joe's plate and silverware. Her movements were hushed and graceful. She was perfect for Turner.

"Emma needs you," she repeated. "And you'll never forgive yourself if you don't help her."

Joe's throat clenched and his eyes burned. He didn't want to cry in front of someone as perfect and controlled as Rachel. She laid the dishes on the sideboard and sat down across from him.

"Emma will never forgive me if I try to help her instead of staying here to make sure everyone else is safe," Joe said.

Rachel gazed at a painting of a young beautiful woman and an old fortuneteller that hung above the sideboard. She didn't say anything.

"I don't really have a choice, though," Joe said. "Do I?"

"Of course you do," Rachel said. "You can…" Her voice trailed off. She stood up, staring at the front door. Had someone knocked?

Joe jumped out of his chair. "Stay here!" he whispered then ran to the door—although it was ridiculous to think that Gatherers would knock or wait for an invitation. "Turner!" he said when the door opened. "God, you look terrible."

"Is Rachel—?"

Rachel shoved Joe out of the way and grabbed Turner, who clung to her. Joe closed the door and went into the dining room so they could be alone.

Turner's weak, dry voice followed him. "Joe. Wait."

Joe turned around.

Turner kissed Rachel on the forehead and said to her, "I'm okay. Really. I promise."

Joe tried to pretend he didn't notice Rachel crying. He realized that she wanted to cry in front of him even less than he'd wanted to cry in front of her.

"You have to go back and help Emma," Turner said.

"What the fuck?" Joe was ready to hit something or someone. "At first everyone said, 'Don't go back, Emma is safer without your help.' Now, when I'm trying to do the right thing for Emma, which is to find Mr. Spencer and help him protect what Emma wants me to protect, you're asking me to leave."

"Calm down, Joe," Turner said, sounding more like himself. "I'll find Mr. Spencer and help him."

"Turner," Joe said, feeling unnerved and crazy. "No offense, but even if you can figure out where they went, you look like fucking shit."

"Hey," Rachel snapped.

"I'm fine," Turner said.

"No, you're not," Joe said. "You can hardly stand up."

"I'm fine," Turner repeated. "I'm much stronger than I was."

Joe exhaled and sat down. "What exactly happened?"

"It was just like Aubrey said. I used almost all my energy. The second the wall broke open, I felt like I had some horrible flu. After I got to the refuse containment center," he added quietly, "I couldn't move at all."

Rachel made a soft noise.

"Turner," Joe said, "you can't stay here by yourself."

"I'm here," Rachel pointed out.

Joe rolled his eyes.

"I take kickboxing," Rachel said.

Joe laughed.

"Shut up," Rachel growled.

"I'm not saying you're weak," Joe said, "or that you couldn't defend yourself against ordinary people, but Gatherers—*gemynd*— have super powers. You don't."

"Turner does," Rachel said.

"Turner is too weak to move anything," Joe said. "Don't try to prove me wrong," he added to Emma's brother. "Don't waste your energy showing off. I'm going to find Mr. Spencer and do what Emma would want me to do. Protect her family."

"Emma is at her breaking point," Rachel said softly.

"How do you know?" Turner asked.

"Because of what Mr. Spencer told me. I don't need to be able to read minds to know that Emma would feel overwhelmed if she thought she had…" Rachel stopped. "I'm not going to say it. Mr. Spencer said we couldn't say it out loud and we have to try not to think about it. Emma must think it's all her fault, though. You would," she said to Turner, who was trembling where he stood.

She led him to the couch where he sat next to Joe. "You and Emma are much more similar than you think," she said, kissing Turner on the head. "Significant GPA differential aside."

"If I leave," Joe murmured, "it will be as if I'm abandoning your whole family when you need the most help, and if anything happens Emma will never forgive me."

"You're not hearing me, Joe," Rachel said, and she knelt in front of him. "Emma won't be around to forgive you or not if you don't leave now."

Joe almost exploded. "Do you think I don't fucking know that? Why do you think I want to get back to Commonworld so badly? I *know* Emma is ready to give up, because I heard her. She doesn't know, but I did. Yes, she thinks it's her fault, and no, she can't stop any of what comes next from happening. The *only* thing I can do is protect the thing she can't."

Rachel glanced at Turner. "I think we have a little time before anything like that happens," she said. Then she turned back to Joe. "The longer Turner is with me, the better he'll feel. Then we can go help Mr. Spencer, assuming he contacts us or we figure out where he went."

"How do you know Turner will get better with you?"

Rachel groaned. "Did you ever ask any questions or read anything about the nature of the Soulmate connection, or did you just decide it's enough to experience it?"

Despite everything, or maybe because he was so exhausted, Joe laughed. "You really are just like a girl Turner."

"No, I'm not," Rachel said, lacing her fingers through Emma's brother's. "I'm his other half, like you're Emma's other half. The Singers of the Apocalypse—"

"You know about them?" Joe said.

"The Singers of the Apocalypse will sense Emma's despair," Rachel repeated, out of patience. "They'll seek her out, and she *will* give in unless you go stop her."

"We'll take care of things here," Turner said. He seemed physically better holding Rachel's hand, but his voice was strained. "You have to go to my sister."

"How did you get back here, anyway?" Joe asked.

"A Commonworld woman helped me when I was trying to find a portal tree. She asked me if I was okay. I guess looked bad. I told her I was Soulmated to an Otherworld girl and really sick and didn't know how to get back to the Otherworld now that rights were suspended."

"How did you know rights were suspended?" Joe asked.

"There were Revealer images everywhere," Turner said, "warning everyone to be careful and obey the Gatherers no matter what. Anyway," he continued, breathing slowly, "she took me to a tree that led to Boston Common."

"How the fuck did you get here from Boston?" Joe asked.

"I hitched a ride. You know that guy who drives fish down from Maine and sells it out of his truck on the highway?"

"No."

"You don't have time to drive to Boston," Rachel interjected.

"I'll fly," Joe said. "So, where was the portal tree?"

"Near the Frog Pond," Turner said. "Do you think you can get there before dawn?"

"Maybe," Joe said. "I hope so."

"You really shouldn't fly that far," Rachel said. "What if FAA radar picked you up or something."

"They haven't yet," Joe said.

"Well, you can't fly over Boston Common in broad daylight," Rachel said. "If it starts to get too close to morning you'll have to get into the city some other way."

Joe nodded and left.

CHAPTER FORTY-FOUR

Emma stood still in the detainee chamber while Lukas unlocked the tie. She didn't care what he planned to do with her. He'd said nothing when Hyad brought her into the chamber.

She and Hyad had returned here without saying much. How much was there to say? Thalia and Rede had gone home. Hyad promised he would make sure their memories of her and her family were erased, and if Thalia's energy was too unstable to erase her memory he swore to make sure she'd be sequestered somewhere until he could. Emma would have broken the tie as soon as Thalia and Rede were safely away, but she didn't want Hyad to watch her die if this method was so horrible. Rede had made her believe it was. She would figure out how to let go as soon as she was alone.

She tried not to think of Joe. She couldn't think of Joe. She knew she wouldn't be able to forgive him if he did what she was about to do, but she couldn't stop herself. She knew it was selfish, and she couldn't help it. She couldn't live knowing what was going to happen, knowing it was her fault.

Sandy.

The idea and the image of his capture smashed into her consciousness. Hyad's arms tightened around her, and Lukas unraveled the last of the tie from her throat. No one spoke. Hyad led Emma to a chair and gently pushed her onto it.

If only they would leave. Emma felt the Singers waiting at the edge of her consciousness. Why didn't they just come back already? A terrible thought struck her. What if the Singers weren't going to let her die? What if they wanted to use her to find Sandy? Could they do that? Thank God she didn't know where he was.

Hyad wrapped something around her wrists and ankles. He said, "You won't be able to move much, but it won't hurt at all." He glanced at Lukas, who was disposing of the leftover energy from the

tie, then back at her. "Do you want me to put you to sleep for a while? You must be exhausted."

"No," Emma said. "I want to stay awake. I want to be able to think."

Hyad nodded, squeezed her shoulder, and left her alone with Lukas, who ran his fingertips over her forehead. Emma flinched.

"What are you doing?" she asked. "You know everything already." Then Lukas dragged a memory out of her head of Joe flying over an Otherworld ocean and begging her not to give up, and she gasped. "He won't come for me. I told him not to."

Lukas exhaled, and Emma felt his regret at hurting her.

"Why don't you act on what you know is right?" Emma asked. "Leave Joe alone. He doesn't know anything."

"You should have let Hyad put you to sleep," Lukas said. "You won't want to think during this."

* * *

Joe reached Boston Common just before dawn. He found the tree Turner had described and moved through it, coming into the Commonworld city of Protepol just as the sun was rising between the highest silver towers. Volucris Gatherers were everywhere, their wings huge and powerful. They were waiting for him.

For a second Joe considered trying to outfly them, but he changed his mind, kept still and prayed that they would take him to wherever Emma was.

In the detainee tower, different Gatherers brought him to a room and accessed all his available thoughts: Rachel, Turner, Newport, Mr. Spencer, Maude, Aubrey, the homeless kid in the laundromat. He didn't resist. They wouldn't find what they were looking for, though, because Joe didn't have that answer. By now, Mr. Spencer and Sandy, along with Elizabeth, Maude and Aubrey, should have completely disappeared. Joe had no idea where they were and no way of finding out.

The Gatherers left, and Lukas, the red-eyed gemynd from whom Joe and Emma had earlier escaped, came into the room.

"I don't know where he is," Joe said.

Lukas looked surprised. "I hadn't realized you had any capacity to hear thoughts beyond those of your Soulmate."

At the mention of Emma, Joe shuddered.

"She's all right for now," Lukas said.

"Is she here?" Joe asked. "I want to see her."

"Perhaps—," Lukas began.

"Now," Joe said.

Lukas sighed. "You're not in a position to make demands. Don't squander your energy. You'll need it."

"You have to let me see her," Joe said, ashamed of the desperation in his voice.

"She's all right," Lukas said again.

"No," Joe said, "she isn't! As soon as she's alone she's going to let go. She's going to give in to the Singers."

"She won't be able to let go of her life force," Lukas said. "When I unlocked the tie I also—"

"What's a tie?" Joe said. "What did you do to her?"

Lukas inhaled slowly and ignored Joe's question. "Emma is connected to something like an Otherworld respirator," he said. "It will keep her heart and lungs working if she tries to let go." He flushed. "But the harder she struggles, the more unpleasant your connection will be."

"Let me see her!" Joe demanded.

Lukas turned away. "As soon the new extrication lights are ready we'll know if anyone has implanted any information about the boy's whereabouts in your head." He looked back at Joe. "Then I will let you see her. She's safe enough for now."

Lukas turned around again, but Joe heard what he was trying half-heartedly to suppress. He liked Emma, and like most gemynd he hated to separate Soulmates. Sometimes it seemed that Commonworlders knew everything but understood nothing.

"When will the extrication lights be ready?" Joe asked.

"In a few days," Lukas answered. "If we're lucky."

"A few days!" Joe repeated. "Let me see her now. Please. How could it hurt anything?"

"I'm sorry," Lukas said, and Joe heard that he meant it. "But you and Emma proved yourselves adept at escaping. I'm sorry," he added and left Joe alone.

Emma, Joe said, and he heard his voice echo in her head as she ignored him. She'd been trying to let go for what seemed like hours. The respirator thing was preventing it. She just didn't know.

Emma, Joe said again. *If you can hear me, the Ones in Power are listening, too, but...* His voice trailed off. *Please talk to me.*

This, he heard her say to herself, *if nothing else, should kill me.*

Emma. She still didn't know he'd learned to hear her thoughts when she didn't want him to, was unaware that he felt her reject him. He sat on the floor. He couldn't leave. He couldn't contact her. He had no choice but to stay connected with her and accept whatever she did.

How could this Soulmate bond be the most revered thing? It was hard enough to sustain yourself, and this... This didn't feel like love; it felt like a prison. The one secret thing Joe had wanted, the one thing he couldn't get for himself, was that someday his father would come into his life and love him and be proud of him. He'd found his dad and lost him just as quickly. He'd found Emma, too. What would happen to him if something happened to her?

This was like the books at home but twisted. Romance. Love. Garbage. Bullshit. Lies. He didn't want to depend on anyone else. Not for happiness. Not for security. Not for anything. This really didn't feel anything like love. It felt like a prison, and he couldn't breathe. How could having an other half be anything but diminishing?

Rachel sent me, he called out in desperation, trying again to make Emma respond to him. Maybe she'd listen to someone other than himself. Maybe other people really were more important to her than he was.

Rachel? Emma said. *What does Rachel have to do with anything?*

Thank God, Joe said, not caring what had gotten her to connect. *Listen to me. I know you can hear me. Rachel was waiting in Mr. Spencer's house. Turner—*

Stop! Emma said. *The Ones in Power are listening. You said they were.*

They already know all this, Joe said, interrupting her before she could say anything further. *They accessed everything they could when I first got here.*

Well, Emma said, her thought-voice high and broken, as if she were much, much younger than seventeen. *What about Turner? Is he okay?*

He won't be if you kill yourself, Joe snapped. *And neither will anyone else. Fuck, Emma, if I'm not enough, if thinking of me isn't enough, think of Maude for God's sake. How much are you going to ask her to lose? Gryphon? Your parents? You?*

Stop, Emma said. *Stop it.*

No, Joe said. *You are being so fucking selfish. No matter what happens, this will make everything worse.*

Stop, Emma begged.

Why? Joe asked. *You obviously couldn't have been thinking about what would happen to me if you died.*

She was silent.

Joe was shocked that his anger had only gotten bigger. He'd expected to be compassionate and consoling, to tell Emma how much he loved her and how much he would miss her, how life was always, *always* worth it, but instead he was furious.

Of course I thought of you, Emma stammered. *I didn't think of anything else.*

Bullshit, Joe said, his voice like fire in his head. *You couldn't have thought about me at all. Because if you had, you never would have been able to consider doing what*—he stopped and smashed his fist into the wall of the empty room, bruising his knuckles—*you've been trying to do for the last several hours.*

Emma sounded shocked. *How did you know?*

Fuck, Emma! I'm your other half, not just some distracting figment of your imagination! Joe shut his eyes so tightly he saw stars and flowers before he could continue. *That's why the Soulmate connection is so terrible. You want to kill yourself, go ahead. But you're also fucking killing me.*

* * *

Emma sank into her chair. Its soft, immovable restraints continued to secrete something into her wrists and ankles.

Her heart kept beating. She could feel it, thick, heavy and rhythmic, thudding in her ears. She felt dead, though. Or suspended. As if she were stuck between worlds, existing nowhere.

Say something, Joe said. *Be angry with me. Fight with me. Tell me I'm wrong. Tell me I'm an asshole. Tell me you're sorry. Just don't be silent.*

I don't know what to do, Emma said. *I can't let go, but I don't know how to stay. Maybe we're too young for this. Maybe because we grew up outside the Commonworld our connection is screwed up somehow. Maybe it's me.*

Is that what you think? That our connection is fucked up?

I don't know, Emma said. *Shouldn't Soulmates have perfect relationships? Isn't that part of it? Isn't that how it works? You've been so secretive and moody, and I feel like I have to handle everything by myself. And then I screw things up and—*

That's not your fault, Joe interrupted.

It is, Emma said. *I thought of him in front of Hyad. Before that, the Ones in Power had no idea.*

We're definitely too young for this shit, Joe said.

Emma laughed.

That's nice, he murmured. *I thought I'd never hear you laugh again.*

Why won't they let me see you? she asked.

The violent upheaval in Joe's chest at her question rose inside her, and suddenly, stupidly, horrifyingly, everything Joe felt, everything he'd been thinking and feeling came crashing down on her. What had she done?

I'm sorry, she said. *I'm sorry. I'm sorry.* Before she'd betrayed her baby brother she'd been so consumed with feeling that she couldn't trust Joe to be there for her, she'd forgot he needed her, too.

She closed her eyes and felt him pacing in a tight circle, wishing he could punch a hole through the wall. Wishing it would hurt. She wished she could do something, that she could break out of this room and stand next to him. Do something. Just be there. With him. Love, or the Soulmate connection, or whatever the hell it was, wasn't an object made of shiny feelings sitting on a private shelf inside you, something you could hold in your hand and examine under the light then put away again. Love was the connection. The connection was love; the sacred energy that lived in the space between her and Joe, looping back and forth, knitting them together. But it needed to be nurtured.

Emma closed her eyes and concentrated on Joe. She tied herself to his thoughts and feelings and slipped inside him, not just his head but his everything. She curled into Joe and kissed the inside of his heart. *I'm sorry.*

Emma, he murmured, and she felt his essence relax. *Emma.*

She felt him breathing, felt his despair at the idea of losing her and his relief that he hadn't.

I love you, she said, suddenly in a very different place. *I don't care if our connection is fucked up.*

Maybe everyone's connection is fucked up, he said. *We're just willing to say it out loud.*

She laughed again, and Joe held on to her as she swam inside him.

CHAPTER FORTY-FIVE

Emma woke up the next day.

Well, she assumed it was the next day. The light in the room never changed. There was no clock and her phone was at Mr. Spencer's. She wasn't tired anymore. She wasn't hungry, either, which was surprising because she couldn't remember the last time she'd eaten. Since she'd connected with Joe last night, the restraints on her wrists and ankles had been secreting less of whatever it was they had been pumping into her.

The door opened in a different place than it had the day before. Lukas walked in. Emma stiffened but said and thought nothing.

He pulled up a chair and sat beside her to examine her restraints. "I see you've decided against ending your life for the time being."

He said it like a question. Emma glanced up.

"You can respond," Lukas said. "I won't hurt you."

"Yes," she said. "I have."

"Good." He stood up, crossed to a counter and began entering information into a reading stone. "We need you."

"I won't help you," Emma said. "I can't help you. You must know that."

He turned, and she felt a scissoring sensation in her brain. *Don't speak or think*, he said, continuing to enter data into the reading stone. Then he exhaled once and raised his head. "You'll feel hungry later." He came over. "When you do, think of a food request and someone will bring you something to eat."

"Where is Joe?" Emma asked. "I know he's here. Why won't you bring him to me?"

Lukas smiled and unlocked the restraints on Emma's wrists. He squeezed her hand. "Don't concern yourself with him. As of now he is well enough."

Lukas left. Emma swore at him, clenching her fists as the door closed, and there was something in one of her hands, something she hadn't felt before. Opening her hand she saw that Lukas had left the reading stone in it.

She ran her finger down the central crevice, and the rock opened like a book. Emma scanned the text to find it was all about her: her vital signs, the shift that came once she'd stopped thinking about suicide, and her distress about being separated from Joe. She was just about to shut the stone when she saw something encarved underneath the text.

The scissoring sensation in her brain grew colder and increased in intensity. It didn't quite hurt. It felt weird, like when a doctor describes an unpleasant sensation as "a little pressure."

The encarved text was in Sacerian. Like the message Eury Vatic had left on the table in Slabsides, Emma could only see it if she looked at it in the right way. Also like Eury's message, she could hear what Lukas was thinking when he wrote it, though she couldn't read Sacerian.

Emma softened her focus and listened.

You and I want the same thing: to spare your brother's life.

The "pressure" in her brain sharpened as a jolt of terror for Sandy and distrust of Lukas heated her chest.

By now, Hyad will have made the case for the necessity of ending your brother's life to the Three Leaders. Although there is nothing to indicate whether the remaining extrication light stolen by your cousin has been destroyed or preserved, the Three Leaders are bound to choose what is most beneficial to the greatest number of Commonworlders. And because you have so ably proven the existence of the Singers of the Apocalypse and their capacity for large-scale destruction if they capture the boy, the Three Leaders, regrettably, must choose his execution over the immediate gain of the first Whole Chronicler in two thousand years.

As soon as Emma read the phrase "Whole Chronicler," the unpleasant pressure in her head became a blinding pain. It finally subsided, and she listened for Lukas's thoughts again, but his voice was fragmented now, like he was on a cell phone driving through a bad service area.

...but I disagree...if you are willing...your brother is not harmed. He will be hidden until he is grown and all of Eury Vatic's...by then...technology will have improved and we should be capable...from your brother without inflicting lasting damage. This

is your only chance to save your brother's life. If you refuse, all the information...will be eliminated from your brain in manner similar...clever cousin pulled... from her own skull.

Protect Sandy?

I'll help you, she said. Whatever he wanted, Emma would do it.

The encarved message disappeared.

* * *

Joe didn't protest when two gemynd came and took him out of the cell. He tried to listen, but their thoughts were locked except for the image of where they were taking him: to see Emma. Breathing slowly, Joe contained his elation.

After a series of doors leading to longer and longer hallways, the gemynd stopped at a blank wall that opened to reveal Emma sitting in an empty room identical to the one where he had been held. She was on the floor eating out of a pale pink bowl. Her wrists and ankles were no longer restrained.

"Joe!" Emma said. She jumped to her feet and ran to him.

His gemynd guards released his arms, and the wall-door shut, leaving him and Emma alone.

She kissed him. He never wanted to let her go.

"Why did they decide to let us see each other?" he asked after a long time kissing her.

"I don't know," Emma said. "I think they believe I'll be more cooperative if you're with me."

"Is that true?" Joe asked.

"I don't know," Emma said. "But I'm so happy to see you."

Joe kissed her and pulled her closer, her breasts pressed against his chest, her open hands on the scars where his wings had been.

"Are you hungry?" Emma asked after he pulled away to look at her. She turned to glance at the pink bowl on the floor. "I don't know what it is, but it tasted all right."

"I'm not hungry," he said, hot, dizzy and completely focused on the feel of her warm against him.

"Are you okay?" Emma asked.

He nodded. She kissed him again, and Joe lost his sense of place in the world. Nothing mattered but her mouth on his and her soft skin warm beneath her shirt. Why had he ever doubted the Soulmate connection?

"Wait," Emma said, out of breath and pushing him slightly away. "Stop."

Joe tried to catch his breath. *I don't want to stop.*

Emma smiled and kissed him. "I know," she said. "I don't want to stop either."

"Why do we have to?" he asked. "There's no one else here and we can't get out." He turned and looked at the place in the wall where the door had been. "*Can* we get out? Have you tried?"

"We can't," Emma said. "I tried."

He pressed his hips to hers, and Emma made a sound that unraveled all his thoughts but those of her.

"Wait. No," she said, pushing him away again. She crossed the room and ran her hand over her forehead, steadying her breathing and not looking at him until she had steadied herself. He couldn't think while he waited.

"I've agreed to something," she said, still on the other side of the room.

"What does that mean?" Joe asked, moving closer.

"I can't tell you what it is," she said. "And I can't explain why. They did something so I can't communicate anything about it."

"So why are telling me?" he almost yelled, frustration making him feel like his blood was made of hot iron.

"Because," she said, not looking at him. "I think they want to make you complicit without telling you anything, and without me telling you, and..." She paused and turned. "And I wanted you to have the chance to refuse. I think I could negotiate for your freedom."

"Freedom from what?" Joe asked.

"From having to help me."

"Emma," Joe said, furious and frustrated at the same time. He wanted to hit something. He turned away and then back, shoved his fists into his pockets and pulled them out again. "Every time you ask me to leave you, it kills me a little."

"I'm sorry," she said.

He exhaled. "Forget it." He crossed to the far end of the room, roared in frustration, and smacked the smooth wall as hard as he could. What else was there to do?

The door opened.

"I see you've kept your emotions in check," Lukas said smoothly, slipping into the room as the wall closed behind him. "You are lucky to be a Commonworlder," he told Joe. "Without the promise and security of a Soulmate, I fear you would be incapable of sustaining any kind of adult relationship."

Joe felt sick and furious. He wanted to tell the red-eyed man to fuck himself.

"That is exactly what I mean," Lukas said, looking at him with curious sympathy, as if Joe were some kind of broken toy. "Your first thought—if one can use that term—is always emotional and reactive. Anger, lust, indignation."

Joe stared past Lukas and retreated into himself the way he had at home and at school when kids made fun of him, when he hated himself and everyone else and just had to stop his head for one second.

"Leave him alone," Emma called out.

"You would be worthier of Emma if you were not in constant need of rescue," Lukas continued.

Joe flew at the gemynd and tried to hit him in the face. A wave of energy like a wall of invisible bricks stopped him, and he fell to the floor. Emma did not rush to help. Joe silently thanked her.

"What do you want?" she asked Lukas.

Joe did not hear the ensuing conversation. He felt Emma respond to something like indecision or vulnerability in Lukas, but when he looked at the gemynd's face he saw nothing.

"You are both to be secreted," Lukas said.

"What?" Emma glanced worriedly at Joe. "No. NO. Why would you bring us together only to separate us forever? What about—?" She abruptly stopped speaking as if something had cut off her tongue.

"To give you a chance to say goodbye," Lukas said.

Joe ran to Emma and grabbed her hand, but the door opened and two Gatherers entered the room.

"No," Emma screamed. "Please. I'll do anything."

"I'm sorry," Lukas said. "There is no other way." Then, as the two Gatherers watched with barely constrained horror, he released a band of spinning red energy.

"No!" Joe shouted, pushing Emma behind his back while punching at the rapidly circling light. It surrounded them and made to break them apart.

"Joe," Emma whispered. Her voice sounded like it was going down a drain.

His grip on her hand softened.

"Joe," Emma said again.

He could hardly see her. The last thing he did see, before he passed out, was Emma's ice-colored hair shrink into blond spikes on the head of a thick, muscular boy wearing a Minecraft teeshirt.

CHAPTER FORTY-SIX

No, Thalia's mother said. *No. I won't allow it.*

Her mother and Hyad were in the living room arguing about erasing Thalia's memory. Thalia was in her room, sitting on her bed doing homework while Rede encarved fos charasso marks on her ankle. She was trying not to listen to Hyad and her mom, but Genna's thoughts kept worming their way into her head. Maybe her mom was doing it on purpose, hoping Thalia would agree with her.

Thalia's fifteenth birthday is only two days from now, Genna continued. *Her energy is too unstable to erase any part of her memory.*

"I know her energy is unstable," Hyad said out loud. He clearly wanted Thalia and Rede to hear what he said. "If the situation weren't so dangerous I wouldn't consider it. But the Three Leaders have issued an edict for that boy's death, and the Gatherers will stop at nothing to find him. Thalia's relationship with Emma makes her a target. And," he added, his voice pained, "the Gatherers will not be careful with an Aponomi. Not now."

Thalia heard her mother cross the room. She must have stopped at the cabinet of music spheres, because a cacophonous protest sang out.

I forgot about this when I gave you Solymi's things, Genna said to Hyad. *I made it for Solymi when he was born and I was seven years old. I didn't know my mother kept it until Solymi met you. She asked me to give it to you when and if you and Solymi had children. It's yours now,* Genna finished.

A child-like song sounded throughout the house, and Hyad's sorrow smashed Thalia repeatedly in the chest. She exhaled and wished she could do something for him, even though there wasn't anything anyone could do. Solymi was gone. So was his nameplate.

Are you all right? Rede asked, glancing up from the floor where he sat at her feet.

Thalia nodded.

What are they going to do?

I don't know, she said.

Rede continued to meticulously carve the luminous fos charasso script into her skin. *This doesn't hurt, does, it? It shouldn't.*

Thalia shook her head. He was so sweet. *No,* she said. *It doesn't hurt at all. How does it look?*

Rede sighed. *I'll let you know when I've finished.*

Thalia watched him concentrate on perfectly forming the ancient letters. His fingers were long and thin, and his movements were graceful.

What are you thinking about? he asked, leaning back to assess what he had just encarved before beginning again.

Nothing, Thalia said, blushing and not yet accustomed to seeing her skin darken rather than disappear when she was embarrassed.

Rede stopped encarving and looked up at her, a wide grin on his face.

What? Thalia asked, blushing more. *Wait. No. Don't listen to what I'm thinking.*

Too late. He laid the fos charasso needle on the floor and climbed onto the bed next to her.

Thalia scooted over. Whether she was trying to get away from him or from herself, she wasn't quite sure. *You're not* that *cute.*

Really? he said. *That's not what it sounded like when you thought about how I—*

Stop, Thalia said, and she kissed him.

After a blissful minute, during which she decided that in the history of the universe there was nothing better than kissing and never would be, Rede pulled away.

What? she asked, breathless, pulling out of the moment more slowly than he had.

I can feel your ankle, he said, looking at her in wonderment.

What do you mean? Now? Thalia checked her feet, which were dangling off the side of the bed. *I can't feel you touching my leg.*

I didn't, Rede said. *I'm not. I feel what* you *feel—or did.* He smiled broadly at her. *That's never happened to me before. I felt where the fos charasso marks entered your skin as if they were entering mine.*

I thought only Aponomi felt what other gemynd felt when they were...kissing. She almost said something else. Something they would surely do when they were older. A rush of excitement careened into a hot wave of embarrassment.

What do you mean? Rede asked.

Thalia tried to clear her head and half succeeded. The tantalizing idea of him waited at the edge of her thoughts, to say nothing of the flesh-and-blood Rede inches away from her on the bed.

Remember when you met Maddie, she said, *and I told you Invisibles develop differently from other gemynd?*

Yeah?

Well, we take in sensory information differently, too, she said. *And that never changes, except during manifestation.*

What does that have to do with me feeling your ankle? he asked.

Nothing, she said, wondering how her face could feel so hot when she wasn't sick. *Well, except it's kind of like what happens when you kiss me.*

What—he grinned, and her face felt ten times hotter—*happens?*

When you kiss me, she explained, *I don't so much feel your mouth on mine as I feel...* She stopped.

What?

Thalia glanced over at her toy sun. She suddenly felt ridiculous, sitting in her room, surrounded by all her old toys on the bed she'd slept in since she was four years old, talking in detail about kissing. With a boy she'd been kissing! It felt like way too many things were happening at once, and faster than she could keep up with.

You don't have to tell me if you don't want to, Rede said.

I feel the kiss all over, she said quickly and turned back to him. *And I feel what you feel when you kiss me.*

Having said that, suddenly everything was perfect, or as perfect as it could be in a world where bad things happened all the time. Rede's eyes lit up and he smiled at Thalia as if she were the most amazing thing in two worlds—which was exactly how she felt about him.

CHAPTER FORTY-SEVEN

Snuggled against something warm and nice, Emma opened her eyes. She was on the floor of what looked like a huge train station with marble steps and an arched ceiling decorated with the constellations. Her snowy hair fell down her tank top and covered most of her chest, but slashes of pink skin shown through the tangled strands.

Emma sat up and turned around. Joe. *Real* Joe, lying on the floor behind her. For a moment she just looked at him, sleeping with his head propped against his hand, his eyelashes like raven feathers on his dark cheeks. He took a deep slow breath, his ribcage expanding and contracting in his black tee shirt, and Emma leaned down and kissed his cheek and his head and his shoulder, running her hand down his back to the waistband of his jeans.

Eyes still closed, Joe took her hand and kissed it then almost jumped to a sitting position.

"We're not secreted," she said. "We're not secreted."

"Thank God," he replied, his voice shaking. "Where are we?"

"A train station, I think. It's big, so we're probably in a city."

Joe looked around but didn't say anything. Emma hugged him.

"Thank God we're not secreted," he said again, his hands in her hair. "How did we get here?"

"I don't know," Emma said. "There aren't any portal trees, obviously. Maybe someone pushed us through a portal opening. Or maybe someone took us? In any case, Lukas must have thought pretending to secret us was the only way to get us here without anyone following."

"He did a very convincing job," Joe replied, his voice still unsteady. "All I wanted to do was memorize your face so I could find you again."

"What did I look like?"

"Different."

"Like what?" she asked.

"A boy. Spiked blond hair. Big arms. A Minecraft teeshirt."

"Still hot though, right?" Emma asked.

"Oh yeah," Joe said, leaning in to kiss her. "Still hot."

Emma licked his throat up to his ear. He sighed and ran his hands up and down her waist.

"You were a very old man," she whispered.

"I guess we would have turned a few heads, then."

She smiled and kissed him again.

Commuters rushed by, not paying them any attention, which was unsurprising with the way they were dressed. They hadn't changed clothes in days, so they probably looked like dirty kids about to ask for money or something.

Joe stood up too fast and swayed a little. Emma took his hand. A woman held out an overturned fist as if she were about to drop something, but seeing that Joe didn't have a cup or an outstretched hand she shot him an embarrassed glance and hurried on. Some of the men who passed still had wet hair. One guy had a curl of shaving cream the color of mint ice cream behind his ear.

"I guess it's pretty early in the morning," Emma said. She stood up, felt dizzy and leaned into Joe.

He ran his fingers through his hair. "We should have taken the money that woman was going to give us."

"Why?" Emma said.

Joe shook his head.

"What?" Emma asked.

"Nothing," he said, turning away and then gazing back at her. "It's just weird to think how different your life was from mine. It's not like I had tons of friends, rich or broke, but—"

"My family's not rich," Emma said.

Joe squeezed her hand. "Nobody thinks they're rich. Everyone who's broke knows it." He squeezed her hand again then let go. "Do you have any cash on you?"

Emma searched her pockets and shook her head. "Do you?"

"A little," he said. "I had to take a bus home from Rhode Island. I stole some money for that. I have a little left."

A fast-walking woman, talking very loudly into her phone, bumped into Emma and didn't even turn around.

"Hey," Emma said, rubbing her shoulder.

Joe took her hand. "Come on. We have to figure out where we are."

They walked toward the main room of the station. There was a cylindrical information booth in the center of a cavernous space swarming with people who were talking and running, smiling and unsmiling. The booth was wrapped in dirty windows the color of tree sap.

"Should we ask there?" Emma asked.

Joe nodded.

"Excuse me," Emma said to a bearded and bent old man behind the glass. He was bald and wore silver-rimmed glasses. He glanced up and put down a copy of *Model Railway Magazine.*

"Yes?"

"Where are we?" Emma asked.

The old man narrowed his eyes and seemed ready to snap at her for wasting his time. Emma saw that the cover article was about building a model railway in your backyard. She smiled at him, and the old man grunted and pushed his glasses up the bridge of his nose.

"Grand Central Terminal," he said, peering past Emma's head at the woman standing behind her, who presumably had a less inane question.

"Thanks," Emma said and then headed back to Joe. "We're in Grand Central Station," she said to him. "That's in New York City, if you didn't know."

"Terminal," Joe corrected. "Grand Central Terminal, because all the train lines terminate here."

"Thanks, Turner."

"Why?" Joe asked.

"Because that's just the kind of thing Turner would say."

"No, silly," Joe said. "Why are we in Grand Central Terminal? Why are we in New York City? Why are we here?"

"Oh," Emma said. "Let's sit down. I need to think."

"Okay," Joe said. He took her hand.

They walked across the main concourse, and for a second Emma pretended they were just young and in love with a whole day of nothing to do in front of them. Joe kissed her head and whispered, *Two out of three isn't bad.*

She squeezed his hand and sat on the marble staircase where several people were sitting, only to be shooed away by a policeman a few moments later.

"I guess that no-sitting sign was serious," she said, glancing around the room. Then, "I...I need to talk to you."

"What? Why can't we talk right here?" Joe asked. "The filter system? Can it really reach the Otherworld?"

"I don't know, maybe sometimes...?" Emma said. "Why else would my mom and dad have put identity shields on us?"

"Then let's go down to the tracks," Joe said. "It will be more crowded, and it's underground—if that helps."

"It's not just the filters," she said. "I don't know if I'm going to be able to say what I need to say. I couldn't when we were in that room with Lukas, but maybe it will be different here."

He took her hand, and they walked down a dirty ramp clogged with people and choked with hot air. They stood on a platform between a square column and a huge gray garbage can, and Joe said, "Too bad we just can't run through that column and get where we need to go."

"You liked *Harry Potter*?" Emma asked, surprised.

"Why? You think people can't love both Samuel Beckett and *Harry Potter*?"

She smiled. "Did you wait for your letter when you were eleven?"

"Of course I did," he said.

"Were you disappointed when it didn't come?"

"What makes you think it didn't come?" he asked. "After all, I can fly. And I met you, didn't I?"

"Shut up," she said, leaning into him as commuters poured out of a train that had just arrived.

Joe kissed her. "Can you tell me now what you couldn't before?"

Emma sucked in a long breath, tried to speak, and swore. "No. It's like it was with Lukas. Worse, actually. I feel like I'm choking on my words. Shit! How are we going to do what we're supposed to do if you don't know what it is and I can't tell you?"

"It's all right," Joe said, his hands in her hair. "We'll figure it out."

"Nice pink skin, ya freak!" someone called out to Emma, one of a passing pack of laughing assholes.

Joe spun around. Emma grabbed his hand. "Forget it," she said. "What the hell do I care what some jerk thinks?"

"I care," Joe said, staring after them.

A girl with a black leather miniskirt, red horns, bright white hair and deep red skin rushed up to them. Joe pulled Emma back.

"Can I walk to Fanime from here?" the girl asked. "I can't believe they added an East Coast con! So awesome, right?"

It's makeup, Emma said to Joe. *She's wearing a costume. She's not a Commonworlder.*

"I don't know," she said to the girl, who looked at a smartphone then held it up for Emma to see the address.

"Do you want to walk with me?" the girl asked. "I've never been to New York City before and my friends bailed on me. So I'm alone."

"Sorry," Emma said. "We'd love to go with you, but I promised my aunt we'd have breakfast with her. Maybe we'll see you later."

"No worries," the girl said. "I'll look for you." She smiled and waved and left.

"Okay," Emma said to Joe when the girl was out of earshot. "Let's try again."

"Okay," he said, running his fingers through her hair. "Not for nothing, but I love your hair and skin."

"I love yours, too."

He kissed her then said, "What if you told me indirectly?"

"Like, how?"

"Say the essence of what you want me to know using related words or ideas. Like 'Brainiac' for Turner or 'Sex King of All Known Worlds' for me."

Emma burst out laughing. "Okay. But it's not about you, so no talk of sex kings."

"Not yet, anyway."

"What is up with you?" Emma asked.

Joe eyed her, smirking. "I'm not going to touch that."

"Me neither," Emma said. "Well, maybe later. If you're really nice to me."

He pulled her close and kissed her. "Is this nice enough?"

"Always," she said, leaning into him then exhaling. "But we have to do what we came here to do first."

Joe stepped back and nodded. "Okay. Try again to tell me."

Emma took a deep breath then whispered in a slow, strained voice, as if she'd just run up five flights of stairs. "The one I'm thinking of loves Captain Underpants and just lost a tooth." She stopped and struggled to breathe. "We have to find him. That's why we're here."

Joe dug into his pocket and gave Emma two dollars. "Go over to that guy selling water," he said. "I'm going to say what I think you mean. Listen, but not attentively, kind of like the way you read that message on the table at Slabsides. If I'm right, or close to being right, buy a bottle of water. No filter should pick *that* up."

Emma nodded and walked over to the man selling beer and water out of a silver cart. She kept within hearing distance.

Joe approached a nearby homeless man who was asking people for money. While giving him a dollar he said, "You've agreed to find Captain Underpants and bring him to the Commonworld."

"I didn't agree to anything," the man said.

"Whoever asked you to do this promised to save Captain Underpants's life," Joe continued.

"I'm not crazy," the homeless guy said. He stuffed the money into his pocket. "I'm just broke. I lost my job. Can you find me a job?"

A policeman appeared and asked the man to move along.

"Can *you* find me a job?" the guy asked the policeman, who ignored him.

Emma walked back. She'd bought water and was drinking it. She took Joe's hand, glad they were on the same page. They went up the ramp and outside onto the busy sidewalk.

CHAPTER FORTY-EIGHT

"I told you we should have knocked."

Hyad's voice broke into Thalia's thoughts a few seconds after he'd spoken.

She never would have heard it, Genna said. She and Hyad were standing in the doorway of Thalia's room. Thalia had no idea how long they'd been standing there or what they'd seen.

"*He* would have heard it," Hyad said.

By this time, Rede had slid so far away from Thalia he'd almost fallen off her bed.

Hyad pulled a chair close to Thalia. "You know why I'm here, don't you?" he asked.

Could something bad happen to Emma if you don't erase my memory? she asked. *Is that why you're doing it?*

"I'm doing it so something bad doesn't happen to you," Hyad said. He glanced at Rede.

"What?" Rede said. "You think I'm going to alert the filters?"

You shouldn't erase her memory at all, Genna spoke up. *It could fragment.*

"The Gatherers are already aware of Thalia's brief connection with Emma," Hyad said. "Because of me they're willing to leave Thalia alone for now. But if they think she knows something about Emma's little brother, if they even suspect it, they'll use extrication lights," Hyad said. "Even without the ceremony, the energy produced by her manifestation will draw the Gatherers here. You know that. If they come at the wrong time, her memories will be hanging everywhere for them like fruit. She won't be able to stop that. And you and Zeph won't be able to stop the Gatherers. This is the only way."

Rede stood up. Thalia thought he was going to argue with Mom, but he said, *Thalia isn't fifteen yet.*

"I know," Hyad said, clearly trying to keep his frustration under control. "Obviously, if she had manifested, her energy would be stable and we wouldn't be having this conversation. Zeph would have erased her memory and yours already."

Thalia isn't fifteen yet, Rede repeated. *Our connection is vulnerable,* he added when Hyad opened his mouth to interrupt.

No, it isn't, Thalia said. *I know you're my Soulmate.*

Rede smiled sadly at her. *Yes,* he said, *but until you actually turn fifteen, the physical connection is vulnerable. That's one of the reasons the Soulmate revelation and connection are protected. Only a few gemynd are aware of their Soulmates before they turn fifteen. If you do meet and understand each other beforehand...well, the connection is like baby born prematurely. Everything is fragile for a while.*

Hyad turned to Thalia's mom, an expression of horror in his amber eyes. "I don't know what to do," he said, breathless. "That's right. I'd forgotten. How could I have been so stupid?"

Genna laid her hand on his shoulder. Both of them were silent. Thalia struggled not to involuntarily Mask herself into Solymi, as his laughing, handsome face was so painfully and powerfully present.

"How does secreting work?" Rede asked. "How *exactly?*"

Hyad gasped. Genna stared at him, surprised, accusation lighting her apricot eyes.

"Don't bother to pretend you don't know," Rede said. "Thalia told me you told her."

Hyad glanced over at her, terrified.

I told him in the in the inaccessible spot, Thalia said.

Hyad stood, but Rede asked again, "How does it work?"

Hyad said nothing.

Why did you tell her anything about that? Genna asked.

Yes, Thalia said. *Why did you tell me? It's horrible.*

Is this the reason you want to erase her memory? Genna asked. *Does knowing about secreting put her in danger? Why did you burden her with something like that? What were you thinking?*

"Stop!" Rede said. "It doesn't matter. It's done. What matters is protecting Thalia *now.* Hide her in the Otherworld. Until her manifestation. It's only three days from now. Then you can erase her memory. And mine."

Genna made a mournful sound. Thalia stood next to her.

What? she asked her mom. *I'll be safe and we'll all be together. Maybe we can have a small party or something there.*

Zino and Maddie and I can't go with you, Genna said. *Aponomi and their families have to appeal to the Ones in Power any time they want to leave the Commonworld. The process can take weeks. Hyad can cover your traces, but he couldn't cover all of ours. If we didn't apply and got caught, Zino and I would lose our jobs and you and Maddie could be taken from us. So, you'd have to go alone. You'd be all alone. In a strange world. For your manifestation.*

"She wouldn't be alone," Rede said. "I'd be with her. I'm not Aponomi. I can leave the Commonworld any time I want."

"How can you even think of asking me to secret you?" Hyad asked in an odd voice, as if he hadn't been listening to anything after Rede's question about the process.

"I'm not asking you to secret us," Rede said. "Misos! I asked you how it worked. Maybe the process can be altered or diluted so it's temporary."

"It can't be altered," Hyad said, his voice shaking. "And it can't be undone."

Genna glared at Hyad then walked over to Thalia's desk. The song sphere she had made for Rede sat between Thalia's properties-of-energy-harnessing school project and her lesson reader. Mom lifted the sphere, and incandescent music filled the small room.

Let me access you, she said to Rede. *For real this time.*

Why? he asked.

I want to know if I can trust you.

"You don't think I'm really Thalia's Soulmate?" Rede said hotly. "Do you think I'm so klasisa as to take advantage of her like that?"

I know you're her Soulmate, Genna said. *I want to be sure you can look after her. And yourself.*

"Of course I can!" Rede snapped.

I don't doubt your intentions, Genna said slowly, controlling her evident exasperation. *But I have to know if you're capable of carrying them out. Let me access you.*

Exhaling rapidly, eyes blazing, Rede walked over to her, and Thalia's mom handed him the music sphere. She touched his heart and forehead and closed her eyes. The blue and silver sphere changed color, and the intricate music fell as if to the floor, tinkling like icicles landing on hard snow. The music that emanated now was dark and sorrowful, shot through with threads of hopeful beauty and strains of longing.

Genna finished. She handed the now green and purple sphere to Thalia, who gazed at it in awe.

"Well?" Rede said, still wounded but not as belligerent as before.

I don't know, Genna said, but she was looking at him differently.

Grimacing, Rede stared at the floor.

What do you think? Genna asked him. *Do* you *think you can deal with whatever happens and keep a cool head?*

Rede looked up, and Thalia couldn't believe the expression on his face. *I don't know,* he said.

I can look after both of us, Thalia volunteered, taking Rede's hand. *You don't know anyone stronger than I am,* she said to her mother. *Uncle Solymi told me.*

"Rede could take care of her physically if she needed it," Hyad said. Thalia groaned in frustration, but he ignored her. "And she could take care of him if the situation became emotionally overwhelming." He sat on the bed and spoke in a very small voice. "I can't endanger their Soulmate connection. I just can't."

Genna crossed her arms and leaned against the door. *You should have taken time for yourself. You're not thinking clearly. I don't know how I'm going to tell Zeph about what you said to Thalia, and the possible danger you put her in. Get Thalia safely to the Otherworld then take some time off before you do something you'll really regret. You're not yourself, Hyad,* she said, some empathy returned to her voice. *Take some time to grieve for Solymi.*

"I couldn't take any time off," he said. *I can't.*

"Well?" Rede asked. "What are we going to do?"

I'll talk to Thalia's father, Genna said. *Hyad will smuggle you both into the Otherworld tonight. I can't see any other way.*

CHAPTER FORTY-NINE

People were lining up on the sidewalk to wait for taxis. Joe glanced around.

"Have you ever been to New York City before?" he asked Emma.

She shook her head. "Have you?"

"No," he said. "Actually, I was here once when I was a baby. Right after my wings were cut off. But I don't remember anything."

"Why were you here?" Emma asked.

"I don't know." He pointed in the direction the taxis were headed. "Let's start walking."

They passed a hot dog cart. Joe turned around and bought two and another bottle of water.

"This is awesome," Emma said, nearly finished with her hot dog before they'd walked half a block. "Maude won't eat these."

"Why?" Joe asked, consuming his more slowly. "You have ketchup on your nose, by the way."

"*Charlotte's Web*," Emma explained, rubbing her nose with the back of her hand. "She won't eat bacon either. Is it still there?"

"We have napkins," Joe said, laughing. "And no, it's gone. You're all clean. Well, maybe not your hand." He passed her a wad of paper.

"You're the worst," she said, licking the ketchup off her hand and drying it with a napkin. "Satisfied, Captain Perfect?"

"Yes," he said. "And it's Sex King of All Known Worlds to you."

"Hmm," Emma said. "We'll see about that."

"Not all hot dogs are made of pork, you know," Joe said, finishing his. "That was really good." He looked back at the cart. "These are made of beef. Did Maude love any kids-book cows?"

Emma smiled and took his hand. "I don't think so. I guess we never saw any."

After they'd walked a few blocks she said, "Look!" Someone was drawing a jungle scene on a huge chalkboard laid out on the sidewalk. Emma grinned at the artist and said, "Wow!"

"Wait here," Joe said. "I have an idea about how we can communicate about the thing you can't talk about." He left Emma on the sidewalk and entered a store with art supplies in the window. A few minutes later he came back out with a little chalkboard, a box of chalk, and a sponge.

"Is there any water left?" he asked.

"This one is half full," Emma said, handing over a bottle.

Joe soaked his sponge in water and wrung it out. He knelt near the artist. "Is this a copy of something?" he asked. "It looks familiar. My mom's an artist," he added, not wanting to sound snotty.

"Rousseau," the woman said. "'The Equatorial Jungle.'"

"Cool," Joe said.

The artist nodded then went back to her work. "Thanks."

"Have you ever heard the story of Tolstoy's brother?" Joe asked her.

"What?" The woman was filling in silver grasses at the bottom of the painting.

"Tolstoy," Joe repeated. "He wrote *Anna Karenina* and *War and Peace*."

The woman sighed. "I know who Tolstoy is."

Joe ignored her irritation and obvious lack of interest in anything he said to say. "When Tolstoy was a kid, his brother told him he had to stand outside until he could stop thinking about white bears."

"That wasn't very nice," the woman said, adding what looked like a speck of moon to the pale sky. "It's pretty cold in Russia."

"Yeah, it is," Joe agreed. "How can anyone think and not think about something at the same time? It seems impossible. Right?"

The woman leaned back on her heels. She gestured to the drawings and watercolors lined up in boxes on the sidewalk. "Do you want to buy something?"

"No," Joe said. "Sorry. Thanks, though." He stood up and wrote, *I know you can. That's how you got out of the detainee tower the first time. Remember?* on his chalkboard, showed it to Emma, and then immediately erased it with his sponge.

Emma nodded once. "Let's keep walking," she said.

Joe tucked the damp chalkboard under his arm and followed her to the corner. Across the street was a huge building with lion statues in front.

"Hey!" he said. "That's the New York Public Library. Did you ever read *CATNYP*, by Delia Sherman?"

"No," Emma said.

"It's a really cool fantasy set in the New York Public Library. A changeling girl named Neef makes a bet that humans know more about love than fairies, so she goes to the library for help to prove it. CATNYP is the library's search engine. He's a lion on a marble pedestal. When you ask him a question, he gives you mice who tell you the answer. I was obsessed with it when I was eleven. I so wanted it to be true at the Wolfeboro library. I kept hoping I was a changeling."

"You kind of were in a way," Emma said.

"Yeah," Joe replied. "I guess I was. Not like I thought, though."

A bus passed so noisily that they both jumped.

"Can you talk more about why we're here," Joe asked, "and how we're going to accomplish what we need to accomplish if you both think and don't think about it? Do you want the chalkboard to try?"

Emma took the chalkboard but could only scribble nonsense. She tried to speak but again seemed to choke on her tongue. She exhaled and said, "Remember when Gryphon touched my mouth and made me talk about Maude without knowing I was doing it?"

Joe felt a wave of jealousy remembering the handsome young gemynd running his thumb over Emma's mouth. "Yeah."

"This is the opposite," Emma said. "Instead of saying things I don't know I'm saying, I can't say what I want to say. Even if I'm trying to hide it by thinking about something else at the same time."

"What?" Joe said, stepping nearer as she made a strange face and stepped away. "Are you okay?"

"I wonder if that's how secreting works."

"What do you mean?"

"Secreted gemynd can't communicate anything they want or need except basic requests for food and shelter," Emma said. "I wonder if whatever Lukas did to prevent me from saying anything about why we're here works on the same principal."

Joe watched a group of tall, backpack-wearing people climb the library steps and position themselves at the feet of the lion statues, while one of them laughed loudly and took pictures. He said, "Why would Lukas send me here with you and make it impossible for us to talk about why we're here?"

"I don't know," Emma said. Her face was emotionless, but Joe knew she was terrified that they wouldn't be able to find Sandy in time.

Sandy. He cringed as the name rang through his head, but nothing dire happened, no buzz of awareness that someone was listening or that Commonworld filters had somehow picked up on anything.

"*I* can think about it," he said.

"What?"

"I can think about what you can't say," he told her. "Maybe Lukas did something to me so I could safely think about it. It seems ridiculous that he wouldn't stop both of us unless there was a good reason. He doesn't seem the type to under-think things."

Both Joe and Emma stood pondering. The crowd across the street and at the corner moved in unison as soon as the light changed. An old woman holding an empty soda bottle and standing near a garbage can stared at them. She looked crazy. Moving her mouth oddly like she was trying to say something, she leaned over the trash can, shaking her head and saying something.

"That's so sad," Joe said. "Nobody should have to live on the street. We suck hardcore at taking care of the people who need the most help, and we're only getting worse. That's one thing they do a little better in the Commonworld. Although, Aubrey would probably disagree."

The light changed again. The old woman tried to run across the street into oncoming traffic. A big man wearing a beautiful suit pulled her back. She stared at Emma and Joe once more then shook the last few drops of liquid out of the bottle, rubbed the mouth on her shirt and crossed the street to the library.

Emma suddenly grabbed Joe's hand. "Let's follow her."

The woman ran up the library steps and in through the doors. Joe turned to see if someone was chasing her, but no one was left on the wide stair except for him and Emma. Inside, a security guard searched the woman's bag and made her leave the water bottle even though it was empty. She tried to argue with him and then gave up.

She never turned to look at Joe or Emma, though they were right behind her.

Why are we following her? Joe asked.

When she looked at me, I felt something, Emma said.

Isn't that a bad thing? Joe asked. *Maybe it's some kind of trap.*

It wasn't, Emma replied.

How can you tell?

I just can, Emma said.

They followed the woman through the library. She never turned around or acknowledged them. In front of a door marked RESTRICTED she stopped and squeezed her eyes shut tight, shaking her head back and forth as if she was trying to escape something or decide something. With an expression of frustration that didn't sound like a real word, the woman finally banged her head once against the door and wandered off, again without talking to or looking at Emma and Joe.

"Wait," Emma called after her.

The woman stopped and shuddered slightly then kept walking.

Turn around, Emma said. *If you can hear me, turn around.*

"I'm thirsty," the woman called out, still walking all the way down the hall and back to the wide stairs. "They took my water. I'm so thirsty."

Emma shook her head. *I guess I was wrong,* she said to the woman who apparently couldn't hear her. *I thought I knew who you were. I thought you knew me. Maybe I just wanted it to be true.* Then, giving Joe's hand a squeeze, she opened the door and went into the restricted room.

"God," she whispered. "This is Maude's dream room. Old books, shiny wooden shelves, and library ladders."

A woman wearing a lipstick-red sweater glanced up from an old-fashioned desk. She looked like a librarian in a picture book, from her straight, chin-length black hair to the black cat-eye glasses hanging from a glittery chain around her neck. "This is a restricted-use room," she said to Joe in a smooth, tart voice. "You have to get a pass from registration."

"We just wanted…," Emma began, and the woman's attention shot to her as if she'd just uttered an unforgivable curse word. The woman put down her long pen, stared at Emma then looked away, chewing her lip.

Joe pulled Emma a little closer and turned to see if the door was still open. The woman stood up without saying anything and pulled a blue leather volume from a shelf near a sunlit window. The title on the cover was etched in delicate, swirly gold letters like the name of an old king. The woman put on her glasses and handed the book to Emma, whom Joe felt contort with a shiver of electric awareness.

Symbols in Art and Poetry of the Romantic Period by Fen Elos.

"What kind of room is this?" Emma asked.

The woman raised her head and examined Emma through her glasses. "What did you come here for?"

"We followed someone," Emma said.

The woman cocked her head and glanced out the still open door. "There hasn't been anyone near this room in months. Except for you."

"We followed an old woman," Emma said. "She smashed her head on the window of the door. You must have heard it."

"That's not what I meant and you know it," Red Sweater said. *"What did you come here for?* This room is restricted. You have to tell me why you're here or I cannot let you stay."

"I can't tell you," Emma said.

"Then I'm sorry." The woman shook her head. "I can't allow you to stay." She took the book from Emma, returned it to the shelf and sat again at her desk.

"She can't tell you," Joe said, "but I can."

Red Sweater smiled kindly at him. "You can't tell me anything," she said, "as your lovely friend is well aware." *He seems very sweet for an Otherworlder,* she added to Emma.

Emma was scanning the titles on nearby shelves. "We don't even know what to look for," she said to Joe before turning back to the woman. "That's why we're here. Something—something important—is lost. And…" She stopped, unable to continue.

"And we don't know where it is or how to find it," Joe said.

"What is lost?" the woman asked, still patient but not persuaded.

"She can't tell you," Joe said. "She can't tell anyone. Not even if she wanted to. Not because she's afraid, but because she is physically incapable of saying anything about it."

Red Sweater looked harder at Joe.

"Why is this place here?" he asked.

"This is a safe room, isn't it?" Emma said. "You're..." She gazed penetratingly at the woman, who stepped back. "You're Fen Elos's many-times-great-granddaughter. This is a kind of sanctuary." Emma looked around again. "The entire room is an inaccessible spot."

The woman spoke quietly. "How did you know? There are protections in place."

"She's a Thoryba Exocho," Joe said. "A super-powerful one."

"And what are you?" Red Sweater asked.

Joe felt hot. "I'm a Volucris," he said. "My wings were cut off. I'm wearing an identity shield."

"I can't see your shield," Red Sweater said. "I can see hers."

Emma kept staring at the woman. After a few moments she turned to Joe, clearly wanting him to say something for her.

"I can't hear what you want, Emma," he said.

Emma turned back to the woman and stared pleadingly at her.

Joe ran both hands over his hair. He felt dizzy. "Okay," he said to Emma, deciding on a course of action. "I'll speak very slowly. If I start to say something other than what you want me to say, hit me or something. Okay? I'm just guessing," he added, shoving his hands in and out of his pockets. "I can't hear what you want me to say."

He turned to the woman. "Is Emma right? Is the whole room inaccessible?"

Red Sweater nodded. She went to secure the door.

Joe glanced back at Emma, his heart pounding in his throat. "I don't know," he said. "I don't know what you want me to say."

The woman scrutinized Emma. "Do you want to know if you can trust me?"

Joe watched Emma's face and saw nothing but desperation to communicate.

"Someone...," he began haltingly. "Someone innocent is in danger. The only way we can save him is to bring him to the Ones in Power."

Red Sweater's expression of sympathetic expectation shut like a door. "I'm sorry," she said. "I can't help you."

Emma made a sound of despair, and her dark blue eyes were impossibly wide.

"*Please* stop me if I'm wrong," Joe whispered to her. Red Sweater's arms were folded across her chest, covering the cat-eye glasses and shining chain. Joe took a short breath and said, "I'm...Sfodro Vatic. I'm Eury Vatic's son."

The woman dropped her arms and opened her mouth. "Oh," she said, nearly inaudible.

Joe stared hard again at Emma. "Emma," he said, looking at her, "is my Soulmate."

Emma was almost panting.

"God," Joe said. "*Can* you stop me if you have to?"

"My grandfather trusted me to protect this place and all the gemynd who come here seeking some kind of refuge," Red Sweater said. "I haven't failed him."

Joe felt like he was going to cry or puke or both. "Okay," he said to Emma, whose wild expression yielded nothing. "Okay," he said again, and turned back to Fen Elos's granddaughter.

"Emma's little brother Sandy is my father's Whole Chronicler. The Ones in Power know, and the Resisters will know soon if they don't already. Because of my father's death and the destruction of the extrication lights they used on him, Emma's brother is the only link to any possibility of understanding how Whole Listening works until the next Whole Listener is born two thousand years from now."

Emma's breathing slowed. Red Sweater looked astonished.

"But that isn't everything," Joe said, glancing once more at Emma, who was pale and trembling. "The Singers of the Apocalypse failed to—"

"The Singers of the Apocalypse are a myth," Red Sweater interrupted.

Joe growled. "Whatever. We don't have time to prove anything about that," he said to Emma then turned back to Red Sweater. "Can you help us figure out where Sandy might be hiding? There's been an edict."

The woman paled. "What can *I* do?" she asked. "How can *I* help you? I'm a Chronicler like my grandfather. I'm a guardian of this place. I am no warrior."

"You must know a lot about the Commonworld," Joe said. "Maybe you could help us figure out where someone could safely hide from Gatherers. Sandy is with a Crossworlder, a Soulskin, a Revealer, and an Anaxio who is probably smarter than all of them combined. Wherever the safest place is, they will have figured it out. Now we have to."

CHAPTER FIFTY

Thalia laid one hand on the rough bark of the portal tree and turned around. In the dark, Hyad's fierce amber face looked tarnished and thin. Rede had insisted on moving through the tree first, in case there was anything dangerous on the other side. Thalia would have argued, but he moved through without giving her a chance. She'd never moved through a portal tree before. She'd never been to the Otherworld.

Her birthday, her manifestation, would happen at midnight tomorrow night. Before she and Rede left, her mother had told her that she might feel the changes begin as early as tomorrow morning. Thalia felt like she'd already experienced too many changes, but maybe that was part of it. She wished she'd known more about manifesting before it happened. When she had kids she'd tell them everything about it so they'd be prepared.

Zino had been even more reluctant than Genna to let her travel to the Otherworld alone with Rede, but he relented when Hyad told him that the Gatherers would use extrication lights on Thalia if they captured her to learn everything they could about Emma.

Are you staying with us? Thalia asked Hyad, who had placed his hand on the branch above Thalia's.

"No," Hyad said. "I'm going to see you safely situated, and then…" He stopped and turned around. "Move through," he whispered. "Someone is coming."

Thalia passed through the tree. It felt a little different—thicker, sharper—than she thought it would. Maybe her manifestation was already beginning. Maybe somehow her parents had confused her actual birth date and she was going to turn fifteen inside this tree. It had been almost midnight when they left her house a little while ago.

She emerged in the Otherworld and saw Rede's worried face. He helped her down.

Are you okay? he asked, placing her gently on the uneven ground. *Did it hurt or something?*

Thalia blushed. *I'm fine.*

She stepped away from the tree to make room for Hyad. They stood on a rocky hill near a narrow stone archway. It was brighter here than it had been at home; there was a weird gray humming light, as if this world wasn't capable of real darkness. Or maybe it was closer to dawn here, though that's not what it looked like. Was there a time difference? Thalia suddenly wasn't sure.

We're in a city, Rede said as Hyad emerged from the tree and jumped down. *That's why it's so bright.* He pointed to a wall of lit buildings lining the sky above the trees then asked Hyad, "Where are we going? Are we sleeping here in this park?"

"No." Hyad looked around but avoided Thalia's gaze. "Solymi and I kept an apartment near here. Before our Soulmate revelation my family was"—he brushed a cluster of dirt and leaves from his pants—"inhospitable to Solymi because he was Aponomi. My mother refused to accept him until after the revelation, and even then she didn't like him, although she was never unkind again." He exhaled and then added, "Solymi and I came here to be alone." He looked around once more. "Come on."

He led them through the brush and over small hills and rocks until they came to a bridge spanning a neck of dark water freckled with light from the buildings above.

What is that noise? Thalia asked.

"Cars," Hyad explained. "Vehicles similar to a kima. Most of them run on combustion and produce a considerable amount of noise and smoke."

Thalia made a face and crossed the bridge. At the top of a little rise was a smooth black roadway. She didn't see any cars, noisy or otherwise.

"The cars are on the street outside the park," Hyad said, pointing to a gate.

Were her unspoken thoughts so loud? Thalia wondered.

"Now," Hyad said when they reached the gate. "Remember what your parents said. Stay indoors until your manifestation is complete." Thalia moved to speak, but Hyad interrupted, answering the question she hadn't asked. "You'll know. It isn't subtle."

Thalia tried not to blush.

"After it's over," Hyad continued, "come back here." He pointed down the hills to the arched stone bridge where the portal tree was. "Memorize this gate and how to get back to the tree. I'll make sure you have enough food for a few days."

"Where will you be?" Rede asked.

Thalia turned. Hyad's beautiful amber face seemed to fall apart.

You? she said, reading his thoughts before he had time to block them. *You have to fulfill the edict and execute Emma's brother?*

She felt suddenly hot and sweaty. Somehow she had stopped thinking about Emma's little brother. All Commonworlders were taught from infancy to strive constantly for the good of as many gemynd as possible. The killing of this little boy—as tragic as it was—meant saving everyone else. Wasn't every other life worth one? The phrase "acceptable consequences" rose violently in her head, and Thalia felt sick.

It's tragic, yes, Hyad said in an empty-sounding voice. *But necessary. Nomos Apodektos, Acceptable Consequences. That doesn't make it any less horrifying.*

I didn't think it would be you, Thalia replied. *I didn't know I'd have to see it. If it's you, I'll have to see it. Because of Uncle Solymi and my protanosi, I'll have to see it.*

Rede laced his fingers through hers, and Thalia sensed something more than his need to protect and soothe her.

What did my mom see when you let her access you? she asked him. *What did Emma see when we met her on the street with Hyad?*

Rede looked away for a minute. *If it's okay with you, I don't want to talk about it yet.* He turned back to her. *I will. I promise. But not yet.*

"Come on," Hyad said, glancing over his shoulder though no one was there. "I want to get you two safely into the apartment."

They walked through the gate and onto something like a footpath.

"Is the apartment inaccessible?" Rede asked as they crossed the street under a light that periodically changed colors. Green, yellow, red.

"No," Hyad said, "but it's protected somewhat. It used to belong to a Crossworlder, who instead of making it inaccessible embedded strands of energy into the walls and floors and ceilings every time she came here. For decades. If the filters tried to access the interior, there would be too much mingled energy to easily distinguish any one thread from another. And there has never been a large singular energy release here that would have warranted a more thorough access."

"What about Thalia's manifestation?" Rede asked. "That's a huge, singular energy release."

"The apartment is now so embedded that Thalia's manifestation will be readily absorbed into the chaos of the energy already present," Hyad replied. "That's why her parents and I think it's the safest place for you to hide."

Thalia had stopped walking.

Do you need to rest? Hyad asked.

Please don't do it, she said. *There has to be another way. There has to be.*

"You know there isn't," Hyad said. "The Ones in Power can't place any one life above all others. It has to be done now, and quickly. I'm the only one."

What if it was Solymi's? Thalia asked. *Would you have killed him to save everyone else in the world?*

"No," Hyad said. "But no one would have asked me to."

No one said anything more as they walked past restaurants with humans eating outside, talking and laughing.

Why do you think he's here in the Otherworld? Thalia asked.

Hyad turned around, that terrible expression in his eyes again. "The less you know, the better. Come on. This is it."

They entered a building and rode an elevator up five floors. Walking down a hallway, they stopped before a door. Thalia felt Hyad shudder as he forced himself to unlock it with a carved, flat metal object, and then as he forced himself to enter the room beyond.

Oh, she said, jerking back.

What? Rede asked, perpetually concerned of danger to her.

Can't you feel the intense concentration of energy in here? She crossed her arms over her chest.

Kind of, Rede said, *but it's more like a distant sound than something right up close.*

I can feel it like it's inside my skin, Thalia said.

Well, you're a Mask, he said. *I'm a Chronicler. Our sensitivities are different.*

It wasn't a particularly brilliant thing to say, but something about how Rede said it acknowledged their differences and the way their differences touched and intertwined. And the way Rede looked at her when he said it made Thalia feel hot and cold, heavy and light, drawn inexorably to him like he was the shore and she was a curl of ocean water.

She didn't mean to kiss him, not in Uncle Solymi and Hyad's secret house, and not so passionately, but the instant Rede's cool skin touched hers, Thalia forgot where she was until Hyad's pain at Solymi's loss threaded into heart and reminded her that she and Rede were not the only gemynd in the world. Again, without meaning to, the impulse to Mask herself into Solymi was so urgent Thalia had to struggle against it.

Inside Hyad's thoughts of Solymi, and his sorrow, and her own fight to keep from Masking herself into Solymi, Thalia heard something else. Maybe because there was so much noisy energy in the room already, or maybe because Hyad's emotions were so close to the surface, but for whatever reason Thalia heard what Hyad had been successfully blocking since Rede suggested hiding in the Otherworld: Emma was coming here with Joe. Someone, one working for the Ones in Power, was working *against* the edict and was sending Emma and Joe here so that they could find Emma's brother and bring him back to the Commonworld unhurt. Hyad knew this, and he planned to follow Emma and find her brother before she could save him.

Almost without effort, Thalia opened herself up and Masked into Solymi, young and incomparably beautiful on the day of his Soulmate Revelation. In response, Hyad made an unearthly sound.

"I'm sorry, I'm sorry," Thalia repeated in Solymi's lilting baritone, and she was successful. Hyad's sorrow was so intense and overwhelming that he never realized what she had heard.

Or that she planned to stop him.

CHAPTER FIFTY-ONE

After hours spent looking through books and talking, Emma, Joe and the librarian, whose name was Una Elos, came up with nothing.

"The library closes in fifteen minutes," Una said, glancing at a clock.

"We have nowhere to go," Emma said, feeling embarrassed.

Una gathered the last few books they'd looked through and put them back on the shelves.

"How did Lukas think we'd be able to do anything with no money?" Joe asked quietly.

"I don't know," Emma said.

"You can stay with me tonight," Una suggested. "And I'll give you some money. But after tonight you'll have to stay somewhere else."

Joe's face darkened.

"That this library succeeds as a sanctuary is due to the careful work of generations of gemynd who have protected its secret," Una said to Joe. "I cannot put that at risk."

Joe stood up. "You do realize what's at stake?" he said, his eyes flashing.

"Yes," Una said. "I realize what's at stake. But I can't help you any more than I have already." She turned off the lights in the main section of the room and retreated to the back corner where one other still shone. "Wait outside. I'll be right there." She stopped walking and turned around. "Only this room is inaccessible. Please keep your thoughts and voices quiet in the hall."

"Okay," Emma said.

She left with Joe, who tripped over a book on the floor just outside the door. He quietly cursed and brushed off his knees.

"Who left a book here?" he muttered.

Emma picked up the green clothbound tome. "*The Poems of John Keats*," she read out loud, carefully turning the browned tissue paper that separated the title and dedication pages. She held the open book to Joe. "Look at this. The editor dedicated the book to his wife because Keats was the first poet they loved together. Sweet."

"Nice," Joe said, "but what was it doing on the floor? And you sound like Maude."

Before Emma could respond, Una came out. "Where did you get that?" she asked, turning around to lock the door.

"It was on the floor," Emma said, and handed her the book.

Una pushed her glasses up her nose and frowned. "It's from the general library," she said. "It's not one of ours." She tucked the book under her arm. "We'll have to return it to circulation before we leave."

They walked down the hall and the wide steps. Una said, "My grandfather loved Keats."

"So does my dad," Emma said.

Joe and Una walked ahead. An idea chewed at the bottom of Emma's stomach, but she kept it at the edge of her thoughts as she ran to catch up. "Are there rules about who can come into the library and how long they stay?" she asked Una as they entered a cavernous room.

"Anyone can come into a public Otherworld library," Una said, sliding the Keats book onto a table. "You must have a library card to borrow a book. And you cannot enter the stacks. But anyone can come and read and stay as long as the library is open."

Emma stared at the Keats book. The idea in her stomach made her heart beat too quickly, and she took a calming breath. Then she looked at Una. "Do you live near here?"

"Good night!" Una called to a security guard. "Not far. About thirty blocks. I like to walk, if that's all right with you."

"Sure," Emma said, looking around.

"What?" Joe said. "What are you looking for?"

Emma ignored him. "Is your apartment…anything like the place where you work?"

Una regarded her strangely. Emma felt Joe watching her, too, but she waited and did not look at him.

"Is it inaccessible?" Joe clarified, guessing at last what Emma wanted.

"No," Una said. "That's why I can only let you stay one night. Come."

"What?" Joe whispered to Emma.

She shook her head.

The homeless woman they'd followed into the library that morning was leaning against a wall near the revolving door. A security guard was telling her that the library was closing in five minutes. The woman nodded her head but didn't move to leave.

She was thin and younger-seeming than Emma thought earlier. Her skin was lined and her features angular. Her sharp chin hung like a pendant at the end of her face. Beneath feathery gray bangs, the woman's dark eyes were penetrating and bright.

When she saw Emma, Joe and Una, the expression on her face didn't change at all, but Emma saw her narrow chest rapidly rise and fall. Emma glanced at Joe and then moved toward the woman.

"Do not give her money," Una said. Her voice was hushed and piercing in Emma's ear. "Look at her. She'll use it for drugs. The kindest thing you can do is let her alone. There are agencies to help people like her. Professionals. Leave her."

The whole time Una was talking, the woman never took her eyes off Emma.

"We have to leave," Una said. "The library is closing."

The security guard looked at the homeless woman and pointed to his watch.

"Wait," Emma said through clenched teeth. She walked up to the homeless woman and took her skinny hand. Dry, cracked skin scraped against Emma's palm, but the hand felt incongruously strong and heavy for an instant.

Joe took Emma's other hand. The woman opened her mouth to speak but said nothing.

"'Heard melodies are sweet,'" Emma said, reciting a line from her father's favorite Keats poem, "'but those unheard/Are sweeter; therefore, ye soft pipes, play on."

Tears poured from the woman's eyes.

Emma choked back a sob. "Dad?"

CHAPTER FIFTY-TWO

The woman said nothing but kept crying. Emma just stared at her.

"What are you doing?" Una asked, her voice quiet now.

"Let's go outside," Joe said, leading all of them through the revolving door. As soon as they were outside he asked, "Is there a safe place to talk around here? It's too bad we can't go back inside."

"Any place is as safe as the next," Una said, watching the security guard lock the door. "It's not like home. The filters aren't everywhere all the time, and they have to work a lot harder here when they do latch on to something. We're safe enough. Just be careful."

The four of them sat at the base of one of the lion statues.

"*He* left the book in front of the door," Emma said, pointing to the homeless woman. "I think it took him all day to do it. Are you hungry? Are you tired?" she asked.

The woman nodded. Emma stood up and paced. She heard Una ask Joe, "What is going on?"

Emma sat near the homeless woman, who still hadn't taken her eyes off her. "My dad is bald," she said, gazing back. "He has blue skin, and he teaches environmental science at a college near our house. He loves Emerson and Keats, and my mom, and my brothers and sisters and me."

The woman, her expression unchanged, did not wipe the tears from her face.

Emma moved closer. "When I try to talk about the reason I am here, my tongue feels fat in my mouth and I can't breathe. No matter how hard I try, I can't say what I want to say. The feeling disappears as soon as I try to say anything else."

The woman pulled a surprisingly clean wad of Starbucks napkins from her pocket. Taking a deep breath, she pressed the napkins to her eyes then sat up straight and stared intently at Emma. Kissing the top of Emma's head, she said in a clear voice, "I'm hungry. I like sandwiches. I'm thirsty. I want water. I'm cold. I need a blanket. I'm hungry. I like soup. I'm thirsty. I want juice. I'm tired. I need a bed."

Emma burst into tears, and the woman held her, kissing her head and brushing her hair from her eyes. Una glanced from the two of them to Joe.

"What do you know about the secreting system?" he asked.

"It began as a weapon," Una said, seeming stunned that Joe would know about it. "Developed after the Fourth Revolution as a deterrent to target the worst threats, it later became a secret prison." Una stared at the homeless woman with an expression of growing disbelief. "There were rumors that developing the weapon required experiments on gemynd that broke Sacerian law far exceeding any boundaries of Acceptable Consequences. After gemynd protested in huge numbers, the Ones in Power abandoned work on the weapon— or so we were told. All records and chronicles were destroyed."

Joe rubbed Emma's back and nodded to the homeless woman. *"This* is the secreting system," he said.

As the four of them walked to Una's neighborhood, Joe explained how the secreting system worked and Emma explained how she'd realized that the woman walking with them was not a woman at all but her father, unalterably Masked by the Synektos weapon to look like this middle-aged female human.

"There is no way for the Ones in Power to track them," Emma said suddenly to Una. "They didn't want to risk revelation in any way. So you and my dad would be safe if he stays with you. If that's okay."

Emma's father stopped walking.

"How could you help us?" Emma asked him, guessing at his reason. "I know you want to, but you couldn't say anything you want to say. You couldn't advise us, and you couldn't warn us if you thought we were doing something wrong. Stay with Una. She has books. I'll find Mom and I'll…" Emma choked, curtailed from saying what she wanted about Sandy. "I'll find Mom as soon as I can. And I'll bring her to you."

She took a long breath. "You won't recognize her, you know. Ever again."

"I'm so hungry," Dad said—in the saddest voice Emma had heard since Maude told her about Gryphon's book. "I'm so hungry. I'm so hungry."

"Una could take you to her library sanctuary, Mr. Mathews," Joe suggested. "Every system has a flaw or a weakness. Maybe you could figure out how to say what you want from there."

Dad said nothing.

"You can stay with me," Una confirmed.

Emma turned her head and watched the cars in the street stop and move forward again. She clenched her teeth and rubbed her eyes then turned to Joe. "I don't know what I would do if we were permanently separated."

"And yet," he said, his voice full of sorrow. "That's what you were going to do to me. You were going to give in to the Singers. And you would have, too, if Lukas hadn't prevented it."

Dad grabbed Emma's face and gazed hard at her. "I don't want that bread," he said. "Not that bread today."

"Come," Una said gently. "This is my building."

Once they were inside, Una said to Emma's dad, "You must want to take a shower." She looked him up and down. "I think we're nearly the same size, though I'm a little taller."

"He only looks the same size," Joe said. "This is a version of a Mask. Mr. Mathews is the same size as I am." *I wonder what happens when a secreted person takes off his clothes,* Joe added to Emma. *Do they look like themselves, or like a naked version of who they've been secreted to look like?*

I don't know, Emma replied, *but I don't want to think about my Dad as a naked man or a naked woman.*

Una was silent for a minute. "All right," she said, "I'll see what I can find. I'll leave the clothes on the bed. And unless you have a reason not to, throw away what you're wearing. It's too filthy to wash."

"Thank you," Dad said as she disappeared into the other room.

Emma smiled at him, and he smiled back before going to take a shower.

"Do you think his clothes were Masked, too?" Emma asked Joe. "Like when he takes off the clothes that look like women's clothes they'll look like his own again?"

"I'm going to make dinner," Una said, appearing after finding something clean for Dad to wear.

"Did my dad's clothes look like men's clothes after he took them off?" Emma asked. "I mean, if he left them where you could see them before he took a shower."

"Yes," Una said quietly. "The clothes he left on the chair were men's clothes. A blue plaid shirt and jeans."

"Do you need help with dinner?" Joe asked.

"No, thank you," Una said. "Sit down for a little while. Rest."

Emma and Joe both sat on the couch. Emma kicked off her shoes and laid her head in Joe's lap. He stroked her hair, and she wished she could sleep. She also wished she could magically figure out where Sandy had hidden himself.

"It seems that your dad can say whether he wants or doesn't want something," Joe pointed out.

"Yes," Emma said, "but only if it has something to do with food or shelter." She rolled over and looked up at him. "Why? What are you thinking?"

Joe looked down at her. "I love you. Don't ever leave me."

She reached up and caressed his cheek. "I love you, too."

Joe kissed her fingers and sighed before continuing. "When Una mentioned your mom, your dad clearly wanted to say something about her, but all he could say was 'I'm so hungry.' When I mentioned the Singers and how you wanted to surrender to them he said, 'I don't want that bread.' I think he was trying to tell you not to do something, probably to not give in to the Singers. So…maybe he can indicate yes or no, no matter what the question is."

The shower turned off, and cooking smells drifted out from the small kitchen. In a few minutes Dad came out of the bathroom, his longish gray-brown hair hanging to his shoulders. He was wearing brown corduroy pants that only came down to his calves and a long black shirt that looked like a nightgown.

Emma ran over and kissed him. He hugged her back, tight.

"Hey!" she said suddenly. "What about mirrors? Is your real face visible in a mirror?" She pulled him over him to a large mirror hanging on a wall, the story of Saint George and the dragon told in pictures on the red wooden frame. "Oh," Emma said sadly at the false face reflected in the glass. "I guess they thought of almost everything."

"What do you see, Mr. Mathews?" Joe asked. "Can you see your own face?"

"Yes, thank you," Dad said, staring sorrowfully at the mirror. "I feel clean now. Thank you."

"It's okay, Dad," Emma said, moving him away from the mirror. "We know who you are and you know who you are. We'll just explain it to everyone else."

Dad turned. "I'm hungry. I'm hungry!"

"Maude—," Emma began, but Joe took over.

Maude, Elizabeth, Sandy and Mr. Spencer are hiding with an Anaxio named Aubrey, he said. *I believe I can think about what Emma can't say without filters picking it up, and your thoughts aren't accessible by anyone. At least, they shouldn't be if what we believe is true.*

"Aubrey helped us when we went back to the Commonworld to find you and Mom," Emma said.

Dad winced at the mention of Mom.

"I think Turner is with Rachel," Joe said. "When I left, they were together and he was okay."

"Joe thinks you can communicate yes or no," Emma said to her father. "He thinks you were trying to tell me not to surrender to the Singers when you said you didn't want bread."

Dad's gray eyes lit up. "I'm hungry," he said, smiling hopefully.

Emma looked excitedly at Joe. "Maybe we could create a code made up of the words he can say. Maybe it's even better than just yes or no."

"I think we could," Joe agreed, "but we don't have time now. We have to figure out how to find Sandy."

"Joe's dad is dead," Emma told her father, trying to catch him up. Neither of her parents would know what had happened to Eury Vatic. "And he didn't give in to the Singers."

"But," Joe added, knowing what Emma could not say, "Sandy is hiding and in danger, and we have to find him."

Emma watched a realization form in her dad's eyes. He hadn't known Sandy was Eury Vatic's Whole Chronicler, but Sandy's obsession with making comic books and his weird presentiments in combination with needing to hide had always been strange. She was pretty sure Dad would put two and two together. If not, however, she couldn't explain it, so she looked to Joe for help.

"Yes," Joe said, answering the unspoken question in Mr. Mathews's eyes. "The Ones in Power know. And they know the truth about the Singers as well." When Joe exhaled, Emma realized he didn't want to tell Dad the worst part, that there was an edict for Sandy's execution.

Dad's eyes widened. "I don't want to wear this shirt," he said, pulling at it wildly but not taking it off. "I don't want to wear this shirt."

Emma made a deal with the Ones in Power, Joe said, putting his hands on Dad's shoulders. *That's why we're here. That's what she can't talk about. We're here to find Sandy first and bring him back before any other Gatherers or the Singers find him.*

"But we don't know...," Emma began. She couldn't finish, so she began again. "We spent the day in the library."

"Maybe your dad *can* help," Joe said. Then he turned and explained what they'd been looking for in the library. "Mr. Spencer had to choose a place to hide where the Singers and the Gatherers wouldn't think to look, and he had to think of it quickly. He had Maude and Aubrey to help him, though. Like Maude, Aubrey is really well-read. Unlike Maude, he's read almost everything about the Commonworld." Joe glanced toward the kitchen doorway. "If you're wondering how an Anaxio got books, Fen Elos gave them to him."

Dad sat on the couch.

"Dinner's almost ready," Una called from the kitchen. "You and Joe should wash your hands, Emma."

Una's cadence was so like Mom's at first, Emma smiled. Then Dad's anguished eyes caught her. She sat beside him on the couch, and he picked up a strand of her hair and then let it drop against her shoulder.

"We'll find Mom," Emma promised.

Dad squeezed her hand and stood up.

CHAPTER FIFTY-THREE

"Why did you do that?" Rede asked Thalia as the Mask of Uncle Solymi dripped off her. "You must have known that he couldn't bear it. That was your Uncle Solymi, wasn't it? It had to be, to have caused that kind of reaction."

Thalia pulled away and ran to Hyad, who sat on a chair near the door, his head in his hands. She knelt at his feet.

I'm sorry, she said. *I'm sorry. I don't know what's going on. I can hardly control myself.*

Hyad breathed slowly and pushed her away. "Just give me a minute," he said in a hollow voice. "Just a minute."

Thalia stood up. She and Rede left Hyad alone and went into the living room.

They sat on opposite ends of a casement alcove, their feet almost touching. The broad, high window overlooked a huge park, which seemed to cut the city in half.

Uncle Solymi was so different from Hyad, Thalia remarked, keeping her plans to help Emma out of her thoughts until Hyad was gone. *He was always laughing at something, and he said everything he thought.*

Rede pressed his toes into hers. She smiled at him.

My mom said that after their revelation they were almost constantly kissing. Everywhere. The statue in Syndesi Park is of the two of them. After the last power shift, one of the Three Leaders felt that the Soulmate connection should be publicly commemorated. She commissioned a Transformist who lived near Hyad and Uncle Solymi to make that kissing statue of them.

Rede leaned forward and held Thalia's hands, swinging them a little in the moonlight pouring in through the window. *Are you sad about manifesting alone?* he asked. *With just me?*

Thalia glanced at him. *Yeah,* she said. *I am. Even though I pretended to my mom—and to myself a little—that I didn't care about the ceremony, that it was mostly for her, I never imagined I would be separated from my family and no one would be with me.*

Except me, Rede said.

Thalia sighed and pushed her feet into his, forcing him to bend his legs.

Hey, he said. *You definitely feel stronger.*

Thalia looked at her legs, and she pushed Rede's feet so hard that his knees almost touched his chest.

Hey! he said, laughing.

You're right, she said. *I am stronger.* She stared at her arms and legs and hands. *Do I look different?*

Rede crawled toward her. He slid her onto her back and lay on top of her. *You look perfect,* he said, kissing her neck.

Thalia felt strange, so she sucked in a mouthful of air. Rede kissed her throat and her mouth, and she kissed him back but as if she were two gemynd existing in one body. She felt him twice, his mouth on hers, and his kiss everywhere. It was greater than before. Not like at home when she'd kissed him; now Thalia felt like she was actually more than herself alone. Like she was Rede *and* herself *and* their connection. Like she was the love that existed between them. This was even better than the kiss she'd wanted, the kiss she'd dreamed of when she read *The Uske*. It felt so much better than she'd ever imagined.

Rede's breathing changed. He pressed his weight more urgently into her then raised himself onto his elbows to stare. *You feel different,* he said, roughly and out of breath.

I know, she said, running her hands over the small of his back. *I feel different to me, too.*

He kissed her neck. Thalia opened her eyes. She watched flashing lights from street below play with the glass ceiling lamp.

Rede made a sound like a song and seemed to melt into her again. She slid the tips of her fingers into the waistband of his jeans and pulled him closer. *He* felt different pressed so tightly against her. Someday, someday soon, when she was a little older, they would do more than kiss. Would it hurt? Would it be scary? Would she like it? Would it be even better than swallowing fire?

Rede brushed the hair from her cheek. *I don't know,* he said, answering Thalia's unspoken thought. *I hope it doesn't hurt. It didn't hurt me when I had sex with the Fallwell. Is it supposed to hurt?*

I don't know, Thalia said.

It wasn't scary, he said. *It was kind of weird. But she wasn't you.*

The sweet weight and heat of him on top of her mixed with her fear of the unknown. *Maybe it's a little bit of both,* she said, *raising her hips slightly into his.*

He sighed. Then, *What do you mean?*

"Scary and awesome," she said. Like trying anything new. She kissed him. *Sometimes scary is part of the awesome.*

Rede hummed and kissed her back, longer and harder than before.

Hyad, Thalia said, struggling to pull herself away from surrendering completely to the moment. *If he comes in,* she explained to Rede. *It might be painful for him.*

You're right, Rede said, up on his elbows again. *You're right.* He groaned and pushed away.

Do I look different? Thalia whispered, unable to help herself.

Rede exhaled and pressed his long back against the alcove wall. *You already asked me that.*

Did I? Thalia said. *I don't remember.*

Hyad walked in. She turned to the doorway and repeated, *I'm so sorry. It won't happen again.*

"It's not your fault," Hyad said in the papery voice of someone who has been ill for days and just come out of the sickroom. He took a calming breath. "This is the beginning of your manifestation. Your powers will increase, but your ability to control them will diminish. That's why you accessed Solymi so readily." He closed his eyes, and Thalia saw he had something clutched in his hand. "Why you couldn't stop yourself from Masking into him."

Is there anything else I should be prepared for? Rede asked, coloring slightly. *I didn't know anything—anything* true*—about Invisibles before I met Thalia.*

Hyad exhaled again. "Her emotions and her thinking will become increasingly erratic as manifestation gets closer. She'll worry more, feel anger more intensely, feel…feel love more intensely."

What's in your hand? Thalia blurted.

Hyad smiled. "That's a bit of what I'm talking about." He squeezed the thing once then opened his fingers so Thalia and Rede could see. A small reddish stone lay in the palm of his hand. "Carnelian," he said. "Fleshstone."

I thought fleshstone was luminous, Thalia said, glancing at Rede. *Does it look luminous to you? Can I not see it as it really is?*

It doesn't look luminous to me, Rede said in a reassuring voice.

Reassuring? She felt thunderously angry. *Are you telling me the truth?*

You know I am, Rede said. *You can hear what I'm thinking.*

Thalia dropped her head and stared at the floor.

"Fleshstones are luminous when they're cut and polished," Hyad said, cradling the stone in his hand again. "This one isn't. I gave it to Solymi on the day we met. He kept it with him until we bought this apartment. Then he insisted that we keep it here." Hyad smiled and frowned almost in the same moment. "To ward off bad luck."

He turned and went into the kitchen. "There is no food here now," he called out after a minute, sounding somewhat recovered. "I'll go out and get something. Then I'll leave you two alone." He reentered the living room. "Remember you have to go home as soon as Thalia's manifestation is complete."

You're not sleeping here? Rede asked. *It's the middle of the night.*

"I can't stay," Hyad said. "I can't waste any more time."

Where are you going to get food? Rede asked. *It's the middle of the night.*

"In this city," Hyad said, glancing at Thalia with concern, "a food business is always open somewhere."

He walked over to Thalia, who was sitting on the windowsill staring at her knees, which looked darker and more opaque than they had a few moments ago. He kissed her head and lifted her chin so that she gazed directly at him, and he said, "Some of what you're going to feel will be exaggerated to the point of being untrustworthy. Don't act or make any decisions based on those feelings. Let Rede guide you."

He turned to Rede next, who looked anxiously at Thalia. After a moment, Hyad glanced back at her. "Did your parents prepare you?"

Yes, Thalia said. She leapt off the windowsill and crossed the room to a table covered with reading stones and Revealer images of Hyad and Solymi preserved in crystal. *No. I don't remember. I think they did. I feel like we talked about it forever. I feel like we talked about this until my ears fell off.*

"How can there be a celebration of this?" Rede asked quietly. "It seems horrible."

It's not horrible! Thalia shouted before sitting on the floor.

"At the usual ceremony," Hyad said, "all the guests combine their energies to soften the worst of the emotional and physical volatility. You'll have to take care of her on your own. I had hoped that the embedded energy here would dull her feelings, but I'm afraid it seems to have had the opposite effect. And there's no time for me to find you both better accommodation that will also protect you from the filters."

Rede nodded. "Hurry back with some food," he said. "Maybe that will help."

"I'll be back as soon as possible," Hyad promised, and he left the apartment.

Rede moved to sit on the floor next to Thalia, but she didn't look at him.

I want my mom, she said. *I want my mom.*

CHAPTER FIFTY-FOUR

"What did your grandfather tell you about the Singers of the Apocalypse?" Emma asked Una. She and Joe and Dad were just sitting down to dinner. "In the kitchen a few minutes ago it seemed like you were saying that he told you the truth at some point."

"He told me they were a myth," Una said, pouring a lemony-smelling sauce over chicken and vegetables, "and I didn't have any reason to question him. No one did. But a few years ago I found a book he'd misplaced in the library here. It belonged in the Otherworld section of the library. It was a small book about their Utopian ideas—Robert Southey's and Samuel Coleridge's pantisocracy plans, among others. When I went to return it, several sheets of very old paper fell out. They meticulously chronicled the retreat from Sacerian culture by a group of Crossworlders after the death of one's Soulmate."

At the mention of Southey and Coleridge, Dad glanced up from his food.

"Dad loves poetry," Emma said. "My sister Maude does, too. I'm sure she would know what pantisocracy means."

Dad squeezed Emma's hand.

"What are your brothers' and sisters' powers?" Una asked.

"Turner is telekinetic, Maude is a Soulskin, Elizabeth is a Revealer, and…" Emma exhaled forcefully and glanced at Joe.

"And you know what her youngest brother is. Did the notes you found talk about the Singers?"

"Not exactly," Una said, "but there were allusions to destruction and 'purification' that I found confusing. When I asked my grandfather he refused to explain, which was so uncharacteristic that I researched on my own."

"So you discovered the truth on your own, and eventually your grandfather had to admit it?" Joe asked.

Una smiled at him, and then at Dad, who seemed to understand what that smiling meant. Emma certainly didn't. Unless it was the OMG-kids-are-so-cute smile that irritated anyone under twenty.

"It's been a very long time since I met a young Commonworlder," she said. "Most gemynd who've come to the library are grown."

Joe blushed and took a bite of his food, his eyes down.

"I'm not trying to embarrass you, Joe," Una said. "I like your questions. I like your energy and your enthusiasm."

Joe sighed. "Thanks," he said, still not looking up.

"Well, to answer your question," Una said, "after centuries of witnessing the horrors we in both worlds inflict on one another again and again, seeming to learn nothing, a group of Crossworlders and their Soulmates seceded from Sacerian culture and set up a kind of new world for themselves modeled on Otherworld utopias. They chose a lush valley between two granite monoliths where they could manipulate the abundance of quartz to render filters almost useless. They didn't want to be followed or found by anyone who didn't share their disgust with Sacerian and Otherworld culture. The new society they created fell apart when Ioletta, a Lucent and the Soulmate of Sidiro, the Crossworlder founder of the utopia, died. I don't think she was much older than twenty-two. No one had chronicled the failure of that utopia in centuries, and I thought the perspective of a middle-aged gemynd who had not yet met her Soulmate might prove interesting."

"How did Ioletta die?" Emma asked.

"She fell into a very large, unidentified portal that was uncovered when a field was being plowed," Una said. "Only a Soulskin can see an unidentified portal, and a Lucent cannot safely travel through any of them."

"That still doesn't answer my question," Joe said, seemingly recovered from the embarrassment of having his energy and enthusiasm enthusiastically admired.

Una swallowed her smile. "You're right," she said, "it doesn't. When I was finished, I wanted to work with a Revealer and make the chronicle public. My grandfather told me I couldn't, that it would raise too many questions. I was angry and said I would make it public anyway. Finally, he told me why I couldn't. What I had meant to be a story to ease the pain of gemynd who had lost their

Soulmates, or who, like me, were older and hadn't met them yet, turned out to be the reason for a danger too powerful to be widely known. So, except for the reading stones and chronicles that my grandfather hid somewhere, there are no chronicles, nothing written anywhere, to link the Singers of the Apocalypse with that failed utopia. Nothing to prove that they are real."

Dad jerked back suddenly and accidentally spilled his wine.

"Are you okay?" Emma asked.

Dad stared at Una. "More juice, please."

"Of course," Una said, standing up. "But it's not juice. It's wine. I thought you'd rather have something that tasted familiar."

"More juice please," Dad said again, emphatically.

"Of course," Una said, blushing.

"Wait," Joe said before she went into the kitchen. "He understands you. He knows it's wine. He wants something else."

"Yes, please," Dad said, "more juice."

"The story," Emma said. "Something about the story you were telling."

"There isn't anything more," Una said.

Dad, his eyes frantic, looked from Emma to Joe.

"We don't know what you mean," Emma said.

Dad got up from the table and paced the room, staring down at the carpet and repeating, "I'm so hungry. I'm so hungry."

"Is it...?" Emma began, but she couldn't finish.

"Is it about Sandy?" Joe asked.

Dad exhaled. "More juice, please."

"Something about the story made you think of where Sandy might be?" Joe said.

Dad said nothing.

"Or Mom," Emma said. "Something about the story made you think you know where Mom is?"

Dad looked at Una.

"I haven't met my Soulmate yet," Una said gently. "I don't know how—"

"More juice, please," Dad said excitedly. "More juice please."

"What were you going to say?" Joe asked Una.

"Just that, although I haven't felt what he feels being separated from his Soulmate," Una said, "I can sympathize..."

She stopped talking, and Dad's eyes blazed.

"Sidiro and Ioletta," Una said. "Sidiro never returned to the place where Ioletta died. He couldn't bear it. And because my grandfather made the Singers into a myth, very few Commonworlders, even those who work in Information Extraction, would know anything about the real origins."

"Juice," Dad said, almost ecstatic with relief. "Juice."

"Did you say your sister Maude is a Soulskin?" Una said.

Emma nodded. "Yes."

Una covered her eyes with her hands and thought for a minute. "If your friend Mr. Spencer only had moments to decide where to hide, he would have wanted to utilize his powers and your sister's. A Crossworlder has the benefit of centuries of reading and knowledge, and a Soulskin can see unidentified portals. Mr. Spencer would have had to think of a way to use Maude's power and his own."

"Aubrey is smarter than all of them," Joe spoke up. "He probably started looking right away for remote places difficult for the filters to access and within a day's drive of Warwick."

Una frowned a little. "I thought you said today that he was Worthless."

"He has read almost everything there is to read about the Commonworld," Joe said. "Your grandfather gave him books and reading stones. Is knowledge worthless?"

Una blushed. Probably because she'd never thought of Anaxio as anything other than something to be dismissed.

Joe took a deep breath and turned to Emma's dad. "Do you think that, because Maude lost Gryphon so recently and she's a Soulskin who can see unidentified portals, she and Mr. Spencer and Aubrey thought the failed utopia location was a safe hiding place even though it's in the Commonworld? They can all move through a portal. Even Aubrey. You just have to think yourself through."

"Juice," Dad said with some effort, and Emma realized he could only repeat his limited vocabulary when a physical need was immediate or hadn't been mentioned in a while.

"Do you know where it is?" Joe asked Una.

"I know both locations," Una said. "Sidiro wasn't satisfied with the small number of able hands in the group. He wanted to persuade like-minded humans to join them. He'd seen enough of both worlds to know that there were humans just as disgusted as he was with an endless history of cruelty and immoral behavior. A few weeks before

Ioletta's death, he and the other Crossworlders expanded the utopia into the Otherworld."

"Where is it?" Emma asked, glancing at Dad. He was clutching the edge of the table like he might fall.

"In the Commonworld it's between the two great forests," she said. "Here in the Otherworld it's in Massachusetts. In Concord. My grandfather, in fact, thought the enormous portal and the manipulated quartz on the other side might have been what attracted the great flowering of thinkers there."

"Thank you for dinner," Dad said.

"Concord?" Joe said. "Where in Concord?"

"I'm not sure," Una said. "I spent more time thinking about the Commonworld side of the portal. But it should be easy to figure out." She walked over to a huge bookcase that covered the wall separating the main room from the bedroom. "There are almost always stories of what Otherworlders call 'the supernatural' connected with a portal."

"That's what Aubrey guessed when I was trying to find a portal to get back to the Commonworld and Emma," Joe said, gazing at her. "I'll bet he reminded Mr. Spencer and Maude about that, too."

"I'm sorry," Emma said to him.

"About what?"

"About trying to give in to the Singers," she said quietly.

Dad had followed Una to the bookcase. He turned, his lined face calm but his eyes full of sorrow.

"I'm sorry, Dad," Emma said.

Dad closed his eyes for a second and breathed deeply.

Una handed him a book. "If you find something useful, will you be able to show me?" she asked.

Dad opened his mouth but couldn't speak.

Emma walked over. "I think he might be able to find something useful," she said, keeping her eyes fixed to her father's face, "but I don't know if he'd be able to show you. Today in the library, whenever I found anything I thought might help I had to concentrate really hard to be able to ask either of you to even look at it."

"Can you write what you want to express?" Una asked. Her face brightened. "Can you impart what you want to say onto a reading stone? I have several."

"He can't write or impart anything," Emma said. "The Ones in Power made sure there would be no way out for victims of the secreting system." She smiled at her dad. "But I don't think it ever occurred to them that someone might find their way *into* it."

Joe stood up and said to Emma, "If he finds something, he can leave the book open on the table."

"Why are you telling me?" Emma asked. "He can hear you."

"I think if I tell you instead of your dad it might be easier for him," Joe pointed out.

Dad handed back the book Una gave him and took from the shelf a brown clothbound volume with a bird on a tiny branch embossed on the cover.

"In the same way he was able to leave that book on the floor in the library," Joe said, his eyes still on Emma alone, "I think, if he finds something useful and then immediately thinks about wanting food or sleep or shelter, he'll be able to leave the book open on the table and walk away. Indirect progress. It's our best hope."

CHAPTER FIFTY-FIVE

Maybe you should try to sleep or something, Rede said to Thalia. *Until Hyad gets back.*

Thalia laughed and jumped up. *Wow,* she said, beaming wildly at him before staring down at her feet, then stomping loudly on the floor. *I feel like I could break anything in either world.*

That's a weird thing to say, Rede said.

She jumped onto the windowsill then off it again. "Look!" she said, "I didn't fall." She burst out laughing. "I feel great!"

Rede glanced at the door.

"He won't be back for a while," Thalia said. "Wow!" she shouted once and then again. "My voice is *loud.* I sound like a Synithi. Misos!"

"Should you calm down?" Rede asked.

"Don't be scared," Thalia said. "I'm not going to hurt myself. Or you."

"I didn't think you would hurt me."

Thalia stood nearer to him. For a second, a shimmer of clear light rose from her hair and skin.

"Oh," Rede said in awe. "You look so…"

Thalia smiled then frowned and shook her head like there was something in her hair.

"What?" Rede said.

"Emma," Thalia replied, glancing at the door. "Emma is here in the Otherworld—or if she's not here now she'll be here soon. She's going to try to save her brother." Thalia walked to the door and listened. "Hyad is here to stop her."

"How do you know?" Rede asked.

"I heard it," Thalia said, "under his thoughts. That's why I Masked into Solymi, so he wouldn't know I'd heard." She made a noise and shook herself again, as if she wanted to physically force her manifestation to completion. "He feels terrible about it. It shouldn't be him. Not now. Not so soon after Solymi's death. But there wasn't anyone else. The Three Leaders are trying to severely limit the number of gemynd who truly know anything."

"Wait," Rede said, terrified. "You're not going to try to help her, are you?"

Thalia said nothing.

"Thalia," he implored. "You can't. He'll figure it out and stop you. And you're vulnerable."

"I...," she said, her throat full of her new beautiful voice. "I am stronger now than I have ever been or ever will be."

Rede turned away.

"Emma's brother is only a few years older than Maddie," Thalia said.

"Children die all the time," Rede almost shouted, desperate to change her mind.

Thalia stepped back. "I know Emma. We're friends."

Rede wanted to tear out his hair. "I promised your mother I'd protect you."

"I'm going to help Emma and her brother," Thalia stated. "I'm—" She stopped, and the new deepening color of her face paled. "He's in the hall. Misos, I wish there was an inaccessible place in this apartment. I have to access Emma and warn her before he goes after her. But, how?"

Rede almost sobbed. Then he swore and said, "Stand where the energy is most intense."

* * *

Thalia ran to the place where she felt the thickest web of energy and tried to warn Emma. She sent out a call with her mind that Hyad was looking for her.

Hyad opened the door and entered the room. Rede moved to stand in the way, but Hyad made a motion with a hand then ran to catch him as he fell toward the table. "He's not hurt," he promised as he lowered Rede to the ground. Then he grabbed Thalia's head.

"Stop it!" Thalia screamed, trying and failing to block Hyad from accessing her thoughts.

Effortlessly—as if she were made of spiderweb—Hyad picked her up and sat her on the floor next to Rede. She felt Hyad sever her connection to Emma as easily as cutting a piece of string. Thalia jumped to her feet and tried to hit him, but Hyad held her back with a wave of energy she couldn't penetrate.

"Misos, Thalia," he begged. "Do not force me to injure you." He grabbed at his hair and stared frantically around the apartment, as if this was all a dream and soon he would wake up with Solymi beside him. Turning wild-eyed from Thalia, he went into the hall and brought in the food he'd gone to acquire. Thalia wondered what to do next.

"He's falling apart," Rede said when Hyad disappeared into the kitchen to put the food away. "This is what your mom meant when she said he needed to take time for himself before he did something he couldn't undo. We have to be careful."

"What's wrong with you?" Thalia asked, hearing how strangely exhausted he sounded. She dropped down next to him and propped him against her. "What did he do to you?"

"He drained my energy," Rede said, sounding like he was going to pass out. "It's…kind of like the opposite of drawing up someone's adrenaline."

Hyad returned to the living room, where he silently began applying something nearly invisible to the floors and walls and ceilings of the entire apartment. Thalia considered trying to stop him, but she couldn't get through the wave of energy he'd made, and she didn't want Hyad to hurt Rede in order to stop her. At this point she wouldn't put anything past him.

"I've left enough food for three days," Hyad said. "And the apartment has its own water source. The preventatives I just applied will dissipate after three days. By then I will have accomplished what I came here for, and you can return home." He pressed his hands to his face then looked at Thalia. "I'm sorry for trapping you here," he said, his voice breaking. "I'm sorry for the rest. I'm sorry it has to be done, and I'm sorry it's me. But one life—even an innocent one—isn't worth every life." Hyad shut his eyes and whispered something Thalia could not hear. Then, laying the carnelian on the table near an image of Solymi, he left the apartment.

Thalia slid away from Rede, who fell to the floor, banging his head.

"Oh!" she said. "I'm sorry."

With effort, Rede slipped a hand under his cheek and separated it from the floor. "It's okay," he said slowly. "I hardly felt it."

Thalia lay on the floor facing him. He smiled at her, and she kissed him. She shivered as another burst of light erupted from her skin and then disappeared, leaving a stain of darker color behind.

"You're beautiful," Rede whispered, elongating every syllable so it seemed to Thalia that he was singing instead of speaking.

She kissed him again, and a scent of something—spice, flowers, and animal—rose thick and heavy between them. Embarrassed, she moved away, but Rede murmured something soft and breathed in the scent as if he were drinking her out of the air.

Oh, he said in his singing voice.

Thalia folded him into her arms. They lay there for what seemed to be both too long and much too short a time.

"Do you think it's wrong?" she asked after long while, reluctant to break the silence but unable to stay still any longer.

Rede breathed slowly. "What?"

"To try to save one gemynd at the possible risk of everyone else."

Clumsily Rede lifted his arms and wrapped them around her. "That's an unanswerable question," he said, kissing her head and hiding his face in her hair, which was steadily darkening, coloring itself, lilac-like, in an imitation of the dawn now fat and threatening between the buildings.

What happened to you? she asked, thought-speaking because she didn't want to hear her voice in her ears.

"I can't tell you yet," he said, his mouth and face still hidden in her hair.

Was it that terrible? she whispered.

Rede sucked in a mouthful of air and said nothing.

What if you weren't here? she asked.

He pushed away slightly to look at her and stroked her cheek.

There is an Otherworld way of thinking, she said, *that I read about during one of those interminably long events forbidden to Invisibles at school. They make us wait in the Otherworld section of the library where we can't access what's going on. It's supposed to be humiliating, but most of us believe we're so much stronger and smarter because we don't have everything handed to us. Sometimes we write chronicles or create Revealer images that mock everyone else. But we always destroy them before the Enforcement Director comes to* beneficently *take us back to class. I hate her.*

Rede shuddered and opened his mouth to speak.

"Quiet," she said, kissing his forehead. "You didn't make the world. And anyway," she added, realizing it was wholly true, "I'm happy with myself the way I am. I felt sorry for Synithi before I knew they felt sorry for us."

Rede laughed softly and kissed her.

He was shaking, so she rubbed his arms. "Are you cold?"

He nodded.

Thalia got up and found a blanket. She brought it to her face before draping it over Rede and said, "It smells like them. Solymi and Hyad."

Rede sighed at the warmth of the blanket. Thalia lay beside him again.

"That Otherworld way of thinking says that if you save one life, it's as if you save an entire world," she said.

Rede turned away.

"That's what I believe," she continued. "I don't believe in acceptable consequences. I believe every life has value. I have to help Emma save her brother."

"Okay," he said.

Thalia kissed his slow, exhausted mouth then stood up. "Do you know how Hyad drained your energy?"

"Not really," Rede said. "Worse, I don't know how to replenish it."

Thalia looked around the small apartment. "Do you think we could use the energy in the walls?"

"Maybe," he said. "But it would have to be similar to my own. How would—?"

Thalia beamed. "I know everything about your energy," she said. "I feel you swimming inside me every time we kiss."

"Really?" Rede said, moving to get up then deciding against it.

"Yes," she said, more invigorated than she'd ever felt. "And I think I could differentiate and identify the embedded energy threads here." She spun once on her heels. "I feel like I can hear everything, see everything, feel everything."

"Well, that sucks for me," Rede said, almost laughing. "I can't get off the floor."

"You can't touch me once the last stage of the manifestation begins," she pointed out, leaning smilingly over him. "Only after it's complete."

Rede muttered a soft curse and closed his eyes.

Thalia began searching the floors and walls and ceiling for a thread of energy that matched his, keeping at the back of her thoughts her fear about how little time they had to find Emma.

CHAPTER FIFTY-SIX

"Why do you have so many books about Concord, Massachusetts?" Emma asked after she and Joe and Una had been looking for nearly an hour. Dad sat alone, painstakingly turning the pages of the brown book he'd taken from the shelf.

"I wanted to include something about the Otherworld side of the portal," Una said, "but I never had time. The chronicle was only half-finished when my grandfather told me why I couldn't make it public." She closed the book she was looking through. "I had to destroy it."

Dad pushed himself away from the table, so slowly and so clumsily Emma thought for a second something was seriously wrong.

"I'm tired," he said, sounding exhausted and then walking unevenly away from the open book on the table.

"Of course," Una said, rushing over. "Come. You can sleep in my bed. I'll sleep on the couch and Joe and Emma can sleep on the floor."

Dad's eyes flashed.

"They're young," Una said. "They'll be fine."

Dad swayed and glanced painfully at Emma. "No, thank you," he said to Una. He spoke with difficulty, as if his mouth were filled with open sores. "I'm not tired."

"Dad," Emma said. "You look terrible. You should sleep."

"No thank you," he said again. "I'm not tired."

"I'm sure you'd rather be home in your own bed," Una said soothingly, "but—"

Dad turned his head quickly and almost lost his balance. Una caught him. He just stared at her, his eyes blazing.

"Can he go home?" Una asked Joe and Emma. "If secreted gemynd can't be traced or accessed, why couldn't I bring him to your home? I could explain who he is to friends or family. Are your family all Resisters? Eleytheria are more than ready to believe in the perfidy of the secreting system."

Emma watched her dad's face as Uma spoke, exhausted and emotionless except for his eyes, which were almost impossible to look at. "We don't live in the Commonworld," she said. "We live here. In New Hampshire."

"What? Why?" Una said. "Why would any gemynd who isn't a Crossworlder choose to live here?"

"You do," Emma said, surprised at the woman's vehemence.

"I made a promise to my grandfather," Una said. "I miss home every day of my life."

Dad exhaled and faltered. Joe moved to help Una hold him up.

"Well, our home is here," Emma said, glancing gratefully at Joe. "Is that what you want, though, Dad? Do you want to go home?"

"Who would watch over you?" Joe asked him. "No one in New Hampshire would recognize you, and we couldn't explain who you are to anyone left. The family is gone."

"Except Turner," Emma said, keeping her attention on her Dad's face. "You said you thought Turner was with Rachel. He can watch Dad. And maybe he and Rachel could help Dad find Mom."

"I want a blanket," Dad said suddenly.

"We don't have time to take him home," Joe said. He turned. "I'm sorry, sir, but I know you want us to find Sandy first."

"I'll take him to New Hampshire," Una said. "I'll explain the secreting system to your brother."

Dad sighed and said, "I am tired."

Una gave him a kind look. "Joe, will you help Emma's father…?" She paused. "What is your name?" she asked Dad. "I'm sorry. I never thought to ask."

"His name is Peter," Emma said. "Peter Mathews."

Dad's eyes lit up.

"Joe," Una said again, "will you help Mr. Mathews into the bedroom?"

Joe took Dad's arm, but Dad wouldn't move. Panting and concentrating as if he were about to jump out of an airplane or run through hot coals, Dad slowly turned his head toward the open book on the table.

"Oh my God," Emma said. "We're idiots. The book."

She and Una ran to read it.

"There isn't anything about ghosts here," Emma said, about to turn the page.

"Don't," Una said, stopping her. She read the pages to herself. "Why do you think the answer is here?" she asked Dad.

"What does it say?" Joe asked, not letting go of Dad's arm. His knees were shaking.

"Let him sit down," Emma said, but her dad wouldn't move.

"What does it say?" Joe asked again.

Una kept her hand on the page Dad had left open and closed the book in order to read the title. "It's a biography of Henry Thoreau." She opened the book again, tracing sentences with her finger. "The pages are about Louisa May Alcott as a child, Thoreau's love of frogs and spring, paragraphs about a day at Walden Pond when he fed squirrels and crows out of his hand."

"Do you think the portal is at Walden Pond?" Joe asked Dad.

Dad said nothing.

"Is there anything else?" Joe asked.

"Emerson and a group of women sitting in the shade while Thoreau helps children find berry bushes," Una said, glancing up at him helplessly.

Emma leaned over the book. She slid Una's fingers off the page and read aloud, "'On Lexington Road, Bronson Alcott had purchased a small farm.'"

Dad exhaled. "I'm ready for bed," he said slowly.

"Wayside," Joe said. "The Alcotts lived at Wayside on Lexington Road. They called it Hillside. They planted crops across the street. The inspiration for *Little Women* came from the years the Alcotts spent there."

"How do you *know* that?" Emma said.

Joe blushed and glanced into the kitchen where dirty pots and pans were still strewn all over the single countertop. "When I was little, my mom, my Otherworld mom, only bought books she had read before. Her family was poor. They only had a few books in the house, and their town had no library. I've read *Little Women* about ten times." Still blushing, he turned to Dad. "Do you think the portal is at Wayside? It's a museum now."

"I am very tired," Dad said.

Joe nodded. "In the morning, Emma and I will go to Concord and Una will take you home to Turner."

Emma was about to thank Joe when a thought-voice pierced her ear like a single, electric shock.

"Oh my God," she said. "He knows we're here. He followed me."

CHAPTER FIFTY-SEVEN

Rede slept all day and into the evening. Thalia did not.

"I think I found it," she called out at last, turning away from a bit of wall space between the bed and the bedroom window. She went back into the living room and knelt beside Rede, shaking him gently until he woke up.

"What?" he said breathlessly. "Are you all right? What time is it? Was I sleeping?"

"Yes," she said, kissing his forehead. "Calm down. I'm fine. Are you okay?"

He nodded. She smiled at him and stroked his cheek.

"I think I found several energy threads that are a near enough match to yours," she said. "I just don't know how to extract or inject them." She frowned and touched Rede's still cold forehead. "If I figure it out, I'm going to inject a small thread into myself first to make sure it will be safe for you."

"No," Rede said, attempting to sit up and groaning.

"I'm only going to use a little," she said. "I can't experiment on you."

"Yes, you can," he said. "I'm fine."

"Shut up," Thalia said, standing. "You're not fine."

She spun once again on her heels. "*I'm* fine," she said, grinning at him then shaking it off. "It's so weird to feel terrified and sad and happy at the same time. I've felt all those things since we came here. Almost constantly."

"Which is why you shouldn't inject yourself with strange energy," Rede said.

"A little," Thalia clarified. "Just a little."

"Please." Rede shook his head. "Don't. Your energy is unstable. You don't know how it might react."

Thalia considered for a minute then shrugged. "I have to do it anyway."

Rede groaned and mutely smashed his fist into the floor.

"I just don't know how to get it out of the wall," Thalia said, ignoring him. "I don't think an ordinary puncture will do anything."

Rede sat up. "Please."

"Stop," Thalia said. "I'm going to do it. If you were stronger you could stop me. If you were stronger I wouldn't have to do it myself!" She exhaled like an overworked animal. "While I'm trying to extract the thread, you can work on figuring out how to get out of here."

Trembling and moaning slightly, Rede pulled himself to a standing position.

"No," he said. "If you're going to inject yourself with strange energy at the very moment your own energy is utterly volatile, I'm going to stand beside you in case you need help. What if you fall or collapse or can't control yourself?"

"Okay, fine," Thalia muttered, wrapping her arm around his waist, "but let me help you into the room."

She ushered him into the bedroom and sat him on the bed. She looked at the two pillows on the mattress and realized that Hyad would never kiss Solymi again here, or anywhere, never hear him speak again, never see his face again. Glancing gratefully at Rede, Thalia suddenly remembered…

"A fleshstone can act as an energy conduit, can't it?" She ran into the living room and grabbed the stone from the table.

Rede frowned. "Yes."

"Okay!" she said brightly. "I'll use the fleshstone to extract the thread and to scrape it into my skin. Then I'll listen to the way it reacts to the energy I feel from you, and if it reacts favorably I'll scrape another thread into your skin."

Rede closed his eyes. "That won't work. You'll have to have my energy inside you right then, not a memory of it, no matter how vivid it is, to be able to hear whether the thread matches."

"Are you trying to trick me into kissing you while I do this?" she teased.

"No," he said, not smiling. "I'm serious. It won't work any other way."

"Okay," she said, "I'll pull out the thread, kiss you, and then scrape it into my arm."

"Not where the dilitirio knife poisoned you," Rede ordered. "Use the other arm."

"How did you know about that?" Thalia asked.

Rede rolled his eyes. "Just because I'm not a genius Teknasma doesn't mean I'm an idiot. I know you, too. I feel things that have happened to you. Things you loved. Things you hated. The connection works both ways."

Thalia blushed. "Fine. Yes, I'll use the other arm."

She stepped close to the wall and took a deep breath, focused on where the thread of energy lay buried and tried not to be distracted by the strange wrongness of kissing for a practical reason.

"There is no bad reason for kissing," Rede argued, a slight smile in his voice.

Thalia exhaled and struck the stone into the chalky substance that made up the wall. Gently using the sharpest edge like a spoon, she caught a tangle of energy and pulled out a luminous vibrating thread, gasping to see it. Grinning briefly at Rede, whom she loved more than anything in the infinite universe, Thalia coiled the thread around the stone, kissed him, and cut the stone into her arm.

The swirling light disappeared into her skin with a sucking noise. Thalia tried to break away from Rede, but he held her close.

"Not yet," he whispered into her mouth. "Wait until the energies react. Stay with me."

Like she was on fire and freezing, flying and drowning, Thalia trembled, overwhelmed by thoughts and sensations in fierce conflict with one another. Hyad had been right; there were decades of energy contained within the wall's threads. She concentrated, trying to determine whether the new energy matched well enough with Rede's. What had she gotten herself into? Why had she thought this would work? Why had she thought she would know the right thing to do?

"Well," he said, pulling away at last. "Did it work?"

"I don't know," she said, her voice uneven. "I think so? I feel like I have a lifetime of moments occurring at once inside me."

Rede held her waist with one arm and took the still-vibrating fleshstone from her hand. Digging the stone into the opening in the wall, he pulled out a longer thread, coiled it around the stone, and sliced it into his calf.

He pushed Thalia violently away, suddenly drained of color and gasping for air.

"No," Thalia said, trying to get near him, but he wouldn't let her. "You took the wrong thread, didn't you? You should have let me do it! Why didn't you let me do it?"

Rede was still sucking at insufficient air, as if he'd lost the use of his lungs.

"No," Thalia repeated, glaring at him in disbelief and still fighting to get close. "You should have let me."

"I'm fine," he said at last, his voice dry, still holding her back. "I'm fine. I took more than I needed. I just have to calm down."

Thalia stepped back. After a few minutes Rede lowered his arm and let her come close. She pressed her hand to his chest and said, "Your heart is beating way too fast!"

"I know," he said, drawing in slow, steadying breaths. "Let me calm down."

He stared blankly out the window where the sun was beginning to set. Terrified, Thalia watched, praying all would be fine. The color indeed returned to Rede's face, if slowly, and when he finally looked at her again she threw her arms around him.

"Thank Misos," she said.

Rede kissed her head and exhaled once more. "We don't have much time. Hyad must be on his way to find Emma. Whatever she knows about her brother he'll get out of her and then incapacitate her until he can do what he came here to do. We have to get to her before he does. He has a head start, and we don't know how to disarm the preventatives he put up."

"The window," Thalia said, her thoughts coming clearer and faster, the air on her skin soft and palpable, the feel of her feet in her shoes and her shoes on the thick carpet almost incomprehensibly vivid and present. "The window."

"He did the window," Rede said. "I saw him do it."

"The way he did it, those preventatives only hold when the window is closed," Thalia said with a laugh. "They stay with the frame and glass."

"How do you know?"

"My parents taught us how to escape in different situations," Thalia said. "All Aponomi parents do."

"Why?" Rede asked.

"Sometimes Synithi imprison Invisibles for fun," Thalia said.

"But, Hyad—"

"I don't know," Thalia said as Rede grimaced. "All I know is that he didn't open the window and shield the opening. He probably hoped I'd be too distracted by helping you, or maybe he was thinking too erratically to realize his mistake. It's much, much harder—and more time-consuming—to shield an opening than something solid."

"So, what about the door?" Rede asked. "Can't we just open the door? It's the same principle and—"

"We can't *open* the door or the window," Thalia said. "We have to break the glass."

CHAPTER FIFTY-EIGHT

"Who is here?" Una asked. "Who followed you?"

"Hyad," Emma said. "I think Lukas has been trying to warn me about it since we got here, but whatever he did to make it seem that Joe and I were secreted worked well enough that he couldn't access me until now." She stopped and listened. "I couldn't hear the voice very distinctly, and now the connection is broken. I don't know what Hyad knows, if he knows exactly where we are, or if he just knows that Lukas sent me here."

"Who are Hyad and Lukas?" Una asked.

"They work in Information Extraction for the Ones in Power," Emma said. "Hyad is the one entrusted to fulfill the edict. Lukas..." She stopped and, swearing, turned away from the table.

Lukas is disobeying the edict, Joe said, continuing to explain where Emma could not. *He wants Emma to find Sandy and bring him back to the Commonworld.*

Dad made a noise like he was drowning.

Una glanced around the apartment. "You have no idea what Hyad knows other than the fact that you are here, and why you're here?"

"No idea," Emma agreed. "All I heard Lukas say was, 'Hyad knows and he followed you.' That's it." She paused. "It didn't sound like his voice, though. He must have distorted it somehow."

"Can Hyad access you?" Una asked.

Emma thought for a second. "I don't think so. Not yet anyway, though he will be able to soon, or the Ones in Power wouldn't have chosen him to fulfill the edict. I don't think he can access Joe at all unless he's physically near him. I think Lukas did something to protect Joe. That's why you didn't know he was a Commonworlder when you saw him."

"Hyad could access me, though," Una said. "If he knew about me."

Emma nodded.

Una closed the Thoreau biography and put it back on the shelf. "I'll take you to Concord tonight. It's nearly seven now and it's about a four-hour drive." She turned to Dad. "And then we'll go to New Hampshire."

Dad said nothing.

"Can either of you drive?" Una asked Joe and Emma. "I can drive and have a car, but it's getting late. It would be easier to share the trip."

"I can," Emma said, "but I don't have a lot of experience at night or on the highway."

"I can drive," Joe said, "but I don't have a license."

"I like my sweater," Dad mentioned brightly.

"Dad can drive," Emma said to Una. "You can trade off. But Dad has to sleep first. You drive to Concord, and Dad can drive home from there."

* * *

"Even if we can break the window," Rede said, "how are we going to get out? We're five floors above the ground."

"We'll make a rope," Thalia said distractedly. "You're good with your hands, right?"

"Yes," Rede said, "but—"

"But first we have to break the glass," Thalia said. "And, because of the preventatives we're only going to be able to do it with a knot of volatile energy."

"What!" Rede said.

"We'll have to pull a bunch of threads out of the wall, roll them into some kind of cohesive clump and throw it at the window." Thalia put her hands on her hips then shook her head impatiently. Was Rede too thickheaded to be any help at all?

"Are you crazy?" he said. "You can't just ball up random threads of energy and expect to touch them unscathed."

"Well, what do *you* think we should do?" Thalia shouted.

"I don't know," Rede said, taken aback. "Not that."

Thalia began pacing the small living room, feeling like an ember before a bellows. She felt like she could just run through the apartment door and it would break for her. She was sure of it, and she had nearly decided to try when Rede interrupted.

"Do you think Emma heard your warning? Do you think she knows Hyad followed her?"

"I don't know," Thalia said. "I couldn't tell. Hyad stopped me before I could hear a response."

"Before we do anything else, you should make sure Emma heard you."

"I can't," Thalia said, shaking her head again and moaning with frustration. "The preventatives completely seal off the apartment. We can't access anyone else, and no one can access us. We're helpless here. And useless. Unless we break free."

She sat on the floor and started to cry. Rede sat beside her and took her hand.

"Don't touch me," she screamed. "You can't help me."

He stood up and stepped away.

"What about a small amount of energy?" he asked after a moment, staring at the wall. "Do you think a small break in the window would be enough for you to be able to access Emma?"

"Maybe," Thalia whispered. "I don't know."

She stood up then cried out. Waves of colored light and a vibrating discordant sound poured like blood from her skin.

"Oh, Misos," Rede said, staring at her in horror and wonder.

Thalia looked down at her arms and legs and chest. "I'm scared," she almost whimpered.

"What time is it?" Rede looked around, frantic. "Where is the periskata clock in here?" He ran to the kitchen. "It's six-thirty. There are still five and half hours left before midnight."

"I'm scared," Thalia said again.

Rede ran back to her.

"No!" Thalia shrieked. "You can't touch me now." She looked down at her hands and her hair, and her feet, all shimmering with changing light and sound. "I wish my mom was here."

Rede stood close by. His hands, clenched into fists, circled slightly, as if he could hardly keep himself from reaching out and grabbing her. "We have to just stay here. It's too late. We can't leave now, not with you like this. Emma and her brother—"

"No," Thalia said again, and it sounded like she spoke with a thousand voices. All were her own. "No."

"We can't get out," Rede said, his arms pressed tightly to the sides of his body.

"Try your idea," Thalia gasped. "Use the fleshstone to pull out a single thread and try to make an opening in the window. Small or big, it doesn't matter."

Rede shook his head. "No. We have to stay."

"Oh," Thalia said in a cascading noise, the word falling rhythmically and melodically out of her mouth. "Oh," she sang again. "I see it. I see what you didn't want to show me."

She gazed at him, and her formerly pale eyes burst into bright color; she saw her reflection in the broad glass of the window, her green skin almost entirely opaque and her eyes like two violet moons beaming from her face.

Rede gasped.

"Break the window," Thalia commanded. "I can't touch the carnelian anymore. I see what you don't want to show me," she said again. "Please break the window. Let me try to help Emma's little brother."

Rede obeyed. He went into the bedroom and pulled a thread of energy from the hole in the wall. He glanced at Thalia, who kept repeating the same phrase like a single note, like a song that began too far back to remember and would continue to sound in a future too distant to comprehend, "I saw what you didn't want me to see. Break the glass."

With a terrible noise, Rede drew back his arm and smashed the stone coiled with bright energy into the window. The glass groaned and undulated. Panting and bent over, Rede stepped back. The fleshstone fell from his fingers.

The window undulated again. Then an opening the size of an egg yolk let in the noise of the evening city, and a rush of warm air circled Thalia like a caress.

CHAPTER FIFTY-NINE

Emma, Joe, Una and Dad were walking to the garage where Una kept her car when, hushed and feathery, a voice Emma almost didn't recognize sounded in her ear.

"Thalia?" She turned around.

Beside her, Joe looked up and down the empty street. Una and Dad stopped and waited beside him. "There isn't anyone else here," he said.

"I hear Thalia," Emma said as the voice continued to half-sing and half-whisper to her. "Wait."

While Joe explained who Thalia was to Una and Dad, Emma listened to the soft thought-voice.

Hyad knows you're here and he knows why you're here, Thalia said. *He's the one.*

I know, Emma said. *Lukas warned me. You shouldn't be talking to me. It's dangerous for you. I have to go.*

No. I warned you, Thalia said, not letting Emma break the connection. *Hyad hid Rede and me in an Otherworld city. He brought us here to protect me, but he's come to take care of Sandy.*

What about your manifestation? Emma asked.

It's begun, Thalia said. *By midnight tonight it will be complete.*

Are you in a safe place? Emma asked.

We're in an apartment Hyad and Uncle Solymi used when they wanted to get away, Thalia replied. *Yes, it's safe for me. But I want to help you. You can't stop Hyad on your own. Is Joe with you?*

Yes, Emma said. *But you can't help. It's too dangerous. Stay where you are. I have to go.* She took a breath. *Thanks, though, for wanting to help.*

Thalia ignored her. *Hyad is too powerful. You'll fail. He'll easily incapacitate you and Joe. You need Rede and me.*

Emma looked at Joe. He said, *What?*

"Thalia is somewhere in the Otherworld. Hyad hid her here for her own protection until her manifestation is complete. She wants to help us."

"How could she help us?" Joe asked. "We don't know where she is, and we don't have time to find her."

Emma glanced worriedly at Dad and Una. "She thinks Hyad will easily incapacitate both of us."

Dad sucked in air through his teeth.

"What is Hyad's power?" Una asked.

"He's a Seer," Emma said. "A Chamura. He works in Information Extraction in the detainee system."

Una looked at Dad then back at Emma. "She's right. You can't defend yourselves against a Chamura, especially one high up in the government." She shook her head. "Your only option is avoiding him. Let's go."

He'll find you. Thalia's voice sliced like a warm knife through Emma's heart. *Let me help you.*

How? Emma asked. *We don't have any time. We have to leave now. I don't know where you are.*

We're in an Otherworld city, Thalia said.

There are tens of thousands of Otherworld cities! Emma snapped. *I have to leave. I'm sorry. Thank you for trying to help.*

Thalia refused to break the connection.

Please, Emma said, terrified that this would somehow alert Hyad to where they were. She felt Thalia look out a window and down at a street filled with hurrying, chatting people coming home from work or going out for the night. Then she felt—as if Thalia were beside her or inside her—the girl dip swiftly into the thoughts of the people below until she had the information she wanted.

We're in New York City.

The girl accented the words oddly, as if she had never heard them before—which, Emma realized, she probably hadn't. A shiver went through her.

"They're here," she said to Joe. "Here in New York. Which means two things. Hyad is definitely close enough to find us quickly. And Thalia and Rede are close enough to help."

By reading other minds, Thalia quickly discovered where she and Rede were, and then she described how they had come up to their particular apartment. She passed this information on to Emma;

and as Emma, Joe, Una, and Dad drove to the address Thalia gave them, Una explained how the preventatives worked that Thalia described Hyad using. They could, she believed, get Thalia and Rede out of the apartment easily if Hyad had only applied them to the interior and not the outside of the apartment door.

The address was not far from Una's parking garage, but it seemed to take forever to get there. When they did arrive, going up inside the building and walking to the particular apartment door, Dad examined it.

"I want to sleep in there," he said.

"Are the preventatives on the outside?" Emma asked, looking at the smooth, mushroom-colored door and seeing nothing.

"I want to sleep *inside*," Dad said.

"We need a key," Joe spoke up. "Even if the preventatives are only on the inside, we can't just open a locked door."

"Could Thalia unlock it?" Emma asked.

"I don't know," Una said. "It depends on how carefully or hastily Hyad applied his preventatives. Wait. How did Thalia access you?" Una asked, as if the question had just occurred to her. "These preventatives are meant to block all access."

"Rede broke a window," Emma replied.

"He shouldn't have been able to," Una said. "Even if Hyad forgot to shield the opening, that glass should be nearly impossible to break."

Joe shook his head. "Who cares?" he said. "This is all irrelevant. Ask Thalia to unlock the door. If she can't do it, or if she can't hear you, we have to leave. There's no time."

Dad held the doorknob as Emma began trying to communicate with Thalia again.

"This is taking too long," Joe muttered.

"Wait," Emma said.

Finally, Thalia answered her. The lock clicked on the other side of the door, and Dad opened it.

"Oh my God," Emma said. Thalia stood inside. She looked almost completely solid, and she throbbed with light and soft sounds that were near to music.

Emma ran to her, but Una and Rede both called out, "Don't touch her!"

Why?" Emma asked, angry. Was this the reflective revulsion ordinary gemynd showed when encountering an Aponomi?

"She's in the last stage of her manifestation," Rede said. "No one can touch her."

Una nodded, fascination and disgust both written on her face. Emma breathed in a strange scent of sweat and fruit, flowers and animal and spice. Thalia blushed and did not speak.

"That scent is part of it," Rede said. "I think."

Una nodded again.

"We have to leave now," Joe said.

"Who are the two women?" Rede asked, and Emma realized he did not want Thalia to help them.

"This is Una Elos, Fen Elos's many-times-great-granddaughter."

Rede's eyes flashed, and Emma thought to Thalia, *Aythentia?*

Thalia smiled at her. *I know. Weird, huh?*

Yeah, weird, Emma said. Then she turned to her tall, strong father, hidden in the Masked shrunken body of a middle-aged woman and said, "And this is my dad, Peter Mathews."

With considerable effort, Dad reached out to shake Rede's hand.

"Misos," Rede said, staring in horror. "So it's really true? Synektos is a real weapon?"

Emma nodded. "Yes."

Rede shook his head and repeated, "Misos. I can't believe it. What happened to his Soulmate, your mother? How is this permissible?"

Dad inhaled brokenly.

"I'm sorry," Rede said. "I'm sorry."

"We have to leave," Una said. "All of us together will be harder for Hyad to incapacitate but much easier to find."

"Yes," Joe said. "Let's get out of here."

CHAPTER SIXTY

They'd been driving in Una's brown, wood-paneled station wagon for nearly four hours.

Dad slept against the door in the wide backseat next to Emma, who sat next to Joe and Rede. So she wouldn't be accidentally touched by anyone, Thalia sat in the front seat next to Una, who seemed both embarrassed and thrilled to watch an Aponomi manifest.

"Can you tell if Hyad has accessed you yet?" Joe called out.

"No," Emma said, shaking her head. "I don't think he has, but I don't know if I'll be able to tell when and if he does." She looked at Thalia, glad they were driving at night on empty roads where no one could see a green-skinned girl with gleaming purple hair and music rising visibly from her skin like she was a human laser show. On the way down to the car they'd covered her with a blanket. She stayed under it until they were safely out of New York City.

"If he does access me," Emma continued, "he'll know that Rede and Thalia got out of the apartment."

No one spoke about where they were going. Una, Joe, and Emma all worked hard to talk about other things and keep their destination at the back of their thoughts. No one was certain if that would help.

Una talked to Thalia about her library sanctuary, and she argued with Rede about the changes in what Chroniclers were permitted to write about since the last power shift. Rede looked shaken when Dad woke up for a minute and hugged Emma.

After he explained to Emma and Joe how fos charasso marks worked, Rede recited the whole of the Idrysi song. Thalia turned around and beamed at him, and a rush of brighter light and sweeter music filled the car. The light from Thalia made the car even more conspicuous, Emma knew. They should have asked Rede to stop, but the song was so beautiful she didn't want it to ever end.

Back at the apartment, Dad must have realized that Rede and Thalia would be hungry. Before they'd left he packed up food for them and poured water into glass jars. Rede ate gratefully, but Thalia couldn't eat or drink anything until her manifestation was complete.

"When we're closer," Una said to everyone, "and I'll let you know when we are, keep a constant narration in your heads. A narration about unrelated things. Shut your eyes so you don't read any road signs."

They drove in silence for a little while longer, and just outside Concord Una whispered, "Now."

Emma closed her eyes and thought about her every moment since meeting Joe, from the first time she saw him outside the guidance office at school to this very moment of Una's whisper. Joe slid his hand under her thigh.

The road was bumpy and curving, and the car was filled with the layered fragrance and strange music of Thalia's manifestation. Emma started to feel sick. She wished she could open her eyes when the car turned and stopped on a graveled surface, but she knew that would be a mistake.

The engine shut off. "Don't think," Una said.

One by one they got out of the car. Rede gazed at Thalia in concern and awe, and tried to avoid looking at Emma's dad. Emma fought back her fears. She couldn't believe that it was wrong to save Sandy, but she also didn't know what would happen if anything went wrong. Like if the Singers got to him.

They were standing in an empty parking lot. Across the street, its black shutters appearing deceptively wet in the light of the moon, stood a pale yellow house with a broad tree-covered hill behind it. To the right, past a few pine trees, was a pink Victorian house, a single light glowing upstairs.

Emma looked up at the protruding bay window. Sandy's little face peeked between lacy white curtains, his fingers spread wide and pressed against the glass, and his sweet voice sounded in Emma's ear as two hands pulled him out of sight.

I told you they'd be here!

Emma grabbed Joe's arm and indicated the tall pink house to Dad and Una, Thalia and Rede. Silently the six of them walked around to the building's side door, all keeping their eyes down to avoid absorbing unnecessary details of their location.

Mr. Spencer, his handsome young face terrified, ran barefoot onto the soft green lawn. "Come," he whispered.

One by one, everyone followed him without speaking. The pink house turned out to be a quiet inn, no one on duty, nearly all its occupants asleep. A fat gray cat purred loudly in the corner of a red-painted, enclosed staircase, whisking its fluffy tail in irritation as they passed and watching Thalia with curiosity.

Emma heard rapidly approaching footsteps from the stairs. Mr. Spencer whispered urgently to whoever it was to be quiet.

Dad disappeared around the corner and up the stairs, and Emma and the others followed. In the middle of a long, flower-patterned carpet in a wallpapered hall he picked up Sandy and kissed him repeatedly. Sandy, dressed in his monster-shark pajamas and clutching his ratty blue blanket, stared at Dad. He didn't say anything, but he didn't struggle or ask to be put down.

Mr. Spencer took Sandy out of Dad's arms. "Come," he said to all of them. "I've made the rooms as inaccessible as possible."

They walked quietly through the darkened first room. Dad gasped with joy at the sight of Elizabeth and Maude sleeping quietly together in a huge four-poster bed canopied with lace and covered with a patchwork quilt. Emma saw Aubrey asleep on a trundle bed, his delicate features fierce even in slumber.

In the adjacent sitting room, Mr. Spencer put Sandy down and half closed the connecting door after they'd all entered.

Still holding his blanket, Sandy ran over to Joe and Emma. "I knew you'd be here," he said, pulling her to a small, black, roll-top desk positioned against a wall. His thumb was wet in Emma's hand. "See?" he said, opening his comic book and pointing to the last few squares.

Emma read the square where Sandy had drawn Thalia luminous and beautiful. Sandy turned around and looked at his subject.

"Cool," he said, then stuck his thumb back in his mouth.

"I'm Una Elos," Una said, reaching out to shake Mr. Spencer's hand. Sandy cocked his head and watched her, sucking his thumb and thinking.

"Will Spencer," Mr. Spencer said, shaking Una's hand. "I'm so sorry about Fen."

Una colored. "Thank you."

Emma felt a wash of prickling guilt. She had never even thought to express any sympathy for Una's loss.

"This is Thalia Salic," Joe said to Mr. Spencer. "She helped us when we returned to the Commonworld."

"They helped me first," Thalia offered in her layered voice.

"Cool!" Sandy said. "But I know that already."

"How?" Emma asked, tugging playfully on the corner of Sandy's blanket. "Don't fib. Mommy doesn't like it."

Sandy pulled his blanket away. "I'm *not*. I knew it already. Just like I knew you'd come here. Pinky swear." He put his thumb back in his mouth.

"I think intuition about the near future and some events of the present might be a part of his powers," Mr. Spencer said. "A kind of protection. I don't know. The records concerning the last of his kind are not extensive."

"Hey," Thalia said to Sandy, who was still nervously sucking his thumb. "Watch this." She shook her head and hair, throwing splashes of light and color all over the walls and windows.

"Awesome," Sandy said.

Thalia smiled at Emma, who said, *Thank you for coming with us.*

"I'm Rede Onerio."

Mr. Spencer swallowed a look of sorrow and shook the young gemynd's offered hand. "I'm happy to meet you, Rede."

Dad stood in the darkness of the half-open doorway, alternating between gazing in at Maude and Elizabeth and watching Sandy.

"Will Spencer," Mr. Spencer said, holding out his hand.

Emma's heart broke. "This is my dad," she said, but Mr. Spencer gaped at her in disbelief. "Secreted gemynd aren't detained. They're Masked so their identities are impossible to detect. They can't communicate anything except a need for food or sleep or shelter."

Mr. Spencer turned and stared hard at Dad's expressionless, female face. Watching, Emma exhaled and bit the inside of her cheek. She added, "They can't recognize their Soulmates or be recognized by them." She glanced at Sandy's comic book, open on the desk. "They're totally lost inside other faces and bodies unless someone figures out who they are. That's what we did."

Mr. Spencer made a noise that was half disbelief and half misery.

"They're dumped in Otherworld cities, too," Joe added. "Dependent entirely on the generosity of Otherworlders to feed and shelter them."

"Misos," Mr. Spencer said, shaking his head and glancing from Emma to Joe and then finally directly at Dad. "Petros?"

Dad looked at him and said nothing. He couldn't. Emma bit back a sob.

"What has happened to us?" Mr. Spencer whispered. "How could we have lost sight of everything?"

Dad's eyes blazed, but he said nothing. His thoughts were inaccessible forever.

Sandy came over, his thumb in his mouth and the dirtiest, thinnest edge of his blanket pressed to his cheek. Dad knelt in front of him. Sandy sucked his thumb and stared at Dad's face for a long time then turned to Emma. "Like Beauty and the Beast?" he said. "Like the prince got turned into the beast, but on the inside he was still the prince?"

"Yes," Emma said. "Just like that." She took Sandy's free hand. "Do you see Daddy's eyes in the strange lady's face?"

Sandy took his thumb out of his mouth and looked harder then stuck his tongue through a space between his front teeth. "I lost a tooth," he said to Dad.

CHAPTER SIXTY-ONE

Though his female face remained stoic, Dad reached into his pocket and pulled out his wad of Starbucks napkins, which he must have kept even after he got rid of his filthy clothes. He opened the napkins and pulled out three shiny quarters, which he handed to Sandy.

"Daddy!" Sandy said, throwing his arms around the old woman's neck. After a second he pushed him away. "Hey!" he said. "I thought the tooth fairy brings the money."

Dad shuddered and pulled Sandy closer, kissing his head. Sandy dragged him over to the desk to show him his comic book, and talked without seeming to take a breath.

"We can't hide here forever," Mr. Spencer said to Emma. "How did you find us?"

Joe explained how they'd figured it out, and why he and Emma were here. And that they'd been followed from the Commonworld.

"With everyone helping, we might be able to hold off a single Chamura," Mr. Spencer mused. "But as soon as he realizes how many of us there are, he'll send for help." He turned to Emma. "If you bring Sandy back to Lukas, he'll be a prisoner to the Ones in Power for the rest of his life."

"And if she doesn't," Thalia asked, "how can she save him from the edict?"

"I don't know," Mr. Spencer said, covering his face with his hands and then pacing in the small room. He glanced at Sandy chattering happily to Dad, who seemed more his real self in Sandy's presence. "Your mom?" he quietly asked Emma.

"I don't know where she is."

Mr. Spencer spoke to Thalia. "Are you all right?"

She nodded.

"I'm sorry you're separated from your family," he said. "Were they afraid that your connection with Emma put you in danger?"

Thalia nodded again, then turned her head, gasped and covered her ears.

"What is it?" Rede asked, stepping closer, clenching his fists and crossing his arms tightly over his chest.

"I can hear *everything,*" she whispered. "I can hear everyone in this house breathing, and their hearts beating. I can hear the currents of energy moving through the walls. I can hear mice chewing scraps of food. I can hear insects burrowing into tree bark, and worms digging in the ground."

"Hyad said that at a manifestation ceremony all the guests would combine their energies to help her," Rede spoke up frantically, talking to Mr. Spencer but never taking his eyes off Thalia, who was pressing her hands to her ears. "Can we do that?"

"We could," Mr. Spencer said. "But…"

"Anything we do might alert Hyad or the Singers to where we are," Joe said.

If they don't know where we are already, Emma thought to him alone.

Joe glanced at her and sat on the pink velvet couch by the bay window.

Rede turned to Joe, and Emma thought he looked very very young, and very very scared. "Look at her," he whispered fiercely.

"How can we stop the Singers?" Emma asked. "If we figure out how to stop the Singers, the edict would be cancelled."

"I don't know," Mr. Spencer said, still looking at Thalia.

"Even if the edict is cancelled," Joe said softly, "both the Resisters and the Ones in Power will want Sandy."

Dad rested his hand on Sandy's head, and Sandy beamed up at him, talking about his lost tooth, asking if the tooth fairy was real, and telling Dad that Mr. Spencer bought him all the Captain Underpants books even though he already had them at home.

Thalia exhaled and dropped her hands from her ears. "I'm okay," she said to Rede. "I'll be okay."

Rede opened and closed his fists like he was trying to crush the air in the room handful by handful. He lowered his head and walked in a tight circle.

Una had been watching Dad and Sandy since they arrived. She went now to the desk where they both were standing and spoke gently to Dad. "I'll go to New Hampshire and stay with your son and his Soulmate until this is over."

Dad exhaled heavily and stroked Sandy's hair.

"Thank you," Emma said. Sandy looked at Una and smiled knowingly. Una blushed. Emma gave her directions to Mr. Spencer's house, and she left.

Everyone else found a place in the room to sit. Sandy drew a new square in his comic book. When he was finished, Emma looked at it. Instead of a drawing of Turner or Rachel, there was picture of Una wearing a long white dress and smiling adoringly at a woman with spiky gray hair and a beaded hippy skirt.

"Who is that?" Emma asked, leaning over the picture of the gray-haired woman, who looked vaguely familiar.

"The lady from the bookstore at home," Sandy said impatiently. "The one with the toy dragons in the front and the jewels hanging in the doorways. She gave me a purple lollipop once, remember? When I fell and my knee was bleeding and Mommy wasn't home."

"Georgiana?" Emma said. "She has long hair, Sandy."

"She got a haircut," Sandy said disdainfully. "Who did you think she was?"

"I didn't know," Emma said. "Why did you draw a picture of her? And don't talk to me in that kind of voice. You know Mom doesn't like it."

Sandy blushed and dropped his head. "Sorry."

"It's okay," Emma said, stroking his soft cheek.

Sandy didn't say anything.

"What are you going to buy with your tooth fairy money?" she asked.

"Dad is the tooth fairy, Emma," Sandy said—disdainfully again, before changing his tone. "Lemon cookies. There is a store here with lemon cookies that have icing on them."

"Good idea," Emma said. "I guess you can't give me a bite because you only have enough money for one."

"I'll give you a bite," he said.

Emma smiled and looked again at the comic book. "Georgiana's dress is really pretty."

"Thanks," Sandy said. "It has to be pretty, because she's getting married."

"Oh," Emma said.

"Your friend with the black glasses loves her. She's been looking for her for a really long time."

Dad came and carried Sandy to bed in the other room. He stayed there for a long while, sitting on the chair in the window, watching Elizabeth, Sandy, and Maude sleep. Emma sat next to Joe and held his hand.

Rede had continued to pace, looking worriedly at Thalia. When Dad finally came back into the sitting room and closed the door behind him, Rede stopped walking and spoke.

"I think the only way to stop the Singers is to tell everyone about them and what they want. And not just Commonworlders. Otherworlders, too. If everyone knew what the Singers wanted and why they want it, maybe the Singers wouldn't be able to seduce very many. The gift of knowledge. The opposite of what Fen Elos imagined. Otherworlders are shaped by fear and superstition. We're shaped by understanding. This is the argument of the entire second book of the Idrysi. Understanding danger is the only way to conquer it."

"How would we tell humans?" Emma asked.

"The same way we'd tell Commonworlders," Rede said. "Revealer images."

"We can't just fill the streets here with hanging, three-dimensional images," Emma said. "People would be terrified. They wouldn't accept it. Or, worse, they'd blame their enemies. Like blaming gay marriage for terrible hurricanes."

"What?" Rede said. "What the hell does that mean?"

"Nothing. Never mind," Emma said. Then she reconsidered. "Some people think it's wrong for a man to love a man or a woman to love a woman, so they try to find evidence to support that in the occurrence of natural disasters."

"I can't believe you'd be joking at a time like this," Rede said. "Especially about something as sacred as the Soulmate connection. Love is sacred, regardless of gender. Don't joke about it."

"I'm not," Emma said. "Some people really think that."

Rede shook his head. "That doesn't make sense. At all."

"Okay," Joe said. "Let's try to focus. Even if Emma is wrong about human fear, which I don't think she is, what about the language barrier? Humans speak thousands of languages. It's just luck that the Commonworld is linked most heavily in English-speaking areas."

"Fine," Rede said, his voice rising and his green eyes back on Thalia. "Do you have a better idea?"

"No," Joe said quietly. "I think you're right in theory. I just don't think it's feasible."

Dad was now sitting at the black desk reading Sandy's comic book. Emma heard him breathing heavily and rhythmically, and she turned to see him staring down at the pages, slowly drawing in great mouthfuls of air.

"What is it, Dad?" she asked, laying a hand on his shoulder and leaning over to see what he was eyeing. It was a drawing of Elizabeth sitting at the computer at home in the family room. Tiny images were crammed into every bit of space in the square. Only Elizabeth and the desk and the computer were clear.

"The Internet," Emma said, and Joe came over and looked at the book with her. "The Revealer images wouldn't have to hang inexplicably in the air. Revealers could project their images onto the Internet. Like a virus, or a viral video."

"Is that possible?" Joe asked Mr. Spencer. "Could a single Revealer project an image onto the Internet and send it to every connected computer, even to countries where online access is limited and restricted? And, again, the language issue."

Mr. Spencer looked at Dad. "I wish you could talk to me. I wish you could tell me what you thought."

"He wanted us to see this picture," Emma said. "He must think it's possible."

"Maybe we wouldn't have to limit it to the Internet," Joe said. "What about books, too? And comics? And videogames?"

"How would it work in the Commonworld?" Thalia asked, turning. "Your youngest sister is a Revealer, but how could she— even with help from all of us—project an image all over the Commonworld? Rede is a Chronicler, and I guess your little brother is, too. But I'm a Mask, and your sister is a Soulskin."

It was an excellent question—but one that seemed irrelevant a moment later. Emma's chest contracted. Without thinking, she ran to the window and looked out into the yard below.

"They're here," she said. "Both of them. Hyad and Lukas are both here."

CHAPTER SIXTY-TWO

Everyone but Thalia ran into the other room and stood in a circle around Sandy's bed.

"Maude," Emma said, shaking her sister. "Elizabeth. You have to wake up. We need you."

Aubrey popped up in the trundle bed and was shockingly quickly to his feet.

"It's all right," Rede said.

"Who the hell are you?" Aubrey asked.

Preceded by a flood of green and lavender light, Thalia walked into the room.

"Oh, Misos," Aubrey said. He gazed at her as if there had never been anything more beautiful and there were no words equal to what he saw. Emma felt the same way.

"Elizabeth and Maude, sit on the bed next to Sandy," Mr. Spencer directed. "Everyone else, hold hands and face out."

Dad grabbed Mr. Spencer's arm with a ferocious expression in his eyes.

"All right, Peter," Mr. Spencer said. "You and Elizabeth sit next to Sandy."

"Dad?" Elizabeth asked.

"We'll explain later," Emma said, helping her sister onto the bed. "Someone is here to hurt Sandy." She glanced down at her brother's sweet, sleeping face. "We have to protect him." Then she looked at Joe. "I can say it. I can say why we're here!"

"Hold hands," Mr. Spencer directed. "You, too, Aubrey."

"I don't have any powers," the Anaxio said. "I'd be a weak link."

Maude took his face in her hands. "Do you want to protect Sandy from gemynd who want to murder or imprison him?"

Aubrey scowled. "Of course I do."

"Then that is power enough," Maude said, taking his hand and spinning away from the bed. On his other side, Aubrey took Mr. Spencer's hand.

Thalia stood in the doorway between the two rooms, spilling colored light onto the dark floor and white doorframe. "I can't breathe," she said. Her voice was frantic and disconnected. "I have to get outside. I can't breathe."

Aubrey looked at her and shook his head. Taking Maude and Mr. Spencer's hands together in one of his, clearly trying not to break the chain, he produced a small metal clock he'd apparently hidden in the trundle bed. Its skinny black hands read 11:55.

Looking once at Thalia, he threw the clock as hard as he could at the window. The glass shattered. Warm spring air floated in with the sounds of bullfrogs and distant cars. Thalia drew in a great breath of it.

"Thanks," she said.

"Everyone," Mr. Spencer called out. "Think of protecting Sandy and protecting yourselves. Don't think of anything else. Don't be distracted."

Sounds of fighting drifted up to them, filtering in through the broken glass. The noise was loud enough that they heard the innkeeper go outside. He demanded over the barking of a big-sounding dog, "What the hell is going on out—?"

Without any other sound, both the dog and man quieted.

"Ignore it," Mr. Spencer hissed. "Sandy and yourselves. Protect Sandy and yourselves."

A ring of energy ran through their linked hands, rising up between them as if the desire to protect Sandy had created a physical shield. Whether that shield would be as impenetrable as the shell that had kept Eury Vatic captive while the extrication lights drained his life away, Emma didn't know.

Sandy continued to sleep between Dad and Elizabeth. Except for the noise of his sucking his thumb, and the quiet music of Thalia's manifestation, the room was silent and waiting.

The fighting outside went on. Hadn't Rede said that understanding danger was the way to conquer it? Emma strained to listen. Apparently Gatherers sent by the Three Leaders had come to support Hyad. They outnumbered Lukas's supporters, Gatherers who had left the Ones in Power to fight with him and protect and exploit the Whole Chronicler. Frantic thoughts from everyone on the ground outside burst intermittently through the roar of battle like a radio station registering clear for a moment in a remote area. Trying to keep half-focused on Sandy, Emma listened harder.

Syndesi Sacere, Lukas said. *Of anyone, especially now, you should know that, Hyad.*

Not at the expense of everyone, Hyad shouted back. *Not at the expense of all of us.*

Emma had never heard anyone, gemynd or human, sound so wild and despairing, not even Eury Vatic.

Mr. Spencer turned to her. *Protect Sandy,* he said.

Emma nodded. *But what does Syndesi Sacere mean?*

Rede answered. *Every life is sacred. It's the last line of the Idrysi.*

The Synektos order shouldn't have fallen on you, Lukas said outside, and Emma felt Hyad stand still amidst the fighting.

It didn't fall on me. Solymi was investigating Synektos and he'd gotten close to uncovering it. I made a deal. I agreed to perform secretings if Solymi wasn't punished. He would have been secreted, or executed, separated forever from me if I hadn't.

Emma saw Lukas now. Was she completely inside Hyad's head? Hyad jumped back as his red-eyed boss came within inches of his face, and Emma glanced down, reassured to see her own hand still tightly clasping Joe's. She wasn't somehow inhabiting Hyad's body too.

Syndesi Sacere, Lukas hissed, drawing a knife. *I'm sorry, Hyad.*

Cutting him off, Hyad thrust a blade of light through his throat.

Emma gasped and broke her connection. Joe squeezed her hand, but with an unsettling sensation like simultaneously throwing up and kissing, Emma felt the sudden arrival of the Singers of the Apocalypse. They circled and dove in a chorus of whispers so gorgeous and alluring that she almost cried.

No, she thought.

"Don't be distracted," Mr. Spencer commanded. "This was inevitable. They must have found a link through Lukas or Hyad. Or even one of us."

The sounds of fighting outside increased. It seemed that more gemynd had come—whether to help Hyad or Lukas, Emma did not know. Would Lukas's supporters still fight now that Lukas was dead or injured? Would they give up? Who would help fight for Sandy's life?

From the soles of her feet and climbing up her legs Emma felt nothing but intense pleasure, and she longed for peace. The peace only the Singers could offer. The peace of oblivion.

"Resist them," Joe said.

"What's happening?" Sandy asked, suddenly sitting up. "Why are you all around my bed? Hey," he drawled, the fear in his voice draining away. "What is that? Is Mommy here? I want Mommy."

Dropping their hands but immediately linking up again, the six of them turned in unison to face him.

"Mommy is *not* here," Maude said. "Those are bad guys, those singers. Don't listen to them. Don't listen."

"But I want to," Sandy said. "I see Mommy. I see her! She wants me."

He stood up, but Dad pulled him down.

Rapid footsteps sounded on the stairs. The innkeeper's wife shouted but was silenced. The sound of her body falling to the floor made Emma feel sick.

The door burst open. "It's over," Hyad said. "I'm sorry."

A blade of light sprang from his hand, and he aimed it at the circle of those surrounding Sandy. At the same time, loudly and just out of sync, grandfather clocks from the rooms adjacent and below chimed twelve o'clock.

A wave of bright energy wove wildly through the six gemynd protecting Sandy and washed over him, Elizabeth and Dad. Thalia stepped forward, joining the circle and linking her hands with Maude's and Rede's, and the circle of energy became more of a protective dome. Simultaneously, a chaotic choir of Thalia's desires, her fears, and her beliefs filled the room; Revealer images of her at every stage of her life opened and burst in a succession of luminous bubbles: baby Thalia laughing silently as she saw the sun for the first time; tasting a raspberry; listening to Zino sing at night in the summer; successfully blocking Hyad and Solymi from accessing her thoughts as they clapped for her in the living room; holding Maddie when Genna brought her home; winning top Teknasma marks for the third year in a row; kissing the Uske in the kitchen; kissing Rede; and finally, choosing to help Emma fight against the edict to execute

Sandy because there were no acceptable consequences, not really. Not if you really thought about it.

Hyad's blade of light bounced off the circle of seven and burned a wide hole through the ceiling, attic and roof, letting in the black sky and bright stars, and in a voice of incandescent loveliness Thalia spoke.

"You'll have to kill me first."

"I want my Mommy," Sandy said. "I see her. I want to go to her. Let me have her!"

Hyad aimed the blade of light again. This time, at Thalia.

Rede pulled her toward him, downward, and the ring of gemynd collapsed over Dad, Elizabeth and Sandy. The light blasted the entire bay window out of the wall and into the yard below. Tinted by the soft green and violet glow of beautiful Thalia, white flames shot up and then died down.

Emma felt Sandy desperately reaching to follow the Singers of the Apocalypse.

"Mommy isn't here," she whispered to him, stroking his damp cheek. "They're lying. They don't have her."

"No, they're not," Sandy said. "I see her. I *see* her."

Emma heard Hyad prepare a third light blade, but she kept her voice calm. "They're tricking you," she said. "They want to take something from you. They want to take your stories from you. They want to steal your comic book and keep it for themselves and never let anyone see it ever again."

Hyad's third blade of light skidded over their dome of protective energy like a flat rock across the surface of a pond.

Emma felt Thalia shiver and heard her say to Rede, *Don't let go of my hand. Don't let go.*

I won't ever let go, he said. *I love you.*

"If she's not really here," Sandy asked, "how come I can see Mommy?"

"Because they're so good at tricking," Emma said.

"Like a bad dream?" Sandy asked. "Like when I was little and I was scared that I was sleeping for my whole life and I would only wake up the second that I died?"

"Yes," Emma said.

"Okay," Sandy said very quietly.

The voices retreated. But for how long?

CHAPTER SIXTY-THREE

Hyad fell to his knees. Dad let go of Sandy's hand and crossed the room to reach him. The circle of the others closed again.

"I'm cold," Dad said to Hyad. "I'm very cold."

"Is Daddy mad at that man?" Sandy whispered to Emma.

"Yes," Emma said. "He is."

"Why?" Sandy asked.

"Because he tried to hurt you."

"He didn't hurt me," Sandy said. "See?" He growled and bent his arms to show Emma his muscles. "I'm strong. Like Captain Underpants."

"Yes," Emma said. "You're very strong."

"I'm cold," Dad said to Hyad again, but it sounded like he wanted to kill him.

"Don't," Mr. Spencer said to Thalia, sensing she wanted to intervene. "There are still Gatherers outside who want Sandy. When the ones who want to kill him have beaten or been defeated by the ones who want the Way of Listening, the victors will be up here. The Singers were not the end of this."

Thalia, heedless but bright and beautiful, her skin and hair opaque, her feet noisy and weighty on the floor, let go of Rede's hand, and the circle of energy protecting Sandy broke for good. Elizabeth burst into tears, and Aubrey sat beside her.

Maude hugged Sandy and kissed him on the head. "What's all over you?" she asked. She wiped her mouth, looked at her hand and leaned closer. "Does it hurt? Did something hit you?"

"No," Sandy said, rubbing his forehead. "I'm okay. Why are you so close to me? You smell like raspberries. Do you have candy? Can I have some? Dad, can I have some of Maude's candy? I already brushed my teeth, but I can brush them again. Please!"

"Stop talking and stand still, silly," Maude said. "It looks like someone with dark red lipstick on kissed you all over your forehead. Are you sure nothing hit you or stung you?"

Dad leaned aggressively into Hyad. Hyad didn't move.

Thalia inserted herself between them and spoke to Dad. "They would have executed his Soulmate if he didn't agree to secret you."

Dad roared like a caged animal.

Hyad secreted my Mom and Dad? Emma thought to Joe. *He knew the whole time what they looked like and where they were?* She took a step toward Hyad, but Thalia shook her head.

"What would you have done in his place?" Thalia asked Emma's father. "Would you have risked your Soulmate's life to save anyone else? Would you have risked her life for anything? Anything at all?"

Emma gasped as the secret Joe had kept from her—the one she had taken out of his head but hadn't listened to—unfolded inside her. She saw everything. The little house they were hiding in when Eury Vatic was still alive and they were all except Gryphon trying to save him. She saw Gryphon, so injured on the bed under the thistledown blanket Mom had made, his hand in Maude's. Then later, after he'd escaped to find Eury and bring him to the Ones in Power, Emma saw Gryphon wrapped in a cocoon, dying. The thistledown blanket, made by her mother and tucked around the gravely injured sixteen year old boy was woven through with the lethal threads of a life-link.

Emma ran to Maude. *Mom?* she said to her sister alone. *Mom life-linked to Gryphon to save Eury and that's why Gryphon died? How long have you known? Why didn't you tell me?*

Maude's soul shivered over the surface of her skin. *I heard her decide to do it when we were in the apartment and I was remembering the last time I saw Gryphon alive. She was willing to do anything to keep the Gatherers from capturing Joe's dad. She was afraid if they did he would give in to the Singers of the Apocalypse. She knew Gryphon was my Soulmate. She lied to herself about it, though, to be able to do what she did. The life-link threads were woven into the blanket she made him.*

How could she? Emma asked. *She knew what would happen to you if Gryphon died.*

She didn't think he would die, Maude said. *You know how she is, always thinking she's right. That she can do anything. She didn't mean to kill him. It was a modified life-link. She made it almost endlessly long, which was why traveling to the Otherworld injured him but didn't kill him right away. She thought she'd be able to undo the life-link safely as soon as Eury had time to get away from the Gatherers. She thought Gryphon was too weak to escape and there was nowhere to go. Joe's dad—what you saw—was trying to save Gryphon, not kill him. That cocooning web was filled with medicine and something to safely break the tie.* Maude's soul spiked with red and black ridges. *It doesn't matter though. Not now. Not ever.*

Dad made an incoherent mournful sound at Hyad then crossed the room to his second oldest daughter. He hugged her and cried into her hair.

"It's okay, Dad," she said. "I know you didn't know. I know you were trying to help Gryphon. It's okay."

Dad kissed Maude's head.

"I can't forgive her," Maude said. "No matter what happened to Mom or what she's like when we find her, I can't forgive her."

Dad nodded.

Emma held Joe's hand. *You were right,* she said. *I wouldn't have wanted to know. Not then anyway.*

Joe kissed her hand then turned to Sandy. "Hey, little brother, are you okay? You look a little pale." He knelt. "Do you feel sick? I know that was scary, but it's over. The Singers, I mean." He turned to Maude. "These marks do look like lipstick kisses. Some wasted kid in Newport the other day stole lipstick from a random purse in a laundromat then put the lipstick on himself. It was the same color. He kissed the pay phone I was talking to you on. I had to fight to get the receiver away from him. So nasty. Sad, but nasty."

"Mommy," Sandy said quietly.

Elizabeth walked over. "We'll find her. Don't worry."

Sandy sat on the floor and started crying. Threads of clear red light emerged from the marks that looked like kisses on his head, swelling into a Revealer image above him.

"Hey, that's the kid!" Joe said, pointing to the scene unfolding in the air. "And that's the park. And the destroyed portal tree. The clock tower on that church says this was fifteen minutes ago." He turned to Dad and Mr. Spencer. "What the hell is going on?"

Sandy lay on the floor. He didn't suck his thumb or hold his blanket.

In the image, a tall, skinny kid no older than Maude stood under a streetlight in a city park, traces of lipstick and dirt smeared around his mouth. His expression was fierce. He looked like he'd been crying. For a second he looked like he might cry again.

Flickering as if it might burn out at any moment, the image was bathed entirely in red light. The boy in the park was flickering, too. As if he might disappear. As if something inside him was trying to get out. Then female features, older and more desperate, appeared inside his face.

"The Uske," Thalia whispered.

"What?" Rede asked.

"Like the story," Thalia said. "You know, *The Uske*. Didn't everyone in your school read it?"

"I guess," Rede said.

"His face changes when he's about to kiss someone," Thalia explained. "When he kisses his Soulmate, his real face appears."

Still on the floor, Sandy drew his knees up to his chest.

"Are you okay?" Emma asked.

"Mom," Elizabeth whispered. "It's Mom."

Emma looked up at the image again.

The drug-addled boy disappeared. Mom stood in his place.

"See, sweetie?" Emma said to Sandy. "There's Mommy. She tried to find you. "She must have been secreted to look like a teenage boy." She turned to Joe. "Maybe that's why she smeared lipstick kisses all over the phone. Secreted gemynd don't lose their powers. I think they're probably just harder to use. My mom must have figured out how to turn the lipstick into something that would send a message or find us because Sandy was in the house with Mr. Spencer when you were talking to him. She sent him kiss-messages because he's the youngest and the one in danger. You were right, Elizabeth," she continued. "Mom's power is awesome."

"Mom looks crazy," Elizabeth said.

Dad made a strangled noise.

"Imagine what this has been like for her," Emma said, her voice gentle for her youngest sister. Then she waited for whatever her mother wanted to say.

On the floor, Sandy closed his eyes.

"It's okay, honey," Mom said, bathed in the red light of the Revealer image, the lipstick tube in her shaking hand. "It's okay.

Don't cry. It's over. It's over, baby boy. I won't let them get you. Come with me. Come with me, Sandy, and everything will be all right. I promise."

Then she dropped the lipstick onto the sidewalk, pulled a knife from her pocket and slit her own throat.

CHAPTER SIXTY-FOUR

"That wasn't real, right?" Elizabeth said as the image disappeared. "That was some kind of trick. The Singers of the Apocalypse or whatever. Right?"

Emma couldn't breathe. No one else said anything.

Rede knelt beside Sandy, who hadn't moved or made a sound. "Hey," he said, shaking Sandy by the shoulders. "Hey."

"Is he okay?" Maude asked, kneeling as well. "Did he faint?"

Emma stared at her baby brother lying so still, and she flashed on a memory of the day she met Joe, months ago, ten lifetimes ago, when Sandy was doing his math homework on the kitchen floor. She'd been setting the table, helping Mom get ready for dinner. When she shook out the red tablecloth, Sandy and his homework sheet were shadowed in scarlet. He'd looked up and smiled at her. *Cool,* he'd said, and she'd shaken the cloth over him again.

Everyone but Emma and Hyad now huddled around Sandy. Emma couldn't stop shaking.

Joe came over and held her. *I'm sorry,* he said. *I'm so sorry about your Mom.*

Sandy, Emma said. "Sandy."

"He's safe now," Joe said. "Everyone will take care of him." He stroked Emma's hair and spoke to her alone. *Your mom must have been going crazy. She must have thought Sandy was going to die, that the Gatherers or someone was going to kill him. I didn't recognize her in Newport, not that I really could have, but I wish...* He sighed and kissed Emma's head. *She must have somehow heard about the edict when we were in the laundromat. That's why she was crying so hard when I left. I'm so sorry, Emma. I wish I could have known it was her, seen something or sensed something the way you did with your dad. I could have taken her with me. I'm so sorry. She must have thought Sandy was going to die and she couldn't save him.*

No, Emma said, afraid to listen to her own voice but more afraid to hide from the truth. *No. That's not it. That's not it at all. You have to willingly surrender to the Singers when you die in order for them to incorporate you. Mom knew that. And she knew how powerful they are. She knew they would convince everyone in both worlds to surrender if they could reach them at the same time. That's why she was willing to kill Gryphon to keep your dad from surrendering even though it would destroy Maude, her own daughter—*

Emma stopped talking and pushed away from Joe as the reality of what had happened sank in. She could hardly breathe. "Sandy is going to let go of his life. Now. Before the Singers have a chance to try to get to him again. That's what she wanted. That's why she killed herself. She didn't want the Singers to use Sandy to figure out how Whole Listening works. She sacrificed him."

* * *

Thalia stepped closer as Rede knelt over Emma's little brother, stroking his face and whispering.

"Hey," Rede said. "Hey, little brother. Your mom doesn't want you to die. Emma and Maude and Elizabeth and your dad don't want you to die. Your mom made a mistake. She was trying to protect other people, which is a good thing, but she did it in a bad way. Grownups make mistakes. Sometimes grownups make terrible mistakes." He brushed the sweaty hair off Sandy's forehead and said, "My mom and dad made a terrible mistake, too. And I'm sad about it all the time."

Sandy stared at the fos charasso marks on Rede's arms, which caught the moonlight from the window, and Thalia watched Rede turn them so the boy could see better.

"That's the Idrysi," he said. "The song of how the worlds were made. Why we're all lucky to be alive. Even when things suck. It's pretty rad, right, little brother? I could show you how to do it. Then you could carve fos charasso pictures on your arms or legs or wherever you wanted."

Sandy touched a luminous word with his finger.

"That's Eynosyndeo. It means Soulmate," Rede said. "That part of the song goes like this…."

He sang, and Sandy closed his eyes, keeping his fingers on the ancient words on Rede's wrist. Emma and Joe held hands. Maude had her arms around her dad. Rede kept singing.

Rede. It didn't matter what he'd called her when they met, or what he'd called her mother. Love had nothing to do with never making mistakes or being perfect. Thalia would have loved him whatever and whoever he was. Whenever she met him. There was no one like him in either world.

Sandy took Rede's hand and pulled it to his chest. From a corner of the room Hyad made a soft noise, and lured by his despair the chorus of the damned returned: the Singers, hair-thin, biting like nettles but singing of peace and salvation.

Thalia heard them differently than she had before her manifestation was complete. Inside the soothing seduction of their false promises, they were arguing amongst themselves, over what she couldn't quite hear. Aubrey, too, looked up from the huddle surrounding Sandy. He listened intently to the Singers, like he was figuring out a puzzle, not falling for their beautiful lies.

Hyad got to his feet and staggered to the door, the Singers' voices all around him.

Thalia called out, *Don't. Don't give in.*

Hyad dropped his head and said, *I've disappeared, Thalia. There isn't anything left of me, anything I value or know about myself. Solymi would not recognize me.* He turned and gazed directly at her. *I used the Synektos weapon on Emma's parents. I killed Lukas to save myself. I tried to kill you. If Rede hadn't pulled you down, I would have killed you. I can't live knowing that. I have to go. I have to let go.*

Something flashed outside. If they had briefly parlayed, the two sides of Gatherers were back to fighting. Screaming and more blasts of light filled the open window.

Emma's dad picked up Sandy and carried him to the bed. He hugged him tight.

Rede looked outside then came to stand beside Thalia. "The victors will be up here soon." He turned sharply on Hyad. "You have to help us. Your powers are the strongest, and the loyal Masevo think you're on their side."

Hyad said nothing.

Rede grabbed his shoulders and shook him. "Look around, periskata. You think you're the only one here who's lost someone? You think you're the only one here who's done something they'd give anything to undo?" Swearing, he pushed Hyad away and turned to Emma's little sister. "Elizabeth. Please help me."

"What are you doing?" Thalia asked.

Rede shook his head and stared at Elizabeth, who turned pale.

"Did you hear me?" he asked her. "Will you help me? Will you do what I asked?" She nodded, and Rede, his green eyes lit with rage and sorrow, turned back to Hyad and waited.

Just above Elizabeth's head, a younger Rede appeared, no older than ten or eleven, nervously clutching the hand of a little boy who was chattering on about a story they were making up together, asking Rede dozens of things as they walked together in Protepol. Rede answered all of his brother's questions, his attention fixed on the footpath.

Threads of a life-link glittered on the younger boy's throat. The young Rede glanced back at a couple watching them.

"Don't let go of his hand," the woman begged.

"Don't tell Rede what to do," shouted the man. "He's nervous enough already. This isn't going to work. It can't be undone. A Hate Match can't be undone. Just accept it. Let's take the boys home and untie the life-link. Allasso! Rede! Come. We're leaving."

Rede turned to face his father as a dog darted past. His grip on his brother's hand loosened slightly, and Allasso ran laughing after the beast. Rede screamed and gave chase. It was too late, though. He reached his little brother just as Allasso collapsed.

The image disappeared.

Rede glared at Hyad. "Are you going to help us?" he asked. "Syndesi Sacere. Every life is sacred," he added, his voice full of everything he couldn't say about that terrible day in his past. "That has to mean something, or nothing has any meaning at all. Grow the fuck up. Nobody has it easy. Not in this world or any other."

Slowly, Hyad nodded. He stepped into the middle of the room.

"Emma, Joe, and you," he said, pointing to Mr. Spencer. "Come here. You, too, Rede. I'm going to implant the process of energy depletion into your heads. Follow me outside and drain as many Gatherers as you can. It's our only hope. The rest of you stay here and guard Sandy."

The others obeyed, and a moment later Thalia watched the five of them leave the room and go outside.

Aubrey was still listening to the thwarted Singers, who hovered, quieted but not beaten. Thalia heard their running argument clearly now, and one side finally won out. She felt the chorus switch directions and descend to the combat below, no longer promising peace or pleasure or salvation of any kind. She ran to the window in time to see gemynd on both sides gape in horror, for the Singers of the Apocalypse sang the truth of Synektos, the unspeakable severing of Soulmates and the inescapable prison of being locked forever inside a Mask of someone else, an irrefutable horror that gemynd had perpetrated on themselves.

CHAPTER SIXTY-FIVE

Thalia watched gemynd collapse on the lawn outside. Supporters of Lukas and the Ones in Power alike let go of their lives, one by one, equally horrified. At first intending to fight but now on the defensive, Rede and Hyad changed tack and tried to silence the Singers by using shielding energy, but the more gemynd surrendered, the stronger the Singers of the Apocalypse became. Emma, Joe, and Mr. Spencer the Crossworlder faltered.

Terrified, Thalia turned away from the window. Emma's dad was sitting on the bed in the other room with Elizabeth and Maude. He was talking to Sandy, who had opened his eyes but not spoken.

Elizabeth came outside and shut the door. She stopped to watch Aubrey pace and talk urgently to himself. Her face said it all.

It's over, Thalia realized. *The Singers are too strong. They'll defeat everyone outside and then come in and take Emma's brother. It's over. It was all for nothing. It's over.*

Aubrey stopped pacing and raised his head, his eyes bright with a sudden revelation. He caught Thalia's glance…then immediately looked away.

"What?" she said. "Did you think of a way out?"

"No." He refused to look at her. "I did, but there has to be another way," he said, half to himself. "I'll figure it out. There has to be a better answer. There's always another answer. It's just a matter of finding it."

"What did you think of?" Thalia asked. "Tell me."

"No. There's another way."

"Tell me," Thalia insisted.

"No!"

"I'll access you," Thalia warned the Anaxio. "I'll listen to whatever you're thinking."

"No!" Aubrey wailed. He covered his head with his hands as if he could keep his thoughts inside by physical force. "No! I won't let you."

"You can't stop me."

"Don't," Aubrey begged. He was crying. "It's a bad idea. It won't work."

"What are you doing to him?" Elizabeth asked, running over.

Aubrey shrieked in protest. Thalia had pulled the thought out of his head.

It wasn't a bad idea. It would work, too.

Rede. She had to tell him.

Silently, she called him. Rede dropped what he was doing and rushed back up into the inn. She heard his footsteps on the stairs.

"Are you all right?" he asked, bursting into the room.

"Don't let her do it," Aubrey said. "I'll think of something else."

"Do what?" Rede asked.

"It won't be your fault," Thalia said to Aubrey. "I understand your resistance, but it won't be your fault."

"What's going on?" Elizabeth asked. "What did you do? Why is he so upset?"

"She didn't do anything to me," Aubrey said, sitting hard on the pink couch and furiously wiping at his eyes.

"It isn't your fault," Thalia said again. "You didn't force me to listen to your idea, and you're not making me follow it. That's the point. This is my choice, Aubrey. Maybe there is another answer, but there isn't time to find it." She sat next to him. "This is my decision. Freely and consciously chosen. This would always be my choice, no matter who figured it out."

"How are you going to do it?" Aubrey asked.

"Just like you thought it through," she answered, standing up. "You're right. It all seems so clear now. Manifestation is a mutation created from elements of every Commonworld power, including those of a Lucent and a Crossworlder. It's to ensure we Aponomi find our Soulmates. Until then, and for a year after that, we can connect to the energy fabric because we have something of all gemynd powers inside us. You're the first one to figure that out, Aubrey. You're the opposite of Worthless. Don't ever let anyone call you that again."

You really are the smartest of all of us, she added to him alone.

"You still haven't told me how," Aubrey said hopefully, as if Thalia might not understand how to do the terrible thing he'd imagined.

"The Singers of the Apocalypse absorb the energies of gemynd who let go of life," she said. "I can do the same thing in reverse. Because I'm a fully manifested Aponomi, I can absorb the Singers into myself."

"Wait! What?" Rede said.

"It will kill you," Aubrey said. He jumped off the couch and crossed the small room. "You understand that, right?"

"No!" Rede said. *You can't.*

"If I don't do it," Thalia said, "the Singers will get to Sandy. Everyone will die."

"You don't know the Singers will get to Sandy," Rede said. "And even if they do, the worst possibility can't happen instantly. Listen to Aubrey. There is another answer. There has to be. You just had your manifestation. You just met me. You've been waiting your whole life for this time. Right now. Don't sacrifice that."

"Yes, I thought about it a lot—kissing and meeting you, I mean. But I did meet you," Thalia said. "And I kissed you and you kissed me. And all of that was better than I ever imagined."

"So that's enough for you, then?" Rede said. "Less than a week?"

"Of course it isn't!" she said. "I don't think it'll ever feel like enough. For anyone. Do you think Solymi thought, 'Oh, I had enough time to love Hyad. I had enough time to do the work I wanted to do,' as the fucking train was burning?"

Rede shook his head and stomped across the room and back.

"It's not the amount of time you have," Thalia said. "It's what you do with it. That you don't waste it."

"Isn't that what you're doing?" Rede asked. "Wasting it? If Aubrey can figure something out but you quit now, you're throwing your whole fucking life away."

"I'm not throwing it away," Thalia said, quietly furious while she felt the direness of the situation below on the lawn. "Do you think I made this choice without thinking about it?"

"I'm not finished," Rede said, equally angry. "You're also throwing away your potential to do things. Not just with me, like feeling the very best life and our connection has to offer." *Every day from here forward,* he added silently and just to her. "You're throwing away whatever you want to do with the Ones in Power. Whatever you want to do to make the world a better place. To fight for Aponomi. To fight for Maddie. To fight so Anaxio aren't treated like garbage. To do the things your uncle knew you could do from the time you were little."

"I know," Thalia said. "I know." She could feel it, just for a second, the urge to give in. Not to the Singers and their twisted views of life and death, but to Rede. And kissing. And having her whole year as a manifested Aponomi. And ice cream. And raspberries. And growing up. And having an important job. And making her parents proud. Making herself proud. And Maddie.

Maddie.

"No," she said. "This is what has to happen. How could it not be? I'm the only one who can do it."

Thalia, Rede begged.

"It doesn't matter whether I'm supposed to or not," she continued. "I don't see things that way. Zino always tells Maddie and me that we're responsible for our own choices. That we, all of us, drive our own destinies. And that's an amazing thing, to create your own life's path." She took Rede's hand. "Hyad and the Ones in Power are demanding sacrifices of others, sacrifices that are decisions only they get to make. And they keep the truth from others. That's wrong, even if their reasons are right. Like Emma's mom's attempt to sacrifice Sandy to keep him from falling into the hands of the Singers. But Sandy's life is his to do with what he wants. Just like mine is. And yours is. And Maddie's is. But if we who can help don't, if we wait and hope to be saved instead of saving, then how are we any better than the ones who take our choices away?"

Okay, Rede said. "Okay. *Okay.*"

"There's another answer," Aubrey pleaded. "I know there is."

"We don't have time to find it," Thalia said simply. "Listen to that wailing outside. Almost everyone is dead or dying. We're all fighting to save something. This is what I can do. This is what I *will* do."

"Not alone," Rede said. "I won't let you do this alone."

"Are you sure?" Thalia asked.

"Yes," Rede said. *Yes. Always.*

"Okay. Take my hand."

* * *

Out on the lawn, Mr. Spencer was trying and failing to convince the remaining Gatherers to ignore what the Singers had revealed about Synektos. When a young female gemynd with dark eyes and darker hair died in his arms, he sat on the ground with his head in his hands.

Even without Rede, Hyad was still trying to shield everyone from the terrible chorus of despair.

"Could we use that thing you and Lukas used on me when I tried to let go?" Emma asked. "So no one can kill themselves no matter how much they want to?"

Hyad turned to her, his eyes full of regret.

"Would that work?" Emma asked.

"Yes," he said.

"If you let the Three Leaders know, could Emma and I go to the Commonworld and bring it here?" Joe asked.

"Yes," Hyad said. "Yes."

"Maybe they'll be understanding about Sandy," Emma said.

Hyad shook his head. "I can't promise anything."

"You made a deal to save your Soulmate," Emma shot back.

"That was different," Hyad said.

"I don't see why. Unless he's Loveless, Sandy has a Soulmate. And Syndesi Sacere means *every* life. How can you live by that ideal and still support Acceptable Consequences?"

"Do you really think things are that simple, Emma?" Hyad asked. "If the Singers get to Sandy and he surrenders to them, that's it. As soon as they understand how Whole Listening works, they'll connect to every human and every gemynd and seduce or terrify them into killing themselves. One life. *One life,"* he repeated. "At the expense of all life? Sandy included. Even if you save him today, he'll be in danger every other day."

"Why didn't you kill him then?" Joe asked furiously. "Why don't you go kill him now? You're still the most powerful gemynd here. We could slow you but we couldn't stop you. But you're still here. Fighting this losing battle. How many gemynd are left alive out here? How many are trying to resist the Singers? Twenty? Thirty? But you're still fighting. You're still here. Why?"

"I can't take another life," Hyad said simply.

More gemynd fell. Mr. Spencer lay down beside the woman who had died in his arms, a woman whom Emma realized suddenly looked like the beautiful young gemynd in the painting in Mr. Spencer's living room, his Soulmate who had died more than one hundred years ago.

It got quieter and quieter.

The Singers dove in and around the few remaining gemynd, tossing images of lost Soulmates and imprisoned identities into the air like poisoned garlands of fragrant flowers. Emma reached for Joe. He walked over from where he was standing between the Singers and a screaming gemynd who gave up at last, and he grabbed Emma, picking her up and kissing her hard on the mouth.

Even without the Soulmate bond I would have chosen you, Joe Castellaw, she said, her fingers in his hair. *The time we had together was enough—and never enough.*

I would have chosen you, too, he said. *Always.*

The Singers suddenly silenced.

Incredulous, Hyad stopped pushing at two gemynd huddled on the ground and said, "Something is drawing them off. Nothing should be able to affect them at all. They're untouchable, part of the energy fabric that makes up everything. They..." He paled and looked up at the inn.

A blinding light burst from the window, and a thunderous noise shook the earth. Pinecones showered out of the trees, thumping onto the ground like heavy rain. Sandy screamed.

Hyad ran into the inn. Joe, Emma and Mr. Spencer followed close behind.

CHAPTER SIXTY-SIX

Green and purple smoke poured from the room upstairs as the four ran in.

"Daddy!" Sandy cried from the other room. "I can't see you."

"I need a blanket," Dad called through the smoke. "I need a blue blanket.

"I have a blue blanket!" Sandy said. "I'll save you."

Rede and Thalia were lying on the floor, their arms wrapped around each other. Purple smoke poured like blood from deep gashes all over Thalia's skin. Green smoke bled from Rede's eyes and nose and mouth. His fos charasso marks were black.

Maude and Elizabeth sat beside them. Maude stroked Thalia's hair. Elizabeth held Rede's hand.

"They're dead," Aubrey said.

Dad picked up Sandy.

"You found me," Sandy said.

Dad kissed him.

Mr. Spencer sat on the couch. Emma buried her head in Joe's shoulder.

"A fully manifested Aponomi can connect to the energy fabric," Hyad realized. "Thalia took the Singers of the Apocalypse inside her. How did we never think of that?"

"Aubrey thought of it," Maude said.

"I didn't mean to," he protested.

"Thalia wanted this," Maude said. "You helped save everything."

"I didn't want to. Not this way."

"What if it was the only way?"

"I'm Nomos Apodektos," he shouted. "*I'm* Acceptable Consequences. There was another way! She just didn't give me time to think of it. I could have done it. I know I could have."

Maude continued to run her fingers through Thalia's hair. "It's so pretty, isn't it?" she said quietly. "Like irises."

Emma sat beside Maude and took her other hand.

"Rede gave her his Nevma," Maude said, her voice tight. "She was clearly dying, and he wanted to see her for a few more minutes, so he gave her his life force. He died just after she did."

"Everything has to follow fundamental laws," Aubrey said, more to himself than anyone else. "Nothing exists outside those laws. That's why there's always an answer, if we don't always know it. Hell, we hardly ever know it, but it's always there." He lowered his head and walked rapidly from the window to the door and back again. "Energy can't be created or destroyed. It can just be converted from one form to another."

He stopped suddenly and looked at Rede and Thalia on the floor. "She has the Singers inside her," he said, kneeling beside them. "Move out of the way!" he commanded Maude and Elizabeth. "Please."

"And Rede's Nevma," Hyad said thoughtfully. "Thalia still has that. It's still there." He knelt beside Aubrey. "What made you think they both died?"

"They stopped breathing," Aubrey growled, irritated as always by stupid questions. "I couldn't find a pulse in either of them."

Hyad ran his fingers up Thalia's forearms, and then Rede's.

"Can you feel anything?" Aubrey asked in a small voice.

"No," Hyad said. "But neither one of them is dead."

"What?" Aubrey said. "How?"

"I don't know," Hyad said. "Maybe the Nevma. Maybe his life force mixing with hers when she was in her fully manifested state, them working together... Maybe the energy of the Singers. I don't know." He leaned closer. "It's almost like their life energy is hiding or waiting, as if they're in a state of suspension."

Dad put Sandy down. He knelt next to Hyad, who shuddered but didn't say anything. Maude, Elizabeth and Aubrey moved away as Dad gently pulled Rede and Thalia apart and laid them on their backs. He opened Rede's shirt.

"Do you feel a pulse or something, Dad?" Emma asked.

Dad exhaled slowly and said, "I'm not tired anymore."

"What does that mean?" Emma asked.

"Sh!" said Aubrey. "He's concentrating. Do you even have schools in the Otherworld? How can you learn anything when you're always talking?"

"Seriously?" Emma said. "Here? Now?"

Aubrey huffed and said, "Shh."

Dad put his hand on Thalia's chest, just below her throat.

"Only a Soulmate can give a Nevma, Dad," Maude said gently. "Remember?"

"Your father has been severed from his Soulmate," Hyad said. "The bond is cut."

Dad moaned, but he didn't move his hand or turn away.

"He might be able to act as a conduit," Hyad murmured, turning to Aubrey.

"Yes!" Aubrey shouted. "He will."

Dad pulled Rede's Nevma from Thalia's chest. Rede's green and silver Spirit Sphere contained a leafless tree with iron branches, and a green glass bird singing the Idrysi. A translucent blue girl emerged from the base of the tree. Still singing, the bright-winged bird dove through the black branches and landed on the girl's sun-touched fingers, her bones visible just inside her twilight-colored skin.

On the floor, Thalia suddenly sucked in a mouthful of air. Hyad cradled her head in his lap.

Dad laid the Nevma on Rede's chest. It disappeared like a stone dropped into a pond, but Rede didn't move.

Elizabeth took Rede's hand and put it into Thalia's. She held their hands together. Thalia opened her eyes and squeezed. Elizabeth smiled and let go.

Rede sat up, out of breath and panicked. "Thalia!"

"I'm right here," she said, sitting up beside him.

"Are you all right?" he asked, feeling her arms and legs and examining the deep gashes no longer bleeding smoke. "What happened?"

"Are you all right?" she asked.

"I asked you first. And no, I'm not all right—unless you are."

"That's your answer?" she said, laughing.

"Yes," he said.

Thalia looked around the room until she found Aubrey's face. "Did it work?" she asked. "Are the Singers gone?"

Aubrey nodded and smiled. "Yes."

Thalia turned to Rede and kissed him. "I am all right," she said. "Me, too," he replied.

CHAPTER SIXTY-SEVEN

Emma, Joe, Mr. Mathews and Sandy returned to the Commonworld with Hyad to appeal to the leaders of the Ones in Power and the Resisters for joint protection of Sandy, who would still be a commodity in danger of being exchanged for money or power. Mr. Spencer took Maude, Elizabeth and Aubrey back to New Hampshire.

Thalia and Rede went home to Protepol in the Commonworld. Before they left, they privately decided with Emma and Joe to work together to expose the truth of the Synektos weapon so the Ones in Power would have no choice but to live up to their reputed ideals.

Back in the Commonworld and walking to her house, Thalia felt Rede watching her.

"You don't have to talk about it until you're ready," he said. "The experience, I mean. You waited a long time for me to talk about what happened to Allasso."

"You didn't *tell* me," she pointed out. "I saw. When my manifestation started in Hyad's apartment, I saw. Remember?"

Rede tugged her hair. "I would have told you eventually."

"I know," she said, closing her eyes for a second to feel his fingers in her hair.

"I just wanted you to know I'm not going to pressure you to talk about it."

Thalia breathed in the familiar scent of the city. "I don't mind talking about it with you, but I don't want to tell my parents. Not yet, anyway."

"How are you going to explain the gashes all over your arms and legs?"

"I'm not," she said.

Rede nodded thoughtfully. "Okay. Do you want to wear my jacket? They won't see your legs, but your arms are exposed." He took off the garment and handed it to her.

"Thanks," she said, putting it on and checking to see that none of the gashes were visible. "I think this is the chrimest thing I've ever worn. It probably cost more than all my clothes put together."

"Yeah, well, don't get it dirty then," he said, grinning.

"Oh, I'm going to roll around in the yard as soon as we get home."

"I think I'd like to see that," he said.

"Shut up," she said and took his hand.

* * *

A few blocks from her house Thalia said, "I think it will last forever."

"What?"

"The music of the Singers inside me. And I don't think I'm ever going to be an ordinary Aponomi again. I think I'll always be in this manifested state. I won't revert."

"Well, that's great, isn't it?" Rede asked. "Everything will be easier for you. You'll never have to worry about being weak or fragile again. You'll always be visible."

"I was happy with myself before," she pointed out.

"I know," he said. "But won't this be easier?"

"It's not just the music inside me," Thalia said. She pushed up the sleeves of his jacket and raised her arms so Rede could see again the series of gashes running up and down her skin. "They look like connector scars, don't they?"

"Yeah," Rede answered. "But connected to what? A connector scar has to be linked to someone else."

"Everyone," she said.

Rede stopped walking. "What do you mean, 'everyone'?"

"If I let myself pay attention, I feel the sadness, and pain, and suffering of everyone. I'm hyper-aware—more than I ever was before, even as a really strong Teknasma or even during the peak of my manifestation—of the suffering in both worlds. I mean, it's always there for anyone who takes the time to think about the hardships everyone faces. It's not like it's a mystery. But hardly anyone thinks about it. Or feels it."

"I do," Rede said quietly.

Thalia smiled. "I know. That's why, Soulmate connection or not, I would have chosen you."

"I would have chosen you, too," he said.

"Yeah." Thalia laughed, tugging his hair. "As soon as you got your pretty head out of your butt and saw me as an equal."

Rede grabbed her waist. "You're the worst."

"I'm the best," she said, and she kissed his chest.

He exhaled and shuddered under her kiss then said, "We have to hurry. Your parents have surely been worrying since you left."

"Okay," she said. "But remember, I don't want to tell them anything yet."

"I remember," he said.

They'd just passed her neighbor's dark house when Thalia heard Maddie singing in her head. She squeezed Rede's hand and rushed to open her front door.

"Mom!" she cried, running to her beautiful, transparent, apricot-colored mother who was sitting in the living room, waiting.

Genna hugged her, and Thalia was shocked to feel how feather-light she seemed.

"Did I feel this insubstantial?" she asked Rede.

"You never felt insubstantial to me," he said shyly, closing the front door behind him.

Genna held Thalia at arm's length. *I can't believe I missed it,* she said. *Look at you.* She turned and smiled at Zino, who walked in holding a sleepy Maddie. *She doesn't look like my mother at all. She looks like Solymi.*

Thalia! Maddie said, reaching out her chubby arms.

Thalia took her little sister and spun in a circle on the floor.

Do it again, Maddie said.

Thalia did, and her sister laughed.

You look funny, Maddie said. *And I'm glad you're not a boy.*

Thalia kissed her sister's curls, so delicate that they seemed almost ephemeral.

Don't tell Thalia she looks funny, Genna scolded.

"That's okay," Thalia said. "That's what I always thought." *I always thought we Invisibles were prettier, too,* she whispered to Maddie.

He's pretty, Maddie whispered back, glancing sidelong at Rede.

Shhh, Thalia said. *Don't tell him. He'll get a big head.*

Maddie stared openly at Rede, waiting for his head to swell.

Are you hungry, chichi? Zino asked Thalia. *You must be. Are you hungry, Rede? I'm making raspberry pancakes.*

And I get to have them, too, Maddie said. *And take bites. With my own fork.* She glanced again at Rede, and Thalia realized her little sister was trying to impress her Soulmate.

I am hungry, Mr. Salic, Rede said. *Thanks. And I wouldn't want to miss Maddie's awesome fork.*

Maddie laughed in her little thought voice.

Thalia put her sister down. When she looked up, Genna and Zino were gazing at her.

Hyad contacted us. To let us know what happened and that you would be okay, Zino said to Thalia alone. *You don't have to talk about what happened—unless you want to.* He glanced at Genna, who looked like she was going to cry but picked up Maddie instead.

Why are you sad? Maddie asked, putting her chubby pink hand on Genna's cheek.

I'm not sad, little peach, Mom said. *I'm so happy Thalia is home that I'm almost* too *happy, and that makes me cry a little.*

That's silly, Maddie said.

It is, Genna agreed. *Let's go practice your song. Maddie learned a special song she wants to sing for you,* she added to Thalia.

Okay, Maddie said. *But I already know all of it.* She glanced at Rede, who smiled at her.

Thalia watched her mom and sister leave the kitchen.

"In my life," Zino said, "I've never been more proud and terrified and grateful than I am right now." He closed his eyes for a moment then stared at the door where Genna and Maddie disappeared before turning to Thalia again. "I just wanted you to know."

"Thanks, Dad."

Zino nodded. "I'll leave you two alone," he said, squeezing Rede's shoulder.

Before he left the kitchen, he turned back to Thalia. "I can help you manage those receptors or whatever exactly they are on your arms and legs. If you want. I wasn't invading your privacy, chichi, but I can't help seeing them. Even with Rede's chrimy jacket covering them up."

Thalia laughed. *Okay, thanks.*

After the door closed and they were alone, she said to Rede, "It's weird."

"What? Everything?"

She laughed. "No. Well, yes. But that's not what I meant.

"What did you mean?"

"If I concentrate I can feel things other gemynd are feeling."

"You mean, more than just their pain?" he asked. "And couldn't you always do that to some degree? I mean, isn't that exactly what a Teknasma does?"

"Yes," she said, "but now I can feel gemynd who are nowhere near me. Like Emma is wrecked, probably about her mom, and confused probably about how to help Maude. She has to think through her mom's betrayals, killing Gryphon and trying to sacrifice Sandy. I don't know how she's going to do it." Thalia's heart beat faster and faster. She started sweating as the emotions of others swelled inside her. "Sandy won't let go of his dad, but something else is helping him. I don't know what it is, but something is making things easier for him. Maybe it's Hyad. He so concentrated on making things right. If I keep opening myself up I can feel Emma's brother Turner, whom I've never met, and what's left of her cousin Isohel, and—

Stop, Rede said taking her hand. *Give yourself a break. Eat some pancakes and listen to Maddie's song and let your dad help you manage those receptors.* "Just because you saved the world last night, Lady Teknasma, it doesn't mean you have to do it again right now. Especially with Maddie's mad fork skills coming up."

"All right, Lord Handsome," she said.

Ribbons of pink sunlight feathered through the tree in the backyard and fell on Maddie's harness, and Thalia said, *I want to watch the sunrise before breakfast. I've never seen myself in the sun like this. I want to know what it looks like before I go outside anywhere by myself.*

You're amazing now, Rede said. *But the first time I saw you in sunlight we were in your kitchen; you sweetly held my arm and I saw the bones through your skin...and I realized I'd never seen anything really beautiful before. Not like that. You were like a mystery revealed in flashes, like the secrets of the universes whispered through the trees. You in the sunlight is the Idrysi made manifest.*

Thalia couldn't speak.

I just wanted you to know that, he said.

"I haven't kissed you," she said.

"Yes, we have," Rede corrected, coloring slightly. "Have you forgotten? Is that a manifestation thing?"

She laughed. "No. I remember every kiss."

"Good," he said, taking her hands. "Me, too. And the ones I thought about when you weren't with me."

"Really?" she asked, letting go of his hands and holding him by the waist. "How am I at imaginary kissing?"

"Amazing," he whispered.

She stroked his cheek and gazed at his fiery green eyes. *I meant, I haven't kissed you as a fully manifested Aponomi yet.* Then she pulled him close, so that she could feel his stomach and chest and heart, all warm and alive against her skin.

Rede made a low noise in the back of his throat and brushed his soft mouth over hers. He grabbed her head and kissed her fiercely, and the fire of the kiss sang inside her blood and hummed through her bones and muscles. With her mouth on Rede's, and his on hers, Thalia knew she was more than herself alone. In this infinite moment, kissing Rede, her Soulmate, her other half, Thalia was every woman and every man, part of the swell of the ever-expanding universe.

And she was herself, too.

ABOUT THE AUTHOR

Mary Beth Bass is an author of science fiction and fantasy romance novels, and a mad lover of 19th century poetry and 21st century punk rock. She frequently considers the awesomeness of the octopus and without too much prompting can talk about the unexpected perfection of lobster sex like a half-drunk natural philosopher. She worships the old gods. You've probably heard of them.

Want to know more? Find Mary Beth Bass at one of these fine virtual locations near you:
https://www.marybethbass.com
https://twitter.com/marybethbass
http://marybethbass.tumblr.com
https://www.pinterest.com/marybethbooks

Did you enjoy this book? Drop us a line and say so! We love to hear from readers, and so do our authors. To connect, visit www.boroughspublishinggroup.com online, send comments directly to info@boroughspublishinggroup.com, or friend us on Facebook and Twitter. And be sure to check back regularly for contests and new releases in your favorite subgenres of romance!

Are you an aspiring writer? Check out www.boroughspublishinggroup.com/submit and see if we can help you make your dreams come true.

www.ingramcontent.com/pod-product-compliance
Lightning Source LLC
Chambersburg PA
CBHW061314170626
46817CB00001B/179